I0720542

ALSO BY SEBASTIAN DE ASSIS

Nonfiction

Sailing Against the Wind

Spiraling Madness

ZENior CitiZEN: Mastering the Art of Aging

rEvolution in Education

Teachers of the World, Unite!

Fiction

The Heat of the Sun

The Beast

The Alchemy of Time

I'LL NEVER COMMIT SUICIDE AGAIN

Sebastian de Assis

Blooming World Books

First Edition

ISBN 978-1-7323285-1-8

Library of Congress Control Number: 2023930021

Published in the United States of America

Blooming World Books
Opening a World of Possibilities
www.bloomingworldbooks.com

For Anne

PART I

BEFORE

It was the first time I attempted to commit suicide—but not the last!

Looking down into the emptiness of an endless darkness, with my eyes half-closed I stood on the edge of the abyss of despair. I could hear the small pebbles tumbling down toward the crashing waves below as I slowly shuffled my feet forward in the direction of my impending death. The headlights of my car parked behind me faded in the distance like faint spotlights on the shadow of a hopeless future I could no longer endure. Whether I looked ahead toward the ominous horizon that my life had become, or below where truculent waves roared like famished beasts eager to devour my flesh, my indifference remained unperturbed. Not even the insidious whirring of the VW bug's engine running could muffle the chilling silence of my last moment on Earth. The time to put an end to my misery had come.

"Wait!" A commanding baritone voice that seemed to have echoed from the depth of a canyon resonated in my ears. It felt as though a storm was building up and a thunderous warning heralded its approaching.

"Don't make such an irreversible mistake," a soothing raspy voice now whispered in my left ear as I felt a strong and yet gentle touch on my right shoulder.

Startled by the unexpected visitor, I turned toward the towering male silhouette standing next to me, but before I could say anything, he continued.

"Once you do this, there is no coming back; no time for regrets and no chance for redemption," he said as I watched his breath wafting in the light that illuminated us from behind. Then, he tilted his head downward the cliff as though he could see something that my eyes were incapable of perceiving. "It looks very dark, cold, and painful down there."

"Yes," I said dismissively looking down at the dark abyss below where the sounds of crashing waves made the ill-omened unseen sight visible to the imagination. "But it feels very dark, cold, and painful up here, too. The difference is that down there it all ends."

"Does it?" He questioned my reasoning insouciantly and I resented the subtlety of sarcasm in the intonation of his voice at such a pressing moment. I turned my head toward him trying very hard to identify his facial traits, but all I could see was his shimmering bright eyes. They looked like a pair of miniature Suns in the twilight at the end of a long stressful day. All the other details of his countenance were obscured by the shadow of the night and the mystery of the moment.

"Who are you? And where the hell did you come from?" I barked at him beginning to feel irritated by the unexpected interference in such a momentous decision-making time in my life; a life that I was determined to end.

"What does it matter to you?" He replied as brashly as I addressed him. "Considering what you are about to do, who I am or where I came from is as irrelevant as wanting to know which of those waves will smash your wrecked dead body against the rocks. The only thing worth knowing right now is that there's no coming back from where you're heading to."

"Maybe, but on the other hand, I'm getting away from a situation that I already know is worthless," I said looking down the pitch-black chasm below wondering, fretfully, what I'd find there.

"It might not be any better than where you are at now," he said. "In fact, it may turn out to be much worse. And once you take the plunge and embark on this mysterious journey, it'll be too late to regret. There is no coming back."

All of a sudden, I felt extremely annoyed with his presence.

"Listen, mister, I've had with you. I didn't ask for your advice and I don't need your meddling in my personal affairs. I'm experiencing excruciating emotional pain and I've made up my mind to put an end to it. I'm not turning back now because a ghost-like figure shows up out of nowhere to intrude in the last minute of my life. Please go back to wherever you came from and let me carry on my business."

A long unnerving silence permeated the moist nightly air. As an onshore breeze wheezed by my ears, I felt his presence moving toward the razor-thin edge of the precipice as though he was trading places with me. Suddenly, he pivoted and I gasped startled by his abrupt move thinking he'd plunged to his death. With his back to the steep drop behind him, he spoke to me and the somber tone of his voice was infused with an ominous enigmatic message I could not comprehend.

"I am invested in you, and so are many others," he said standing immovably as though he spoke to himself. "If you jump to your death, we'll all suffer the consequences of your desperation-based impulse to put a premature end to your life at a moment of emotional vulnerability. If you fail to triumph over this challenge, we'll all pay the price and lose an extraordinary opportunity to succeed. It's not worth it."

Although his hodgepodge made absolutely no sense to me at the time, I felt terrified with the prospect of bearing such an immeasurable weight of responsibility; a responsibility that it was completely oblivious to my consciousness. And yet, I felt as though iron anvils of accountability weighed heavily on my shoulders. I intuited that something of foremost importance would be wrought by my decision. But I was determined to put an end to my life and there was no turning back. I could not go on living any longer. The weight of my pain was significantly heavier than the symbolic iron anvil of accountability on my shoulder.

I could feel he sensed my determination when he took a step toward me. Then, he placed his gentle strong hand on my shoulder before speaking again.

"Well, there is only so much I'm able to do to avert this unnecessary tragedy. My duty is to make recommendations, but you're the only one who can make decisions," he said while letting his hand slowly slip off my shoulder. "I must get going now. I don't want to witness what I failed to prevent from happening."

I did not utter a single word. I just paid attention to the sounds of his footsteps on the gravel road fading away behind me, until I felt an irresistible urge to turn around to see his vanishing in the same mysterious way he'd appeared. Suddenly, his footsteps were haltered and only the deadly eerie sounds of the waves crashing on the rocks below filled my ears with dread. I knew he was standing there and I couldn't resist turning around to take another look at him. However, the bright headlights of the car obstructed his silhouette in the distance. Then, to my astonishment, he spoke again and his last words would haunt me for many years to come.

"We shall visit again in the future, but I'm afraid it'll be at a time of even more dire circumstances," he said and the somber tone of his voice was almost visible in the haze. "We shall see how it'll all pan out. Having nothing else to say to you, I bid you farewell, for now."

After he disappeared as mysteriously as he had showed up, I stood at the edge of the cliff for what it felt like an eternity. I looked up staring at the stars spangled sky as a shooting star crisscrossed the firmament as though to tell me that I didn't have to die, at least not at that moment. Almost involuntarily, I began shuffling my feet backwards away from the razor-thin edge of death. Next thing I remember, I was driving the winding road down the canyon heading back home.

This event happened 18 years to the day until I attempted to commit suicide again; but the second time around I would not fail.

Excitement took over me when I heard the revving up of the engine of his Porsche 718 Boxster approaching the circular driveway of our posh residence. After stopping under the covered area by the wide stairway leading to the imposing double front door, he shut off the vehicle, slammed the door, and rushed inside our beautiful home calling my name out loud. My exhilaration increased at the same pace the crescendo sound of his footsteps punctuated the mahogany hardwood floor in the hallway leading to the library where I waited for him with anticipation. The man I loved was home.

"Lucy, my darling, I have great news!" My husband said chucking his briefcase and a large gift box on the Persian rug under the marble coffee table. Then, he sat down next to me on the red velvet sofa and kissed me with seething passion.

"I can't wait to hear it," I said trying to catch my breath after his fervent display of affection. While waiting for his reply, I surreptitiously glanced at the snazzy silver package with a wide white ribbon around it leaning against the coffee table leg. All of a sudden, my heart started beating faster and I noticed the moisture oozing out the palms of my hands. I felt fidgety. I straightened up myself in an effort to recompose both my posture and my concerned mind. Then, when I looked into his silent eyes, all the excitement I'd been building up in anticipation to his coming home vanished in a nanosecond. I'd seen that look before and I knew what it meant. I sighed inwardly.

"Well, let's get started the right way," he said standing up abruptly breaking the uncomfortable eye contact we shared. He bent down to pick up the silver gift package and handed it to me with a mischievous gaze. "Open it! I think it's going to look absolutely dashing on you."

I took it from his hands, and at a painfully slow pace, I untied the white ribbon before opening the box. Inside, there was this gorgeous black silk dress with a daring low cleavage v-cut in the front with a completely open back circling slightly below the waistline. The openings on the shoulder area accentuated the tight-fit long sleeves and the boldness of the design. My always reliable intuition let me know this was not a gift for me.

"What do you think?" He asked me with wide open eyes looking like an aroused teenager who's about to get laid. Before I had a chance to reply, he continued. "C'mon, try it on! I can't wait to see it on you."

With great effort, I half-smiled and walked to one of the bedrooms down the hallway recalling the last time I went through similar situation. It'd been a few years since the last time this happened; and a seemingly long time when it happened for the first time. The raw memories made me pause as a dismal feeling of helplessness sequestered my heart.

"No time for self-indulgence," I mumbled as I put the dress on while looking at myself in front of the large mirror inside the walk-in closet door. The eye-catching sexy dress felt like a magical garment that possessed its own seductive spell; so powerful that it could render even the most loyal husband unfaithful. It made me look and feel like an irresistible temptress with overpowering seductive authority over the vulnerable masculine sexuality. I took a step closer toward the mirror and established deep eye contact with myself. "You can do this Lucy, one last time," I whispered through my teeth, almost silently, as I felt my eyes well up with tears.

I walked out of the bedroom and headed back to the library. On the outside, I felt seductively attractive wearing the audacious flesh hugging black silk dress. Inside, however, I felt like a miserable condemned witch walking toward the gallows.

"Oh my goodness! You look like a sex goddess!" Daniel exclaimed in awe staring at me agape as soon as I stepped in. "You look like Aphrodite storming out of Mount Olympus to seduce helpless warriors. No man could resist such a sexy appeal. You look sexually delectable; absolutely irresistible!"

He started walking slowly toward me with devouring eyes as if I were a defenseless prey on the path of a hungry predator. As he got closer, I could feel the heat exuding from his eyes flaming with desire. Then, he paced slowly around me scrutinizing every single detail of my appearance.

"You look stunning!" He said gawking at me as I felt his strong hands holding my waist tight and pressing my body against his aroused manhood. He started nuzzling his nose around my neck until abruptly kissing me with impetuous desire.

"Wait!" I said gently pushing him away as he started undressing me with uncontained arousal. "You said you had something important to tell me."

"I'll tell you all about the great news later, my darling," he said with his eyes blazing with irrepressible sexual excitement. "Right now all I want to do is to have passionate sex with you."

And so he did.

Almost every day I came home from school I witnessed the same dissonant arguments.

"Damn it! How many times have I told you not to talk to me like this?" My father yelled at my mother who cowed on the corner of the kitchen floor after being smacked in the face. "I've told you bitch, I'll do whatever da fuck I want with the television, furniture, or any other piece of crap in this shithole place. Someone's got to put food on the table and I ain't seeing you doing shit about it. Now leave me da fuck alone!"

At the age of seven it was a scene hard to comprehend. Later in my life, I was amazed at how I managed to get used to it, albeit with enormous difficulty. I also got used to going to bed many times without eating dinner, which became more often after my father was laid off from his automobile manufacturing job during a bad economic downturn that put him in a chronically unemployed status that he seemed unable to overcome. As his financial situation deteriorated, my father took on gambling and my tenuous family life became, as if it were possible, even more precarious. At that time, it seemed to me that every day I came home there was one less item in the already under-furnished one bedroom apartment we lived in the outskirts of town. My father was pawning everything we owned in a desperate attempt to recoup his losses on the poker tables and horse racing tracks he frequented. It'd become his new disreputable full-time job, which not only he didn't get paid, but it was impoverishing us further and beyond the material necessities of life. As a child, I felt as though the lack of money was severing the fragile thread of hope that I so desperately hung on to, until it broke off for good.

"What's the matter, mommy?" I asked my sobbing mother who sat on the floor of the empty living room cuddling a worn out green blanket. "Daddy will get all this stuff back some day."

She raised her chin to face me and her red swollen eyes told me he wouldn't. She beckoned at me to sit in her lap and enveloped me in the green blanket with her loving arms. Then, in a soft whispering voice that attempted to soothe both of us, she let me know of the new challenges ahead.

"Your father has left us; and like all the furniture in this apartment, he's not coming back. But don't you worry, my baby girl, we're gonna pull this off somehow." She sniffled while dabbing her fingers under her puffed up eyes. "We're gonna make it, my baby girl, I promise you, we're gonna make it. Just be strong as we take on this challenge."

I don't have a clear recollection of the time between that afternoon and the day we moved into the public housing project in the outer reaches of the city. Neither do I remember the last time I saw my father. All I recall is the emptiness of his absence in my life and that I never saw him again. Later on in my adolescence, I found out that he had been arrested for armed robbery and beaten to a pulp by prison gang members. His damaging brain injuries left him in a vegetative state and my hopes to ever speaking with my father again ended as quickly as he left my life. As for my mother, she struggled continuously trying to eke out a living with nary success.

By the time I was 10-years-old, I could clearly tell that something was not right with her. She seemed to be spiraling into the darkness of her inner turmoil. I could feel a whirlwind of despair swirling around our downtrodden dwelling as I witnessed my mother succumb to utter despondency. I felt compelled to speed up my growing up process as insecurities of all sorts were threatening my survival in a world I had no one stable to rely on; well, except for my devoted imaginary friend who always seemed to show up at my darkest hours. Whenever I felt completely helpless and alone in the hostile environment I existed, he appeared literally out of nowhere to console me. I never saw him physically and he never told me his name, but I could feel his presence and hear his voice in my head with utmost clarity. My nameless invisible friend exerted an enormous influence in my life at a time I needed the most.

"Lively up, my friend," he'd say to me whenever I moped about my distressing situation. "Like everything else, this too shall pass; and in the end you'll be stronger and better because of the challenges you overcome. Giving up is the only danger in the face of life's trials and travails."

I tried to heed his words and absorb his guidance with the devotion and faith of an apostle. Alas, sometimes my distressful state of being was so pungent that taking in his message felt like an impossible task. Then, one day he offered me an advice that forever changed my life.

"Really? Can you do that?" I reacted in disbelief to his comment about the potential to developing new invisible friendships that could yield great rewards.

"Of course you can!" He said enthusiastically. "In fact, you can even befriend people who have died many years before you were born. Books are filled with the written words of authors whose thoughts, emotions, and ideas that resonate with you can lead to extraordinary friendships. Once you establish genuine bonds with your favorite authors, you have lifetime friends at your fingertips, literally."

"Really?" I said again marveling in the possibility of making reliable friends, even if I could not see them.

"I cross my heart," he said and I could feel his mirth jiggling inside of me. "Books have the power to connect minds and hearts far beyond the limitations of time and space. They're like magical bridges connecting readers and authors over the banks of the great river of knowledge. And once you take up the habit of reading, you'll never feel alone again. You should give it a try."

And so I did. I was in desperate need of friends, especially at a time when my life was spiraling down into hopeless destitution. Once I learned there were places called libraries where people could borrow books at no cost, I paid a visit to the small dilapidated branch in my neighborhood and started a lifelong habit. Reading became my refuge from my troubled fledgling life. But as good as books were, I very much needed a down-to-earth bridge to the reality of my daily life, too. Although my nameless invisible friend was always there for me, my child self was growing terrified of what untoward event could happen next. My mother was gradually reaching rock-bottom, and she was dragging me along with her. I was scared.

"I can't believe I'm unable to land a job anywhere," my mother said stumbling her way into our hovel. I could smell her alcohol-infused breath from afar. She managed to stagger her way to the refrigerator without falling down, opened it, then she released a jarring sigh that sounded like a mournful wailing to my ears. I knew what she was sighing about, for I had opened the fridge moments before she did. There was nothing in the refrigerator but a couple of brown bananas, a half-loaf of sliced bread, and an open box of baking soda.

The financial burden was weighing heavily on her shoulders. After enduring insidious unemployment, regular lay-offs, and low-paying gigs for a long stretch of time, my mother started coming home drunk more often. It was evident that she was reaching the end of the rope of hope. In the face of what I perceived to be a growing existential threat, I increased my self-imposed commitment to hasten my growing up process in order to be able to be there for her. However, in spite of my valiant efforts, there was nothing the well-intentioned 10-year-old child could do to fulfill the role of an adult in a critical situation. I felt utterly impotent and at the mercy of my unfortunate kismet.

Many times throughout my life I wondered whether my mother couldn't get a job because she'd become a drunkard or she took on drinking to soak up her poverty-stricken miserable existence. But the fact that I do not recall ever seeing her take a swig of alcohol before my father left us was evidence of what came first. Eventually, it made sense to me: how can a lonely person burdened by economic privation and the responsibility of caring for a child cope with the challenge? After all, how many times can someone walk into an empty home, open an empty refrigerator, go to bed on an empty stomach, and wake up with an empty heart just to resume the tribulations of an inauspicious empty life? Not very long, I soon found out. And as the heiress of her misery, it was a matter of time for me to inherit the burden of growing up on my own in utter destitution.

"Does anyone else live here with you?" One of the two police officers who showed up at the door late at night asked me.

"My mommy," I replied with trembling lips while lowering my head and feeling an ice cold fear run through my spinal cord. I'd been waiting for her a long time before falling asleep on the torn and stained brown couch we got at the Salvation Army a few days earlier.

"You must come with us, my child," the other policeman said putting his large comforting hand on my scrawny shoulder before leading me out the door.

"I can't go without my mommy," I said halting my steps. "I need to talk to my mommy first. She told me never to walk alone with strangers."

The officers look at each other in silence. As soon as I noticed the dejected expression in their faces, I intuitively knew that, like my father, I would never see my mother again. I burst into uncontrollable tears. One of the officers picked me up and enveloped me in a protective embrace as they took me away toward a frightening unknown future.

The circumstance of my mother's death haunted me for many years into my adulthood. Although the police records stated that she'd been hit by a car while crossing a busy street, the testimony and cooperation of the driver and witnesses led the investigators to conclude that she had intentionally walked into traffic. I refused to believe that my mother would commit suicide and leave me alone in this vile world to fend off hostilities by myself at the tender age of ten. She couldn't possibly do this to me. But since the autopsy revealed an elevated alcohol content in her blood stream, I surmised that perhaps she'd lost her sense of direction and accidentally staggered into the high traffic without noticing it. However, after many years mulling over the conditions of my mother's death, I realized that more than a sense of direction, what she really lost was her will to live.

The next three years of my life following my mother's passing became what I later called my "foster homes tour years." Within that timeframe I lived in seven different households; some of which, as if it were possible, much worse than my original home experience. Some of those folks willing to take me in as a foster child did it so for the allowance they received from the state, as well as having me as an additional helper for household chores. They had me clean, cook, mow the lawn, and even help with the caregiving of a disabled bedridden man who had suffered a massive stroke a few weeks before they took me in. There was one lady, however, Mrs. Holliday, an old grandmother-like figure who saw in me what both of us desperately needed: love. She catered to both my emotional and physical needs with utmost loving care; and we even had a large white Siamese cat in the house, Lilly, whom I became quite fond of. I remember falling asleep on the couch at night leaning against Mrs. Holliday's bosom with Lilly asleep in my lap. I was beginning to feel a false sense of security in my first experience in a stable home environment. Alas, the stormy winds of my tempestuous childhood would blow my fragile stability away. One night when the three of us fell asleep on the couch watching T.V., Mrs. Holliday never woke up again. Suddenly, my six months of home bliss came to an abrupt heartrending end.

The next two years of my foster homes tour intensified as I moved from home to home in different towns and counties, which made it impossible for me to establish friendships with other children, not to mention developing an even remotely stable schooling experience. It was at that time that I became appreciatively grateful to my invisible friend's suggestion to make new invisible friends with authors of books. Thus, in the prepubescent years of my life I'd become a voracious reader, which greatly offset the lack of traditional schooling.

As bad as my situation was, my life took a drastic turn from dreadful to unbearable when the state placed me in the McLean's home. Mr. McLean was a chubby mean-looking older man with a scraggly graying beard who spent the entire day drinking beer in front of a television set while his wife worked. From the moment his pallid emaciated wife came home from work, she started drinking bourbon while filling the living room with billows of cigarette smoke. It was a toxic environment in every sense of the word, which made me wonder how the state could place a child under the "care" of such crass people. But one night, a few weeks after I'd moved in, they sneaked into my bedroom drunk out of their wits and raped me in most ghastly fashion. Horrified by the sexual violence, I ran away as soon as they passed out in the ignominious bed tainted with sperm, blood, and shame where I brutally lost my feminine innocence.

I do not recall the details of that traumatic experience, for I had to block it out of my memory in order to survive at the most basic psychological level. All I remember is walking for miles in the dark trying to get to an unknown destination; any place far away from the living hell that I wasn't aware I carried inside of me. After weeks of aimless wanderings, begging strangers for chump change, crying myself to sleep on the cold cement of empty streets, and hitchhiking for the sake of moving toward nowhere, I ended up in a neighboring state where my life was about to take an upswing change, at last.

After a few days in a different town, I was still trying to get acquainted with the nooks and crannies of homeless survival in a new unfamiliar environment. It takes time to get settled in the harsh jungle of life in the streets alone, especially for a young girl preyed upon by vicious unscrupulous people. With neither basic resources nor a single friend to rely on—except for my invisible nameless friend who always seemed to hang around in quietly eerie fashion—the mind can take some strange twists and turns around the corner of insanity as escapism from unforgiving experiences of reality. Hunger, cold, and loneliness, all seem to pave the way to the alluring path of madness as a palliative to utter desolation that can lead, not only to mental breakdown, but also to a potential collapse of the understanding of what it means to be human. But then, there is always a chance of coming across loving people who can make you turn around from a self-destructive path. It happened to me when I was walking in the back alley of Main Street scouting my new territory. It was when I stuck my head inside the kitchen of a closing hour restaurant asking for a piece of bread that my life unexpectedly changed.

"Hmm, the young lady is hungry," the middle-aged man with dark hair and handsome features said looking at me with empathetic eyes. "C'mon in and I'll fix something to eat."

Although both his eyes and demeanor inspired confidence, I stepped into the kitchen with much trepidation. But as he kept on talking to me, the mellifluous tone of his voice assuaged my concerns while mollifying my suspicions.

"So, what's the young lady doing this time late in the evening roaming a dark back alley asking for a piece of bread?" He asked while serving me a full meal on a wobbly metal table on the corner of the kitchen. I was so flabbergasted staring at the succulent steak, baked potato, vegetables, salad, and the large glass of lemonade in front of me that I didn't answer his question. I hadn't eaten a meal like that in time immemorial.

"Alright," he said chuckling in childlike manner as he walked away toward the stove. "I'll get some work done while you eat your meal and we can talk later."

And talk we did. Joseph Burton, the loving father-figure man with compassionate blue eyes owned the restaurant I fortuitously stumbled upon that evening. After listening to a summary of my fledgling life's travails and learning about my challenging situation at the time, he was seemingly so moved that he offered to put me up at the in-law apartment over the garage of the house he shared with his wife. It was supposed to be a temporary arrangement, but it was a matter of short time for the childless couple and me to grow closer and more fondly of one another. As our bond strengthened with the passing of time, he and his wife took all the necessary legal steps with the local authorities and I started living with them. Soon, I was working at his restaurant, going back to school and, for the first time in my life, I had a stable domestic situation in which I could thrive. I felt as though my life had begun in my early adolescence.

Meeting Mr. Burton was the most auspicious serendipity of my life—and the reason I attempted to commit suicide for the first time at 20-years-old.

"Oh my God! This was absolutely awesome!" Daniel exclaimed after falling off the top of me to the side. I could feel the hot air of his breathing heavily, and I wondered whether he noticed that I was barely breathing at all. It'd been a long time since I enjoyed having sex with my husband. It seemed that the richer we got over the years, the more distant we became from each other.

"You're so beautiful," he said twirling my hair with his fingers. "I love your long dark hair and how it frames the delicate features of your face."

I shunted aside his comment as uninterestedly as I did his sexual advances.

"Look at me," he said holding my chin while turning my face toward him. "Let me look into your bright emerald eyes. You know you are very precious to me, don't you?"

In the earlier years of our marriage those words flattered me and made me feel madly in love with him. For someone with my background who yearned for love like a thirsty lost wanderer in the desert craves water, his words used to soothe my parched heart and invigorated my limp spirit with hope. Now, each sylla-ble sounded more like threatening incendiary sparks that could trigger devastating wildfires in the dried up landscape of my be-ing. The truth, however, is that I'd been burning inside quietly for quite some time.

He laid his head on my breasts and started running his fin-gers in gentle circles around my belly button. The pervading si-lence that ensued screamed loudly in my ears with anticipation of what was about to come. I delayed the inevitable for as long as I could until it became unbearable to restrain myself from asking. I needed to hear directly from him what I already knew.

"So, what's the good news of the day?" I asked.

I could feel his smiling even before he slowly raised his head off my breasts to face me.

"Honey, we're in for one of the greatest opportunities of our lives; a real game changer that will catapult us to the stratosphere of financial gains like we've never seen before. You won't be-lieve with whom I met today."

Staring at the ceiling with a dry throat while trying to hide my moist eyes from his view, I did not venture to say anything. The memories of painful past experiences raced through my head rendering me momentarily mute.

"C'mon, make a wild guess," he insisted now leaning over me in a futile attempt to make eye contact. I turned my head slightly to the side so he wouldn't notice my clammy eyes.

"Senator Robert Faradell," I said with great difficulty.

"Senator Faradell? Oh please, hell no, he's so passé; and besides, he's no game changer. He's past traveled trails, honey. We've already squeezed every drop out of that old lemon and drank the lemonade a long time ago. I'm talking about some real high stakes chips on the table; someone that can introduce us to the top echelons of Wall Street elite club.

For a moment my mind went into a state of stupor. The sheer mentioning of his name was enough to make me feel literally sick to the stomach. I utterly despised the septuagenarian Senator Faradell. Everything about that swinish man disgusted me. From the contemptible idiosyncrasies of his sociopathic nature and immoral character to the repulsiveness of his physical body and slimy personality, he epitomized everything I found repugnant in a man. I recalled Daniels' previous dealings with him and I loathed the slumped old shriveled man with utmost indignation. Like many of his class, he was a dishonorable politician who would do anything to further his own self-interest, which was the reason he got into politics in the first place. I learned, directly from him, that he'd crush anyone who stayed in his way to wealth and power. Daniel had teamed up with him once in a deal that annihilated the national economy of a third world country while enriching both men handsomely—and indirectly me. I carried an enormous amount of guilt for benefiting from that tacit crime that victimized millions of poverty-stricken people. I dealt with assiduous daily pangs of guilt for my indirect participation in that corrupt scheme in the unfettered pursuit of individual profit in detriment to the welfare of millions of people.

"O.K. the guessing game is over," Daniel said breaking the nerve-racking silence while assuaging my quiet distress recollecting past events. "Honey, today I met with the top-dog mogul of international real estate development; the man who will help us move up to the billionaire's rung in the ladder of success."

I finally made eye contact with Daniel silently urging him to get to the point and put an end to the charade.

"Today, I visited with the one and only Anthony Menlo; one of the wealthiest men in the world," he said glowing with greedy enthusiasm. "And we talked business; I mean some serious big money business."

I suppose he expected me to get as excited as he was before he had sex with me moments earlier. But instead, I rolled my eyes under shut eyelids while nibbling on the corner of my lower lip with trepidation for what was going to come next. To my credit, I concealed my anguish with savvy deception; a skill I had developed over the past years of our troubled marriage.

"It sounds very exciting," I said showing none of it in my voice. "So, what's the next step? Are you planning a similar tactic as the one you applied to cajole Senator Robert Faradell into doing a deal with you?"

The room was silent. He didn't reply right away. I turned my head sideways to look at him and he was grinning with absent-minded eyes staring at the distant wall. It looked like he was daydreaming, perhaps about times of great riches to come at the expense of others' misery, including my own. Suddenly, he turned toward me and kissed me on the lips.

"It worked like a charm, didn't it?" He said. "Why should we change a strategy that has proven to work so well in the past? Yes, my darling, we're going to do it again; but this time we're going to hit the jackpot."

It was my turn to stare at the wall with vacant eyes. But unlike him, instead of grinning in reverie, I was brooding with a grimace. The thought of participating in another skullduggery business deal that would likely ruin the lives of innocent people along with my own ever-depleting self-esteem weighed heavily on me. However, what troubled me the most was my disillusionment with the man I loved; a love that was gradually turning into self-hatred. After all, I was going along with all sorts of shenanigans he pulled off to close his businesses deals; and I did it, because I loved him.

"Alright, Daniel, we'll do it again; but this time will be the last," I said looking at him straight in the eye. "I mean it."

"Honey, after I close this deal with Anthony Menlo, we'll never have to do anything we don't want again, ever!" He said with jubilance resonating from his vocal chords. "We'll be wealthy beyond our wildest dreams. We'll be able to do whatever we want in luxury for the rest of our lives."

Suddenly, he got up and walked to the bathroom whistling a popular tune of the early 1970s titled *For the Love of Money*. In my turn, almost immediately after he left the room, I started humming Billie Holiday's *I Love my Man*, though I was beginning to question whether I loved him or just loathed myself; or where the fine line between the two crossed. What I did know was that I'd become helplessly infatuated with him from the very first time we met. He was an ambitious handsome man who swept me off my feet at a time I was on the brink of self-destruction. In hindsight, I guess I fell in love not with Daniel the man, but with a romantic idealization of a brave knight in shining armor who rescued me at a critical time in my life when I first attempted to commit suicide.

But as time passed by, the truth is that throughout the years of our marriage I harbored many doubts about our relationship. I was always wondering whether he ever loved me at all, or was I just another useful adornment placed on the egocentric mantel-shelf of his self-centered interests. This disconcerting dichotomy persisted through the years; and like a swinging pendulum, my feelings and perception oscillated regularly. However, on days when he showered me with fashionable sexy garments and talked about business strategies, I knew that in our marriage I was the only spouse in love. To him, I felt like I was mostly a valuable business partner with whom he had sex at will. But back in the day when we first met, I thought he was the most attractive man in the world; the epitome of the prince charming that came to my rescue when I needed the most.

◄5►

"Hurry up Lucy or you'll be late to school," Mr. Burton hollered through the half-open window of his humming VW bug on the driveway where he waited to drive me to school.

"I'm coming, I'm coming," I yelled running out the door holding a piece of peanut butter smeared toast in one hand, my satchel in the other, and a broad smile of absolute joy in my face.

Since that fortuitous evening when my destiny led me to the backdoor of Mr. Burton's restaurant, I'd been experiencing happiness I had no idea existed in the world. Except for the brief six-month sojourn I spent under the foster care of Mrs. Holliday, I had never enjoyed such a loving home environment. What was supposed to be a temporary assistance for a young girl in distress, it ended up becoming an official adoption. Shortly after moving in the apartment above Mr. and Mrs. Burton's garage, it was a matter of months for our growing closer to one another; and that's when they decided to follow the legal protocol to have me living with them on a permanent basis. By the time I turned 16-years-old, some three years after moving in with them, my life had a quantum leap of possibilities.

It was during that time that I had the most expansive growth of my life—in every level. Physically, I grew up to be a beautiful 5 feet 10 inches tall brunette with long straight hair that cascaded down to my curvy waistline. With strongly shaped athletic legs that I maintained with regular biking and exercise, I was growing up to become a truly sexy feminine force of nature to be reckoned with; a force exacerbated by a pair of voluptuous breasts. And in my face, the delicate contours of my slightly upward slanted nose blended in with my high cheek bones that gave way to deep dimples below every time I smiled. However, of all my seasoning physical attributes, it was my eyes that seemed to monopolize the attention of onlookers. Yes, my bright emerald green eyes that I genetically inherited from my mom, shone in my countenance like inward lighthouses that could guide strangers to the tempestuous story of my life; storms that had long been blown away by the winds of kindness of a loving man and his wife.

Intellectually, I'd progressed at an equally astounding pace. Not only I resumed my schooling, but also augmented my bibliophilic passion that had begun in my lonely childhood at the recommendation of my devoted imaginary friend, who was still a part of my life and visited me occasionally, albeit now only in my dreams. By the time I turned seventeen, I was right on schedule to graduate from high school with honors and a well thought-out strategy to attend college, which Mr. Burton was helping facilitate in my behalf. At that time, among all my goals and ambitions, there was one that emerged to the top of the list: I wanted to make Mr. Burton proud of me as if he were my father. I started working for him at his restaurant and my life was running at an all time high gear. Everything was going really well, except for one facet of my life in which the growth spurt seemed to be oddly truncated: the psychological aspect of my being. Perhaps because of the traumas I endured in childhood, I felt emotionally vulnerable and unable to overcome my insecurities. And as I grew older, I began longing for attention from the opposite sex; not because of my physical attributes, but for the intelligent and sensitive woman I was blossoming into being. Unbeknownst to me at the time, I was searching for security outside of myself; a faulty foundation upon which to build self-esteem. Later on I came to understand the psychological nuances of that phase of my life. It was the little girl in me who, robbed from a healthy paternal relationship, started seeking fatherly love in a male dominated world.

"Hey Lucy, come here for a moment will you?" Mr. Burton whispered at me as I walked by him on my way to the serving station on a busy Saturday evening at the restaurant. I placed the tray down on the counter and approached the kitchen door where he stood with sleuthing eyes.

"What can I do for you, boss?" I said in good jest.

"Did you notice that man sitting at table 7; the tall blond guy who's about to leave?"

"What about him? I asked on stand-by mode of curiosity.

"He must be a new patron. I've never seen him here before. Have you?" He asked looking at me from over the brim of his tortoise round-framed glasses as if I were about to make a confession.

"Why are you so interested in that customer?" I asked wondering about the ulterior motive of the question.

"Well, he seemed to be quite infatuated with you; you know, he was giving you a good share of attention," Mr. Burton said as the tone of his voice took on a paternal timbre, which made me feel overjoyed sensing his protective mantle. "Have you noticed him here before?"

"I'm not sure," I said coyly and embarrassed that he'd noticed the dapper good-looking man surreptitiously flirting with me as I waited on him. He called me several times asking for something or other; and each time I approached his table I felt as though he was undressing me with his penetrating eyes. He tipped me very generously when he left.

"Whether he is a first timer or not, I'll bet you anything that he'll be coming back," Mr. Burton said before heading back into the kitchen. Suddenly, he stopped by the swinging doorway and turned around with one final comment. "And I don't think it's because of the food."

Mr. Burton was right. The youthful-looking older man started coming almost daily; always sitting at table 7 whenever it was available, which was located across from the serving station where I had to make frequent stops throughout my shift. After several visits to the restaurant, one evening he showed up 20 minutes prior to closing time. He sat at his customary table staring at me for the longest time while I put pots of coffee and water pitches away at the serving station. When I approached the table to take his order, I was consumed with mixed feelings of excitement and consternation.

"Please sit down for a moment," he said looking me in the eye before I had a chance to say anything. His wide blue eyes felt dangerously alluring.

"I'm working, sir. I'm not supposed to mingle with my customers," I said feeling semi-hypnotized by his gaze.

"Please have a seat," he insisted. "Just for a brief moment, please."

I discretely looked around the almost empty room, cleared my throat from the uneasiness of the situation, and with my fingers fidgeting on the note pad and pen in my hands, I sat down in capitulation to his persistence.

"I would like to go out with you on a date," he whispered leaning toward me as soon as I awkwardly sat down at the table. His straightforward statement was as direct as the way he looked at me in the eye. I could feel the blood rushing to my face and I thought I probably looked as reddish as the burgundy tablecloth. At first I looked away, but then I plucked some nerve to look into his eye and the intensity of his penetrating gaze triggered a flood of shivers all over my body. I knew right then that I had fallen under his masculine spell.

"You choose the day, time, where you want to go, and any other stipulation you wish," he said without budging. "What do you say?"

I looked at him in silence for a long time until I succumbed to his magnetism and smiled at last. There was something intriguingly impish about that man. He had a boyish demeanor but with the clout of a full-fledged man. I liked him—a lot!

"Does it mean yes?" He questioned my smiling.

"Let me think about it," I said while standing up. "Maybe next time you come here I'll have an answer for you."

"Wait!" He called out as I was walking away. "What's your name?"

"Lucy," I answered curtly.

"I'm Daniel, Daniel Trapp."

It took me several months until I mustered the necessary chutzpah to accept Daniel's invite. Once I turned 18-years-old and was officially a college student, I felt quite mature and ready to step out of my confining comfort zone. Although my adoring surrogate father expressed initial reservations about my dating a 40-year-old man, he eventually acquiesced to my decision letting me know that he trusted my judgment. In my turn, I hoped that one day I'd love, respect, and admire a man at similar high standards I reserved to Mr. Burton.

I still remember the early days of my getting acquainted with Daniel. Since that Saturday night we went out on our first date, we became close friends and started a steady and gradually developing relationship. His dashing good looks, his sharp mind, and irreverent wits captivated me from the get-go. There was also another characteristic of his that seduced me in a peculiar way: his ambition. I'd never met any person in my life who was as boldly driven as Daniel. His determination to become wealthy was such an irrepressible force that he was willing to do whatever it took to reach his goal. As soon as I became aware of his ultimate life's aspiration, I felt both thrilled and edgy to one day embark on that adventure with him. Perhaps it was the trauma of my penurious childhood that intoxicated me with his desire to be rich no matter what it took to accomplish the socially accepted concept of success. From the very early days of our relationship, I knew that his greed was a dangerously pervasive attribute of his personality that could eventually have a destructive impact later on in my life. Nevertheless, I'd fallen for him like a tantalizing ripe red apple in the hands of a lascivious man who was the personification of the serpent of sin in the Garden of Eden.

"I have good news to share with you," Daniel said as we walked on the park savoring mouthwatering chocolate chips ice-cream cones on a hot summer afternoon. "Today I made a very promising acquaintance in the business world. I hooked up with a real estate attorney who's going to set me up with a potentially lucrative deal." His voice oozed exhilaration.

"It seems that every time you tell me you have good news it involves making a profit of some sort," I remarked wondering about his priorities.

"It's all about making money, Lucy. Everything else is cheap talk bullshit,"

"Do you really think that making money is what life is all about?" I asked while halting my steps.

"Of course not!" He exclaimed with his lips engulfed on the rapidly vanishing ice cream ball atop the waffle cone. Then, he suddenly started laughing before speaking again. "Making love is almost as important as making money."

Indeed, those were the two main priorities in Daniel's life: making money and the hedonistic experiences that having money ensures. But after dating him for awhile, I eventually learned that, albeit not as nearly as dramatic as my childhood ordeal, he, too, grew up in a very dysfunctional environment. His father, who left Daniel's mother when he was a little boy and two other wives after the first, was a womanizer obsessed with accumulation of wealth, and he passed on his materialistic and hedonistic values to his son. Like his father, Daniel grew up obsessed with going after all the money and breasts he could get his hands on. From the very beginning, it was obvious to me that he could not possibly be a good husband to any woman. However, as a boyfriend of a troubled solitary girl he was a fantastic companion. He was pleasant, smart, and he made me laugh, which chased away the sorrows of my past; at least temporarily. But as far as a future with him was concerned, I never thought to be possible that we'd go anywhere together beyond our shared walks and casual dates. I was wrong. When the unexpected iceberg of tragedy appeared once again on the icy waters of my life, the fragile hull of my battered emotional vessel hit it head on leaving me drowning in hypothermic freezing waters of grief. At that time, Daniel proved to be the life raft that rescued me after my first suicide attempt.

Alas, years later he would become the allegorical iceberg that sank my ship into the deep mysterious waters of death.

The years I spent living with Mr. and Mrs. Burton were the best I'd ever known. For the first time in my life I had a loving stable home where I was able to begin the healing process of my heartbreaking past. Although I never fully recovered from my childhood traumas, the nurturing love I received from Mr. Burton and his wife was like an emotional medicine that prevented my painful experiences from festering into irreparable damage to my being. Instead, in spite of all the hardships and limitations of my upbringing, I was able to thrive to a level I never thought possible for someone with my background. As an inevitable consequence of my good fortune, I developed an enormous gratitude for them, which I strove to pay back with the currency of my love. My feelings were significantly augmented when I found out that in the equation of our blended lives we shared the common denominator of family misfortunes; and in their case, unbearable sorrow.

"She was only 16-years-old," Mrs. Burton said as her eyes welled up with grief when the subject first came up one evening after dinner, the time we often got together to chat. "Rose was a loving beautiful girl; a little flower child that was plucked out of the garden of life way too soon."

I don't remember how the conversation led to the topic of losing their only child in a most tragic way, but out of respect and commiseration, I refrained from asking any questions about Rose. However, it was obvious that they embraced the opportunity to process their excruciating anguish. I was under the impression that my presence allowed them to undergo a sort of impromptu therapeutic engagement, as though they talked to Rose through me. I silently acquiesced and obliged to the emotional needs of my loving surrogate parents.

"When she asked me to go to a friend's sleepover birthday party out in the country, I remember hesitating to answer," Mr. Burton said with an utterly absent-minded expression. With his chin facing up, his eyes were fixated on the white ceiling as though he watched a video recording of that dreadful day on the despondent screen of his memory. There was an uncomfortable silent pause before he resumed speaking.

"Although I had no legitimate reasons to object, I kept having this weird uneasy feeling in my gut that I should say no. Oh, how I wish I had," he said releasing a sigh of regret in his breath.

"You can't keep on blaming yourself for something you did not know," Mrs. Burton said touching his crossed hands in his lap. "You could not have interfered with her destiny; or ours for that matter."

He lowered his head slowly, looked at his wife, and a solitary tear rolled down from his bloodshot eyes.

"I know," he said. "But it's hard not to imagine what could have been had I...; well, you're right."

I sat there quietly gazing at them with utmost love and compassion. I didn't know what to say in a moment like that. I just allowed them to sort out their grief-stricken hearts as best suited their emotional needs. I learned then that often times the best way to support someone you care about is to hearken, not their words per se, but their feelings.

"It was a very bizarre sensation," Mr. Burton said staring at the ceiling again with hollow eyes that seemed to see nothing but darkness. "I remember waving good-bye from the porch as she drove away with her girlfriends. I felt my stomach clump, my heart started beating faster, and even the temperature of my body seemed to have risen. It felt like a bad dream in which I wanted to shout for her not to go but my voice was paralyzed by an involuntary demand to remain silent. Somehow I knew that I was waving at my child for the last time."

I wanted to ask him what happened but I could not muster the nerve to do it. He must have intuited my interest—or more likely had an ardent urge to process his pent-up anguish—for he disclosed it shortly after I thought about it.

"A few hours later, I answered that shocking phone call from the hospital letting me know that my baby girl was in the ICU with life-threatening injuries incurred in a head-on collision," he said drying up tears with the back of his hand. "We rushed to the hospital and as soon as we arrived they sympathetically told us that they were not able to save her. It was the most agonizing evening of my life."

I'd had many bad evenings of my own, but I have to say that listening to him while witnessing the harrowing sorrow of such a loving man turned that evening into one of the worst I've ever had. Right then, I promised myself that I'd devoutly love him and do everything in my power to attempt assuaging his grief. Although neither I nor anyone else would ever be able to replace his daughter, I committed myself to being a source of joy and comfort for his battered soul.

After that evening, both my love and gratitude for my surrogate father grew exponentially. And because of the trauma of my past marked by constant losses and travails, the mere passing thought of not having him in my life triggered a terrifying feeling of despair. Unfortunately, the self-fulfilling promise of my worst nightmare became a reality as Mr. Burton became my version of his Rose. As this precious fatherly rose in the garden of my life was yanked away from me, the spiky thorns punctured deeply through the delicate membrane of my heart. Badly wounded and bleeding anguish, I realized I had no choice but to follow on Rose's footsteps on my own terms.

"What a bunch of bull!" Daniel said as we engaged in one of our customary philosophical conversations.

"Do you really think that we live in a death-denying society? Look at all the popular movies, TV crime shows, gory video games; for Pete's sake, even the news broadcast glorifies death as a most valuable commodity that they profit from at will. No, Lucy, we don't live in a death-denying society; we live in a death-worshiping society!"

The last thing I wanted to talk about on my 20th birthday was death. I was celebrating life—my life—which at that time was reaching a plateau of happiness I hadn't experienced in a long…; well, really, I had never felt that mirthful ever. I was on schedule to graduate from junior college in a few months; I'd just been promoted to be the manager of Mr. Burton's restaurant; I'd recently joined a yoga practice group that was fun and kept me fit; it was a beautiful sunny afternoon; and, to top everything off, my relationship with Daniel was soaring higher than the hawk I could see up above circling what was likely its next meal-to-be prey. In fact, my life seemed to be in an upswing motion with each passing day and I was finally optimistic about the future. But since he seemed to be so enthusiastic and interested in discussing the morbid subject of death, I gave in to his intellectual desires with the same willingness I'd later do to the yearnings of his physical passion.

"I think what really matters is how you feel about the inevitable ending of life, not what our culture presupposes it to be," I said. "In the end, no pun intended, it's about accepting the finite nature of life and coming to terms with the fact that death is a fundamental component of the human existence."

"C'mon, this is as close to death-denying as it gets," he objected frowning at me. "Your argument is based on a philosophical concept of what death is supposed to be, not the actual experience of it, which at the individual level nobody knows what the outcome is. But having to deal with the death of a loved one or the anxiety of knowing that our own demise will sooner or later arrive; now, that changes the conversation. It's easy to talk about death, but to experience it is a completely different ball game."

"Well, according to Freud the goal of all life is death," I remarked.

"Yes, I've read about it, too," he said. "But I also remember that Freud believed that even though people typically channel their death instincts outwards in form of anger and violence, sometimes these instincts are directed inwards. It's like a bizarre type of survival instinct acting against itself in a self-destructive pattern that can even culminate in suicide."

At the sound of his last word, I decided I could no longer continue the conversation. It was too close to home. The haunting memory of my mother's death and the suspicion that she might have committed suicide gave me chills and clouded my beautiful sunny birthday. Besides, I was aware that Freud's theory postulated that people who experience a traumatic event would often reenact that very same experience; and that was something I was not willing to talk about, especially on my birthday. I remained silent for awhile watching a hawk flying in circles high above me as if I were its prey. I wondered whether it was an omen.

"Happy birthday, babe," he said kissing me on the lips unexpectedly while breaking the silence in a sweet way. "I'll swing by your place at around eight and we'll go out for dinner to celebrate your special day. Why don't you hop on and I'll give you a ride."

"Thanks, Daniel, but I think I want to walk home. It's a beautiful sunset and some fresh air will do me good," I said. "I'll see you later at around eight."

"As you wish, babe. You're the birthday girl," he said while mounting on his black Triumph motorcycle as if it were a wild stallion. Then, he turned on the ignition and blew me a kiss along with a mischievous wink before accelerating away.

I started walking home facing west marveling at the gorgeous chameleon crimson hue continuously changing before my eyes. The fresh and exquisite fragrance of night blooming jasmine drifted in the air penetrating my nostrils with olfactory pleasure. The chirping of birds sounded like they were communicating with one another to announce it was time to ensconce in their nests in the surrounding trees. I looked up and the hawk was nowhere to be seen, probably already savoring the reward of its hunting in some cozy arboreal dwelling. Everything around me looked and felt magnificently alive; and yet, inside of me an eerie inquietude disturbed the joy that I so much wanted to experience on my birthday. Perhaps it was the conversation about death that Daniel unwittingly brought up that affected my spirit and made me recall the passing of my mother. But the farther I walked the more I realized there was something else going on that I could not fathom; some sort of uncanny prescience that ignited an unwelcomed unsettling feeling. I tried to divert my mind from any negative thoughts to no avail.

As I turned around the corner of the last block leading to my street, I noticed from afar that there was another car parked on the driveway next to Mr. Burton's beloved VW bug. I frowned with suspicion while feeling my facial muscles tense up for no apparent reason. Without even noticing that I'd picked up my pace, I was walking faster as if my feet rushed trying to catch up with the speed of my heart. By the time I was able to identify the kind of vehicle on the driveway of my cherished home, my feet outran my heart by a long shot. I ran nonstop until I barged in the open front door in quasi-desperation mode.

"What happened?" I asked breathing heavily. The sight in the living room left me stricken with horror.

"C'mon sir, stay with me, stay with me," the paramedic repeated frantically while performing cardiopulmonary resuscitation on Mr. Burton splayed on the living room floor.

Instinctively, I moved toward my loving surrogate father but the other paramedic put his arms around me and gently stopped me on my tracks. Looking at him lying unconscious on the hardwood floor, I began perspiring and shivering unremittingly.

"Please don't do this to me, I can't live through this again," I mumbled to myself with trembling lips as panic took over my terrorized mind. Then, when I noticed that the paramedic performing CPR had stopped the pumping and counting, I felt lightheaded on the verge of fainting.

"I'm very sorry." It was all he said before standing up leaving my Mr. Burton dad lifeless on the floor. I extricated myself from the paramedic's gentle hold and lunged on top of the body of the only real dad I'd ever had, and for such a brief time. With my face smashed against his silent chest while my hand caressed his soon-to-be cold face, I burst into uncontrollable tears.

"Are you his daughter?" The paramedic asked me after I finally regained a modicum of self-control.

"Stepdaughter," I replied curtly without moving as my fingers ran through Mr. Burton's hair.

"Is there anyone else related to him?" He asked again.

"His wife, but she's out of town visiting her elderly mother," I answered between intermittent sobbing while still embracing his lifeless body. Suddenly, it dawned on me how the ambulance got to our home in the first place.

"How did you get the call for this emergency?" I asked.

"Somehow he managed to call 911 in the midst of a cardiac arrest," the paramedic answered. "Unfortunately, he was not able to give the full address and that delayed our arrival trying to figure out where the call came from. I wish his wife had been home today. We might have been able to save his life if he had the address available."

As soon as he finished speaking, I felt the pangs of guilt stab me deep into my gut like a murderous dagger slicing my viscera open. Had I not spent my time leisurely with Daniel, I might have been able to save Mr. Burton's life. Besides, I had promised Mrs. Burton that I would keep an eye on him while she was gone. I felt like I'd failed everyone who counted on me; the ones whom I was most grateful for being there for me when I needed the most. Albeit unjustifiable, I felt as guilty for his death as I'd felt for my mother's when I was a child.

"We're going to need to get in touch with his wife," the paramedic said.

Without replying, I stood up and walked to the small desk next to the kitchen table, opened a rectangular red telephone notebook and handed it to him pointing to the number to call.

"I cannot deliver this news to her," I said.

"I'll take care of it, ma'am," he said looking at me in the eye and his gaze exuded commiseration. "Try to get yourself some rest now."

Dejected and distraught, the last thing I could imagine being able to do was to rest. I needed to do something to alleviate the excruciating pain and the unbearable guilt hammering my mind to a useless pulp. Then, as I was closing the drawer, I noticed the VW bug's spare key inside. Without hesitating, I picked it up, put it in my jean's pocket and surreptitiously walked out of the house. I got in the car and sped away as if I raced for my life, though my genuine pursuit was death. I could feel the perspiration soaking up my countenance and my damp hair sticking to the back of my neck. My sweaty hands every now and then slipped off the steering-wheel causing the vehicle to veer off the dangerous windy canyon road. My muddled mind and dilacerated heart were confabulating against any common sense I had left. My feet felt heavy on the gas pedal and soon I reached the top of the canyon—and the zenith of my despair.

Next thing I remember was staring down into the darkness of my soul from a high cliff overlooking the turbulent sea that my life had suddenly become. The blithe mood I'd experienced earlier on the day of my 20th birthday had vanished without a moment's notice. I knew that my birthdays would never be the same again, so I decided that this would be my last. Never would I have death for a birthday gift again. But as soon as I had made up my mind and became determined to put an end to my misery, that strange man showed up literally out of nowhere to put the kibosh on my determination to end my life. His words would haunt me for years to come; and his assurance that we would meet again in the future stalked my thoughts eliciting a great deal of anxiety for what was yet to come. He made me wonder what is like to wager my life as I struggled.

A year after the traumatic death-changing experience of losing a loved one and staring at my own death in the eye for the first time, my life took another upswing turn as love embraced me again in full-force. As I battled continuous bouts of depression, Daniel proved to be the best cornerman in the ring where I fought fierce inner demons. He was there for me every step of the way, tending to the aching wounds of my heart while replenishing the oozing energy of my mind with his loving care. That's when I really fell in love with him; and he, I thought, with me. Thus, on my 21st birthday, in an effort to help erasing the harrowing memories of what used to be my special day, we got married with great fanfare.

Within a few years of marital bliss, it was a matter of time for the ambitious Daniel Trapp to immerse himself completely in his life-long pursuit of increasing wealth, influence, and power.

His efforts panned out and he would go on to accomplish his objectives beyond his wildest dreams. In my turn, though I benefited from extraordinary material abundance, my relationship with him was irremediably compromised by the manner in which he involved me in his unscrupulous business deals. Soon I became but a valuable resource to his business transactions; an appendage to his financial interests. After years of neglect, I realized that I had lost my husband to his indomitable greed. If only I had not lost myself to my own loneliness and despair, maybe I would have not considered putting an end to my life in the future.

◄9►

I was taking a nap in the well-cushioned brown leather couch in the living room when the phone rang. I rubbed my closed eyes in an effort to open them and reached out to the phone on the marble coffee table.

"Honey, I'm here at the penthouse of Anthony Menlo's downtown office building waiting to meet with him," Daniel said almost in a whisper but with unambiguous exuberance percolating through his voice. "If I can persuade him to get me onboard a multinational real estate deal with a select group of foreign investors, we'll be adding an enormous amount of wealth to our investments portfolio."

"That's very good, Daniel," I said nonchalantly.

"Very good? This can be the deal of a lifetime!" He said expressing subtle disapproval of my blasé reaction.

"I'm sorry, Daniel, I didn't mean to minimize the significance of this opportunity. Of course I realize how important this meeting is to you; after all, you've spoken about it all the time in the past month. I'm excited for you," I said in half-truth.

"Of course, I'm going to invite him over for dinner. I'll let you know of the details when I get home later this evening," he said hastily as if he were about to be called in. "Wish me luck."

When I hung up the phone, I slumped on my back with a whistling thump on the fluffy couch. Staring at the ceiling looking at the emptiness in my mind, I wondered how I'd muster the mettle to pull it off one more time. The prospect of participating in his filthy monkey business made me sick to the stomach, even though he assured me this would be the last time we'd have to do it. But I knew it better. For a man with Daniel's irrepressible ambition and greed, there is never a last time; to the contrary, the last time is only the prelude to the next. At this stage in his life, it was not about money anymore; it was about the pursuit of power, domination, and manipulation of others. Like a hunter whose thrill of the chase is more meaningful than killing the prey itself, Daniel's desire to cajole and conquer the powerful Anthony Menlo's attention was where his real gain was; the ultimate reward of his selfish actions. Of course the money was an enticing motivation and a welcome addition; but it was mostly that, the fat red cherry atop the ice-cream sundae of his cold ego.

I stood up and started pacing around the living room as if propelled by anxiety of things to come. As I moved back and forth wondering how this new business deal was going to affect my already bruised self-esteem, I realized there was a similarity between Daniel and my biological father that I'd never thought about before: both were irredeemable gamblers. While my father recurred to small and even petty gambling in order to eke out a living under financial hardship, Daniel's wagers were at a much higher level of operation. Nevertheless, in a sort of bizarre mathematical equation of compulsive behavior, they shared the common denominator of being gambling addicts. While my father played for survival, Daniel played for wealth and power. My father's bets involved furniture and household items he managed to pawn for money to take his scanty chances of temporarily improving his miserable lot. But Daniel played with a much different type of chips he placed on his high stake gambling table. Unlike my father's turning our family's belongings into chump change for gambling, Daniel turned people into capital he invested in his multi-million dollar deals that often times destroyed numerous livelihoods, shattered individual lives, bankrupted businesses, and even obliterated the welfare of underdeveloped nations. At that moment, as I paced in the silent luxury of my living room, I realized that the difference between an ordinary gambling addict and an inveterate capitalist is the degree of their vile disease and the number of lives they devastate with their selfish dealings. Either destroying a family or a nation, they are indifferent to the damage they mete out on their innocent victims.

I was about to step outside to get some fresh air when the phone rang again. I hesitated to pick it up, for I did not want to talk with Daniel again. But when I looked at the caller ID I answered the call with welcome relief and excitement.

"Samantha, my dear friend, you're a bad girl. I haven't heard from you in weeks," I said attempting to disguise the signs of my forlorn mood. "What's my best girlfriend been up to these days?"

"Oh, c'mon Lucy, did anybody break into your memory bank? I told you last month that I was going to be vacationing in Europe with my new squeeze for three weeks. I just got back last night and I'm calling you today. That proves that I'm not that bad of a girl; well, except when I'm in bed with Sean," she said bursting into a jovial laughter that I so badly needed to hear.

"I miss talking with you, my friend" I said in a tone of voice that might have unwittingly revealed the tension I was trying to conceal. I didn't want to bother Samantha with my troubles.

"What's the matter?" She asked clearly picking up the vibes of my turbulent emotions.

"Daniel is setting up another 'the-greatest-deal-of-his-life' move and I've been bracing myself for the occasion," I said feeling relieved and thankful to have someone with whom I could share my innermost anguish. She was the only person I trusted and could rely on.

"What?" She bawled.

Anticipating her condemnation, I remained silent unable to muster the courage to say anything.

"You can't do this again, Lucy. You hear me? You cannot allow yourself to go along with his shenanigans again," she said sounding like an army officer commanding a reluctant private who seems unable to change her old ways.

"This will be the last time, Sam. Daniel and I agreed that after this one we'll be done for good and set for life," I said after an awkward pause.

"Are you trying to lie to me or to yourself? Either way you know it's foolish because neither one of us believe it," she said.

Another long moment of silence ensued followed by a deep despondent sigh. I felt emotionally exhausted just thinking about the burden that my life had become.

"Sometimes I feel like I owe him my life and I have to go along with his desires, needs, and whims," I said. "But the truth is that I'm at my wit's end."

"Not another word," she said but now sounding more like a four-star general delivering an official order. "We need to talk in person and pronto. What about lunch tomorrow at *Bon Appétit* restaurant around one o'clock?"

"I guess I may be…," I said unable to finish my sentence.

"Good! I'm glad you can make it. I'll see you tomorrow at one," she said ending the call abruptly.

Samantha was not only my best but the only real friend I'd ever had. She was like an older sister who advised, guided, and watched over me with intrepid determination to protect me from harm and danger. Since the early days of our budding friendship when she learned about my troubled past, she took upon herself to serve as my *de facto* guardian angel on Earth. Although she came from a socioeconomic background of privilege, she seemed to relate to my deprived pecuniary upbringing in a vicarious way that at first astounded me. It was a matter of time for me to realize that it was her enormously compassionate heart that allowed her to see me as very few people in my life ever had. But when it came to my state of affairs with Daniel, she had a very personal bone to pick, for she had experienced similar situation in her erstwhile marriage, though not nearly as ignominious as mine.

◄10►

"**Y**ou cannot allow yourself to put up with this crap anymore, Lucy. I can see how the mere anticipation of going along with his monkey business again is affecting you," Samantha said while sipping on her mint ice tea. "Really, this is having a heavy toll on your physical, psychological, and emotional health. You cannot continue carrying on this concubine role. The time to put an end to it has come."

With my tuna sandwich inside my mouth, I paused in mid-bite lifting my chin to look at her. Her eyes were blazing with the same intense conviction that her words expressed. Knowing that she had gone through a similar situation in her life, though not quite as egregious as mine, I could not help but heed my friend's advice. After a brief pause, I bit on my sandwich and started chewing while looking into her eye without saying a word.

"How much longer do you think you can go on like this?" She asked placing her cold glass on the table. "You know as well as I do that this is not going to end unless you put the kibosh on it. You are the only one who can put an end to this sham."

"I don't know how," I mumbled almost inaudibly.

"What? You're telling me you don't know what you need to do to put an end to abuse? Well, my dear, it's very simple: you just refuse to do what goes against your principles," Samantha said frowning with a stern look in her face that made me feel embarrassed. "Listen, this is your life and you're the only one who has sovereignty over it. You cannot allow Daniel, or anyone else for that matter, to decide what you should or should not do. In the end, you're the only one who must live with the consequences of your actions, or the lack thereof as the case may be."

I wiped off my mouth with the napkin and kept it over my lips as if it were a white cotton muzzle that hindered my ability to speak. I tried to ignore her unyielding stare that demanded something from me that I wasn't sure I had to give. Not flinching, she raised her eyebrow silently telling me to speak my mind.

"I've made up my mind, Sam, this will be the last time and I'll never do it again," I said unsure if I was trying to convince her or myself of something neither of us believed.

Her intense gaze was piercing through the falsehood my eyes were likely displaying as I uttered unconvincing words. Suddenly, she turned her head sideways and nodded in disapproving fashion.

"I don't know, Lucy, I don't know," she spoke softly without looking at me. "I've been through similar situation and I feel for you. But at this point in my life, just the thought of having to go through it again makes me cringe to my bones. It's hard to believe you don't feel the same way."

"Of course I do!" I said brashly.

"Then, why do you hesitate to do something about it? Why don't you take action right away?" She asked still demanding a straight answer from me.

"Because…, well, because…I owe it to Daniel. I'm in his debt for what he's done for me," I said.

"Lucy, my dear, please, look at what he's doing to you now? He's leading you back to a life of trauma that you long have left behind. If you allow this to continue, you might end up seriously damaged in more than one way," she said as I shivered hearing her harsh warning.

"One last time, Sam, I promise you; one last time and I'll never do it again," I said striving to sound resolute.

She said nothing for a long time. I vividly remember the cold eerie silence preceding Samantha's words. It felt as though the air had been permeated with a presage of things to come; an unofficial announcement of my kismet.

"Well Lucy, I don't know what else to say. You're a big girl and should make your own decisions. But I'll tell you something, my friend, if it were me, I wouldn't be able to play the filthy game anymore," she said and an ill-omened pause permeated the air. When she resumed speaking, an uncanny prescience captured my attention in a way I wish it had not. "Personally, I'd rather die than have to submit myself to such indignation again."

Later that evening I struggled to fall asleep. I lay in bed with my eyes wide open thinking of Samantha's words while listening to Daniel's dissonant snoring as it reverberated in my raucous mind. I tossed and turned at every thought of what was coming ahead. I sweat and shivered at every memory of the past times I was enticed to participate in his business deals. This was going to be the third time I'd agreed to take part in his sordid business scams; but this time, it was going to be the last.

Third strike and I'd be out—for good.

◁ 11 ▷

The first time it happened was around the year of our fifth anniversary. At that time, Daniel's business ventures were beginning to take off and he desperately needed capital; lots of it. I'm not sure how he managed to infiltrate the inside circles of high-powered financial bankers. All I know is what he told me the night he planned to set up the first scheme that he would repeat twice again in the future.

"Honey, I think we're finally beginning to move in the right direction," Daniel said while pouring himself a double whisky at the drink cart in our recently remodeled spacious living room. "Remember that shopping center project that I talked with you about last month?

"I do. How's it progressing?" I asked uninterestedly while leafing through a magazine. I'd reached a point of complete indifference to his business projects.

"Well, today I met a real pooh-bah in the financial industry who has shown a great deal of interest in learning more about the project. If he decides to come onboard, I should have the building up and running in no time. If this goes through, we'll collect hundreds of thousands of dollars in rental income of which a fraction will go to pay the loan at a ridiculously low interest rate. It will be a homerun with bases loaded."

"It sounds great, Daniel, I'm so excited you're making this happen. Is there anything I can do to be of help?" I suggested in my naïveté of the early years of our marriage.

He didn't answer right away. Instead, he kept walking slowly toward me with a pensive expression and a sly smile delineating his handsome face. I noticed how he held the whisky glass in his right hand as if it were a symbolic trophy of success; a silent statement of accomplishment in the business world. In my turn, I was proud of him for going full-on after what he wanted most in life: money and power. In fact, I admired his resolution and the way he applied his unfettered ambition as the fuel to propel him forward. I was also very grateful to be a beneficiary of his unstoppable drive to achieve economic success. But that was then, when I didn't know yet what would be required of me in the course of his path to riches.

"Perhaps, we should start it with a casual strategy; an informal approach to bait the hook," he said sitting next to me with vacant eyes as if he mulled over his scheme.

"What do you have in mind?" I asked.

"I'm thinking about inviting him over for a get-to-know-each-other dinner; something casual, informal, and entertaining; a sort of an icebreaker," he said still not looking at me. Suddenly, he turned around and looked me in the eye. "What do you think about having him over for dinner this weekend? I'm going to see him tomorrow and I can invite him then. What do you say?"

"Sure," I said. "Why not?"

"Good. I'll make arrangements," he said standing up abruptly and walking away.

The weekend arrived not a day too soon. I finally got to meet the famed investment banker that would catapult us up to the higher rungs of the coveted economic ladder. Charles Belstein, was a short, pudgy, bald, and very white man with an extremely unattractive personality to match his repulsive physical attributes. His large squared black frame spectacles seemed to slide continually down the bridge of his elongated nose, which added another peculiar element that exacerbated his ungainly appearance. He was, indeed, an odd specimen; a sort of a human and hog hybrid. But he was rich—filthy rich. And he was the fuel that would propel our rocket of fortune through the stratosphere of abundance. Thus, my role was to be a charming hostess who would help open the gates of opportunity for my husband's ambitious business transactions.

"Mrs. Trapp, you have a lovely home," Charles Belstein said as we sat on the couch in the living room after dinner. "Your decorative flair is absolutely exquisite."

Something was not right. As soon as he finished his last sentence, he touched my thigh, just above the knee, and winked at me with surreptitious mischievousness. As soon as I noticed the subtle malice in his eye, I turned my glance away instinctively. I felt very uncomfortable, both with Belstein's manners as well as Daniel's impassive reaction. He clearly witnessed the incident, for he was sitting right across and smiling as though he enjoyed the banker's inappropriate fawning behavior. Later in the evening, I let Daniel know of my disappointment with his indifference.

"How could you remain so passive watching that repugnant man make a not-so-subtle pass at me?" I said at the end of the evening as we were getting ready to go to sleep.

"Oh, c'mon Lucy, Charles is just a nerd goofball. He doesn't have any sense of how to communicate with the opposite sex. He wasn't really flirting with you; he was rescuing himself from embarrassment," Daniel said walking out of the bathroom naked with only a white towel around his neck.

I looked at him with a slew of mixed feelings. There was the man I loved but whom I did not seem to know anymore. His sole life's purpose was all about accumulating more and more wealth, and the wealth itself was not even the main reward. I began wondering what I meant to this man in the scope of his grandiose ambitions. I wasn't sure if or where I fit in his life. But at that moment it was about me and the conflicting feelings I was experiencing simultaneously: love and repulsion; admiration and abomination; pride and disappointment; trust and suspicion; all happening at once as though a dam of emotions broke loose inside of me inundating my overwhelmed being.

"Come babe, let's celebrate this promising night," he said getting under the sheets and pulling me toward him. My body gave way but my mind stayed behind immersed in a murky pool of conflicting thoughts and feelings.

He passed out almost immediately after having sex with me, and I didn't even become aware of the sex act until he fell asleep on top of me. I stayed awake for a long time thinking about the evening and how uncomfortable I felt with that creepy man sitting next to me on the couch acting randy, uttering suggestive words, staring at me in insinuating ways, and making assertive moves while casually touching my thigh. But worst of all, I was deeply saddened that my husband, the man I loved and admired, was utterly indifferent to our guest's inappropriate behavior. Although I knew how much Daniel needed the financial support of the investment banker, I didn't expect to be delegated to a secondary level in his interests, which was painful to realize where I stood in the grand scheme of his priorities.

And just when I thought it couldn't get any worse, it did.

<h1 style="text-align:center">◀12▶</h1>

"Lucy, Lucy," Daniel barged in the house calling out my name with excitement exuding through his voice. "I have a present for you."

I smiled feeling great joy. The year of our fifth anniversary was going so smoothly and I was excited about what the future would bring. After all, they say the fifth year of marriage is of special significance for the couple. Supposedly, it's the milestone in which the union transitions from newlyweds to a bona fide common life partnership, though in many cases it might not be as romantic and committed as it seems.

"Here," he said handing me a large white box with a wide red ribbon around it. "It's something very, very beautiful. I think you're going to like it."

I took it from his hands with my eyes smiling at him.

"C'mon, go ahead and open it," he said as I stood there loving him with my eyes.

I placed the package on the sofa and gently removed the red ribbon around the edges. For some schmaltzy reason, I didn't want to damage it. Inside the box, a gorgeous silk red dress blossomed before my eyes like a blooming rose surrounded by glossy soft white wrapping paper.

"What do you think?" He asked lasciviously.

"It's dazzling!" I said holding the thin spaghetti strap dress in front of me.

"It's for you to wear for our special celebration dinner tomorrow," he said.

"Well, where are you planning to take me wearing a dress like this?" I whispered in his ears with my arms around his neck.

"We're not going anywhere in particular, except up and up," he said before kissing me on the lips. "Tomorrow we'll host the signing document of my business partnership with one of the leading honchos in the real estate investment banking industry."

"What do you mean?" I asked dropping my arms from around his neck with a heavy thump in a vacuum space of disappointment.

"Charles Belstein agreed to partner with me and requested that we sign the document at a dinner celebration here at home tomorrow before he leaves for Europe the next day," he said.

"But tomorrow…, tomorrow we had planned to go out just the two of us," I said with subdued objection. "I thought we were going to celebrate it in some special way, just the two of us."

"I know, babe, but Charles is going to attend an international banking conference overseas the day after tomorrow, so I obliged to accommodate his schedule. And considering what this business partnership will mean to us, I thought you'd be O.K. with this arrangement," he said trying to validate his decision against the passive opposition of my dispirited demeanor. "I'll make it up to you; I promise."

I was dumbfounded. I was expecting to be dined and wined wearing a beautiful sexy red dress that he would rip off my body for desert. I thought our marriage; I thought I was important to him. And perhaps I was, but not in a manner I romanticized. I was valuable in a very peculiar way directly related to his unbridled ambition. I knew he'd compromise anything to achieve his financial goals. I just never had imagined that I'd become a sacrificial pawn in the chess game of his business dealings.

The next day when Charles Belstein came over for dinner, I answered the door wearing the alluring dress my husband had purchased for the special occasion. I still remember with a great deal of disgust the old man's drooping face when he saw me. With his eyes wide open, mouth agape, and his left hand inside his trousers' pocket subtly touching his crotch, he took my hand and kissed it for what it felt like a repugnant eternity. I led him in the house while rubbing off my hand on the silk dress to dry up the slimy slobber he managed to generate with his sodden mouth. Waiting for us in the living room, Daniel welcomed his guest with disingenuous hospitality, though I could see how excited he was with the prospect of the benefits of Belstein's visit.

Determined to impress his new business partner, Daniel made arrangements to cater the dinner. We had lobster for dinner, *Don Pérignon* champagne to wash it down—plenty of champagne—chocolate mousse with strawberries for desert, and then we moved to the living room for some *Louis XIII de Remi Martin* cognac in preparation for the most coveted item of the evening. The titillating anticipation of the signing of the financial investment agreement had finally arrived for Daniel. As for Belstein, his own apotheosis moment awaited shortly after the ink dried on the contract paper.

"Honey, why don't you entertain Charles for a moment while I put these documents away in the safe," Daniel said shuffling his feet out of the living room. Clearly, he had too much to drink.

After Daniel left the room, a brief awkward silent moment ensued. Suddenly, Belstein scooted it over closer to me on the couch and placed his right hand on my inner thigh with a strong grip. I jolted backward with his unexpected audacity, then immediately grabbed his hand off me. He looked at me with defying eyes as though I was the one infringing upon his rights. He was visibly inebriated.

"What's the matter?" He asked running the back of his fingers on my neck and down my cleavage. "Now that we've closed the deal I need to be compensated."

"Compensated…," I repeated to myself looking at Belstein in disbelief while thinking of Daniel with utmost disdain. I wanted to scream but I knew it would be in vain. After all, I was the unwritten clause of the financial agreement that allowed my husband to close a very lucrative business deal that left my self-esteem impoverished and my marriage bankrupt.

It was one of the most miserable nights of my life—and alas, I've had plenty. The old disgusting codger had his way with me in my own bedroom while my husband celebrated his big business achievement in the room next door; alone with his despicable greed. At the end of the nightmarish evening, I swore to myself nothing like this would ever happen to me again. I was wrong. A few years later, Daniel set me up on a high stakes business deal that revealed to me the sordid human nature; and the unscrupulous world of economic transactions; and the immoral makeup of politics; and on a deeply personal level, my disillusion with marriage and romantic love.

That evening was an inflection point in my life. After that second experience, I began losing my will to live.

◄13►

After a period of great prosperity, Daniel's expanding entrepreneurial ventures came to a screeching halt. The markets, well known for their tidal nature to ebb and flow at the whims of volatile financial events, slid down the slippery slope of uncertainty toward the cyclical pattern of economic recession. But this time around it hit hard and long. Both businesses and individuals were filing for bankruptcy in droves. The wealthy became terrified of losing their financial advantage. The middle-class began falling like bowling pins in the back alley of unemployment. And the poor were the only members of an economic class that remained the same, albeit with significant more numbers joining their inauspicious rank. It was a time of economic chaos, and Daniel was scared stiff of potential financial misfortunes that could befall on him. That's when he knocked on the backdoor of politics hoping to find a secure entryway out of trouble.

Afraid of sinking his cargo vessel in the turbulent sea of economic volatility, he knew that he had to keep his business investments afloat, lest he'd end up like many of his peers who sank to the bottom of the financial ocean floor. Thus, in order to rescue the cargo ship of his wealth, he docked it at the safe harbor of politics; the special place the privileged resort to ensure protection from the storms of the market. And as I witnessed, the inside shenanigans worked like a charm.

Daniel's first foray into the political marketplace was as a lobbyist for a multinational housing development company. Having been in the real estate business for quite some time and with investments around the world, he found a way to associate with an international group that needed special deregulation initiatives in the legislative branch of government. Being a schmoozer extraordinaire who touted himself to be a bellwether of all trades, he was a perfect fit for the job of political mongering. It was a matter of time for him to be hobnobbing with the most influential politicians in the nation; and among them, Senator Robert Faradell was at the top of the totem pole of political corruption. He belonged to the privileged political class where influence is bought and sold; not with the cheap currency of people's votes, but with large sums of capital from interest groups.

Senator Faradell was a towering and burly septuagenarian with the disposition of someone twice his junior. The only thing larger than his physical presence was his colossal ego, which could be gratified only by accumulation of wealth and power. In spite of his well manicured appearance adorned by expensive suits and colorful ties, he looked to me like an anthropomorphized version of a human hog. And I despised everything about him. Although his slimy demeanor was abhorrent, it was the immorality of his character that gave me the heebie-jeebies. I'd learned through Daniel about the debaucheries and chicaneries that Senator Faradell managed to pull off in both his personal and public dealings, and I was appalled long before I met the man. Thus, when Daniel told me that he was closing in on a business deal with the high-powered politician, I became anxiously concerned about my wellbeing. After my traumatizing experience with Charles Belstein's business deal years earlier, I intuitively knew that it would be a matter of time for Daniel to engage me in another demeaning scheme. Sure enough what I dreaded the most came into being in no time.

"Remember that bailout contract I told you about?" Daniel said while chewing on a bloody rare bite of fillet mignon steak at a swanky restaurant dinner table. "Well, Senator Faradell and I are flying to Africa next week to close the deal. We're going to make hundreds of millions in this transaction."

"I don't understand how Senator Faradell can be involved in a business transaction that involves purchasing the national debt of an impoverished small African nation," I said expressing what had been baffling my mind since the first day Daniel told me about the potential business deal. "After all, he is a politician and for what I know he's supposed to be representing our country, not his personal interests."

"Of course he's representing our national interests," Daniel replied with a snarky smirk that matched the tone of his voice. "Under a private consulting contract, I'm the one who's carrying out his personal business interests in his behalf; for a big share of the loot, of course."

He paused to take a sip of wine and then continued.

"You see, this is why we partnered in the first place. He established the political connections and opened the way to introduce me as a member of the business community that will help this impoverished nation recover from insidious economic hardship. Then, with the money of a behind the scene coalition of investors that include Senator Faradell, we'll buy out their massive national debt so that we can sell it to other investors vying to explore the country's vast natural resources, especially their gold and diamond mines, both of which are immensely more valuable than the national debt itself. It's a devilishly ingenious strategy."

I looked at the ebullient expression in his face wondering how in the world we've come to turning millions of people's misery into a handful of millionaires. I mused on how our economic system manages to generate extraordinary wealth for a few while at the same time producing widespread poverty for countless many. It is such a wickedly fashioned economic system that even poverty itself becomes a commodity for profit. Be it the debt of an individual or the debt of a nation, the people behind the financial institutions know how to capitalize on the vulnerability of the dispossessed. And backing up their unbridled initiatives, the political system, which has become a sort of public corporation for private corporations' agenda, succumbs into mediocrity, corruption, and shame.

As I brooded over the disreputable means of carrying out business as usual, suddenly I became aware that I, like poverty, had been turned into a commodity of trade as well. The thought jolted me back to the present moment reminding me that I was in imminent danger of becoming involved in the negotiations. In fact, it was very likely that I was already an unwritten clause in the agreement. At that moment, Daniel raised his chin to look at me as though he was prescient of my feelings. His eyes pierced through my fears bursting my dreaded bubble into reality.

"By the way, honey, I invited Senator Faradell to have dinner with us this Saturday," he said nonchalantly as if attempting to masquerade his hidden intention.

"This Saturday," I repeated feeling my throat dry up with traumatic trepidation.

"Yes," he said with exuberance oozing from every letter of the word. "We want to celebrate this lucrative business deal with festive zeal. After all, this is a momentous occasion."

"Are you signing any agreements on Saturday as well?" I asked already knowing the answer.

"Yes," he said, but this time the exuberance was replaced by subdued enthusiasm as though beseeching me not to balk.

I lowered my head in shameful submission and didn't say anything else. A long uncomfortable silence filled the air with unspoken matrimonial discord.

"Listen, honey, I know I ask too much of you, but this is huge; I mean really big, especially in this difficult financial times we've been going through," he said holding my chin while looking me in the eye trying to inveigle me. "Since that day you came to my office and Senator Faradell laid his eyes on you he was, in his own words, 'bewitched with your charms.' And once he found out about Charles Belstein, he pretty much demanded to have a similar deal. We have no way out."

Listening to my husband telling me how a despicable man referred to his wife in a sexual context could have been heart-wrenching. And yet, in the grand scheme of my humiliation, it didn't bother me at all. I remained silent with my head down in order to avoid making eye contact with the conspirator. I interlaced my fingers and squeezed them between my thighs as my eyes moistened with sadness.

"This time around it's even more complicated," he said attempting to convince me of the importance of my sacrifice. "Senator Faradell knows of my inside trading deals and he's insinuated several times that he'd turn me in if anything goes awry in this deal; anything."

A long silence ensued as I remained unmovable. Suddenly, he resumed his untrustworthy cajoling talk.

"This time is not only about money, Lucy; it's about my freedom. Do you realize what's at stake? You don't want your husband to go to jail, do you?" He asked.

At that moment, in the privacy of my jumbled thoughts and turbulent emotions, I felt wicked to wish I did. Maybe it was the only way to my own freedom.

"Please, Lucy, say something," he insisted.

"I think it's time to go home," I said standing up abruptly.

On the silent drive home, I felt like a lonely sheep heading to the slaughterhouse aware that I was going to end up on the dinner plate of another powerful man. Infallibly, on the following Saturday I was the *"plate du jour"* of the African nation exploitation deal dinner party. Daniel served me garnished in a low cleavage black mini dress, and Senator Faradell consumed me with voracious sexual appetite. After being digested and eliminated, I sympathized with the population of the poor African nation they were going to carve out and serve for others to profit. We shared something in common: we were all disposable human commodities at the mercy of ravenous human vultures.

With my self-esteem crushed and my sense of self-worth utterly dilacerated, my life had become a meaningless experience of disappointment and futility. My appreciation for Daniel had faded away and turned into bitter resentment. And yet, I held on to my love for him as if he were a vine on the edge of the precipice of my insecurities. But I knew that any jerking motion would cause me to fall down into the frightening abyss below.

Alas, a couple of years later Anthony Menlo became the sharp knife that severed the fragile vine that kept me from succumbing to my untimely death.

◁14▷

"**B**ut this Friday is our anniversary and my 38th birthday!" I said in subdued protest against a last minute arrangement I was not ready to accept. "We've talked about going away to the coast for the weekend, remember?"

"I'm so sorry, honey, but this is the only day he can make it," Daniel said dismissing my objection with casual indifference. "I'll make it up to you, I promise. Once we close this deal, I'll take you to *Côte d'Azur* in the French Riviera. There we can celebrate everything: our anniversary, your birthday, and this milestone business achievement, which shall be one of the most profitable of our lives."

After years of marital transgressions and disappointments with the man I thought I loved, I should have gotten accustomed to knowing that his business interests always preceded mine, our marriage, or any other for that matter. But this time it bothered me more than ever. I felt I'd reached the tipping point of my tolerance threshold. This was going to be the third time I'd be made into a bargaining tool Daniel wielded to facilitate his business transactions. Like a chip on a gambling table, I was tossed about, moved around, and piled up on high stake bets in which I always lost everything, including the smattering of self-worth I had left.

The first time I was wheedled to participate in his business deals I was shocked that he enlisted me; and even more so that I submitted to his wiles. The second time, because of the threat to Daniel's inside trading revelations, I was numbed by the circumstances and apathetic to a situation I'd lost control. But the third time was different; it was about my reaching the saturation point; the point of no return. I felt like it was the *coup de grace* I needed to put an end to it once and for all. Like the denouement of Giuseppe Verdi's *La Traviata*, I wanted to exit the stage in a grand finale leaving a memorable impact to the tragic opera that my life had become. However, I would not go out alone. I was going to take everyone who contributed to my premature and premeditated death along for an unforgettable ride into the shame I knew so well.

15

"Oh please, Lucy. We've been on this road before. It's become the beaten path of futility," my good friend Samantha said one afternoon when I invited her over for tea at my sprawling property. "In fact, we've been talking about this for years and you just seem incapable to muster the chutzpah to disentangle yourself from this morass. What else do you want me to say to you?"

I looked at her while digesting her words and the truth made me feel blameworthy of my subservient weakness. She was right. I had been unable to extricate myself from what had turned into an unbearable situation I could no longer endure. I'd become a morally spineless woman beleaguered by shame and guilt.

Although the ignominious incidents happened intermittently through the years, the lingering negative psychological effects persisted with festering consequences. My love for my husband had been tainted with loathsome sentiments of resentment and disdain, which eventually spilled over to my own self-esteem. It was a matter of time until I began feeling overwhelmed with self-contempt. I had to do something about it if I were to survive.

"Listen, I totally understand that your lifestyle has entrapped you in this unbearable situation, but you have options to freedom, if you choose to do so," Samantha said after a brief moment of silence. "Look at my own example; I'm a living testimony that it's doable. Since I bailed out from my miserable marriage I never looked back, and I've been much better off ever since. I trust you can do the same if you muster the courage to take action."

"I remember one option to freedom that you mentioned a few years ago," I said as if I were musing out loud.

"I don't recall ever suggesting any options to freedom to you," she said staring at me with an inquisitive frown. "What's it I said?"

"You said that 'personally you'd rather die than have to submit yourself to such indignation again'," I repeated her words verbatim as she'd voiced them to me years back. They had become indelibly etched in my memory.

"What are you talking about?" She asked leaning forward with a startled raised eyebrow.

I avoided her intimidating eye contact that demanded an explanation. I looked up toward the trees as though attempting to find a hollow space to hide my gaucherie.

"I don't remember ever saying anything like that to you; but if I did, it was figuratively speaking. It'd never be my intention to have such words taken for face value," she said as the tone of her voice switched to a crescendo filled with apprehension.

"Of course I know it, Sam, of course," I said lightheartedly in an effort to assuage her evident uneasiness. "I guess the reason I remember it is because it reminds me of how vitally important this issue is; so much so, that it must be resolved pronto."

I was guilt-ridden to have lied to my best friend, but I had no choice. I could not have shared my plans with her, for most certainly she would not have allowed me to carry them out. I had to contrive it alone, in the solitude and privacy of my anguished soul without anyone's complicity to the planning of my crime.

Later that afternoon after she left my home, I spent hours on a lounging chair by the swimming pool with a yellow pad and pen in hand. I started working on what ended up being a long piece of writing; a well designed plot for my post-mortem goals. For the first time in my life I felt like I had the luxury to plan for my future according to my own will; and I premeditated it with thorough minutiae.

After meticulous preparation and gathering all the necessary components to effectuate my strategy, when the ill-fated day arrived I was ready for it. Nothing was going to stop me this time.

◄16►

"He is here," Daniel yelled out as soon as the door bell rang. "Hurry up!"

"I'll be down there in a minute," I replied from the bedroom upstairs while arraying myself in the stunning black satin dress.

I hurried fastening the emerald necklace adorning my torso and noticed how it screamed attention to my bold cleavage. The shiny green gem dangled slightly above my breasts like a suspended lighthouse directing coveting eyes to the tantalizing harbor of my bosom. The truth, however, is that it was more like a deceptive lure of a mermaid's enchantment leading hopeless sailors to their imminent demise. I looked in the mirror one last time, adjusted the matching emerald earrings, and then looked at myself in the eye.

"The moment has finally arrived," I whispered before turning around to head downstairs where my perpetrators eagerly waited for me.

I walked down the circular stairway feeling like a luxury harlot geared up to perform my lascivious duties. But it didn't matter anymore. This last time I got into it and I was determined to make an indelible impression. I was going to deliver a performance for the ages before exiting the stage for good. It was my final role in another dreary act of the tragedy of my life. I purposefully stopped mid-way down so they could behold me in the

◄61►

lavishing black satin dress from the distance; a subtle visual tease to sexual appetite. From where I stood high above, I seductively looked at them as if they were helpless flies caught in the web of temptation and about to be devoured by a wicked black widow spider. I could feel the sexual energy exuding from the core of my being as it bewitched my vulnerable preys.

"You look absolutely dazzling, Lucy; like a Greek goddess descending from Olympus," Anthony Menlo said gawking at me while my husband stood indifferent next to him.

Outwardly, I smiled as though enjoying the compliment. Inside, however, I was crying out for help; screaming from the bottom of my stifled lungs for my husband to do something to save me from what I was about to do.

"She's gorgeous, isn't she?" Daniel said addressing Anthony Menlo with perverted excitement.

Now I knew there was nothing else left for me to do but to carry out my deadly plot.

After downing half-bottle of *Chateau Lafite Rothschild* with my bloody red rare filet mignon dinner, I felt primed to move on to the first step of my compulsive self-destructive plan. I kept the conversation at a casual and friendly level waiting for the cues to take action. Then, when we moved to the living room for the cognac and cigar segment of the evening, I knew it was the prelude to the main event. I decided it was the time to set up the ruse.

"I'll let you gentlemen enjoy your cigars and brandy," I said standing up.

"Oh, please don't leave us," Anthony said staring at me with lustful eyes. "The cigar and brandy will not taste the same without you in the room."

"I'm going upstairs to slip into something more comfortable," I said with a contrived sensual tone of voice accompanied by a randy look in the eye. "I need to get ready for my bed time, Anthony. You excuse me, don't you?"

"Of…course," he stuttered while dropping the cigar he held between his fingers on the floor.

Like a sailor walking the plank on a pirate's ship, I climbed the circular stairways with tremulous knees. Every step up punctuated by the sound of my stilettos reminded me that it was the last time I'd be going in that direction. I was at peace with it; after all, I was about to put an end to my misery.

After ingesting a cocktail of barbiturates I'd carefully prepared, I placed a flash drive and a note on Daniel's desk and ensconced in bed to wait for my last business assignment. Not a minute too soon the door opened, without a knock, and the exuberant Anthony Menlo walked in as if he'd entered a heavenly harem of one.

"Come, Tony boy, come to your mamma," I said beckoning at him with my indicator finger and a tantalizing gaze while kneeling on the bed in a provocative pose. He had succumbed to my feminine spell. I was in control.

Agape, he walked slowly toward me beaming with excitement and ardent anticipation. I pulled the thin pink lacy strap off my lingerie and felt it slide gently down my breasts tickling my nipples. Ignited by the visual temptation, he undressed hastily and embraced me with uncontained passion. His malodorous, flaccid, and unshapely body pressing against mine triggered a revolting response that made me shiver, which likely led him erroneously to infer that I was aroused by his caresses. He upped the ante. He started kissing me and the stench coming out of his salivating mouth made me feel queasy. Not even the reek of alcohol and cigar smoke assuaged his repulsive fetid breath and the repugnant taste of the experience. By the time he penetrated me, I noticed I was gradually slipping away into the embrace of death.

The more he stroked me, the more rapidly I fell into unconsciousness, until I was completely gone—for good.

◄17►

"Oh my God!" Anthony screamed in terror from the bottom of his lungs holding my naked dead body in his arms. Sitting on the corner of the bed, I watched the whole drama unfold with great interest.

Obviously startled by Anthony's panicky bawling, Daniel rushed upstairs and barged into the bedroom looking utterly discombobulated.

"What the hell is going on here?" Daniel asked petrified in the middle of the room. "What the fuck did you do to her?"

"She's…dead!" Anthony struggled to say the last word.

"What the fuck just happened here?" Daniel yelled sounding louder, angrier, and more disoriented with every tick of the clock.

"She…she…died on me; in the middle…of the act," Anthony stuttered with a whimpering voice. His extremely pallid face made him look like he could drop dead at any moment, too. "What are we going to do?"

Daniel paced back and forth with his right hand covering his mouth as though he restrained himself from screaming. Anxiety and fear made his eyes look like they were bulging out of the sockets. He looked terrified and every move he made revealed his consternation. In the midst of his uncontrollable pacing, he stopped when noticing my note and the flash drive on his desk.

"What the hell is this?" He said to himself holding my note and the flash drive in his hand. He opened the envelope and started reading it. His face was growing increasingly colorless until he turned even paler than Anthony.

"What's the matter?" Anthony asked looking horror-struck while moving toward the desk.

Without saying a word, Daniel powered on his computer and inserted the flash drive in it. Then, to the astonishment of both men, there I was, alive again, making a compromising statement on video. As they watched the approximately 25-minute diatribe testimony, they looked intermittently at each other in utter dismay. After years witnessing and learning details about their corrupt political and financial shenanigans, I documented on video all that I knew about their lies, chicaneries, tax evasions, briberies, and a slew of other crimes, as well as evidences to my testimony. Then, at the end of the video recording, I listed a summary of media outlets, antagonistic political groups, business rivals, personal enemies, courts, and even wives whom I thought would be interested in learning how much fortune was stacked away in offshore accounts without their knowledge—and the name of mistresses benefiting from the clandestine wealth. I made it clear that everyone on the list received a copy of the flash drive in the mail.

They left the bedroom in complete emotional and psychological disarray leaving my lifeless body on the bed unattended. Babbling incessantly without making any sense, they considered what they were going to do next. I smirked. I felt vindicated.

Suddenly, like a dreadful lightning bolt harbingering a fast-approaching storm, I was struck and swept away into a consciousness that had evaded me hitherto. I was no longer a living biological organism. I was physically dead; and like those men, I didn't know what to do next. I panicked. I stood up and the lightness of my being disturbed me. All of a sudden, the room temperature started dropping significantly while the light kept dimming piecemeal. I hugged myself shivering as the darkness enveloped me like a thick blanket of gloom. I wanted to cry out for help but my vocal chords had been severed off from my will. My heart started feeling heavy with the weight of guilt of what I'd just done. I tried to skedaddle out of the house but my feet were cemented in place; right at the center of a dark circle I could not escape. I felt being siphoned into a black hole where disconsolate wailing echoed from its depth. As I began spiraling faster down into this somber vertical tunnel, I released an inaudible howling of despair amidst loud sounds of despondent weeping. Overwhelmed by the darkness that consumed me into nothingness, I vaguely heard a familiar voice whispering in my ears.

"Remember the time I tried to stop you from jumping off the edge of a cliff on your 20th birthday? I told you then that we'd cross paths again. Well, here we are. But this time you have a formidable challenge to overcome. Death is child's play in comparison to unforgiving regret."

"Oh my God! What have I done? What am I going to do?" I bawled in despair.

"You'll have to relearn how to live all over again."

PART II

AFTER

❰18❱

After travelling at extraordinary speed churning inside a murky cloud in a downward spiraling vortex, I crash-landed on an utterly desolate place that reeked of decomposing organic matter. The insidious odor of death blending in with dense layers of sulfur emanating from the dry lifeless soil made me feel nauseated. I vomited nonstop until my empty stomach convulsed involuntarily. Sick and disoriented, I wondered whether I was having an actual life-like experience or it was just a frightening nightmare from which I'd soon wake up.

Although the lightness of my being corroborated that I'd lost my physical body, I oddly experienced both neurological sensations and bodily functions of my erstwhile bio-organic existence. And even though I was bereft of a body, I felt both physically and emotionally exhausted. I tried to fall asleep but I realized that I was in a permanent theta wave frequency state of being. I was neither awake nor asleep; neither alive nor dead.

Suddenly, I noticed the temperature gradually rising to a crescendo heat wave that enveloped me like a heavy wool blanket on a hot summer day. I began perspiring profusely. The sultry air dried my mouth, scratched my throat, and irritated my lungs with every single breath I struggled to take. My eyes burned intensely to the point of extreme lacrimation. Soon, it became unbearably uncomfortable and I was compelled to cover my mouth and nose with my forearm while closing my eyes in a desperate attempt for relief. It got worse. The heat was intensifying as a bonfire of despair burned inside of me. Then, in my mind's eye I saw a large red rectangular thermometer hanging on a black wall. As I stared at it, the mercury inside kept moving up steadily at the same time the high temperature reached a level that it felt as though I was burning alive at the stake of my misery. When the mercury reached the zenith, the thermometer exploded spattering its poisonous chemical in my face.

"Oh my God!" I screamed as my panicky voice echoed the terror I was experiencing. A grossly deformed large face zoomed in and out within inches from mine while releasing a boisterous baritone evil laughter. The more scared I felt, the more intense the sight and sound became. With my eyes closed, I started tossing and turning in a futile attempt to avoid the visual encounter with that harassing bestial entity. Not only it didn't work but it upset my inquisitor.

"How dare you turn away from me," he yelled and his hoarse dissonant voice made me cringe. "You've given up your right to live and now you must submit your will to the whims of death. I own you now, you fucking cunt! You're my bitch!"

I was completely discombobulated as the harbinger of horror turned up the knob of my affliction to an unbearable level. Suddenly, the frightening sight of his disfigured face, the raucous bawling of his croaky voice, and a continuous counter clockwise circular motion all sped up simultaneously at a dizzying pace. I started throwing up again as my empty stomach convulsed uncontrollably. Lightheaded, spent, sick, and hopeless, I felt like I was experiencing a gruesome form of death. I cried out for help.

"I cannot take this anymore. I beg for forgiveness and assistance," I shouted amidst the clamoring reverberations of the high pitch diabolic laughter.

Then, almost instantaneously, I felt a larger than life presence next to me. I could sense high frequency wavelengths carrying me away as though I'd been ensnared by a powerful gravitational force that hurled me through the lattice of spacetime in slingshot fashion. I landed on a downy turquoise nebula that felt like a most comfortable bed; an auspicious cradle for those destined to enjoy the gentle sleep of death. I dozed off without even noticing; as if I were under the influence of a potent anesthetic. Soon I blacked out only to awaken realizing that relief was nowhere in sight.

I woke up rubbing my eyes feeling as if I had slept for days in a roll. My body ached and my mind was muddled in a state of semi-awareness and I could not comprehend what was going on. It felt as though I'd woken up to another dream and it was impossible for me to discern the difference between them; a multi-dimensional reality I experienced concomitantly. But despite my bewilderment, I was glad that the ghastly creature was no longer harassing me with its terrifying appearance and threatening evil laughter.

Unbeknownst to me how I ended up in such a desolate place, I was behind a dried up shrub on a dimly lit unpaved street in a pitch black night. Surreptitiously, I stuck my neck out to survey the area and noticed that the long street was completely deserted. All of a sudden, I heard a disorderly ruction approaching from the far corner where streets intersected. I immediately retreated and hunkered down gnawing on my finger nails terrified with the approaching unruly crowd. Scared, I remained immovable and quiet noticing that the pandemonium was moving at a rapid pace in my direction. When I peeked through the chinks of the withering bush I hid behind, I swallowed dry and gasped at the appalling sight. A large mob of several dozen people engaged in a brutal mêlée was now within my close view. Watching their exchanging blows willy-nilly, I realized that each fought for himself against everyone else; like a selfish vicious struggle for survival of the fittest in a realm of chaotic violence. I feared that if they saw me, I'd be mercilessly beaten up to a pulp. I curled up within myself in a fetus position mumbling prayers hoping for the best, and yet expecting my ill-fated kismet to ensue.

"Don't worry," a familiar voice whispered in my ears as I felt a gentle touch on my right shoulder, even though there was no one there. "They cannot see you. In fact, they cannot even see themselves. They fight as a survival mechanism for their tormented souls not to think about where they ended up. By engaging in continuous combat with one another, they cannot afford to think about anything else but self-defense, therefore they forget about themselves in the act of fighting."

The soothing melodious tone of the familiar voice I recognized but could not identify was muted by the rowdy uproar of the violent slugfest parading before my eyes. It was total chaos. Bellowing expletives in a loud cacophony of obscenities, each of the dozens of wretched participants in the brawl sucker punched one another indiscriminately. Astonished, I observed this most perplexing fracas noticing how utterly unaware of themselves they seemed to be. It was as though only the chaotic fray had a life of its own in which the partakers were but essential appendages of the conflict. As they moved down the somber narrow street, others came out of dark alleys to join in the skirmish while many fell to the ground trampled and consumed by exhaustion. I watched in awe the miserable throng gradually disappearing in the distance leaving behind a sonorous trail of despair, anger, and hopelessness ringing in my ears.

"As I said, it is the fighting that allows them to cope with the unbearable burden of the new reality they've begotten for themselves. If it weren't for the unending violent distraction of the brawl, they would have to come to terms with their enduring agony; and that would be too painful to bear," said the soothing voice in my ears. "It'll be a matter of time and you will have to make similar choices, too."

I didn't like the sound of it. But even more disturbing was to be heeding advice from someone I could not see, though his presence was filling the space all around me with an enormous intangible energetic mass.

"Your voice sounds familiar. When have I heard it before?" I asked out loud attempting to make acquaintance with my unexpected invisible visitor.

"I spoke to you right before you jumped off the edge of the cliff on that chilly evening," he said dispassionately.

Like a lightning bolt striking at the core of my memory, my emotions jolted my being with the recollection of that dreadful evening. Of course I remembered his voice; in fact, just as clearly as I remembered that dismal day of what used to be my life. The affliction of the grief triggered by a devastating loss had led me to the edge of the abyss of self-destruction. Yes, I recalled the incident and the reason behind it. It was my twentieth birthday. However, it was not on that day I committed suicide. So why did he say "just before you jumped off the edge of the cliff?"

"Because it was the day you committed to the decision to doing part with your life someday," he said clearly reading my mind and sounding just as self-assured as the first time he spoke to me that evening. "But of course, it was not the right time for you to depart the three-dimensional world."

"This is weird," I blurted out loud feeling flummoxed that he responded to my thoughts that I had not verbalized.

"Everything has an intrinsic designed plan; the DNA of destiny if you will. From the nucleus of an atom in a molecule to a massive black hole in the middle of a spiraling galaxy, nothing in the Universe is happenstance," he said. "Of course, as a cosmic subatomic particle, you are no exception."

The rowdy fighting crowd had long disappeared in the distance; and yet, I was feeling uncomfortable in the false sense of security of my solitude. Perhaps, having my thoughts vulnerable to interception was the culprit of my uneasiness.

"As for the unusual communication we share, you don't have to wonder about it anymore. It's just a matter of high frequency and fast wavelengths that the nature of the manifestation of my being exudes, which differs significantly from yours," he said resonating loud and clear in my ears as if I had a set of stereophonic loudspeakers implanted in my eardrums. "Like a radio you need to tune in to the proper station you want to listen, you have to be in synchrony with my purpose in order to receive my message."

"And why can't I see you?" I asked feeling odd about engaging in direct dialogue with the voice in my head. "I remember not being able to see your face that night on the cliff either, but back then it was night and dark."

"You can't see me because I'm not here, just as I wasn't there that night; at least not in the traditional way you're accustomed to companionship," he said. "Both the Earth and its surrounding umbra can accommodate neither the velocity nor the luminosity of the vibration of my being. Therefore, I must operate remotely; or in quantum mechanics terms, in non-locality mode; and I do so because you and I are entangled through a most powerful force."

"And will I ever be able to see you?" I asked beginning to feel curious about meeting my invisible companion face-to-face.

"I surely hope so," he said with a great deal of longing oozing from the cadence of his voice. "But for that to happen, you must come to where I am; and that's a long, long cosmic journey through the lattice of spacetime continuum."

For a moment I lost myself in the realization that I was in a very strange state of being in a most unusual foreign realm. It seemed like an inordinate amount of time had passed since I petered out in that man's arms. Even the journey inside the spiraling vortex and the encounter with that gruesome fiend felt like a past long gone. It was as though my perception of time had vanished in the eternity of the present moment; the only time that really mattered.

"It's time to get going," he said abruptly. "You need to find a way out of the umbral region before it gets too difficult to escape. The discordant gravitational pull of this place can keep those with low energetic frequencies here for a long time. But if you are able to take the quantum leap to the nucleus of a different realm, then you may be able to continue moving toward the inner orbits of The Great Circle of Life."

"What do I need to do to move in that direction?" I asked eager to find out how to get away from that untoward place as soon as possible.

"The journey itself will help you learn to live again, granted that you will not waver in the face of the daunting challenges ahead," he said. "You must be brave, determined, and most importantly, you must persevere."

"I'm really confused," I said as my words trembled out amidst a deep sigh. "I have no idea what I need to do."

"You need to do nothing; nothing but follow the process as it leads you where you're supposed to go. I'll be watching over you every step of the way and providing all the necessary assistance as needed," he said before pausing for a long moment as though to emphasize his next statement. "You may rest assured that you're not journeying alone."

I sighed again, but this time I experienced ineffable relief. Somehow being assured that I was not going to be alone gave me courage and emboldened my self-confidence.

"I must go now," he said as his voice began fading piecemeal. "I'll connect you with a local entity that has been working his way out of this realm for a long time. You may benefit from his knowledge and experience. In the meantime, you are on your own."

Suddenly it became so quiet that I could hear my heartbeat.

◄19►

I started walking without any idea where I was going. The dark empty streets with dilapidated vacant buildings looked like a war zone. With not a soul in sight, I surmised the population probably had fled the desolate town in the midst of brutal combat hostilities. As I passed by a malodorous dumpster scribbled with red ink graffiti, I noticed that my hands were trembling, my brow dotted with droplets of sweat, and my jittery knees made it very difficult for me to move forward. I was frightened. Although I'd been assured that I would not be going alone, which made me feel confident at the time the words were spoken, now that I was actually on my own without even a voice whispering in my ears, I realized the colossal difference that exists between words and experiences; between intellectual understanding and empirical knowledge.

Scared but determined to proceed, I scanned the long deserted street from one side to the other and there was not a shadow anywhere. The mêlée that had happened just a few moments earlier felt like no such a thing had ever occurred. It was quiet, dim, and musky. The air was heavy and tainted with sulfuric acid emanating from the dark dirt soil. Every time I took a breath, I felt as though I was breathing in the molecules of death strewn in the hopeless atmosphere. Even though I had no idea where I was going, I knew I had to keep moving forward. I couldn't just stop and remain stationary in what felt like a lifeless vacuum space. The greatest challenge I faced at that moment, however, was choosing which way to go, since both ends of the street looked exactly the same: ghostly, bare, and seemingly endless. Without thinking, I turned to the left and began walking in that direction. Although I had absolutely no perception of the passing of time, it felt as though I'd been walking for hours on end. The barren blurry scenery of nothingness looked the same in all directions along the way. Then, vaguely visible through the fetid haze, I noticed a fuzzy delineation of some dwellings in the distance. I tried to speed up my pace eager to reach my destination, but my feet would not move any faster. I insisted on forcing the issue on my terms and I toppled on my steps falling flat on my face.

"Patience and perseverance must be strictly observed if you want to get out of this mess you got yourself into," I indistinctly heard in my inner ears as I strove to get back on my feet. "Just keep moving at a steady unhurried pace."

And so I did. Soon I reached what seemed to be the last outpost of life in the frontier of death.

After walking nonstop for what it felt like a very long time, I came across an emaciated barefooted man dressed in tattered clothing on the side of the road. He held on to an old rusty bicycle whose both tires were flat. Next to him on the dirt ground, a worn out sturdy black suitcase tilted against his leg as if it worked to prop the man up to keep him from falling down by the weight of his misery.

"Excuse me," I said approaching him gingerly from behind.

He turned around to look at me but didn't utter a sound. And there was no need for words. His dark circled eyes looked like black holes that had consumed the life force out of him. I tried to look into the faintly brownish iris withering behind the cornea of his eyes, but they were barely visible under the sagging eyelids that magnified his cavernous countenance. There was not a single sign of emotions in that being; not even an iota of hope remained. He was as expressionless as death itself.

After holding a fruitless eye contact with the emptiness of his soul, I simpered, shrugged, and walked away shaking my head. It took me awhile to overcome the negative effect that man exerted on me. But as I kept moving on, I noticed that there were scattered folks on both sides of the street, and facing different directions. They all seemed to be attempting to escape that low-spirited environment. Some sat on their luggage with their thumbs up attempting to hitchhike out of that nightmarish place. They seemed indifferent to the fact that very likely there had not been any traffic on the narrow, grimy, and sinister street for time immemorial. And yet, there they stood the futile test of time that unrelenting hopelessness had imposed on them.

All of sudden, a swirling dark cloud swept through the street in the distance as if a whirlwind of chaos was approaching.

"Run, run for safety," said a frayed-looking woman that appeared out of nowhere dashing down the street. "The beasts are coming in droves; and they are mad as hell."

I looked around and I was flabbergasted. A place that a few moments earlier seemed deserted and lifeless, all of a sudden erupted as if fear had unearthed the dead and brought them back from the grave. A loud cacophony of desperate voices echoed all around me as if I'd been encircled in a bubble of panic. At a distance, angry shouting voices spewing hateful and virulent statements quickly approached like an ominous thunderstorm. The closer they got, the more threatening they seemed to be. Based on the deafening stampede that caused the ground to tremble, I thought that a cavalry of four thousand horsemen of the apocalypse were marching on in a vengeful mission. Frightened out of my wits, I dashed to the nearby slum and scurried away into a decrepit building that looked like it'd been mercilessly bombarded in an airstrike.

"Please let me in," I begged knocking on a door where I saw a young man rushing inside. No reply. I cringed hearing the multitude of fast approaching footsteps stomping so heavily on the ground that made the whole building quake. The thud of terror was reverberating all over the place.

"I'm gonna shred to pieces the first mother-fucker that crosses my way," I hoarse demonic voice infused with odium bounced off the walls like harmful darts aiming at random targets. "I'm aroused by hatred and I'm craving sadistic violence."

"Please, I beg you to let me in," I screamed while pounding on the door with both fists as the terrorizing footsteps of that enraged fiend sounded closer by the second.

Alas, that door was sealed to any commiseration to my despair. I had no choice but run—and as fast as I could. Amidst the horrifying clamor of maddening fury and the agonizing shrills of those who fell prey to their unforgiving subjugators, I hastened through the narrow stairways of the decrepit structure knocking on every locked door I saw along the way. In spite of my frantic crying out for help, there was not a single sign of compassion. I was in danger and I was on my own. My heart started beating so fast that I thought it was going to be ruptured out of my chest in an unexpected explosion. I began feeling so sick that I could taste the bitter bile bubbling up from my stressed out liver. I felt terminally trapped; like a helpless mouse in a maze where a fa-

mished wild cat waited for me at the exit. Driven by sheer desperation, I kept running randomly until I turned around the corner
and literally ran into this hideous looking massive ogre.

"Where da fuck you think you going, you little piece of
shit," he bellowed as I crashed against his tall and bulky physi-
que. Looking down at me with his grossly deformed face and
bulging bloodshot eyes, he sneered and a big blob of dense slimy
slobber fell on my face temporarily obstructing my vision. Wiping the sticky grayish splotch off my eyes, I wanted to run but I
had reached the end of the hallway and had my back against the
wall. I screamed so hard that I felt as if my vocal cords had burst
into coiled smithereens. And yet, the sound waves never made
out of my mouth; they echoed only inside the deep canyon of my
mind where my horrified self had fallen into anguish while being
assailed by threatening terror.

"I'm going to shove my monstrous dick down your fucking
throat until you choke to death; oh wait, you're already fucking
dead you bitch," he shouted followed by thunderous laughter that
made the walls tremble as I shivered in panic. With my arms outstretched pressing against the wall behind me, I cowered staring
at his grotesquely large hands with long bright red finger nails
that looked like sharp blades ready to cut me asunder. His eyes
blazing with murderous desire as he salivated like an aroused
animal engaged in a foreplay preceding an erotic act of violence.
When he lifted his arms and got his hands within inches from my
throat, I felt my body being stretched backwards toward the wall
as if I were a flimsy stretching rubber band ready to burst at any
moment. Suddenly, the thin thread that held me together snapped
and I was sucked backwards into the wall losing consciousness in
the process.

Next thing I knew I was lying on my back with my arms and
legs splayed on the dirt ground. Bewildered and exhausted, I

slowly opened my eyes relieved not to see that bestial creature. Instead, there was a towering amicable-looking entity staring at me with an impassive expression.

◄20►

"What happened?" I asked myself while sitting up and running my hands through my disheveled hair.

"You've just been tunneled out of the coarsest crud of the transitional umbral region," said the tall, svelte, and scholarly-looking handsome man standing in front of me. His bright blue eyes shone like stars through the thin glasses of his round wire-framed spectacles.

"Tunneled?" I mumbled unable to comprehend what was going on.

"Yes, tunneled, like going through a mountain to the other side; or in your case, to another dimension via a zero mass passageway.

"Zero mass passageway…" I repeated inaudibly feeling more confused by the minute.

"I've been here for a long time waiting for you," he said as I continued musing about the incomprehensible.

"And who are you?" I asked wondering about this good-mannered man who drastically contrasted with the repugnant creature I'd just encountered earlier.

"I am your designated guide in this next leg of your journey back to the inner orbits of The Great Circle of Life," he said kneeling to help me stand up. "Right now you are on the far outer orbit of your destination. You have a very long way to go."

"And why are you helping me?" I asked suspiciously holding my hand back and away from his outstretched arm.

"Because I'm invested in your successful redemption," he said. "If you make it, my helping you will contribute to my own liberation."

Although I was no longer suspicious of his intentions, I kept withholding my hand while trying to make sense of what was going on.

"Get up, you can't be lying there all day," he said stretching his arm farther to touch my hand. "As I said, you have a very long way to go."

I didn't ask any more questions. I held his hand, got on my feet, and started walking in silence next to him on the desolate long dirt road. Although the physical environment looked similar to my previous soirée in purgatory, the atmosphere felt significantly lighter. There was no sulfur oozing out of the ground; no sights or sounds of violent marauding crowds; no bestial creatures threatening me, and no signs of imminent danger to my wellbeing. The only thing bothering me at the time was a burning curiosity about my self-proclaimed guide.

"Based on your familiar time measurement system, we should reach the next dust of life post in a couple of weeks," he said walking briskly on the pebble-ridden road. "It's a long stretch, but a worthy effort to make it out of this place. Anything that gives you a chance to get out of here is a welcome sacrifice."

"What is this place you call here?" I asked.

"The umbral; the realm of the shadows; the place that functions at very low vibrational frequency; the space in the farthest outskirts of The Great Circle of Life," he said as I noticed the somber timbre of his voice. "When you are here, the only thing that really matters is to get out."

"You make it sound like we're light-years away from the Earth," I said thinking of my erstwhile planet's 8-minute light-year proximity to the enormous source of the life-giving Sun.

He suddenly halted his steps, looked at me, shook his head, and chuckled before resuming his walking.

"What's the matter?" I asked in my turn to stop and look at him silently demanding an explanation.

"Of course you're mystified," he said. "As a newcomer to the umbral, your awareness is limited to the primordial stages of sensorial perception; otherwise you wouldn't be here in the first place."

"Taking my pithy sense of awareness for granted, you're going to have to be more specific if you want me to be able to make any sense out of the hokum you're talking about," I said somewhat defiantly.

"Alright, I'll be as bluntly clear as I can: the worldly life you've experienced on Earth was but a physical manifestation of the very low energetic frequency of the umbral. You, I, and everyone else who signs up for the adventurously challenging journey of spiritual evolution must traverse through the human experience at least once, which is impossible to do unscathed," he said looking at me in the eye. "From a spiritual electrodynamics perspective, the transient human world is within the realm of the umbral. The planet Earth herself is but the magical living stage upon which the tragic comedy play of human life takes place."

"All the world is a stage, and all the men and women merely players," I spoke out loud the words of William Shakespeare in whose own magical world often I found respite from my worldly distresses.

"They have their exits and their entrances, and one man is his time plays many parts," he segued my quoting of the Bard. "However, when it comes to the umbral, exiting is what matters the most."

Suddenly, I felt an uncomfortable tingling run through my ethereal spinal cord. Obviously, the way I exited the world in my own terms may not have been conducive to an optimum performance in the tragic comedy play of human life, as he called it. Although I didn't expect a standing ovation, never I thought of my resolve to end my life as a compromising factor to my evolution. After all, what some might perceive as a dastardly act, my difficult decision to end my life was triggered by unbearable anguish deeply embedded in long suffering and human weakness.

"Because of the intrinsic trying circumstances of the human experience, those who go through it imbued with courage and determination to overcome the many challenges the worldly conditions present take a step upward in the evolutionary ladder," he said as we resumed walking.

"And those who don't?" I questioned with anticipation.

"They end up here at the lower levels of the umbral; the equivalent of a step down in the evolutionary ladder," he said melancholically. "Oh well, at least we are given a chance to climb it back up."

I didn't say anything after he spoke. I began fretting and wondering whether I'd made a most grave mistake that I could not undo. I started cold sweating and feeling queasy with the prospect of having committed a blunder of great consequences. But as he'd pointed out, there was an opportunity to find the way back; a chance for redemption.

"The Earth herself is an autonomous living being with her own soul and consciousness," he continued talking as we walked along the seemingly endless dirt road. "It is the delusion created by intellectual hubris that hoodwinked humanity to thinking of themselves as independent beings. And as they evolved through centuries of history and progressed in their technological achievements, they became demented with an obsession to conquer and exploit; not only the Earth herself, but also their fellow humans and all life on the planet. And once they established a wicked economic system depended on unfettered consumption, they managed to turn everything and everyone into disposable commodities. It reached a point in which the challenges of both individual and collective survival became overwhelmingly difficult to endure."

"That's why many jump ship afraid it's going to capsize at any moment," I remarked.

"Many, indeed," he said. "In fact, some 800,000 people die by suicide every year, which equates to one person every 40 seconds. It is a dismal global phenomenon. It's estimated that for each adult who dies by suicide there are more than 20 others attempting suicide. From children as young as 5-years-old to elderly folks in their 80s and beyond, people kill themselves at any stage of the lifespan."

"Five-year-old children!" I exclaimed in disbelief. "Even in the darkest hours of my childhood, I can't imagine considering to kill myself at such a young age."

"And suicide is the second leading cause of death among 15 and 29-year-olds worldwide," he added. "Almost 80 percent of suicides occur in low to middle income countries."

"How do you happen to know so much about suicide data?" I asked.

It took him a long time to reply. I noticed his strong masculine countenance drooping. His eyes turned away from mine as he moved a couple of steps ahead of me. He seemed to struggle to hide his shame.

"I was a distinguished professor of sociology at an Ivy League American university at the time I committed suicide myself," he said and the subdued tone of his voice disclosed evident embarrassment. "I guess I became an expert in the field in a desperate attempt to avoid facing my own struggles with chronic depression. I'm afraid I hoped that accumulating information on the subject would somehow deter me from taking the fatal step I'd considered so many times. Well, I obviously failed."

"At least we are given a chance for redemption," I said trying to assuage his evident sorrow by reminding him of his own words.

"Yes, but in the meantime, the calamity of suicide goes on unabated," he said returning to his professorial stance. "In the United States alone at the time of my departure, there were approximately 123 suicides per day; about five every hour. You're actually a minority, for men die by suicide three times more often than women. In fact, according to the data at the time I joined this ignominious statistics, white males accounted for seven out of ten suicides. But it is the rapid increase in suicide attempts among children that is the most disturbing to me."

"What a shame!" I said not knowing what else to say.

"And despite all the technological and economic developments, humanity has turned the world into a madhouse where people have become unable to cope with the growing anxieties of modern civilization," he continued undeterred. "The reason you ended up here first is because the circumstances in the umbral are unrefined manifestations akin to the living conditions on Earth. It is the shadow of the planet; and like the dark side of the moon that cannot be seen in plenilune, it exists in quiet obscurity."

As we continued walking toward what he described as the next "dust of life post," I reflected on my recent experiences in that abhorrent place I'd just tunneled from and compared it to the physical life on Earth I'd left behind. Although they differed in their appearances, the core reality of those distinct worlds seemed to share a common ground: unremitting violence, widespread poverty, indifference to other's suffering, constant oppressive fear, among many terrorizing circumstances of which the feeling of hopelessness can castrate the will to live. Alas, in a world of incomprehensible madness, wide-ranging ignorance, and unmanageable chaos, no wonder so many people commit suicide on an hourly basis. But what was the easy way out when you are stuck in the despondency of the umbral? You cannot commit suicide when you're already dead. At that moment, I realized there was never an easy way out; to the contrary, there is only the difficult way in; and that was where I was heading toward.

We walked in silence side by side for what seemed to be an interminable time. The only sounds I heard were our footsteps hitting the ground and pebbles occasionally rolling down to the side. Although there was no sulfuric fumes emanating from the dry soil, the dust lifted by the light breeze on the road billowed up in a cloud of heavy particles that made it difficult to breathe. Suddenly, he broke the silence with an unexpected uncanny observation.

"At last," he said. "There it is; the next dust of life post."

I looked straight ahead and I couldn't see anything; and it wasn't because dust blew into my eyes making me squint. There was absolutely nothing in the horizon as far as my eyes could see.

"I know it is not perceptible to you," he said likely noticing the befuddled expression in my face. "The scope of my sensorial capability is slightly more accentuated than those who have just crossed the entryway to the umbral. But trust me; it's out there within the inner vision of my perception."

"How can you see something that's not there?" I asked.

"There are many ways of seeing that do not require the use of your eyes," he said.

"Like what?" I asked.

"Common sense," he replied right away. "Way too often, something may be so obvious and even evinced by observable facts; and yet, it's completely oblivious to the mind that cannot or chooses not to see. If there is one truth about common sense is that it is anything but common."

After that brief verbal interaction, we picked up the pace of our walking. I noticed a certain degree of anticipation on his peppery steps, as though he was eager to reach his destination. I also realized that he knew the region well, for he'd been there for awhile. As for me, I didn't feel like I had any destination at all. I felt like one of the particles of dust blowing in the wind toward nowhere.

"I can see it! I can see it now!" I abruptly blurted out excited to spot what looked like a distant township.

He didn't say anything; and neither did he show any enthusiasm as I expected he would. But I was thrilled to see that settlement with my own eyes. There were people moving about and some even hawking their wares on the streets. What struck me, however, was the fact that there was not a single means of transportation anywhere; not even bicycles with flat tires as I'd seen before. Nevertheless, the thick dirty air in the atmosphere felt like the place stood smack in the middle of a high traffic freeway where poisonous carbon monoxide spewed from countless exhaust systems. As for the roaming crowd, it looked entirely different from the unruly masses of downcast individuals I'd encountered in the first leg of my ill-fated journey. And yet, they seemed mistrustful of one another as they walked by scrutinizing their surroundings with utmost suspicion. As my guide had pointed out, it was clearly a place of very low frequency in the spiritual electromagnetic field; a place I should tread around very cautiously.

"I guess this is it," he said stopping at a busy intersection in that bizarre locale. "I've done my job and now it's up to you to do yours. Best of luck to you."

"What do you mean this is it?" I said feeling both saddened to part ways with my walking companion, as well as scared to be left at that place on my own.

"From this point onward, I must take a different route from yours. We each have different evolutionary needs that require taking different paths for now," he said with his eyes skewed to the side to avoid making eye contact with me. I realized he was having a difficult time bidding farewell, too.

"Where do I go from here?" I asked with trepidation echoing through every syllable of my words.

"Do you see that street over there?" He said pointing toward a festive brightly lit street on a hill.

"Yes," I uttered the three-letter word with gleeful anticipation.

"That's where I'm heading. You are going right over there," he said pointing in a direction that immediately deflated my expectations.

"There!" I said monosyllabically looking at the dim-lit sinister street he pointed at.

"Yes, that is the next leg of your journey. I've already gone through that process and there's no longer a need for me to do it again," he said.

Disappointed, I lowered my head without saying anything.

"There is something else I need to show you before we go separate ways. Come, follow me," he said as we crossed the street in the direction I was supposed to go.

We walked toward a narrow shadowy passageway right around the corner of the street. There, parked at the end of the smelly alley, a rusty old car pressed sideways against a graffiti scribbled wall looked like a shipwreck at the bottom of a murky asphalt ocean floor. Puzzled, I looked at him in the eye waiting for an explanation for the bizarre sight.

"Here, take this," he said handing me a warped and badly oxidized key. "This is the key to the ignition of this car."

Reluctantly, I took the key from his hand feeling so confused that the skin in my furrowed brow tickled my forehead.

"The street you're about to enter is actually a circle," he said beginning to explain the peculiar riddle I was facing. "If you can manage to make amends with yourself and learn valuable lessons along the way, by the time you come around through the circle, you'll have fixed this vehicle that will take you to closer inner orbits of The Great Circle of Life."

"How can I possibly fix this falling to pieces car while being far away from it?" I asked feeling more confused than ever.

"The car represents the vehicle, but it's not the car that is the vehicle," he said metaphorically as I squinted while shaking my head befuddled. "Don't worry about it now. You'll understand it without even realizing how it happened. You can become a good mechanic of the soul and I have confidence in you; in fact, I am counting on you to make it."

As soon as he finished speaking, I felt a heavy weight of responsibility on my shoulders. And yet, I had no idea what it meant or entailed, but I was determined to honor whatever it was I could not comprehend.

"Well, until we see again," he said looking into my eye as though he looked into my soul. A time-freezing silent moment ensued. Then, he leaned toward me and gently kissed me on the right cheek. "Good luck to you."

Before I could reply, he turned around and dashed out of the alley heading toward the other side of the street. After hesitating momentarily, I ran after him only to see his specter vanishing as soon as he entered his destination. Turning my head in the direction of the dark street I was supposed to go to and the one he'd just entered, I vacillated deciding which way to move. Impulsively, I rushed to the brightly lit up and festive street where he disappeared. As I got closer and had a good view of it, I realized that bright and festive don't always mean illuminated and joyful. I stopped on the sidewalk looking inside the street and what I saw was disturbing: hookers and drug dealers carrying out their trades; armed robberies happening as people walked by; bloody fist fights outside nightclubs; all happening under loud discordant screaming and yelling of angry people. But among the many alarming events hijacking my attention, none unsettled me more than watching a priest with a salacious expression in his face walking hand in hand with a scared-looking little boy. Dragging the child along toward an inconspicuous dark corner, the hypocritical old man of faith sped up as soon as he noticed my observing them. Suddenly, the boy turned around to look at me and his terrified innocent eyes cried out for help. That was it. I was determined to venture in to come to his rescue.

"Hey, you!" A harsh female voice echoed from the shadows. "Where da fuck you think you going?"

Literally out of nowhere, a dark-haired brawny woman wearing indigo jeans and red t-shirt moved toward me at what I perceived to be a bellicose pace. Right behind her, three mean-spirited looking men holding knives and baseball bats seemed to salivate in their hunger for violence. At that point, the helpless boy and his depraved predator had disappeared from view. I had no other option but to run for my own safety as fast as I could to the other side of the street where I was supposed to go.

Scared, shaken, and saddened for not being able to help that child, I wondered what kind of place that street where my former usher went to was about. What I do know is that it reminded me a lot of the circumstances of the world I abandoned via suicide. Maybe it was a backdoor gateway leading to the earthly world; some sort of a tunnel passageway my ex-companion needed to go through to fulfill his personal destiny. As for me, I had my own share of ordeals to worry about. I had to muster some chutzpah to enter the sinister circle hoping I'd make it around in one piece; and, perhaps, be able to fix the vehicle that would drive me away from that penitent place.

◄21►

The first thing that struck me when I stepped into the hazy street was the high-pitched subtle sounds of mournful wailing in the background. It was as though an invisible macabre choir sang a single-tune symphony of lamentation that permeated the air with sorrow. It was a matter of time for me to be affected by the low-spirited environment aggravated by the morose sound waves. Soon, I started crying and sobbing nonstop. I felt as though I'd just joined the unfortunate chorus with my own out-of-tune resonance of remorse. I looked around and there was not a sign of life anywhere. I was alone. I felt abandoned, depressed, and utterly hopeless. I wanted to kill myself, but I could not reenact what had been already done. I was the living dead roaming aimlessly like a lonely specter in a ghost town.

Heeding the advice I'd received in the past, I kept moving forward in the shadowy, chilly, and barren street that seemed to have had life plucked out of it mercilessly. If it were possible for a geographic location to commit suicide, that place would be, oxymoronically speaking, the living example of it. As I continued moving ahead, I noticed an iron street post with a sign on the top right at the corner where the circle bent. Unable to see it clearly from afar through the murky air, I walked closer and looked at it while rubbing my eyes in an effort to read it. Still sniffling between intermittent bouts of sobbing, I was finally able to get a good look at it. In faint red color painted against a pale black background the sign read: Suicide Orbit Sector, with the letters S.O.S. under parentheses next to it.

Suddenly, it felt as though time had come to a standstill. Puzzled and intrigued, I stood by the sign post looking toward the other side of the circle but unable to see anything through the misty air. I realized that the only clear sensory perception I had was my auditory capacity, which at that point was overloaded by the piercing wailing sounds that was reaching a crescendo. Along with the rising sounds of sorrow, a frigid breeze blew from the hazy circle as I started rotating in place counter clockwise. In untoward synchrony with the tormenting cries of affliction that echoed in my head at deafening decibels, I began spinning faster and faster until I lost consciousness in a freezing spiraling vortex. Numbed by the high-speed icy motion, I felt temporarily comfortable, at last.

"The Suicide Orbit Sector, or S.O.S. as they like to call it around here, offers extraordinary opportunities for understanding both the causes and consequences of voluntary self-eradication," a familiar voice spoke in my ears after the disquieting sounds of wailing had ceased. "It is the next step toward the possibility of redemption."

"It's you, isn't it?" I mumbled out loud.

"I told you would not be travelling alone," he said. "I'll be shadowing you all the way through your journey."

Hearing his words triggered an ineffable feeling of joy and comfort. After a brief pause, I needed some clarification.

"What is this Suicide Orbit Sector?" I asked.

"It is a gathering place for those who committed the iniquitous act; like a neighborhood they temporarily share before moving on their evolutionary path," he said as I noticed his voice fading away in the back of my head. "It is a triage place where suicides both receive and give treatments for the hundreds of thousands of new arrivals who end up here every earthly year. Some must stay for a long time while others just seem to be able to pass through. I hope you'll be part of the latter group."

"What do I need to do?" I asked eager for guidance and consumed by the angst that he was about to abscond at any moment.

The long silence that ensued filled me with trepidation. I feared he'd already departed and I would have to fend for myself with no direction. Alas, fear is the subjugator of confidence.

"We've already gone through this before; and quite frankly, I'm beginning to be perturbed by your inability to grasp the learning that your experiences should have revealed to you by now," he said disclosing a tinge of annoyance with me. "You have to do nothing other than respond to the challenges that come along the way; flow with the events without resisting or judging their purposes; and most importantly, without ever quitting."

I sniffled a couple of times attempting to clear the sound of his vanishing voice in my head. I felt embarrassed but remained agog to receive some guidance.

"If there is anything you need to do is to surrender with unwavering faith to the mysterious evolutionary process of life," he said sounding more like a distant reverberating echo in the deep canyon of my mind. "You must learn to let go of fear, for fear will never let go of you."

As soon as his voice whispered away into the silence of my troubled mind, the spinning motion resumed unabated. This time, however, I was swept off the ground swirling upwards as if I'd been riding on a tornado that had touched down just to pick me up. The wailing sounds had returned, too, but they were not as high-pitched as before. In fact, I was surprised to experience a peculiar melodious feeling about the somber tunes of anguish, as if grief had its own unconventional intrinsic beauty. And as the sounds of swirling winds and static sorrowfulness mixed in the ever-moving environment, I could feel the phonons carrying me away to the most unusual vicinity I'd ever visited.

After riding on sound waves for what it felt like a long time, I arrived exactly where I was before, but at a different spacetime locale. At first I had a difficult time trying to comprehend the paradox of such an abnormal type of journey. However, as soon as I recalled the recent advice to surrender with abandon to the unfolding of my experiences, I realized that besides flowing with the motion of the events, there was absolutely nothing else for me to do. But what I was experiencing at that moment was unprecedented and I didn't know what to make of it.

A pervading chilly night seemed to be the only time and season of that unprivileged place. Scattered leafless trees flanked the sidewalks of the poorly lit street whose dim lights often flickered emitting an electric buzzing sound. The air was equally charged with electricity, which made me feel like the flickering lights with every breath I took. But the most striking element of that unusual street circle was the dwellings and how they were arranged. Even for someone like me who had lived through the extreme ends of the spectrum of wealth and poverty, never had I seen a hovel standing right next to a ritzy mansion among modest suburban houses and shoddy apartment complexes. They looked like strange patterns of a neighborhood quilt stitched together in the same social fabric of despair. Apparently, all the different classes of people in that surrounding area shared one thing in common: they were all residents of the notorious Suicide Orbit Sector. It was obvious that suicide was indifferent to socioeconomic status.

I was about to embark on an extraordinary educational tour of multifaceted aspects of suicide.

◁22▷

As I ventured walking toward that peculiar housing district, the first thing that captured my attention was the large writing crossing over the imposing iron arch over the entrance leading to that out of the ordinary borough. In capital letters it read: *SELBSTMORD MACHT FREI.* I stopped while staring at it for a long time trying to suss out what it meant. Soon, it dawned on me that it bore similarity to the sign at the entrance of the infamous Auschwitz concentration camp where over a million people were executed during World War II. Since I'd learned from my readings that the Auschwitz sign stated *ARBEIT MACHT FREI,* or "work will set you free," I immediately inferred, considering that I was in the Suicide Orbit Sector, the sign said "suicide will set you free." At that moment I realized I was entering a realm of deception.

After walking through the arch, I started moving toward the bending corner of the circle wondering why there was no one out on the street. The unpleasantly cold electric charged air compelled me to seek out temporary shelter from my growing discomfort. Across the street from the sidewalk I treaded on, there was a palatial white manor with a tall bronze gate bearing a glitzy crest on top; and right underneath a sign saying *SELBSTMORD MACHT FREI*; like the one over the arch I'd just crossed. Unfazed and determined to ferret out the hidden meaning of the ubiquitous message, I didn't shilly-shally and rushed to make contact with the residents of the ritzy residence.

I was about to press the golden button under a speaker on the ivy-covered wall when I noticed that the gate was ajar. As I hesitated between ringing the bell or walking into the property unannounced, a light breeze blew by from behind me causing the gate to open slightly wider. I construed it to be an omen; a silent invitation for me to step in without formalities. Heeding the subtle message, I stepped in without even touching the gate and walked through the long manicured yard all the way to the front door. But as I was passing by an eye-catching water fountain in which a sensually posing Aphrodite-looking statue spewed water through her voluptuous breasts, I halted my steps noticing that the only light inside the house came from a window upstairs. It reminded me of my bedroom in the last house I used to live; and the thought of it made me shiver recalling the last experience of my earthly life. I took a deep breath and walked to the front door.

Like the property's main entryway, the front door was also ajar. I frowned with suspicion while nibbling on my lower lip with a great deal of apprehension. But at that point, I'd already gone too far to back away because of my uneasiness. Besides, the air was getting colder and more electrifying by the minute. I desperately needed some respite from the harsh atmosphere.

"Excuse me," I said in loud voice while walking in gingerly into the elegantly furnished foyer. "Is there anyone home?"

There was no response. I kept making my way into the house, snooping around trying to find any sign of life in the sprawling downstairs area of the residence.

"Hello!" I said louder. There was still no answer.

I decided to walk upstairs where I'd seen the light turned on. Climbing up the spiraling stairway quietly and at slow pace, I was disturbed to recall, vividly, the last time I went up a similar stairway. At one point, I thought of turning around and dashing out of that house in a hurry, but I'd gone too far to run away now.

"I'm coming in," I said anxiously pushing the bedroom door open. Once I made my way in the room, I was stunned to find a beautiful middle-aged woman lying naked on an oversized bed with her back propped up by large pink pillows that matched the satin sheet covering her right leg.

"Have a seat," she said without turning around to look at me.

There was a beige sofa near the nightstand where a half-filled glass of wine stood next to an empty container of prescription drugs. I sat on the sofa and gazed at her from a slanted angle without saying a word. Her long dark hair cascading down her slender shoulders barely covered the sweet honey color nipples of her sensual breasts. I observed her body with a tad of envy, for I could not help noticing her curvaceous waist line and the perfectly roundish shape of her exposed bent left thigh. Her physical appearance was the idealized prototype of sensuality that women long to possess. She was a beautiful female specimen.

"Isn't it ironic that a beautiful wealthy woman whom everyone believes to have it all can feel more miserable than the ugliest and poorest woman on Earth?" She said tilting her head sideways to look at me for the first time. "You know what I'm talking about, don't you?"

Hypnotized by her intense gaze that pierced through the privacy of my being, I nodded in silence while feeling her unbearable pain as if it were my own. Not even the exquisite contours of her countenance could cover up the sadness that exuded from her eyes, which resembled fading embers that once burned fiery torches of life. I realized that both her beauty and wealth were but decoys she used to conceal the abhorrent reality of her ugly existence.

"In spite of my distressing childhood, never I thought of doing away with my life," she said. "But from the day my mother committed suicide, I knew that would be a matter of time for my following on her footsteps to a premature and premeditated death. I suppose it was my destiny to end up as I did."

At that moment, I was utterly stunned to realize that the woman lying naked on the bed was me. Like a doppelganger of a sort, she and I communicated as one in an unfathomable frequency of dual existence. In mundane physical world perspective, it felt as though I was talking with myself in front of a mirror while looking into my own eyes. I could not comprehend what was going on, but it was evident that a single source of energy I identified as me was manifesting juxtaposed to each other concomitantly. But as I sat there on the sofa staring at the other manifestation of me, I realized the extraordinary opportunity at hand. By engaging in dialogue with the projection of myself, I would be able to exercise an unusual therapeutic work in which both the therapist and the patient are one and the same with a common dilemma to resolve.

"If it was indeed your destiny to terminate your life on your own terms, what is the take away from your action?" I asked my doppelganger lying on the bed.

There was a long pause before she spoke, as though she collected her thoughts before giving me a useful answer.

"Well, perhaps I should have considered the other alternatives to my problems. After all, there were other options available that I was not strong enough to take them into consideration," she said.

"Like what?"

"I could have disentangled myself from that situation and pursued a life on my own," she replied.

"But you couldn't do it because you were traumatized by past experiences that left you disempowered and weak," I said thinking of my own situation.

"No, it was not so much a matter of weakness as it was desperation. I felt like I had enough and couldn't carry on living anymore," she remarked.

"But isn't desperation evidence of weakness?" I questioned what I perceived to be an intrinsic duality.

"Not at all," she replied without hesitating. "Desperation is a condition spawned from exhaustion, fear, and hopelessness. One can remain strong in the face of despair. Conversely, one can be weak even when endowed by the power of wealth, beauty, and other attributes of a sheltered life."

"Then, perhaps, it's neither a matter of strength nor weakness, but having awareness of what the purpose of desolation is supposed to be in the course of the human experience," I said.

"Oh, please, what a quixotic point of view," she remarked in characteristic sarcastic fashion I recognized as one of my personal traits. "If everybody knew the purpose underlying the trials and travails of life on Earth, the human existence would not be the same. The mystery is arguably the most significant element of the purpose of existence itself; and without it, the magic of life would vanish the moment awareness dispersed the haze of ignorance of the unknown."

"And yet, you had no qualms to let go of the magic of life; and the mystery of it didn't help you save yourself either," I said in rebuke to my double's sarcasm.

"What's the point of this self-disparaging inquisition? What are you trying to accomplish by being judgmental of an action I regret and cannot reverse?" My doppelganger remarked as I felt her indignation within myself.

"What do you expect me to do?" I asked.

"Learn and grow," she replied and her annoyance was palpable. "Maybe you can find a way to catapult yourself out of this miserable orbit of death."

"And how exactly am I supposed to acquire the knowledge, skills, and strength that will help me grow?" I asked oozing the despair and frustration I experienced.

"Go for an investigative walk in this wretched street circle where others who have done what you did perish while waiting for answers from within. You will find out the many reasons, causes, and circumstances that lead a man or a woman, young and old alike, to quit their lives in the face of desperation. Perhaps, by becoming more sympathetic to other people's despondency and understanding their plight, you'll grow to be more forgiving of yourself and find your own way to redemption," she said leaning forward to look straight into my eye.

I was mesmerized by the intensity of her gaze. It felt as though I'd been transposed to the inside of an invisible magical mirror that reflected my own image from the inside out.

"It is time for you to leave," she said turning her face toward the corner window where I saw the dim light flickering from the dark street. "Like the life you lived in your luxurious house on Earth, there is no reason for you to be here any longer. You have a new purpose, as well as a new opportunity to prove that not even a tragic mistake can be fatal in the pursuit of emancipation."

Next thing I knew I was walking on the bleak dark street of that strange circle in the far outer region of the Suicide Orbit Sector. Now I understood why they called it S.O.S.

◄23►

The circle was quite peculiar in the way it bent around the corner. Its elongated curvature seemed to perpetuate in an abstract geometric form as if it were endless. Although I'd been moving for what it seemed like a very long time, I felt as though I'd been walking in circles in a nauseating pattern of futility. And despite the fact that there were dwellings one next to the other on both sides of the circle, the loneliness that permeated the air was emotionally disturbing. Most houses looked empty and dark with ghoulish whimpering sounds coming out of them. It was as though its residents had abandon, not their homes, but themselves.

Suddenly, I noticed a gleaming light in the distance; and in a neighborhood like that, the vaguest twinkle could well be the only lodestar guiding me out of that sea of despair. I picked up my pace and started moving faster, rushing to my intended target like a famished predator after its prey. As soon as I sped up my steps, I stumbled onto my feet and fell awkwardly to the ground.

"It is not the speed toward your goal that will get you where you want to be. It is the steadfastness of the intention of what you want to accomplish that determines the outcome of the journey. The stronger the commitment, the faster you get to your destination," the familiar masculine voice echoed in the deep chambers of my mind.

Upon hearing those words, I got on my feet and resumed walking, slowly and effortlessly. Before I even realized, I was standing right in front of a modest looking two-story building with a natural wooden door and rectangular white curtain-covered windows on the sides. I rang the door bell and waited, patiently, for someone to come to greet me. As I waited, I couldn't help noticing the words *SELBSTMORD MACHT FREI* arching over the bell door button. Although no one came to the door, it opened as if by an automated electric control system.

"Hello Lucy," a mellifluous voice resonated in the air as soon as I stepped in. "We've been eagerly waiting for your arrival here at the Children's Suicide Ward."

As I entered what looked like a reception area of an old hospital, I was flabbergasted to see a bright white-bluish specter of light standing vertically from behind the across the room counter. The lightning bolt-like energy vibrated so fast that its wave length went through me and extended far beyond where I stood. I felt embraced by the magnetic warmth of its aura. It was the most auspicious welcome I'd experienced in my post-mortem time thus far; and a wonderful surprise to learn that even in the darkest of places such a sublime experience was possible. What puzzled me, however, was to be expected to arrive at a children's suicide ward. Unless my spiritual developmental process was at the infancy level, it made no sense to me to be summoned to such a place.

"Among the many inhabitants in this circle of the S.O.S., some of the residents in this ward will offer you the first glimpse into both the psychological and sociological reasons behind self-annihilation," the sound waves emanating from the specter reverberated in my ears. "If you can understand, even if ever so vaguely, what leads a child to commit suicide, you'll likely be able to make sense of the senseless world you once lived in."

Why would I need to make sense of a senseless world I was no longer a part of? I casually questioned myself in the privacy of my thoughts. After all, I'd become a different entity inhabiting a drastically different world; much worse than my physical organic existence on Earth, or so I thought at the time.

"Because you still bear the psychological and emotional remnants of that life in your ever-changing being," the specter answered my unspoken question as if it heard my every thought and replied in response. "It is a fundamental element of the cathartic process you need to go through to achieve your goal of redemption; like an old heavy luggage you no longer need to carry around. These children will help you strengthen your emotional muscle by understanding the underlying causes that leads a child to commit suicide. And because of the particular vibrational frequency of this place of healing, and the educational function we provide to our needy visitors, the children will speak to you in very clear adult-like language that will leave no room for misunderstandings of contextual information."

I wasn't really sure what it meant, but I was willing to do anything that would get me out of the sinister S.O.S.

"If you go straight down the corridor, you will see that there are three doors on the left hand side," the specter continued vibrating the sound waves of its communication. "Inside the rooms are the specific cases we've selected for your particular healing needs. Those children who lost their will to live will help you understand your own reasons for committing a crime against yourself; and hopefully, also help you find self-forgiveness. If you achieve this goal, then you'll be able to forgive those who wronged you as well."

I looked down the shadowy corridor and I felt somewhat intimidated. I felt as if I were a child inside a haunted house trick-or-treating on a stormy Halloween night. I had to knock on three doors and I wasn't sure whether I'd get tricked or treated. Nevertheless, I had no choice but follow the directions as they were delivered to me, for I had committed to surrendering unconditionally to guidance.

"May the stolen innocence of children show you the travesties of life when it loses its will to live; and may it help you to recover yours," the specter voiced for the last time before gradually dissipating in thin air.

Alone in the sudden quietude of the reception area, I took another look at the dim-lit corridor and felt my dry mouth and tight crinkly lips stick together. After standing still for a long time, I slowly began moving forward in the direction of what felt like a frightening hallway, even though there were no signs of threat to my wellbeing. In fact, compared to what I'd experienced before, it was a tranquil environment bereft of creepy sounds or horrific sights. As my steps became steady in motion, I noticed that the physical corridor was turning into a mysterious time tunnel. It seemed that at every inch of space I moved ahead, an extent of time moved back into the past in correlated fashion. By the time I passed far beyond the middle way of what had become an atypical tunnel, I was back to my adolescence and experiencing the related emotions of that time in my earthly life. Then, in an eerie turn of events, as soon as I crossed the tunnel it became a corridor again, and the child in me came back into existence. Now, three doors dotted the sideways of the corridor. I knocked on the one nearest to me.

❮24❯

"May I come in?" I asked after hearing some mumbling inside the room.

"Whatever," a girlish voice replied dismissively.

I slowly pushed the door open and walked in at the screeching sound of the old rusty door hinges. I stepped in the long rectangular shaped room gingerly surveying the utter disarray in the space. Strewn all over the odorous green carpeted floor, there were various pieces of clothing, notebooks, empty soda cans, candy wrapping papers, magazines, among an assorted array of objects, knick-knacks, and odd items of personal use. The place was a consummate mess. It reminded me of one of those garbage patches of plastic waste floating through the Earth's oceans. Across the room in that symbolic sea of pollution, a disheveled single bed with a purple quilt hanging half way down to the floor where a lonely survivor was adrift in chaos. With her back to me, a petite blond girl sat on the edge of the bed impassively looking out the window where the only sight was darkness.

"What do you want?" The girl asked me abrasively.

"I was told I could learn something from you," I said shuffling my feet through the scattered items on the floor careful not to step on anything breakable. "May I have a moment with you?"

She turned around to look at me and I was stunned with her puerile beauty. Probably on the cusp of childhood and puberty, the beautiful blond girl with shimmering blue eyes adorning her rosy high cheek bones gazed at me for a long time without saying a word. I reciprocated the attention in silence while noticing how the fair complexion of her face was overshadowed by the obscurity coming from within.

"What would make you think that someone like me could teach you anything?" She said after I smiled when we were making eye contact. "Look at this place; c'mon, take a good look around and see the reflection of what has become of me. How could I possibly teach someone anything worthwhile? If anything, I can teach you how to put an end to your misery."

"Huh, that's interesting. It seems to me that the misery you claim to be able to help me get rid of is in plain sight for anyone to see," I said sitting next to her on the bed. "No, I don't think you can help me with that; besides, it's not what I came here for anyway."

"What did you come here for?" She asked with a leery look in her eye.

"I'm in the pursuit of peace and redemption," I said. "I need to find my way back to life."

"Then I can tell you for sure that you came to the wrong place," she said turning her head toward the window again. "You'll find neither peace nor redemption here; and definitely not a way back to life."

"I do not expect to find them here, but I have to start somewhere," I said. "This seems as good a place to start as anywhere else. And I have a hunch that you can be of help to me."

She turned around to face me again and the sadness in her eyes pierced through my own sorrow like a needle threading a common fabric.

"What do you want from me?" She asked bluntly.

"Your story. I want to know why and how you ended up here," I said.

"Why? How could learning about me help you in the pursuit of your own lofty goals?" She asked.

"So that I know that I am not alone. Maybe learning about your motives will help me understand why I thought I could get rid of my emotional misery by ending my organic life," I said. "But as we both know, we were unable to eliminate neither the misery nor the life."

She looked at me intently in silence for a long time before a surreptitious simpering delineated on her lips. Then, a subtle twinkle in the eye revealed her acquiescence to my request. I'd earned her trust.

"My disappointment with this whole business of living started at a very young age," she said while standing up. "If growing up in poverty and abandoned were not challenging enough, I had to cope with the trauma of being routinely molested by an unscrupulous uncle since I was 4-years-old. The following four years ruined my hope for the future."

"Abandoned and in poverty?" I asked curious about that aspect of her life that resonated with my own ill-kismet.

"Well, my grandmother took care of me to the best of her abilities, but unfortunately she was not fit for the task when it came to protecting me," she said pacing around with a disheartening expression stamped on her melancholic face. "I never knew who my parents were and my grandmother refused to talk about them. They must have been really bad people; like my uncle I suppose."

I looked at her moving through the cluttered floor as if she swam in a polluted ocean of caustic emotions. As for me, I hoped that listening to her would somehow lead me to a buoy before I drowned in my own sea of sorrow.

"Soon after my uncle was arrested for child sexual abuse, the word got out among the depraved people he hung out with about what he had been doing to me," she said with vacant eyes staring at the ceiling. "And that's when life became unbearable to manage and I didn't want to live anymore."

"What happened?" I asked leaning forward moved by mixed feelings of anticipatory distress and uncontainable curiosity.

"I was only 11-years-old," she said and the despondent tone of her voice disturbed me. "One afternoon when I was walking home from school, an old black van showed up out of nowhere as soon as I turned around the corner. In lightening speed, the door opened and a big strong man snatched me with the ease one would pick up a ragdoll. Then he shoved me inside, duck-taped my mouth and that was the beginning of my end."

"Did he molest you?" I asked ascertained it was the obvious outcome.

"He? Oh hell no, there were many men who had me perform all kinds of sexual acts on them in front of video cameras," she said as the tone of her voice changed from sadness to anger. "And they likely made a fortune with their unspeakable crime."

I looked at her dejected face and my heart was filled with empathy and anger as my mind wondered about the criminal depravity of the human species. It is difficult to comprehend how it's possible for the same species that spawns the likes of Johann Sebastian Bach and William Shakespeare to give birth to despicable primates unworthy of belonging to the *Homo sapiens* group. When she resumed talking, I was incensed realizing how wickedly filthy human nature and the culture it produces can be.

"They dressed me up in skimpy sexy outfits, which I remember overhearing one of the men saying it was good marketing," she said with her anger apparently tamed by her rational mind. "They dressed an 11-year-old child like a cheap concubine they sold as an equally cheap commodity in the black market of depravity. But make no mistake; the profit they collected from their smutty criminal venture was anything but cheap."

I stood up and walked toward her amidst the symbolic mess that her life had become. I put my arm around her and silently commiserated with her emotional ordeal. As we remained in a quiet sideway embrace, I thought of the dominant worldly culture that viewed everything and anyone as profit-seeking ventures. And since sex and violence were venerated among deranged consumers, the demand for inhumane actions and behaviors was insatiable; and so was the desire for profit. I deemed the consumers of sexual exploitation of children to have reached the pinnacle of the most ignominious human depravity. In unexpected timely fashion, as soon as I had this thought, I recalled seeing the old priest disappearing into the darkness while holding an innocent boy's hand. There was no doubt in my mind that the hypocritical man of faith was leading the child to a lascivious escapade in the shadows of shame; the lower levels of existence where malice and falsehoods disguise as pseudo-piety.

"Do you understand now why I had no choice but to kill myself?" She asked gently holding my hand lying on her shoulder. "The truth is that I was already dead; there was no point keeping the body alive. That's why I decided to jump out of the apartment building window where I lived with my grandmother."

"What I do not understand is how a child at such a tender age can even think about killing herself; that's utterly incomprehensible to me," I said as we started moving back toward the bed. "As for having choices, I suppose we always do, but who is to say which is the right one for others when we don't even know what's the right one for ourselves."

"You don't think you made the right choice?" She asked halting her steps to look at me in the eye.

I was taken by surprise and could not answer her right away. Her piercing blue eyes zeroed in on me demanding to give her an answer that I did not have.

"That's alright," she said shifting her gaze toward the window. "I'm not sure I made the right choice either; after all, look where I ended up."

Suddenly, she turned back to face me again and the terror in her eyes reflected within my own fears.

"What if we made the wrong decision? What if this kind of death is but a rebirth to perpetual misery?" She asked with her eyes bulging out of their sockets as if they were being pried open by an invisible force.

"If we made the wrong decision, it's been already done and neither regret nor fear can reverse it," I said. "On the other hand, the decisions we make now will overlap the ones we made in the past; and who knows what good might come out of them."

She looked at me and smiled as if hope had been rekindled in her helpless soul.

"I'm so glad you came by," she said.

"That I know it was the right decision," I replied gently touching her cheek.

"Will I see you again?" She asked with a great deal of expectation in her voice.

"I'm not sure, but I do know that every time we think of each other, we will meet again in our hearts and minds," I said. "We've become entangled by the mysterious circumstances that brought us together, and that's a bond that shall endure through spacetime, regardless of how far apart we may be."

She winked at me and smiled.

"Well, it's time for me to go to meet the girl next door," I said getting ready to leave.

"Actually, it's a boy that lives next door. I hear him all the time; often yelling angry words of revenge. Sometimes I feel scared of the people who live here, even though I never get to see them," she said cowering into the corner of the bed holding the pillow tight against her chest as if it were a protective shield. "I guess we all have our ghosts to exorcise."

"We all do," I said. "We all do."

I stood up and started walking toward the door careful not to step on and break anything along the way. Much had been damaged enough in that room.

◄25►

I didn't recall the doors in that corridor being so close together. I barely walked out of her room and the next one seemed like it was within arm's length.

"What do you want?" A young boy's voice echoed annoyance and mistrust shortly after I knocked on the door.

"I need to talk with you," I said softly. "I need your help."

There was a long pause that I interpreted as a positive sign. I was right. Soon, shuffling footsteps approached the door followed by the unlocking sound of the safety bolt. When he opened the door, a hot muggy air gushed out of the room as if a Sun blazing harsh desert prevailed inside. I could feel the percolating drops of moisture on my brow.

"Are you another counselor they want me to see?" The young boy inquired looking at me askance, almost defiantly. "I'm getting sick and tired of it."

"No, I am not a counselor; if anything I'm the one who needs counseling," I said trying to assuage his suspicion of me. "And I think you might be able to help me."

"Oh please lady; I'm a 14-year-old boy who just committed suicide. I could not help you if I wanted to; and frankly, I have no interest in your need for help. For God sake, I couldn't even help myself," he said leaving the door ajar while moving back inside. I inferred it as a subtle invitation to come in.

I entered the room and closed the door behind me. In blatant contrast with the girl's room, his was tidy and well ordered, but much smaller than hers. It was as though he'd been boxed in a confining place he could not escape. Maybe he was a prisoner of his troubled mind.

"It's much more difficult to help yourself than others; and sometimes helping others is the best way to help yourself," I said walking toward the small desk where he sat at doodling on a piece of paper. "I think we might be able to help each other."

"Really?" He said sarcastically while dropping the pencil on the desk and turning around to look at me. "And how exactly this is going to happen?"

"I don't know yet, but I'm willing to find out. Are you?" I said in a not-so-subtle purposeful ultimatum.

He stared at me sizing me up seemingly still unsure of my trustworthiness. He picked up the pencil again and started drumming it on the desk without losing eye contact with me. I could feel his longing to reach out hampered by his misgivings.

"What do you say?" I pressured on.

"Well," he said while beating the pencil more emphatically on the desk. "I guess we could give it a shot. Besides, what else is there to lose anyway?"

"Good. Let's get started then," I said.

"What do we do?" he asked.

"We talk and we learn from each other's experience," I said.

"O.K., you go first," he said.

I sat on a wooden stool bench next to the desk and started the metaphorical audio book of my former life for him to listen. I told him about the financial and emotional hardships of my childhood not sparing any details of my miserable upbringing. I let him know how poverty pushed my father to the brink of despair, and that both poverty and despair were the only things my mother and I inherited from him. I shared how my mother's suicide may have contributed to my ill-conceived decision to end my own life in adulthood. I gave him a descriptive narrative of my years of homelessness and that I was sexually abused by perverted adults who had taken on the responsibility of carrying for me. But as I was in the process of telling him the rest of my former life's story leading to my suicide, he stopped me abruptly as if he had heard enough; or, perhaps, he felt an irrepressible urge to share his own story with me.

"To live in poverty must be terrible," he said commiserating with my experience. "But maybe it spared you from committing suicide at my age. Had you lived in a household where your parents could afford to give you everything you want, including sophisticated electronic devices, you'd have been tormented to the point of not wanting to live anymore."

"I'm not sure I understand what you mean," I said.

"This," he said holding up a handheld computer commonly identified under the misnomer Smartphone. "This was the vehicle that drove me to kill myself. It's not like it was the culprit itself, but the means through which untenable mockery and hatred turned my life into a daily nightmare."

Suddenly, I recalled overhearing a conversation among the many congressmen that habitually visited my house. I remembered their talking about an emerging crisis in the school system in which more than 2 million children were bullied every year, and some 4,400 of them committed suicide in the same time period to an average of twelve children committing suicide every day—in the United States alone! Now I knew what I was dealing with in that room.

"When I got my first Smartphone I was so excited about being able to connect with my friends through social media. I remember setting up accounts in every platform available, especially the ones my buddies thought to be really hip," he said revealing, for the first time, a modicum of excitement. "At first I was jazzed up posting photos and messages about the cool things happening in my life. Like everyone else, I just wanted to belong to the virtual communities all my peers hung out. It was such an idyllic cyber world where I could present myself as I wished and the information spread at the speed of light. But then, when mean-spirited people started posting hateful lies and harming materials about me, I felt like the information started spreading at the speed of darkness. Soon, I just couldn't cope anymore."

"I have no idea what that would feel like," I commiserated.

"Oh, I'll tell you, it's the worst feeling of all. When you can only be harassed in person, like in the old days of my parents, the moments you are alone in the safety of your home are precious moments of tranquility no one can take away from you. But when you carry a communication device with you wherever you go; an electronic gadget that becomes an integral part of your life like an extra arm or leg you can't do parts with, then the pestering follows you mercilessly round the clock. It is an incessant torment in which insults, abuse, disparaging comments, humiliation, physical and emotional threats become daily routine. And knowing that everyone in the cyber community is receiving the same message is a devastating shame for a teenager to deal with. Eventually, you can't help but snap like a brittle twig."

He silenced and lowered his head, occasionally nodding as if he were in disbelief that people; other children for crying out loud, could impart intentional injury on others. Although I never had experienced that particular type of harassment, I could only imagine what would be like to endure continuous persecution and public embarrassment in the formative years when peers acceptance has such high value to a child's self-esteem. It made me wonder about the intrinsically wicked human nature that expresses its malignant character at such an early age. And if humans are, indeed, morally defective from the origin, then everything they create is doomed to be hazardous, regardless of how it is disguised under the cloak of progress. Not only technological ingenuities can wreak havoc on many aspects of life, it can also push countless emotionally vulnerable young people over the edge of despair. Perhaps, there is some truth to the religious concept of original sin; not in relation to a natural biological order, but to the corrupting nature of malice and exploitation that has made its mark throughout human history.

"Before the bullying, harassments, and threats turned my life into a living hell, I was doing just fine living a carefree childhood. But when I had my first foretaste of puberty, I realized there was something different, or perhaps even wrong about me," he said as his chin dropped lowering his head down as if caused by the weight of his memories.

"It sounds like it was a rather bitter taste of puberty," I said attempting to lighten up the direction of the conversation. "In my book, anything that makes me feel wrong about myself cannot possibly be good."

"Sure, but when others are the ones who determine what you feel to be wrong, then your commitment to be right and true to yourself dies on the vine. You can no longer coexist with the dominant culture," he said with his eyes still fixated on the floor.

"What is this glimpse at puberty that affected you so strong-ly and what does it have to do with your being here?" I asked baffled and agog to find out.

He slowly raised his head and looked me in the eye. I could see the turbulence that confusion, shame, and fear were churning inside of his still troubled existence.

"Long before my pre-teen years I realized that I didn't feel like a boy; I mean the typical boy, the kind that likes to play football, to fight, and be tough. I was sensitive, perhaps even more so than many girls in my school. I identified with gentle-ness and I wanted to express my being that way, but I was not allowed to do it without being bullied, harassed, and threatened. It felt as though I was not allowed to exist as my genuine self," he said returning his gaze down to what felt to me like the depths of the Earth below. "And if you can't exist as you see yourself to be and live on your terms, what's the point of living?"

It was my turn to look down and ponder. In an adult way, I, too, had to deal with a similar situation before committing the same crime to myself as he did. I didn't feel like I could live in accord with the promptings emerging from my true self. I lived as a pawn sacrificed on the chess board game of profit that my abusive husband played so well.

"Once 'the real boys' in my school started looking down upon me, calling me derogatory names, and often times even hit-ting me with their bare knuckles when I walked by the hallway for no reason, I knew I had entered a dark tunnel whose light at the end could only be death," he said as I felt a billowing of heavy somber fill the air. "After incessant cyberbullying and physical aggression, I realized that the light at the end of the tun-nel was in my home's garage with a tight noose around my neck. I thought that from the moment I pushed the ladder away with my feet and hanged freely from the wood frame ceiling, all my troubles would be over. Of course it didn't work quite as I expected. Just look at me now."

I did. And what I saw was a terrified child in search of his identity as a human being in a world where our common humanity has ceased to exist. Hampered by pseudo-morality deeply rooted in archaic religious precepts, the cultural fiber that bonds society together has morphed into an unrecognizable ethos in which hatred has become the fundamental thread sewing discord. Of course I didn't say anything to him, but in reality he was but an example among millions of people who are regularly assaulted in manifold ways by small-mindedness. Despite the extraordinary developments in scientific and technological ingenuity, the wide expansion of modern civilization has not led to the integral development of righteousness in comprehensive human terms. Alas, the wide gate of progress seems to have turned into a narrow door leading to indifference, intolerance, and yes, hatred. The broad scope of love has no chance to make through such a constricted passage.

"Now you tell me," he said. "How could anything I shared with you help either you or me in any way whatsoever? From where I stand, other than venting my sorrows, I see no good coming out of our conversation."

"The good doesn't come out of the conversation itself, but from our willingness to confront and discuss our weaknesses and sadness," I said putting my arm around his shoulders. "Talking and listening to you have helped me in ways that I cannot comprehend just yet; and I'm O.K. with it. I guess I don't have to know everything right away. But I can feel with certitude that it was a positive exchange for both of us."

"In any case, thank you for stopping by," he said smiling tenderly at me for the first time. "I think you're probably right; it may have helped me, too."

I brushed my fingers through his dark hair and walked out without saying anything else. There were no more needs for words, for they already had fulfilled their purpose. The only thing left for me to do was to move ahead toward my ultimate goal of getting out of that low-frequency region they called S.O.S. Perhaps my progress in that direction would benefit that boy somehow, just as his own growth would contribute to mine as well. From the moment he and I connected and shared important aspects of our struggles, a numinous entanglement was conceived in the womb of the mystery of life.

◄26►

I moved on toward the last room I was supposed to visit before departing the Suicide Children's Ward. The last door was near the exit, right next to a sort of nurse station that, though there was no one staffing it, the area vibrated with irrefutable invisible presence.

I stopped in front of the black door with a dark round silver knob and quietly listened to what was going on inside.

"I got 'em! I got 'em all!" A young man voiced his undeniable excitement. "Yeh, the nineteen hours nonstop action finally paid off. There's not one mother-fucker standing."

With my eyebrows nearly touching each other over the bridge of my nose, I shook my head puzzled and consumed with curiosity about what was going on inside that room. I pressed my right ear against the door as if it were a stethoscope I employed to identify and diagnose an unhealthy condition. Suddenly, I detected an inconsolable continuous sobbing followed by a loud cry of despair. Without hesitating or even knocking on the door, I barged in with a sense of urgency.

"What's going on in here?" I asked looking at the young man sitting at a small desk in front of a large computer screen. With both hands lying lifelessly on the keyboard, his neck and head hanging down his drooped shoulders in a physical posture that depicted total defeat. It was the opposite image I associated in my mind with the sounds I heard before walking in. I was confused, even more so after noticing that the computer screen was pitch-black blank.

"Get out!" He commanded without looking at me. "I told 'em not to send anyone to talk with me. I fucked up but it was my choice. I don't need anybody's help."

Instead of heeding his authoritarian demand, I walked forcibly toward him unfazed by his false bravado.

"You may not need anybody's help, but I do," I said standing right next to him. "And I'm not going to get out until I get what I came here for."

Slowly, he lifted his head to look at me. His sunken dark circled bloodshot eyes seemed to bathe in a pool of sorrow. I maintained eye contact trying to ferret out any hints that would give me a glimpse at who I was dealing with. Although he was likely no older than 15-years-old, the distress exuding from his troubled countenance revealed the agony of decades of misery.

"I need to know what happened to you and why you ended up in this ward," I said laying out the terms of my determination. "I don't know about you, but I'm doing everything I can to get out of the Suicide Orbit Sector, and I'm wasting no time in the pursuit of my goal. So let's cut to the chase: how did you end up here? And by the way, I do not want an abbreviated version. In order to get the help I need, I must know the details."

"Details," he mumbled almost inaudibly. "Should I start with my miserable childhood or with my uncontrollable addiction? Maybe the insidious peer pressure and bullying I endured in middle school? Or perhaps I should get straight to the point and talk about the hopelessness I felt about the future that I couldn't bear to think about. Where do you want me to start, lady?"

"From the beginning," I said succinctly.

"Fair enough," he said standing up and moving toward the window that shadowed the outside darkness inside the room. "The tragedy of the individual human experience always seems to begin in childhood; so let me start from the beginning, as you request."

He paced back and forth in silence as though he collected the scattered pieces of his broken self. I gazed at him moving about with his shiny long blond hair falling over his face like a curtain concealing the stage of the drama he was about to unveil. Meanwhile, I, the sole audience member of this ill-fated play, remained quiet and patiently waiting for the performance to begin.

"I'd always had everything I needed as a child; everything but love," he said pacing at the center stage of the room. "Neither my sister nor I seldom, if ever, received any loving attention from our parents who seemed to live for each other alone. They lived in some sort of selfish cocoon of two. To me it felt as if my sister and I were but necessary accoutrements in their idyllic family life. But on the other hand, they gave us everything a child could dream of; everything but love."

"Maybe it was the only way they knew how to express their love for you. Some people communicate love in very peculiar emotional languages," I said. "Sometimes you have to translate it in order to be able to feel it."

"So much for love being a universal language," he said sarcastically. "Whatever love language they spoke it got lost in translation, for never I understood it at the emotional level, though intellectually it made sense to me. Since both my parents grew up in dire financial needs, being able to shower their children with material abundance they never had might have felt like an expression of love to them. It so happens that the child grows up in a house full of goods and amenities but with an empty heart starved for genuine affection."

I wanted to tell him how much worse it could have been if he had experienced an empty heart in an empty home as I did. However, I monitored my impulses and refrained from saying anything. It would serve no purpose under the circumstances.

"By the time I reached middle school age, I'd become a reclusive child with bare minimum social skills. I found comfort and safety in an artificial reality that I could immerse myself in with abandon," he said as if reciting a memorized script. "It's not like I discovered a brave new world on my own; to the contrary, it was the norm all around me. It was not even a voluntary choice, but rather a commanding call I could not resist. It was like a cultural black hole that dragged me in by the powerful gravitational force of a meaningless technological existence. And for an emotionally starved child, the virtual reality of the cyber world was like a forbidden fruit dangling from a magical tree. It so happened that the seductive fruit was contaminated with the virus of death."

"Strong language," I remarked.

"Yes, but more meaningful than the obtuse language of love that no one seems to understand," he retorted with cynicism. "In the cyber world I could invent myself as I wished to be, and that made me feel special for awhile. But once the rejections, judgments, and harassments started bombarding me on social media, I retrieved into the darkness of my isolation again until I started hating people and wanting to inflict violence and pain on all of them, including myself. I found humanity to be mean, vicious, despicable and dangerous."

"It sounds like you started learning the language of hatred at a very young age. It seems to me more obtuse than the language of love," I remarked with a tinge of cynicism of my own.

"How can you not when it's spoken all around you every day?" He said while turning around to look at me in the eye. "It was a matter of time for my becoming very articulate in the language of hatred; after all, everyone around me spoke it fluently."

I had difficulty maintaining eye contact with him. The intense energy emanating from his gaze compelled me to look the other way. I wondered whether humanity is genuinely mean, vicious, despicable and dangerous, or if the circumstances of the life they've created make them act the way they do. I did not know the answer. But in front of me there was a classic example of a former fledgling human being growing up bereft of love in a consumerist culture in which hatred is a valuable commodity. And if the environment of discord were not harmful enough, there were umpteen available tools with which to forge a human beast out of the natural human. And once the individual turns into a socially nurtured fiend, the culture of loathing prevails.

"In order to offset my social media withdrawal syndrome, I took up video games, and that changed my life forever," he continued. "I played for hours on end and it became easy to forget myself and the uncaring world I lived in. I became addicted to video gaming and I got to be very good at all sorts of violent games. It was a matter of time for me to start fantasizing about doing the real thing one day. Then, two things happened in my life that changed the course of my destiny."

"The first...," I said prompting the disclosure.

"Out of the blue, my parents transitioned from selfish love birds into aggressive bats out of hell that started hating each other. Their regular physical altercations got so violent that I was traumatized witnessing their daily fracas. One time, I saw my father knock two teeth right out of my mother's mouth with a sucker punch. Of course, eventually they had the most acrimonious divorce and my sister and I got caught in the middle of their custody disputes; not because they cared about us, but just to spite each other in their divorce battle," he said and I could feel his soul sinking into a swamp of melancholy.

"And the second…," I said expediting the revelations.

He raised his chin and stared at me as I had an ominous feeling. I could see the birth of madness in his eyes.

"I desperately needed some relief from my inner turmoil," he said. "Troubled adults recur to alcohol, drugs, sex, or other more conventional forms of addiction; the socially accepted palliatives to deal with the wretchedness of the world. Kids, they need an outlet, too. And in the electronic age, there is nothing more seductive and effective escapism than video games. It's like being transported to another world where you become its virtual intrepid inhabitant."

"I still don't understand what this has to do with your being here," I said.

He sneered at me as if my naiveté amused him. I suddenly recalled the countless times I discounted the intelligence present in a child; a human being in early stages of development. Even in this most bizarre realm of existence that truth seemed to prevail.

"When the *School Shooting* video game came out, many of us got addicted to it. It was just such a thrill to virtually walk into a classroom full of innocent children and murder them willy-nilly. The game was such a rush," he said and I could feel his sickening arousal for mindless violence. "At that time I was so depressed and disillusioned with life that I began considering killing myself. By the time I made up my mind to put an end to it all, I decided that I was going to die in the most exciting way I was virtually accustomed to, and at the same time get much notoriety to my death. I chose to commit murder-suicide in actual school shooting fashion; like playing the video game in real time."

I looked at him with a mix of pity and contempt. I understood very well what the throes of human anguish can do to a battered person. I was also aware that sometimes the pain is so acute that a desperate way out is the only exit a clouded mind can perceive. What I could not understand was why taking other people's lives in a most ghastly way, especially children, could justify the decision one person makes to himself. It was incomprehensible to me how imparting unimaginable suffering to mothers, fathers, siblings, friends, and communities could add excitement to the act of dying. Something was terribly wrong with the world I'd just departed; and apparently, the similarities were reflected in this dismal place I ended up. In any case, I had enough of talking with that boy, for his action disgusted me.

"I must get going," I said heading to the door. "I need to find my way out of this suicide hell."

"You're judging me, aren't you?" He asked abruptly, which made me halt my steps and turn around to look at him. "You're just like the rest of them. They all condemn me because they are afraid of taking any responsibility for what happens in the sickened society they've created. The blame always falls on the isolated individual; the lone wolf with mental health issues, addictions, or any other deficiencies they attribute to the deranged person. But they never question, much less admit, that they've been fostering a social environment that nurtures the proliferation of unhinged madness, which they turn into profitable commodities. I am the human end product spurting out the conveyor belt of the lucrative industry of violence."

I held eye contact with him without saying anything. Although he made a valid point about the corrupt culture, I still could neither comprehend nor acknowledge the debased act of mass-murdering children as a route to committing suicide. Even when I tried to rationalize how an emotionally disturbed person addicted to violent video games could easily slip off into the abyss of madness, I couldn't help denouncing his murderous approach to killing himself.

"Did you get what you came here for?" He asked me and his sarcasm irked me.

"I'm not sure what I came here for, though I know exactly what I am after; and I'm positive that I'm not going to find it here," I said heading to the door.

"I hope you'll meet others out there who have done as I did for different reasons. Maybe you will no longer be so disapproving of me," he said turning his back to me and walking back to his computer desk. "Now if you excuse me, I need to go back to my video game. It's the only way I can forget myself and find solace from my misery."

I left the Children's Suicide Ward thinking about the reasons underlying the motivations of children who choose to take their own lives. Although they were as diverse as they were complex, the common denominator among all of them was suffering; the unavoidable element of the human experience that was seemingly more intolerable than ever before. Based on the rampant escalation in suicide rates, it was obvious that another common factor in the equation of despair was a well-established culture of selfishness, indifference, contempt, and hatred that had been cemented in the edifice of progress. But as I'd soon learn, there were many other components in the complex computation that adds up to self-annihilation. From economic distress to religious fanaticism, the road to suicide was paved with psychological ruin. I needed to learn about it in order to understand my own shortcut to death. It was my only path to redemption.

◁27▷

The first thing I noticed when I came back out to the deserted circle was a very tall building in the distance. Although I could not see clearly through the dense fog, the enigmatic edifice had an alluring peculiarity that intrigued me. Fueled by irrepressible curiosity, I decided to head in that direction to find out what the mysterious structure was about. And because I'd long lost my perception of time and space in the strange S.O.S. realm, I do not know how long or far it took me to get to my aimed destination.

Standing in front of the building with a frown that made me feel the crinkling of the skin over the bridge of my nose, I raised my eyes up toward the steeple of what looked like an imposing cathedral. At first I couldn't tell if it was a church, a mosque, a synagogue, or maybe even a Zen Buddhism monastery. It was, indeed, an unidentifiable structure that seemed to have common characteristics of various religions. One thing seemed undeniably evident: it was some sort of house of worship. Unhesitatingly, I walked in to find out what it was and who I'd find in there.

"Hello! Is there anyone in here?" I asked while gingerly moving through the long and wide hallway leading to a large open room. There was no response. I kept walking in and the gentle sounds of my footsteps reverberated throughout the building making me feel anxious and uncomfortable. I stopped for a moment just to get a respite from the resonance of my footsteps in that dead-quiet place. Suddenly, a thunderous sound of life erupted from the large room at the end of the corridor.

"Allahu Akbar!" A commanding masculine voice bellowed with roaring passion. The vociferous sound waves carried an intense energy of conviction that resonated through the stifled indoor atmosphere. Faith seems to possess an intrinsic power that exudes from those imbued with it.

I tiptoed into the large room where a man prostrated on a burgundy rug had his back to me. I remained quiet observing him as he exercised his religious ritual.

"Allahu Akbar!" He shouted again after raising his torso to an upright sitting position. Then, he stood up and turned around to face me as if he knew I'd been there watching him.

"I'm sorry," I said somewhat embarrassed. "I didn't mean to disturb your religious practice."

"How could you? I've already been disturbed so many times that I don't notice the difference anymore," he said while slowly walking toward me.

As he got closer, I felt the palms of my hands get sweaty. I was scared. His light brown eyes radiated a dark vigor that made me cower and take two steps backwards when he stopped in front of me. His tanned rugged face partially covered by a scraggly beard accentuated his menacing appearance. But it wasn't what he looked like that instigated the threatening feeling. It was his attire that gave me the heebie-jeebies.

"Never I doubted that I was doing the right thing," he said as if I were a magistrate he was trying to convince of his innocence. "It comes a moment in a man's life when he must rise to the call of duty to his people, and to Allah Himself."

"I understand," I said in a subdued tone of voice while gawking at the bulky suicide bomb vest he wore. "Sometimes a man must die for what he believes to be right, though they say that real courage is living and suffering for what you believe."

"They who?" He bawled abruptly making me cringe with fear. "Whoever said such nonsense does not know what living in anguish without hope really is. There is only so much suffering people can take before life and death join in the same playing field of value. In fact, death takes on a commanding advantage in the struggle for survival. Whoever they are, what do they know about undying misery?"

I felt so intimidated by his menacing demeanor that I chose not to reply to his unexpected outburst of anger. It was obvious that the individual before me was deeply scarred by the traumas of the afflictions of what once was his life on Earth.

"After undergoing oppression from generation to generation, despair finds its roots in the hearts of a hopeless people. And when life loses its face value, death becomes a welcoming alternative to fight for what you believe, not the other way around as you suggested," he said in a toned down voice that assuaged my inquietude. "Besides, who is to define what courage means? To you or to them, whoever they happen to be, courage may mean enduring agony in compliance with the circumstances of the suffering. But to me and to us, my people, courage is what is born out of the womb of despair when there is nothing left to lose but life itself."

At that moment I mustered some courage of my own and looked into his eye searching for his truth. I wanted to learn about his journey to this bleak realm of existence we both found ourselves imprisoned. I needed to know how his motivation to doing part with life and how it was different from my own. Although suffering was the common thread that our lives hanged in limbo before we decided to cut it off, the distinction between his and my drive to pursue death as a delusional solution was something important for me to know. I smiled at him timidly and then started moving toward the large rectangular burgundy rug I found him prostrated on when I came in.

"Come," I said beckoning at him from the center of the rug where I sat on my bent knees. "I want to learn what courage means to you and your people, whoever they happen to be."

He hesitated for a moment before starting moving toward me. Both his eyes and the contorted expression in his face revealed that he seemed suspicious of my interest in him. Yet, soon he was sitting across from me ready to open the book containing the story of his suicide tragedy.

"People living in abject poverty with no hope to guide them out of their misery are people condemned to living death," he started with an ominous preface that disclosed the disillusionment that led him to his self-annihilating act. "When your homeland is occupied, the population displaced, and an oppressive foreign power subjugates your hopes for a dignified life, death becomes a welcome path to liberation, especially when your beliefs suggest that martyrdom is a noble cause. It becomes the only hope you have for a meaningful existence in the face of an unwelcoming future."

For the first time since I laid eyes on him, I felt a strange wave of empathy flowing inside of me. Unlike my own situation in which individual despair triggered my decision to end my life, the man sitting in front of me seemed to be assailed by so many circumstantial forces that made me think his suicide had merits that mine did not.

"As a child growing up in the ghetto of disbanded people, I was indoctrinated to believe that there was a heroic purpose in the act of killing yourself while murdering those who have done you wrong," he said while casually touching the suicide vest he wore. "And if the honor of martyrdom were not enough, you are conditioned to believe that you'll be rewarded handsomely in the next life. Evidently, it is not true."

"What exactly is it that you did that got you here?" I asked beginning to question the possibility of any merit in his suicide.

"After the occupying oppressor's air raid on my village killed my father, mother and siblings, I became overwhelmed with both grief and anger. Yearning for revenge, I joined a training group that was determined to fight back in a way that would deliver serious consequences to our enemies. There are only so many rocks you can cast with your slingshot against machine guns until you realize the futility of the strategy; even if it's the only one you have," he said as his voice began crackling.

"What did you do?" I insisted in learning the details.

"I delivered to them similar pain they've inflicted on me and my people for decades of occupation and oppression. I hit them where it hurts the most; in the loss of family, friends, love and life," he said and I could almost see his grief and guilt dancing to the macabre tune of remorse. "I put on this vest and headed to a wedding celebration in our enemy's neighboring town determined to give them an equal taste of the anguish that I and many of my compatriots had endured for such a long time. I vividly remember sneaking in disguised as a servant feeling the mirth exuding from smiling faces rejoicing the beginning of a new life they didn't know I was about to put an end to. By the time I pulled the triggering device, those who survived the carnage probably envied the others whose body parts were strewn all over the bloodbath I delivered to the marriage ceremony. In a split second, I turned joviality into unspeakable horror."

As I listened to him, I thought of the teenager who committed murder-suicide killing innocent children. Although I deemed both cases repugnant, this man's ignominious action was motivated by a socioeconomic-political cause fuelled by anger, sorrow, and despair. Nevertheless, the killing of others who had no direct link to his purpose was as incomprehensible as it was unacceptable to me. I could not fathom how the bloodshed of harmless citizens celebrating life's special moments was even remotely justifiable, regardless of any injustices or crimes committed against him and his people. No matter how I tried to rationalize his motivation, it was a despicably reprehensible act. I was distraught and he obviously became aware of my indignation.

"I'm not proud of what I did, but I had to carry out both my patriotic and religious duties; and I paid the ultimate price for my action," he said looking down at his fingers fiddling with the detonating ring on his suicide vest. "Both my people and my faith demanded it from me."

"No, I don't think so," I said instinctively as soon as he finished his statement. "Neither a nation nor religious beliefs would coerce anyone to murder innocent people while committing suicide."

"And what do you know about it?" He asked staring at me with a raised eyebrow that made me feel slightly intimidated. "You appear to me to be someone who's never known or cared for either nation or religion."

"Perhaps not in the same way you do; as a copout to my own individual suffering and personal failures," I said trying to muster some nerve to stand my ground while maintaining eye contact with him. "I killed myself on my own terms to put an end to my personal misery. I aspired to be neither a national hero nor a religious martyr; and I did not take any other lives with my decision to take my own. It is just not the way I would serve my country or faith."

"I told you that I'm not proud of what I did, but it was a noble act to give my life to my people's cause," he said in what I perceived to be a desperate last moment attempt to convince himself instead of me.

"I suppose there is some nobility in dying for your country and for what you believe, but not at the expense of blameless individuals' lives whose only fault was to belong to the group you hate," I said beginning to feel impassioned by my argument. "Frankly, I do not see any honor or value in what you did; to the contrary, I think it was a dastardly act unworthy of merit in any level. And the fact that you're sitting here in front of me and not surrounded by 72 virgin nymphs in heaven makes me believe that I am correct in my judgment."

He looked at me with a mix of disdain and shame. I felt as though I had pulled off the trigger on his vest with my words and inadvertently blown his foolish pride away. Unlike the loud clamor of explosion and the ensuing outcry of pain and suffering that his act generated, my words were followed by an enduring uncomfortable silence.

"You should leave now," he said brusquely.

"I don't know where to go," I replied.

"See that door over there?" He said looking in the direction of a tall arching white door at the end of the room.

"What's in there?" I asked.

"It's a passageway leading to the religious faith you're more likely to understand," he said with a tinge of derision. "Maybe you will have more sympathy for a good Christian man who murdered no one but himself because he trusted the Lord would be forgiving and deliver his salvation. He could no longer bear the tediousness of living; and since he was led to believe that the Lord would wash away his sins, he put an end to his life while compromising the life of another person. Perhaps you'll find it less reprehensible than what I did. You can decide it for yourself when you visit with him."

"How do you know about it? I asked puzzled about his acquaintance of the Christian man's situation.

"In the suicide house of worship, we all know one another's case, even though we never open the door of religions we don't subscribe for," he said. "As it is, he knows that I didn't get my promised virgins just as I know that his Lord didn't deliver his salvation either. But regardless of the circumstances, we ended up in the same miserable place. I guess both his God and mine are not forgiving of murder; be it of one or many."

Since I'd never been a religious person in my terrestrial life, I wondered what religious people mean by their individual different gods, and how they claim their wrathful warring gods to be the legitimate guardians of the truth. To me, in my deep-seated iconoclastic approach to belief systems, the only judging god I knew was my consciousness, which had not been in a good space since I committed suicide.

"Please leave me alone now," he said lowering his head and nodding while releasing a subtle mournful sigh.

I stood up and walked in the direction he'd indicated. As soon as I opened the large solid marble door, I was transported to another realm of faith where lasciviousness and chicanery were the objects of devotion.

◀28▶

As soon as I opened the imposing door anticipating to enter an equally impressive environment, I was shocked with the unwelcoming contrast to my expectation. Once I stepped into the room, an unpleasant wave of pungent musty odor invaded my nostrils causing me to pucker my lips in disgust. It was dark and it smelled putrid; a repulsive combination that made me cringe.

As I slowly made my way inside the moldy room, I saw in the distance the feeble flame of a candle burning on the top of what it seemed to be an altar. I moved toward it and noticed that the closer I got to it the less ghastly the rancid smell became. Soon, I could see a young man wearing a white robe and black slacks gently swinging a bowl of incense while mumbling sounds that I assumed to be prayers. The dim light and the soothing fragrance motivated me to hasten my pace toward him, though with a great deal of skepticism.

"Excuse me," I said gently approaching him from behind.

He turned around and the sunken eyes in his youthful innocent face dragged me down to the bottom of the desolation of his existence. I felt like I was standing before a soulless being that had lost the will to live. He stared back at me with his empty eyes without saying a word. I wondered if his mumblings that sounded like prayers were what kept his feeling alive.

"I'm sorry to have disturbed your religious ritual, but I need to find my way out of here. Do you think you could help me? I asked with my eyes piercing through his as I attempted to communicate beyond the limitation of words.

"Only through the Lord you can find your way out of the Suicide Orbit Sector," he whispered. "Only through the Lord."

"Listen, I am stuck in this place and I don't think there is much the Lord can do for me right now. Do you know of any other options?" I said beginning to feel both annoyed and frustrated with his pious gibberish.

"The Lord got me here and the Lord will deliver me from this place," he whispered again now staring at the dark distance as if he could see a vacuum of nothingness with his vacant eyes.

"The Lord got you here?" I repeated to myself confused with a seemingly hokum statement.

"Yes, He did," he replied almost instantly. "Since I was a child I was conditioned to believe that the Lord would not only wash away my sins, but He'd also wait for me in heaven. Because I believed in both, I didn't hesitate to kill myself when the pain became unbearable to endure. I knew I could count on the Lord to rescue me from the hell I lived in. Now I rely on the Lord once again to exonerate my sins and deliver me out of the searing anguish of my guilt and shame."

I looked at that innocent-looking young man wondering what in the world could drive someone like him to put an end to his life. Since I'd been told that learning was a pre-requisite to the possibility of my redemption, I decided that it was important to me to find out the circumstances that led that young man to the infamous circle of the S.O.S.

"Come," I said beckoning at him. "Come have a seat."

His expressionless eyes suddenly showed some signs of life as they smiled at me with a subtle twinkle. Perhaps my interest in him aroused a renewed jest for living. Or maybe he just embraced the rare opportunity to unload his heavy heart and mind. Whatever it was, when he started walking toward the wooden bench I invited him to sit down next to me, I could feel his eagerness to talk it out likely hoping to cleanse the dense emotions that were clogging up his heart. As he got closer, I experienced a strange feeling of being a priestess on the other side of an invisible confession booth where this penitent soul was about to unearth his darkest secrets.

"I was only 28-years-old when I committed suicide, but I felt three times older, and I was utterly exhausted," he said with his head turned away from my face as if to avoid eye contact. "I'd grown up on a farm where the nearest small town 50 miles away had a post-office, a general store, and a church. That's all I knew until I was eighteen and had to move away in order to survive."

"Was there a drought in the region you farmed?" I asked. "What else would make you move away to survive?"

"There was no shortage of water; but there was a dearth of morals that led to the starvation of my spirit," he said as I could sense resentment percolating through his words. "For years I was sexually molested by the man my family trusted the most; the one who was supposed to be a beacon of decency and morality.

And yet, every Sunday, religiously, he sodomized me after preaching the truths of the Bible to his congregation, which included my parents. By the time I grew some sense out of his hypocritical lies and crimes against the innocence of childhood, I began hating him so much that I fantasized murdering him and sticking a stake deep into his ass to make sure that pedophile Dracula would never come back to haunt another child. When it got to the point that I could not look at him without thinking of killing him or myself, I realized I had to leave town for good."

"Where did you go?" I asked feeling intrigued by this man's route to self-annihilation.

"I moved far away to the big city hoping that being among throngs of people would alleviate my loneliness," he said while sighing out loud and shaking his head. "Alas, I only discovered that lonesomeness is but a state of being, regardless of where you are or how many people are around you. In fact, the crowds in the city only aggravated my inner despair, for I felt more alone than ever before. But then one day my fortune changed when the Lord shone a bright light at the end of the dark tunnel of my life."

I remained attentively quiet allowing him to continue without interruptions.

"When I met Elaine I discovered the brave new world of romantic love; that intoxicating state of being that makes you forget your own existence. For the first time in my life, I experienced the loving touch of a woman, which greatly contrasted with the repugnant homosexual assault I endured as a child. She became the solid foundation of my fractured existence," he said gazing vacantly at the floor.

All of a sudden, I became increasingly curious about this young man's reason to ending up in the S.O.S. However, I could not muster the nerve to ask him any questions about it. All I did was to tap three times on the top of his hand resting on his knee to convey support and willingness to listen. He clearly heeded my silent message.

"Eventually, we got married and had children. But it was a matter of time for the romantic illusion to fade away and boredom moved into my life with a vengeance. I was already overwhelmed by the imposing burden to support my family on very limited income earned doing menial jobs I absolutely hated. It was at that time when the haunting memories of sexual abuse started sneaking out of the bleak caverns of my tormented mind," he said before pausing for a long moment as though he reflected on past events. "Suddenly, the traumatic sexual experiences I endured in my childhood hijacked my emotions while disturbing the inner balance of my adult life. When I reached rock-bottom, I began planning a well thought-out exit strategy."

I couldn't help remembering when I started my own exit plan out of what felt like a hellish existence. The insurmountable accumulation of distress eventually had its toll. But if there was one thing I'd already learned in the Suicide Orbit Sector was the common breaking point that pushes one over the edge. I also noticed that most of us caught in the infamous suicide path shared a propensity to give up the struggle to overcome life's trials. I was beginning to indulge in my own distressful thoughts when he resumed talking.

"Unable to bear the burden of constant psychological torment that triggered my miserable daily existence, I decided that it was time for me to be with the Lord. I was sure he'd wash away my sins if I did it the right way."

"Is there really a right way to commit suicide?" I asked intrigued by what I deemed to be an absurd remark.

"Well, if I made sure my wife and children would be alright after my passing," he said sounding convinced of his rationalization. "I was very meticulous in my planning."

"And how exactly you made sure a widow and her fatherless children coped with their loss in satisfactory fashion?" I asked.

"I purchased a large life insurance policy while long-term planning my suicide," he said and I noticed a sense of pride in the tone of his voice, as if he'd been a responsible family man. "Several months later, I rode my bicycle on the shoulder of a heavy traffic road and purposefully swerved onto the speeding cars moving behind me in what appeared to be an unfortunate accident."

I immediately thought of my mother who'd killed herself in a similar way, though she left nothing but sorrow and vulnerability for her orphaned child. Also, for the first time, I realized that by choosing that method of suicide, both this man and my mother involved an innocent party in their act; the random motorist that haphazardly crossed their paths. I felt compelled to voice my condemnation of his suicidal plan.

"Did it ever occur to you that not only you traumatized your family, but also an innocent person who had nothing to do with your troubles?" I asked without subduing my indignation.

"Oh please, spare me from your righteousness," he said striking my indignation with sarcasm. "Look at you; look where you are. We both vibrate at the same frequency of despondence. Yes, my act affected other people's lives, but so did yours. I had no choice, and neither did you."

"And do you think this is alright by the Lord?" I asked questioning his religiosity.

"Of course it is," he replied in a heartbeat. "The Lord washes away all our sins; even those of monstrous human beings capable of violating the innocence of children. Yes, even the criminals proclaiming to be the paragon of morality receive the mercy of the Lord."

"How can you be so sure of it?" I asked.

"Because the priest who molested me when I was a boy is here, too," he said. "He is in another wing of this religious building as the Lord washes away the sins of his soul."

"It seems that the greatest challenge must be keeping yourself clean after the Lord washes your sins off. I suppose even the Lord must get fed up with washing someone's sins over and over again. It's a Sisyphean task that not even gods can withstand too long," I said returning some sarcasm back at him.

"Maybe you should go visit with him," he suggested. "You might be able to understand something that I can't. And who knows, it might even help you take another step to your way out of this place."

"How do I get to him?" I asked enthused with the opportunity to move closer to the exit of that dismal environment.

"See that door at the end of the hallway?" He said pointing in the direction of the dark corridor. "Once you open it, you'll be there."

Without saying another word, I started walking toward the door feeling an electric charge of excitement and trepidation running through my spinal cord. As the chilling mist emanating from the walls of the humid hallway made me shiver, I wondered how many more doors I'd have to walk through before I found my way out for good.

"As many as necessary," a familiar voice resonated in my head as soon as the thought occurred to me. "The real daunting challenge would be to know for sure that no matter how many doors you have to walk through, you'd still never find your way out of the labyrinth of despair. Now, that would be a truly Sisyphean task that would be hard even for gods to withstand. But you are no god, so just keep moving forward."

I immediately quieted my mind's voice and kept a steady pace toward the next step of my journey.

◁29▷

"What are you doing?" I yelled as soon as I stepped into the well-lit room where several candles burned on a makeshift altar.

The tall grey-haired man, whom I estimated to be a mid-septuagenarian, quickly recomposed himself trying to hide both his penis and embarrassment under his white religious garment. He turned his back to me while straightening himself up and repeatedly apologizing for his indecorous sexual misbehavior.

"I'm very sorry," he said looking at me from over his left shoulder before turning around to face me. "I wasn't expecting anyone to come in to witness my disgrace. It's been a struggle to get rid of my perverted addiction. I thought that once I crossed over, I'd be able to recover from this pervasive psychological malaise that has ruined my life, and apparently even my death."

Once his hands dropped down to the side, I started walking toward him to get a closer look at that pathetic old man who masturbated while lasciviously uttering a boy's name. Perhaps disturbed by my encroaching, he moved away from the front of the altar when I noticed a photograph next to a large candle. It was a picture of a group of boys dressed up in ornamented cassocks in which one face in the middle of the photo was circled in red ink. I picked it up to take a good look under the flame of the candle and I immediately recognized the circled face as the young man I'd just met in the other room of that despicable pseudo-house of worship.

"I founded that beautiful boys' choir when I worked as the principal of the St. Anthony's Parochial School," he said looking discomfited. "And that boy was my favorite singer."

"Then I suppose that when I walked in you were singing his favorite hymn," I said with poignant cynicism.

His face turned somberly aggressive and I felt threatened when he slowly moved in my direction. I made a strong effort to conceal my apprehension and looked at him in the eye as he got closer to me.

"Listen, I am a sick man, but I wasn't born this way. I was made sick by a hypocritical society that abused me just as much as I abused those boys," he said as I noticed the hostility in his eyes turn into deep despondency. "I'm a victim of a malignant vicious cycle that replicates itself like viruses in previously healthy host cells."

"A victim!" I exclaimed in dismay. "What does it make of the innocent abused boys when their perpetrator proclaims victimhood?"

"When I was a boy I was abused, too. For years I endured sexual molestation by the priest who preached against the immorality of homosexuality from the pulpit every Sunday. He openly condemned unwed sexual activity and exhorted his own vows of celibacy to the congregation. And while propagating his lies and falsehoods, he molested me and other altar boys on a regular basis," he said as his dejection percolated through every syllable of his words. "Make no mistake; I'm the unholy outcome of a hypocritical society whose decadent culture emerges from the essence of corruption."

"I suppose you adopted a corrupted version of the Golden Rule: do unto others as it was done unto you," I said unmoved by his victimized self-justification. "You became a priest yourself so you could duplicate the wicked perversion you endured. Your spirit must have dried up and become so brittle that broke whatever modicum of character you had into smithereens. No wonder you ended up in this miserable place."

"Yes, and I am not alone," he replied with a retaliatory look.

"Touché," I said acknowledging my own hypocritical comment. In the S.O.S. region righteousness is an unclaimed item in the lost and found desk of redemption.

A long silence ensued and I became pensive. For the first time it'd dawned on me that the contradictory societal hypocrisy he deposed against had various counterparts. Like Christianity, democracy, too, enjoys a holier-than-thou status in social decorum; and yet, it is equally marred by corruption and falsehoods. The same deceiving concept of equality, be it in the eyes of God or the democratic state where each person casts an equal value vote, suddenly seemed like a sham to me; a utopian view of equality in a vast sea of diversity of intelligence, education, character, and even individual merit. At that moment I realized that democracy, like religion, had become a degenerate scheme of manipulation and deception. However, I had to admit that the sordid priest had made a solid point about being the end product of a hypocritical society, though nothing; not even having been a victim himself, could exculpate him from his sexual crimes against children.

"After molesting dozens of choir boys for more than three decades, I was eventually caught, arraigned, and agreed with a guilty-plea bargain with the prosecutors to only a few of the countless crimes I committed," he said breaking the silence. "In the end, I'm aware that I've ruined many lives, including my own."

"How did you transition from the mortal biological sphere?" I asked interested in details.

"I placed the rope of guilt around my shame and hanged myself in my jail cell a few months before my release from prison," he said rubbing his right hand on his neck. "At 76-years-old, life as a registered sexual offender was not something I looked forward to. I'd already lived a long life; I didn't need to perpetuate my suffering. Thus, I chose to die as the hypocrite that society molded me into being. Besides, I believed that the Lord would wash away my sins regardless of how filthy they were."

"You don't really believe it, do you?" I asked with a raised eyebrow and a subtle disdainful sneer at his debauchery.

"Does it really matter?" He said looking at me from the corner of his eyes sneering right back at me.

I hated to have to admit that he had a valid point, again. It doesn't matter what you believe in, but what your beliefs will deliver to you as a compensation for your act of believing. Whether it assuages intellectual anxieties or emotional distresses, the only thing that really matters is the end result, regardless of how preposterous the subject of the belief may be. Whether it's an innocent child who believes in the fairy tooth and Santa Claus, or a fearful religious man who believes in a wrathful god and a burning hell, the intrinsic function of believing in something is the reward it brings to the believer, regardless of the veracity of the conviction.

"Well...," he said staring at me as he waited for an answer.

"I believe that I can make my way out of this place," I said reinforcing to myself the conclusion about the nature of believing that I'd just arrived. "And that I believe it does matter."

"You have lofty ambitions," he said turning his gaze away from me. "I'm afraid I cannot be of help to you; after all, I am a corrupt hypocrite child molester. I'd already committed spiritual suicide long before I hanged myself in that jail cell."

"Yeh, that's a lot of dirty laundry of sin for the Lord to handle," I said sarcastically. I just couldn't hold myself back, for there was something about that man that revolted me.

"Where are you going?" He asked after I stood up and started walking away.

"I don't know," I said turning around to look at him before paraphrasing his earlier question. "Does it really matter?"

"If you believe that you can make it out of here, then I believe that it does matter," he said duplicating the words of my answer.

"I don't have any viable options but venture into the unknown on my own," I said determined to find a way out of the S.O.S.

"You talk like an intrepid warrior; as if you were an Amazonian warrior on a rescue mission," he said.

"Damn right I'm on a rescue mission!" I snarled. "Unlike you, I'm not relying on any lord to save my ass. I must find a way to liberate myself."

"Then you must visit with your kin," he said sounding assured of his statement.

"What are you talking about now?" I asked beginning to lose the thin thread of tolerance I had left for him.

"If you walk up the narrow circular stairway to the tower of this building, you will be at a terrace with a platform at the end of it. Keep moving toward it and you'll get to the threshold of the domain of suicide warriors. If you can manage to cross the barrier of fear, you will meet with those who have lost their fear of death. They vibrate in quite distinct frequency from all other suicides in this penitent orbit. If you can take the leap of faith, you'll put your own beliefs to the test," he said. "It's a tough challenge but definitely worth a try."

"I'll give it a shot," I said.

"Good luck to you," he whispered while walking away.

Soon, I was climbing up the narrow circular stairway with droplets of perspiration in my brow, high tempo breathing, and my heart pounding inside my chest like a war drum.

I was about to enter the realm of suicide warriors.

30

As soon as I opened the squeaky metal door leading to the terrace, I immediately noticed the lighter and fresher air that breezed through. Although I'd climbed up only a couple of flights of stairs, the wide open terrace I ended up at felt like it was located many thousand feet high. It felt chilly and the thin atmosphere made me feel lighter, which was a welcome contrast to the sulfuric-laden air I'd breathed lower below. I kept walking toward the edge of the terrace where a wooden platform protruded out to an area I couldn't see from the distance. Driven by irrepressible curiosity, I picked up my pace only to be reminded by the recollections of past advice to be patient with the process without rushing to outcomes. I slowed down and breathed deeply aware of my feet touching the ground at every step. Soon and without even noticing, I'd reached my next destination: the entryway to a new realm of suicide experience.

As soon as I stepped onto the solid oak platform, I experienced an eerie feeling of standing on an ethereal threshold; a barely perceptible sensory of a new reality. Hesitantly, I moved toward the edge to see what lay beyond the wooden structure. I looked down and I gasped. Triggered by my predisposition to acrophobia, my head started spinning as I looked down at what seemed like an endless abyss below. If that weren't frightening enough, the memory of my first suicide attempt harassed my emotions paralyzing me exactly the same way I experienced that night on the edge of the coastal cliff. It was as though I stood where I'd been before. I was terrified.

"What are you going to do this time around?" A familiar voice resonated inside my head.

Not knowing what to answer, I shivered in the icy silence of the moment. Just as it happened on that frightful night, plunging into the unknown was an intimidating initiative I was not ready to undertake.

"What are you going to do now?" The voice reverberated from the bottom of the depth of my fears as I looked down the treacherous terrain below.

"I do not know," I mumbled. "What am I jumping into?"

"You will find out only if you jump," the voiced replied.

"But what if…," I muttered unable to complete my sentence.

"The meaning of leap of faith is to go for it knowing that the safety net is there even when you can't see it," the voice said.

Suddenly, the answer was clear to me: going back was out of question. In fact, moving backwards in any way seemed like a dangerously detrimental option for someone in my position trying to find the way out of the untoward situation I put myself in. Besides, having not carried out my suicide attempt the first time around and failing to jump off that cliff, perhaps this was a second opportunity to bounce back to a life I had forfeited. I closed my eyes, took a deep breath, and leapt in total surrender to my destiny.

As soon as my feet left the edge of the platform, I was stunned to realize I was falling upwards, as though an antigravity force pulled me up like a feather moving freely through a gentle autumn breeze. I felt like a wingless bird flying up and northward in an effortless migration to a predetermined destination. I was at ease until I landed on an unconventional setting on a majestic mountain top.

"Kiai!" An imposing figure donned in full-on war regalia appeared out of nowhere shouting at me with a long shining blade drawn. I became petrified with fear assured that I was about to die a second death. He started moving slowly toward me and his blazing gaze made me feel like a helpless prey standing still before a starved predator. As he got closer, I could feel the heat wave emanating from his body while his fiery eyes assaulted me even before his blade struck.

"Kiai!" He shouted again wielding his sword with extreme rapidity above my head. I could feel the whizzing of it as I wondered whether my head was still attached to my neck. Suddenly, he stopped his skilful sword maneuvers and started circling me. After scrutinizing every detail of my being, he faced me and his bright right eye pierced through mine as if it were an incandescent blade of energy.

"I…came here because…I was told you could be of…help to me," I stuttered still attempting to recover from the frightening experience. "I was told that…I needed to visit with my kin. I'm sorry I…may not have come to the right place. It doesn't look like we…have much in common."

"Of course we do, though I have to admit that it's difficult to acknowledge it at first sight," he said while sheathing his *katana*, the samurai's sword, in a black leather case hanging across his back. "But the reality is that you would not have been sent here otherwise."

I didn't say anything else. I stood there quietly observing that imposing figure before me. His impressive warrior garment was like a pliable shield protecting both his physical body as well as his undaunted spirit. Around his waist, a woven black rope held the sheath of a well tucked in *wakizashi*, the short samurai sword known for its menacing point suid an edge sharper than a razor. On his head, a magnificently crafted *kabuto*, the samurai helmet, set like a monarchic crown of a true warrior king. Not only was the *kabuto* an exquisite work of craftsmanship, the piece adorned the strong features of his noble masculine face while magnifying the intensity of his awe-inspiring eyes. The more I analyzed that foreboding character, the more I wondered what a warrior of that magnitude was doing in a place like the Suicide Orbit Sector. It was a matter of time for him to start disclosing the mystery.

"I was raised to be a man of honor and wrought to become a samurai," he said pulling the *katana* off his back and placing it on a large granite rock next to him. "I grew up cultivating the martial virtues and learning to be completely indifferent to death and pain. Valor, fortitude, bravery, fearlessness, and courage in all manifestations are the qualities that have nurtured my spirit. But all of them would be worthless if they did not rest on the virtuous principle of loyalty."

"Loyalty?" I questioned. "To whom?"

"Loyalty as a principle," he replied. "Loyalty to the honor of my spirit. The object of the loyalty is irrelevant to the principle."

"Is your loyalty to blame for your being here?" I asked uneasily deeming that I might have been intrusive.

He stared at me and his penetrating gaze made me quiver. For a moment I regretted having asked him the question, though soon he abated my concerns when he resumed talking.

"How could anybody hold loyalty responsible for anything but nobility of spirit?" He observed looking into my eye. "My being in this place of atonement is strictly related to the decisions I've made in my life and in accordance with the principles I've lived and died by. Like you and everyone else in this penitent orbit of death, I, too, chose the suicide route. However, the distinction between your motivation and mine is as incomparable as a dragon and a dragonfly."

"Really?" I said sarcastically. "What would make your suicide more excusable than mine or anyone else stuck in this nauseating orbit of misery?"

"Loyalty," he replied. "Loyalty to the honor of my spirit."

"And yet, you ended up in the same place as the rest of us. There is something wrong with your rationale," I pointed out.

"Of course, if your perception of what suicide means pertains to the basic fact of dying by one's own hand. Yes, in that sense there's no difference between our cases. But because not all suicides are alike, the nature of yours and mine are light-years apart," he said briefly turning his back to me in a subtle gesture that I interpreted as unspoken contempt.

"What do you mean different kinds of suicide? If you choose to quit living on your own terms you are a suicide. I don't care how you may try to embellish the image, you're still a suicide," I said taking on a defiant argumentative stance. Somehow I felt annoyed by his implicit sense of moral superiority.

"You chose to die out of despair, sorrow, and anger, whereas I decided to take on death head on inspired by honor, courage, and tranquility in the face of the most terrifying enigma of the human existence," he said looking straight into my eye as if to assert the truth of his words with his feelings. "From where I stand, I am a suicide warrior whereas you are a suicide coward."

"And yet, here the coward stands in the same place as the brave," I remarked oozing sarcasm. "Perhaps the difference between us is not as black and white as you paint it to be."

"You're obviously taking this way too personally, which prompts me to be more specific so you can understand what I'm referring to," he said starting to pace as he spoke. "Firstly, the reason the coward and the brave are in the same place is because we both have betrayed the life nature entrusted us to uphold. But the motivational factor leading us to commit suicide is not by any means even remotely comparable. I am a dragon and you are a dragonfly. At the historical time and culture I lived, *seppuku* was a highly noble suicidal process that required a great deal of courage in the face of self-immolation in death. *Seppuku* was more than a valiant noble act; it was a ceremonial institution of my warrior culture."

Suddenly, I thought of the great Greek philosopher Socrates who also died by means of suicide; and in some way related to distinct motivational factors this samurai warrior was referring to. In Socrates' case, however, he chose to ingest the suicidal drink of hemlock rather than admitting to a crime he didn't believe he committed; that is, corrupting the minds of the youth of Athens with his philosophical teachings. Under his specific circumstance, would be fair-minded to call Socrates a suicide? I realized the samurai had a legitimate point in saying that dying by one's hand is not in and by itself an acceptable generalization of the meaning of suicide. I would learn more about this concept later on in my journey through the Suicide Orbit Sector.

"After feeling that I had dishonored my shogun by not fulfilling my duties in battle, I knew that the only way to restore my honor would be through *seppuku*," he said and for the first time I noticed his eyes moving down toward the ground. "Thus, I asked my best friend to serve the honor of being my *kaishaku* after I disemboweled my *hara* with my *wakizashi*."

I knew that the *hara* was the place slightly below the navel where the Japanese warriors believed spirit was enshrined in a powerhouse of energy; like the nucleus of an atom. *Wakizashi* was the deadly sharp dagger-like weapon the samurai carried along with his *katana*. *Seppuku* was the suicidal ritual of honor, but *kaishaku* was unknown to me.

"What's a *kaishaku*?" I asked.

Slowly, he lifted his eyes up to look deeply into mine. There was a long unsettling pause before he resumed talking.

"He's the one who has the honor of beheading the warrior committing *seppuku* when the latter reaches the point of unbearable physical agony in the midst of self-disembowelment. The *kaishaku* delivers the final blow to an honorable death."

I remained silent for a long time mulling over the concept of suicide as a painful ritual of honor. While most suicides are carried out as quickly and pain-free as possible, *seppuku* was a drastic exception to commonality. Now I understood why he made a distinction between his suicide method and mine, referring to his as noble and mine pusillanimous. Driven by a strong sense of honor, he chose to die a most ghastly death, while someone like me took the easy way out through the backdoor of ignoble escapism from life's challenges. I suppose he was right when he referred to himself as a suicide warrior and I a suicide coward. Nevertheless, both his bravery and my spinelessness seemed to have the same weight of culpability on life's scale of justice, for at that moment we shared a common shameful place in an off-centered orbit of existence. But regardless of how I looked at it, it became obvious to me from that moment onward that each driving force compelling a suicide act had its own distinct nature, and therefore its own unique set of morals and dishonor. Indeed, the samurai was right when he asserted that not all suicides are alike.

"What does it take for someone to commit suicide in such ghastly way?" I asked wondering how much courage was required to carry out this horrific method of self-annihilation.

"Tranquility," he replied succinctly.

I was stunned by his answer. After all, I was expecting to hear some magnanimous explanation about unwavering bravery required in the face of a gruesome death. He probably read the perplexity in my facial expression as he explained in most cogent fashion.

"Tranquility is courage in repose. It's a statical manifestation of valor as daring deeds are a dynamical. A truly brave man is ever serene; he is never taken by surprise; nothing ruffles the equanimity of his spirit. This level of tranquility is what's required to live and die as a warrior," he said picking up his *katana* and sheathing it before placing it around his back. "Now it's time for me to go, for I must continue my journey."

"Where are you going?" I asked wondering whether his journey bore any similarity to mine. Maybe I could follow him and learn how to develop such high level of equanimity.

"I am journeying back to recovering the honor I lost when I committed what I thought to be my honorable death," he said beginning to walk away. "And you, you must go find your way to another opportunity to conquer the honor you never had a chance to acquire."

"Wait!" I said trying to get his attention as he walked away. "Where do I go from here?"

He stopped and turned around to look at me for the last time. "Your showing up here to visit with me was not a haphazard event; nothing is. Now, you must move on and find your own inner warrior's way."

"And what's the warrior's way?" I asked.

"Tranquility in the face of death," he replied before turning around and vanishing in the distance.

Instinctively, I wanted to follow in his direction but I could no longer see him as he disappeared amidst the cloud-covered mountain peaks in the distance.

Once I realized I was on my own again, I started wondering how I went from walking in a circle street to a mountain top after entering a church-like building. And if my mind were not befuddled enough, I was puzzled to realize that after walking down the mountain for what it felt like a very long time, I ended up at a tarmac with several old warplanes nearby. Hoping that perhaps I could fly my way out of the S.O.S., I entered a large old hangar onsite hoping to find answers to my countless questions.

◄31►

"Excuse me," I said approaching a group of men gathering around parked aircrafts with their backs to me. Talking lively in a language I could not comprehend, they didn't seem to notice my presence. I gingerly walked closer to them before speaking again.

"Excuse me," I repeated in a subdued tone of voice while tapping on the shoulder of one of the men to get his attention. "I need your help."

When he turned around and looked at me, I swallowed dry air wondering whether it was a good idea to have dared to touch him even so lightly. His incisive slanted dark eyes pierced through mine like a Neanderthal's spear puncturing a wounded wild boar. I cleared my parched throat as I looked into his mesmerizing stare as if I were hypnotized by the silent capturing power of his gaze. Feeling my wobbly knees give way to my fear, I wanted to run away but I realized it was too late for that. I stood there, motionless, looking at him unable to utter another word. Noticing the similar facial features of this man in uniform with the samurai I'd just visited with earlier, I was reminded of the latter's reference to tranquility as an act of courage in repose. However, the lofty concept seemed to have evaded me at a time I felt threatened by the sheer power of this man's presence.

"You look like the enemy to me," he said moving his rugged face within inches of mine. "But I respect a brave enemy who walks into the foes den."

"I'm nobody's enemy but my own," I said beginning to understand and experience the concept of tranquility as an act of courage in the face of a challenge. "I just need help to find my way out of this place. I'm hoping that with your aircrafts you might be able to fly me out of here."

He turned around toward his peers, said something to them in the foreign language I did not understand, and they all burst into boisterous laughter that made me feel both embarrassed and concerned.

"And where exactly do you want to go?" He asked me after they calmed down.

"Anywhere out of this place," I answered.

"Anywhere?" He asked raising an eyebrow.

"Well, anywhere safe," I replied with suspicion.

They all laughed out loud as soon as I finished my sentence.

"There is no such place anywhere," he said as his voice took on a serious tone and all his companions displayed solemn facial expressions. "Where life and death walk hand in hand, safety is a figment of the coward's imagination."

It was an awkward moment. I didn't know what to say after he made me feel inadequately out of place. I chuckled, nodded my head in disappointment, and started walking away.

"Wait!" He commanded as I halted my steps on the double. "I can take you on a journey that will not only dispel your illusion about safety but also lead the way to glory."

Now he got both my attention and interest. It sounded like a promising proposition that I couldn't afford to let slip away. I turned around and walked back toward him stopping right before his imposing stature. Looking straight into his eye without saying a word, I felt the statical manifestation of valor envelop me like a protective armor of courage. I was tranquil.

"Good," he said smiling for the first time. "You may come aboard with me."

After speaking in an authoritative tone of voice to the other men in uniform, they all boarded their aircrafts emblazoned with a large red circle on the sides of the vertical stabilizers. I followed my cicerone to his plane and noticed when he picked up a *katana* leaning against the aircraft's wheels before boarding. The sword was similar to the one the samurai wielded in my previous encounter.

"We are warriors," he said probably noticing my surprised expression. "We find honor in death."

I nodded silently before climbing aboard and sat behind him in the close-fitting cockpit. Suddenly, I realized what I'd gotten myself into. I'd just boarded a warplane on a suicide mission. Once he turned on the engine, my heart accelerated and I started breathing heavily as if I were about to take off on my own terms. But as soon as the propellers began whizzing noisily, they muffled the intense inner rattling of my anticipation. Besides, I thought, I was already dead anyway.

"There is a major difference between us, suicide warriors, and the rest of you who commit the act to bail out from your miserable existence," he said shortly after taking off.

"What's the difference?" I asked unconvinced of the self-proclaimed suicide warrior superiority.

"We know that the ultimate purpose of life is death; and how we live and die determine the value of our spirit," he said. "We are aware that the true meaning of life lies on, not only accepting, but also embracing death wholeheartedly as the most dignified act of our temporal existence. Thus, choosing to die for a noble cause is the definitive undertaking of a life well lived. We live like a storm sweeping through the barren desert of mortality. That's why we're called the divine wind."

"It sounds like an unusual moniker for a suicide warrior," I said with a hint of sarcasm.

"That's what *kamikaze* means," he said. "It comes from the name my people gave to a typhoon that obliterated the invading

Mongol ships in the 13th century that saved our country from foreign domination. Now we act as the divine wind in defense of the motherland."

"Except that you've become the invaders; the airstrike equivalent of the Mongol ships the divine wind wiped out," I remarked based on his narrative of historical facts. "You've become the aggressors of other people's motherland and not the defenders of your own."

"Aggressor and defender are subjective interpretations to the purpose one serves. We *kamikazes* volunteer to die for our country, and some 3,800 have sacrificed themselves during World War II," he said as the plane took a deep turn down to the left. "We welcome death as a defying act against the illusion of a temporary existence while becoming glorified in the process."

I mulled over his words and realized that he sounded much like the suicide bomber I'd met at an earlier stage of my journey through the S.O.S. This *kamikaze* warrior's nationalistic attitude did not seem to differ from the religious approach of the man who is willing to die for his faith. At that moment, it became clear to me how foolishly akin religion and patriotism are. Both the pious and the patriotic aficionado are willing to die for their faith, country, or the aftermath of rewards and glory their acts may deliver.

"We are approaching the target," he said interrupting my musing about the spurious nature of religion and patriotism.

As the aircraft gradually descended, I picked up a pair of binoculars and saw a fleet of warships sailing in the middle of a vast ocean. Although I could not see the naval personnel onboard, I thought of the hundreds of husbands, fathers, brothers and sons who were about to lose their lives by the criminal suicide act of people who deemed themselves to be honorable warriors. Of course I was aware they were engaged in war; a criminal act in and by itself, but that was not the point of my experience. What mattered was the act of suicide perceived as a deed of nobility, which did not ring true to me at that moment. Maybe I was just an average suicide who did not understand the meaning behind a higher purpose.

"*Tennōheika Banzai*!" He yelled as the plane plunged down toward one ship while his peers attacked others. The war cry of "Long Live His Majesty the Emperor" didn't sound regal to my ears; to the contrary, it sounded irredeemably subservient. There was nothing divine about that wind, and definitely not noble.

As the warplane headed down full-speed toward its target against a flurry of anti-aircraft fire, I was surprised to notice how cool and collected I remained. Even though I knew I was already dead, the experience was vivid and felt real to me. Maybe I'd realized the meaning of tranquility in the face of death, and learned to not allow anything to ruffle the equanimity of my spirit. But as the final explosive moment of impact approached, I couldn't help thinking if there was any suicide warrior act that would remotely resemble an act of nobility. Then, when the plane made contact with its target and exploded into smithereens of scattered metal and human flesh, my awareness of the moment went into a state of stupor.

By the time I opened my eyes, I found myself lying on a prairie in an undisturbed state of being. It was there that I learned that a suicide warrior could, indeed, be a noble spirit, and his act a laudable demonstration of his power.

◁32▷

Lying semi-awake on the damp grass, I inadvertently slapped my right hand on my nose when an intrusive fly landed on it. The self-inflicted smack brought me to full consciousness as I sat up abruptly. I rubbed my eyes before opening them and what I saw in the distance was the most beautiful sight I'd seen since I committed suicide. It didn't look like anything I'd seen before in the infamous Suicide Orbit Sector. In fact, it was such a magnanimous landscape that I wondered whether I'd been finally transported out of the abhorrent S.O.S. I stood up to get a better view trying to identify what befuddled my eyes. Far away by a wide translucent meandering river, an expansive community gathered around an idyllic environment that was the antithesis of the iniquitous surroundings I'd been wandering through of lately. After beholding the magnificent scenery from afar consumed with great wonder, I could no longer just stand there agape. Propelled by irrepressible curiosity, my feet started moving toward the fascination of my vision.

As I got closer to the magical site, I became increasingly mesmerized by the splendor that captured my senses. There were what I estimated to be several dozen tepees by the river bank where horses, dogs, and other domestic animals roamed about freely among children playing with seemingly uncontainable joy. The mirth of their giggling sounds rang in my ears like bells tolling the celebration of a life infused with unsurpassed contentment. I took a deep breath and the enchanting fragrance of blooming jasmine flowers travelled through my nostrils until it reached the core of my scentless soul. Filled with unexpected joy, I smiled and bent down to pick up a lemongrass along the way and the softness of its texture caressed my fingertips as if nature attempted to love me through a sublime kinesthetic process. Then, I put it in my mouth and its tantalizing nectar flavored my hopes for a future in which joy, contentment, and harmony would be mine again someday when I'd be able to live like what my senses experienced at that time.

All of a sudden, I felt inexplicably fatigued with a strong urge to lie down on the prairie. Since I was still some distance away from the community encampment, I decided to stop for a moment and take a rest. I lay down on my back and stayed there for awhile staring at the resplendent ample blue sky until I dozed off.

"Goodness! What was that?" I said out loud to myself while sitting up abruptly awakened from my nap. I looked up to the sky and lead-colored billowing clouds were moving in heralded by striking lightning bolts followed by thunderous clamor. Suddenly, the blue sky that I fell asleep under had turned ominously gray after I woke up. I got to my feet intending to resume walking, but as I looked in the direction of the encampment, I was astonished to realize it was no longer there. The massive bulging dark clouds had enveloped the site where once was a paradisiacal setting. Now the vast open space was as obscured as my flummoxed mind wondering what happened.

"Did I just dream that I was somewhere else outside the Suicide Orbit Sector, or was I now dreaming to be back to that vile circuitous place?" I asked myself out loud hoping the latter was the case and I'd soon wake up. Either way, I decided to get moving and search for shelter as the storm loomed near.

Although intimidated by the rumbling thunder that seemed to strike in sync with my strides, I kept moving forward through what now had become a dense fog with nearly zero visibility. There was no way I could tell where I was going. However, since I was frightened out of my wits by the deafening sounds of thunder, I had no choice but keep moving, in any direction, and at a steady pace. I felt as though I was running away from a persecuting high decibel army that assaulted my auditory sense while terrifying my spirit. All of a sudden, louder than ever before, an earsplitting rumble erupted in the dark sky as if an earthquake had occurred in the atmosphere. At the precise time of the thunderous explosion, a formidable being appeared before my startled eyes.

"*Hoka hey*!" He shouted and his raspy voice resonated in my ears even louder than the thunder itself. "*Hoka hey*!"

As soon as he shouted for the second time, the fog dissipated and everything around me became visible again. I looked around with despairing astonishment. Where used to be a lively encampment community now resembled a death camp; an opened ground cemetery where mutilated bodies of men, women, children, and animals lay to waste. The arid smoky odor of burned to the ground teepees irritated my eyes and clogged my respiratory track. Looking farther beyond the sight of that unspeakable tragedy, I noticed that what was a large clear water river had turned into a filthy swamp whose color matched the billowing clouds above. Alas, I was definitely back in the S.O.S. again, though in reality I'd never left it but in a fleeting reverie.

"It was not a dream," the imposing figure spoke unexpectedly. "What you saw actually existed before the unscrupulous greedy tyrants came from faraway lands. Like these ominous dark clouds above, they rolled in our country and over our people bringing to us the calamity of destitution, despair, and death. They occupied our motherland, annihilated our culture, and destroyed our way of life. They trampled on our human rights as if we were undesirable crawling insects that must be squashed under their boots of oppression. They turned a beautiful dream into a horrific nightmare in which life was replaced by death."

I stared at this majestic looking man who stood as tall as a mountain an individual can be. His long braided grayish hair fell over his broad shoulders resting on his muscular chest covered by an ornate leather garment. On the crown of his head, two solitary eagle feathers stood up in what I perceived to be a V shape that I interpreted as a sign of victory that eluded his people. But it was his eyes that sequestered my attention. His right bright eye was beautifully serene and conveyed unwavering self-confidence. The left eye, however, created a disturbing contrast to his otherwise handsome facial features. Bloodshot, swollen, shriveled, and devoid of any luminosity, the eye on the left looked like a barren entrance to the dark and humid cavern of his afflicted soul. The egregious contrast in his visage reflected the disparity between the two environments I'd witnessed with my own eyes.

"What happened to you?" I asked looking into his left eye.

He didn't reply. He looked back at me as if I'd spoken bunkum he did not understand.

"What happened to the place that was here before I fell asleep?" I edited my question hoping for a response while switching my eye contact to his right eye.

"It vanished into the past, like everything else does," he replied with a somber timbre in his voice. "But I, I rejoice in the comfort of knowing that I gave my life to it, and in death my honor is unscathed."

"I don't understand," I said puzzled and wondering why this magnificently looking man ended up in a place like the Suicide Orbit Sector.

"Just as there is a variety of manners in which death manifests itself, there are many different motivations leading to suicide; many reasons to kill yourself," he said seemingly aware of what I wanted to learn. "Death occurs all the time at nanosecond pace. Each moment that fades away into the next is a moment that has died and given birth to a new one. It is as though life is but a concatenation of endless succession of moments. As for killing yourself, any time someone willingly forfeits life, physically or otherwise, that person has committed suicide."

"Sure, it seems obvious that anyone who kills herself has committed suicide. What's not clear to me and it's intriguing my intellect is how it is applicable to you. I just can't picture a brave warrior like you committing suicide. How exactly did you kill yourself?" I asked wondering whether I'd stepped out of my boundaries by asking such a personal question.

He closed his eyes and remained in silence for a long time as if recalling the day of his dying. I looked at the noble expression in his face and had a very difficult time believing that such a dignified being could have taken his own life, even in the manner in which the samurai and the kamikaze carried out theirs.

"After they lied, deceived, betrayed, and massacred many of our people's tribes, I realized that it was a matter of time for them to take over our ancestral homeland and turn it into their own wasteland. Once it became clear to me that our country, culture, and way of life were being mercilessly taken away by brutal force, I was convinced that the only thing left to preserve intact was the honor of our people. Aware that we could not win the physical battle with our tomahawks, bows and arrows against firearms, I realized that sometimes the only way to be victorious is by fighting death with death," he said with his eyes still closed.

"I don't understand," I said.

"Although some of our people remained physically alive under oppression in concentration camps the white men called reservations, the reality was that we were already dead as a nation. There was nothing left of us worth surviving but our honor. Stripped of everything we'd valued from time immemorial without a chance to ever recovering what we'd lost, honor was the only attribute of our heritage that we could preserve," he said while opening his left eye only. "By going to battle with nothing but a fearless will to die, we faced bullets and cannonballs with an open chest in a defiant and courageous willful act of suicide in which only our honor would survive, since everything else had already died."

"Wait a minute," I said immediately after he finished his sentence. "What you did was not suicide. You died in battle fighting a war for survival. You were fighting against the oppressors of your people. You did not kill yourself; you got killed by your enemies in battle."

Now he opened his right eye and stared deeply into mine for a long time before speaking again.

"No, it was suicide. I'd lost the will to live under those circumstances. I chose to die a dignified death in which my honor could be preserved. Whoever fights a war that cannot be won is engaged in a suicide act, especially when dying becomes the ultimate purpose of the warfare. The truth is that we were already dead anyway."

I still could not acknowledge his death as suicide, even though the intention to die was, as he asserted, his ultimate goal. I thought of the samurai and kamikaze warriors I'd met earlier, both of whom claimed their suicide to be honorable acts, and I couldn't find a common ground between their behavior and the one carried out by this native brave. In fact, I considered the latter's motive to be both more honorable and courageous than his oriental counterparts. Perhaps disemboweling oneself in devotion to a noble cause, or heading toward a target on a suicide flight as loyalty to country are praiseworthy acts. But to ride toward death with an open mind and chest to preserve the only thing left of a proud people, it seemed an honorable act of defiance that I did not consider to be suicide, at least not in conventional terms. But as he'd pointed out, willfully forfeiting life in any way is, indeed, an act of suicide.

"I must go search for my people lost in this fog of despair," he said walking toward a thick layer of haze as if it were a threshold curtain separating the worlds of the naturally deceased and the suicide dead. "I must gather them for the redemption ghost dance that will revive our lost way of life beyond this miserable orbit of death."

I watched him disappearing in the mist like a specter vanishing in the mysterious ether. Strangely, as soon as he blended in the fog, the air cleared in an evaporation process that felt like rain moving upward instead of falling down. Once the veil-like mist dissipated, I sighed and started walking aimlessly not knowing where to go next.

As I moved toward an unknown destination, I kept thinking about the presumptive suicide case of the native brave warrior wondering whether there were any particular situations in which committing suicide was, if not irreprehensible, at least justifiable by dint of excruciating circumstances. As soon as the thought occurred to me, I noticed a dilapidated hovel in the distance of the deserted place I found myself wandering. Unbeknownst to my perception of how it happened, I was back at the circle from where I started off. Intrigued by the unexplainable geographical transition, I moved toward the remote dwelling with an enigmatic sense of purpose.

"Hello!" I shouted while knocking on the discolored old wooden door. "Is there anybody home?"

There was no answer. The place was eerily quiet and reeked of decomposing organic matter as if death itself inhabited the abode. I knocked louder and waited a brief moment for the slim chance of a response. Not a murmur. I touched the door knob gently turning it open and ventured in the dark and humid place.

"Hello!" I shouted again while stepping inside gingerly. "Is there anybody home?"

Not a whisper. In fact, it was so quiet I could hear my own heartbeat rhythmically in tune with the accelerated pace of my breathing. Shuffling my feet through the squeaky wood floor, all of a sudden I felt nauseated with the foul odor of urine and feces that impregnated the air begetting a putrid atmosphere I struggled to cope with. The stench, humidity, and darkness of the place made me want to step out and run away as fast as I could; and I almost did, until a familiar voice echoed in my head advising me to stay on course.

"If you need to run anywhere, always choose to run into it instead of away from it," the voice whispered in my ears with timely precision with my thought as it occurred. "You're not going to get out of the S.O.S. by moving backwards."

Despite the creeping queasiness and crescendo anxiety, I heeded the advice and kept moving my feet forward as though waddling through a malodorous swamp. As I gradually gained ground inside that uninviting home, I came across a frightening sight that jolted me out of my wits.

"Don't be scared," the old man sitting in an armchair at the end of the living room said. "It's all over now."

I gasped looking at the feeble-looking elderly man covered in blood holding a .38 caliber revolver in his hand. On the right side of his head, a gaping hole oozed blood uninterruptedly in a gory surreal spectacle like a scary scene in a horror movie. I froze in place gritting my teeth.

"It's alright," he said with his voice exuding serenity as if attempting to assuage my trepidation. "I finally plucked the courage to put an end to it."

"What did you do?" I asked surprising myself to ask a stupid question to an obvious fact.

"The same thing you did," he replied insouciantly. "I just used a different method; and of course, under different circumstances."

"And how do your circumstances differ from mine?" I asked still avoiding looking at the ghastly sight of his presence.

"I was informed of your coming and they told me you committed suicide at a fairly young age; and apparently living in very privileged financial situation," he said. "You don't know what's like to grow old, poor, sick, and lonely with nothing left to live for. You killed yourself out of despair in the face of life's travails, whereas I ended a biological organism in which the meaning of life no longer existed."

"But in the end, it seems to me that the underlying motive of both our suicides was desperation and unwillingness to carry on," I blurted out insensitively.

"Perhaps, but the difference is that life had long quit on me before I chose to relinquish the old aching body it left me behind. I guess I could have waited for nature to take its inevitable course, but I didn't see the point in feeling already dead trapped in a barely breathing body," he said placing the handgun on a standing tray next to the armchair. "Besides, other than the emergency personnel and a couple of case workers from the state human services department, no one ever even noticed that I'd passed away; no one."

Out of compassion, I finally had the nerve to look at that old man sitting helplessly in a pool of blood, urine, and feces. Overcoming my own resistance, I gazed into his eye and suddenly his disturbing physical appearance gave way to the equally disquieting sight of his distraught soul. Maybe he was correct when he distinguished his motivation to commit suicide to mine. Not having given myself the opportunity to grow old, I did not know what it was like, as he said, to be old, poor, sick, and lonely. He must have felt my burning curiosity, for he started self-disclosing the agony that led him to pull the trigger on his life.

"I may have decided to kill myself in my late seventies, but the truth is that I'd already died some twenty years earlier," he said struggling to speak out as though the recollections in his troubled mind encumbered his speech. "It all started out when I was laid off from my job at middle age to clear the way to a new generation of cheap young labor to replace me in the workplace. At 58-years-old, I was never able to find work in my field again, much less at similar pay rate. In fact, even menial jobs became a challenge to come by. Then, when my wife was diagnosed with the dreadful disease of cancer, all our lifelong savings were transferred from our bank account to the coffers of the profitable medical care industry and its investors. Shortly after our money vanished, I lost the most valuable asset of my life as my wife passed away leaving me broke and heartbroken. Henceforth, it was a downhill slide into the dark underground of depression and destitution."

"I'm so sorry to hear it," I said feeling deeply touched and not knowing what else to say.

"Yes, that's what they all said at the time, though no one could offer me any meaningful help. But I understand that people have their own problems and challenges to attend to. And society, as it is set up to function on selfish individualistic interests, cannot meet the needs of people like me either. We're left to fend for ourselves," he said while glancing at the gun.

"Well, there are social services available for people in need," I said recalling the difficult times of my childhood when my mother received some basic assistance.

"Sure," he said with a smirk that made me regret my remark. "Other than the occasional help with basic survival needs and momentary words of support, there is only so far an old, poor, sick, and lonely man can go without considering putting an end to his life. But by the time I had a stroke and lost much of my independence, I realized it was time to let it all go. There was no point to continue living a dead life in which only my physical body struggled to remain alive."

I lowered my head unable to keep eye contact with him. I could not fathom an existence in old age with all the heartaches of a lifetime aggravated by the burden of poverty, loneliness, and loss of independence. Although I hesitated to admit it to myself, I couldn't help acknowledging that the circumstances of his suicide were drastically different from mine. If nothing else, at least he'd endured the hardships of the trials and travails of the human experience much longer than I had. Nevertheless, in the end we were both suicide cases who'd quit the game of life because we couldn't take it anymore.

"People tend to be critical of those who take their own lives, but little they know what's like to reach the end of the lengthy human journey with nothing to look forward to but death," he said after a long pause. "I've never been a religious man and I never believed in the frightening manipulative tales of heaven and hell. Thus, I did what I thought it was the right thing for me to do. And even though I've ended up in this bizarre place, I assure you that I have no regrets. To be honest, this is not any worse than what I was experiencing when I was physically alive."

Although in my particular case I did not agree with his last statement, I understood and commiserated with his sentiments. If the piecemeal scourge of the aging process and the oppressing fear of death were not terrifying enough to the average human being, to face these challenges under the conditions this man endured, made me wonder whether in certain situations suicide was an acceptable act. On the other hand, if it were the case, then why did he wind up in the ignominious Suicide Orbit Sector? I did not know the answer yet, but I was determined to ferret out whether there were any circumstances in which suicide was justifiable.

"Oh well, compared to some other folks I consider myself fortunate," he blurted out abruptly.

"Fortunate?" I questioned stunned with his unexpected oxymoronic comment.

"Indeed," he replied nodding his head.

"What make you say that?" I asked unable to perceive a modicum of fortune in such a miserable condition.

"Well, at least I only had to kill myself and not my loved one as well," he said picking up the gun and looking at it.

"Killing someone else is not suicide; it's murder," I said.

"Precisely," he replied right away. "Some folks have to commit murder before committing suicide."

"It's hard to fathom," I remarked.

"I suggest going down the circle and stopping by a small blue house with a brown tile roof," he said. "You'll understand what I mean when I say that I am not the worst case scenario in this heartrending neighborhood of death."

Confused and consumed by curiosity, I walked out of his fetid place and headed out toward the direction he insinuated I'd find answers to my questions. Among the many questions assailing me for answers, the most important one was to find out whether there is a fair-minded justification to committing suicide; if ever there was one.

◁34▷

Because of my previous experiences knocking on doors that were not answered, I walked into the faded blue dwelling without announcing my arrival. As soon as I stepped in, I immediately noticed the strong stench, though not quite as intense as the previous house I visited. I made my way in gingerly and the only sound greeting me was the meowing of an emaciated black cat lying coyly on the corner of the dim lighted empty living room. There were no other signs of life anywhere. I climbed the stairways to the upstairs area where a bedroom door was slightly ajar. I pushed it open gently and the squeaking sound of the rusty hinges magnified my already high level of anticipation. Suddenly, I was jolted by a frightening apparition.

"What are you doing here?" An old man with a full head of long gray hair with streaks of red on the sides and a completely blurred visage came out of the adjacent bathroom holding a shotgun in his hands. "I've already told them that we don't want any visitors and we don't need any help; not anymore."

"Nobody sent me here, sir," I said with a whimper still trying to recover from the startling encounter.

"What do you want?" He asked with his shotgun pointed in my direction.

"Your neighbor down the street told me I could learn something from you," I said with a quavering voice.

"Ah, that bastard! He thinks he's better than the rest of us," the old man said tilting the barrel of his weapon toward the floor assuaging my trepidations. "I have nothing to teach you."

I wanted to tell him that the reason I was there was to learn whether there was a justifiable connection between the murdering of a loved one and suicide. However, I could not pluck the courage to say anything to a clearly irritated man with a shotgun in his hands. I barely managed to be able to stand there silently looking at his threatening presence.

"I have nothing to teach you and you have no business here. Now get the hell out," he commanded.

I started moving backwards toward the doorway with my eyes fixated on him afraid he would shoot me at will. Then, I realized I was already dead and that illusion of being alive was but a bad dream experienced in death. I turned around and started walking out of the bedroom unconcerned with what might happen next.

"Wait!" A woman's voice called out.

I halted my steps immediately and stood still for awhile unable to turn around. I was both frightened and astonished to hear a female's voice; someone I'd not seen in the room.

"Honey, I think you should talk to this lady," the woman said addressing the man in the room. "Maybe you do have something to teach her after all."

Propelled by my inherent curiosity nature, I pivoted on my feet right away eager to take a look at the third person in the bedroom I did not see before. Lying in bed with a pillow over her head and her long white hair over the white night gown she wore, the elderly lady stood peacefully immobile making me wonder how her voice could not have sounded muffled when she spoke. I stood stunned without budging.

"Alright," he grumbled. "C'mon back in and I'll talk with you for a little while, but don't waste my time with any stupid questions. Now, what is it that you want to know?"

The first thing that occurred to me was to ask how in the world the lady lying in bed with a pillow over her head spoke so clearly when the sound should have been muffled. However, I refrained from asking what I deemed to be irrelevant information under the circumstances, especially after being forewarned not to ask stupid questions. Instead, I asked myself how I managed to miss seeing her when I walked in. The answer to my question was obvious: when a man comes out of nowhere holding a shotgun, you can't see anything else but the danger before your eyes.

"I had no choice. I had to do it," he said looking at the motionless lady lying in bed. The coarse tone of his voice scratched my ears with the abrasiveness of sorrow and tormenting guilt.

"What did you do?" I asked meekly.

"I got my loving wife out of her misery, and mine," he said staring at her stationary body. "It all began when she started forgetting names, dates, and where she placed objects such as keys, glasses, and even where she parked her car when she went out by herself. It kept getting progressively worse until it reached a point that she was endangering her life and our safety. There was one day that she nearly burned the house down when she was cooking alone in the kitchen. By the time I smelled something burning and rushed to the kitchen, there were flames spewing out of the oven like an irate dragon's mouth. She'd left a pair of mittens inside next to the pot. That day I realized that the situation was more serious than I thought."

I gazed at her body lying peacefully in bed and contrasted it with the despondency in the man's body language. The only thing they had in common to my eyes was the fact that I could not see their faces. Hers was buried under a pillow; and his blurred like a dark cloud encircling a mountain top.

"I took her to the doctor and he told me that she was afflicted with an aggressive case of Alzheimer's disease, and that it was going to progress and get worse fast. I was devastated." He paused shaking his head slightly, as though recollecting the difficult times he endured. "Without the means to place her in a memory care facility, I had to quit my job to take care of her round the clock. The financial and emotional stress accumulated rapidly until it reached the point of bankruptcy. And as bad as lack of money can be, emotional bankruptcy is an insurmountable debt to overcome. It was a matter of time for me to snap into a madness of my own."

"I assume that's when you killed her," I guessed out loud.

"No, I did not kill her," he reacted defensively. "I got both of us out of what had become a most miserable existence. She'd lost control of all her body functions, could not be left alone for a single moment, and didn't even recognize me anymore; me, her loving husband of more than half a century of marriage. We were no longer living; and worse yet, we were separated by the oblivion of a terrifying disease that robbed us from each other. Oh, no, I assure you I killed neither one of us. I simply eradicated a subtle kind of death that sneaked into what used to be our life."

I looked at that dejected old man, and even though I could not see his face, I felt the immeasurable deluge of grief inundating his drowning soul in a sea of sorrow. How could I or anyone else pass any judgment on his actions not knowing what's like to go through such an excruciating ordeal? But as I was immersed in sympathy for this distressed being, it suddenly dawned on me that thus far he'd been talking about her murder and not his suicide. Furthermore, the fact that she had not killed herself, what was she doing in the Suicide Orbit Sector with her husband? After an uncomfortable moment of silence, he resumed talking and the self-disclosure began.

"One night I finally reached the bottom of the well of despair and realized I was dry and empty. After a long day caring for her and dealing with unpaid bills pilling up on my desk along with harassing phone calls from hostile creditors, I decided it was time to put an end to our misery once and for all. I sat on the bed by her side caressing her shiny white hair until she fell asleep, kissed her forehead, and bid farewell to the love of my life. Then, I placed the pillow over her face and pressed for the longest time, until the quietude of death ceased her struggling to breathe," he said standing next to her lying motionless body. After listening to him, I felt my eyes moistening with tears.

"What did you do next?" I asked right away trying to divert his attention from his painful memories, as well as my emotional discomfort.

He kept looking at her as if they were in different spacetime regions. After a long pause that made me feel as if I were not in the same room with him, he turned toward me and said: "Did you say something?"

"What did you do afterwards?" I asked again.

"I walked into the bathroom, sat on the edge of the tub, put the shotgun barrel in my mouth, and pulled the trigger with my toes," he said as his attention veered toward the shotgun in his hands. "It was the quietest blast I've ever heard."

I lowered my head and felt a teardrop falling on my thigh. My eyes bathed in commiseration; my nose was congested with sympathetic affliction; my ears clogged up with the disturbing silence of sorrow, and my mind shut down wondering about the unspeakable anguish of the human condition.

"So there you have it," he said. "Did you learn anything?"

"I think so," I said. "Except for one important detail that I'm not sure you'll be able to answer."

"Try me," he said.

"I understand the reason you ended up in the Suicide Orbit Sector, but why is your wife here? She did not kill herself," I said looking at her lying in bed puzzled by the incongruity of the fact.

"She's not here," he said dispassionately.

"What do you mean she's not here? She's right there, lying in bed with a pillow squashed over her head," I said pointing directly at her.

"Oh no, that is not her. It's the teleportation of her physical body that she insisted to have it present with me as I work my way out of this place back to the path of redemption," he explained. "She had to plead her case with high ranking entities in the realm where she is now awaiting for my eventual arrival. In the meantime, we communicate, as you witnessed auditorily, via fast frequency sound waves with highly charged phonons in the audio quantum field; audiokinesis that is."

"Teleportation; highly charged phonons; audiokinesis," I mumbled to myself utterly confused with what sounded to me as highly scientific recondite language.

I thanked him for sharing his experience with me and left the small faded blue house back to the dreary street circle. As I trod along, I couldn't stop thinking about that man's suicide as a legitimate case of justified self-annihilation. Considering the in-auspicious circumstances of his life, I deemed what he did to be an atypical dignified act of love and devotion driven by despera-tion. And yet, according to some natural law I could not under-stand, he was supposed to be just another suicide roaming about the infamous S.O.S.; like an errant asteroid lost in the void of infinite space. Perhaps, there were other situations in which committing suicide would be considered a reasonable act in the face of unimaginable suffering. Otherwise, I would have to con-clude that the sole purpose of living is to capitulate to irredeema-ble penitence; and that's not something I was willing to entertain as merciless truth.

As I walked aimlessly through the barren environment that I'd already become well-acquainted with, I wondered whether I'd come across anyone whose suicide would be even remotely as defensible as the two elderly men I'd just met. As soon as the thought occurred to me, I noticed a dim bluish light twinkling in the distance. I decided to keep moving in that direction until I arrived at a modest dwelling with a candle burning on the inside window sill.

It was there that I found the ultimate example of what I be-lieved to be a legitimately justifiable suicide.

A t that point in my journey, I felt as though that mysterious circle had become my own neighborhood where my suicide peers resided. I was so comfortably at ease that I no longer bothered to knock on the door anymore. I walked right in as if entering my own home. Unlike my previous pattern, I did not make a sound announcing my arrival hoping to find someone to greet me. Instead, I tiptoed in as if I were a sleuth secretly investigating a crime scene.

The place was quiet and tidy. But even more drastically different from the last two houses I visited, the ambiance in this one was suffused with a pleasant mist of lavender fragrance in the air. I felt welcomed in absentia. I moved about sneaking through the foyer leading to the living room searching for any sign of existential presence. Suddenly, I heard exquisite violin music coming from a closed door at the end of the hallway past the dining area. Bewitched by the melodious sound waves of beautiful music, I veered effortlessly toward its originating point. As I buoyed along what felt like a sea of harmonious musical notes, an unexpected enchanting experience overcame me with great joy. My feet seemed to be barely touching the floor as I moved forward driven by the luring effect of the music; as if I walked on rice paper I was cautious not to tear. There was something unusual about that place and I wanted to find out what it was.

With my right ear pressed against the door, I heard murmurs blending in with the music I recognized to be J.S. Bach's Violin Concerto in A minor. I tried to eavesdrop on the conversation taking place inside the room. I could tell there were at least three people communicating sotto voce with one another. With willful effort to make sense of what was happening inside, I focused intently until I was able to discern intermittent pieces of the dialogue among them.

"This is your last chance to change your mind," a male voice said. "Are you sure you want to go ahead with this? You know that once you take these pills there is no coming back."

I gasped recalling the night when I took the barbiturates that ended my life. Holding my breath agape, I was terrified that it was about to happen to someone else.

"Yes, I'm aware of what I'm doing. I've been preparing for this moment for a long time," a feeble female voice replied. "I've thought this over very carefully and this is what I choose to do."

"No, don't do it!" I yelled barging in the room in a frenzied state of extreme anxiety reliving my own traumatic experience. "You'll regret it as I do."

Instead of reacting to my outburst and unsolicited warning at a most inappropriate time, they just looked at me with sympathetic eyes without saying a word. I felt utterly embarrassed and out of place.

"Perhaps you should witness this experience," said the man wearing a white smock jacket with a stethoscope dangling around his neck. "It may help you heal whatever has traumatized you in the past."

The late sexagenarian lady lying comfortably in a wide and long armchair nodded in agreement as a middle-aged woman sitting next to her beckoned at me to come in. Feeling quite ashamed by my unseemly behavior, I hesitated to abide by the silent invitation, but eventually I complied and walked in timidly with an apologetic expression stamped on my face.

"Have a seat," the woman sitting next to the lady in the armchair said. "My mother is about to embark on her final journey. You're welcome to witness her departure."

At first I was confused because everyone in the Suicide Orbit Sector was supposed to have already departed. But in what could only have been a telepathic communication, the man in the room communicated to me, without saying a word, that the event was just a reenactment of what already had happened; like seeing a photograph of a cosmological event that occurred millions of years ago. I thought it was some sort of a rewound video recording playing again for my educational purpose. I glanced around at the three of them and their receptivity convinced me to sit down on the wooden chair across from the dying lady's daughter.

"My mother has been diagnosed with terminal lung cancer. She's been in excruciating pain, struggling to breathe, and unable to nourish her body except through intravenous means," the daughter said while holding her mother's hand. "After a well thought-out process, she's decided to exit this life in her own terms, instead of extending her suffering unnecessarily for the few months she has left. She's opted for medical assisted suicide, and I'm here to support her in her decision with loving acceptance of a circumstance that cannot be changed."

"Let's get started with the first step of the process," the doctor said moving toward the old lady with a tiny piece of bright yellow paper in his hand that he placed inside her mouth.

"What is it?" I asked impulsively.

"It's a small dose of lysergic acid diethylamide," he replied. "It will help her see and feel the entryway of a different reality without anxiety and fear before crossing the threshold to a new dimension of existence. Then, once she receives the lethal dose of barbiturates, she'll gradually flow into a gentle state of comatose toward a peaceful death. Think of it as a sort of sleeping pill that will induce her to the last sleep of her life."

Moments later, the doctor administered the barbiturates and we all gazed at the resting lady without saying a word. The only sound in the room was Bach's music that had switched from the violin concerto to the gentle organ music titled *Sleepers, Wake*; a beautiful piece that it felt like a magical musical pathway leading to another realm of existence. Soon, the lady's face looked completely relaxed and her closed eyes seemed to be seeing pleasant visions that made her smile. She was clearly embarking on the final sleep of her life. At that moment I thought of Shakespeare's passage in Act II Scene I of *Hamlet* when he says, *"For in that sleep of death what dreams may come, when we have shuffled off this mortal coil."*

I marveled at how different this lady's experience of death was compared to the nightmare I'd experienced when I shuffled off my mortal coil with utmost indignation. As Bach's melodious tunes permeated the atmosphere with the soothing sounds of his majestic art, I wished I had planned my suicide in similar fashion, instead of the grotesque revengeful route I chose. At the same time, I wondered whether the outcome of my destiny would have been any different.

"She's passed," the daughter said caressing her mother's forehead.

I gazed at her and she looked as serene as her dead mother. There was not a trace of guilt, regret, or the slightest ill feeling in that daughter's face; to the contrary, I noticed a subtle sense of comfort, albeit blended with the natural grief that accompanies the farewell of a loved one.

"Well, the work's been done. It is time for you to leave now," the doctor said addressing me.

"Does what I just witnessed have anything to do with me?" I asked feeling confused.

"It has everything to do with you," he replied. "This was a reenactment of an event that happened a long time ago. This segment of the Akashic Records was open to you in order to assist your perception of the many causes and motivations of suicide so you can find the redemption you seek. This was your last encounter with suicide cases in this low frequency orbit of ethereal existence. Now you must continue your journey if you want to make your way out of this place."

"But I still have so many unanswered questions," I said wondering what I might be able to see in the Akashic Records.

"And do you expect me to answer them for you?" He questioned my resolve.

"Well, I was hoping for some help," I said with diffidence.

"You've already had all the help you need. Now it's time for you to help yourself, for no one else can do it for you," he retorted dismissively. "I and everyone else in this decadent orbit of existence have fulfilled our assignments to show you different facets of suicide. It's time for you to sieve the wheat from the chaff of life and determine what you will want to do next."

"But what comes next? Where do I go from here?" I asked with apprehension in my voice while realizing I was asking the same crucial questions people did in my earthly life.

"Keep moving forward, just as you've been doing all along," he said.

"What about you? Where are you going to? Can I go with you?" I asked in pleading fashion beginning to show my despondence and revealing my weaknesses.

Suddenly, the daughter who had been sitting quietly observing our interaction stood up to address me.

"You can't come with us because we are not from here," she said looking at me with compassionate eyes. "We don't belong to the fabric of this space and time. We are here just to give you an opportunity for you to rethink your own situation. My mother's suicide is meant to be another example for you to discern whether or not the taking of one's own life can be justified under certain circumstances. You'll have to come up with your own conclusions."

"What about your mother? Doesn't she belong to this realm? After all, she did commit suicide," I asked feeling confused about what determined a suicide's kismet.

"You'll have to draw your own conclusions about it as well," the daughter replied serenely. Then, she took a step in my direction and placed her comforting arm around my shoulder that felt like an angel's wing enveloping me under her aegis. "You're so close to completing a full circle of the S.O.S. Keep searching for your answers within you and soon you shall find what you seek. You're very close to reaching the boomerang point. Have confidence and don't give up."

As soon as she finished speaking, Bach's music playing in the background started fading away until it completely vanished along with the woman and the doctor. Left behind in the silence were only me and the deadly dormant body of the older woman in the armchair who had committed the most sublime and legitimate form of suicide I'd ever known. Now it was up to me to determine how far and fair can the validation of a suicide act be. I wasn't sure why such inquiry was important to my potential freedom, but whatever the boomerang point the daughter referred to was, it was clear to me that my conclusion was the turning point to reaching it.

❮36❯

From the moment I walked back to the deserted dark street, I started thinking about my last encounter with a suicide; the one that made most sense to me. Unlike mine and all the others I had come across in the tortuous route of the Suicide Orbit Sector, that older lady's decision to end her life on her own terms posed no doubts in my mind that it was, indeed, a justifiable, humane, and even dignified act of dying. After all, she was terminally ill, in pain, and with a short time left to live a life that was no longer worth living. How could I or anyone else possibly question the validity and righteousness of her decision?

"No one," a familiar voice echoed inside my head as soon as I raised the silent question to myself. "No one, except the laws of nature."

Startled by the unexpected intrusion into my thoughts, I halted my steps and began questioning my own question, which now had escalated to a whole new level I had not anticipated: the laws of nature.

"Shouldn't the laws of compassion be intrinsic to the laws of nature?" I uttered out loud. "A suffering human being should have a viable alternative to assuage unabated agony that is doomed to be consumed by death in due time. Why should nature object to it?"

"Nature is impartial, non-judgmental, and objects to nothing a freewill being of her creation chooses to do," the voice replied in what was the beginning of an intense internal debate with an invisible intelligence roaming inside my head. "Nature simply has her own set of patterns and procedures, which life and death are integral components."

"Then, if there is no judgment or objections, that poor woman has no business being here in the S.O.S. along with people like me," I said voicing my protest to what I deemed to be unfair treatment.

"Apparently, the only one passing judgment and raising objections is you. You have decided on your own terms how life and its inevitable transmutation through death ought to happen. But the reasons that woman ended up here is unbeknownst to you, and it shall remain this way until you realize in earnest why you ended your own life," the voice replied with subtle admonishment to my reaction. "As for inquiring about how and why that woman landed on this lower orbit of transition between life and death, I suggest refraining from speculation and instead minding your own business."

"Why do you talk to me like this? I'm neither judging nor objecting anything," I said resenting what it felt like an unwarranted offensive accusation from an inside intruder. "An older woman in pain on the edge of death throes with no chance for survival should have the right to die on her own terms."

"And she exercised her right to do so," the voice replied.

"Yes, but with the consequence of winding up in this miserable triage place where itinerant lost souls wander aimlessly in the pursuit of redemption," I demurred. "She's been penalized for exercising her freewill to end a life that was no longer worth living."

"You're switching from passing judgment to making assumptions about other people's experiences," the voice observed.

"She was clearly miserable," I said.

"She didn't look miserable to me; to the contrary, she seemed quite comfortable and content in her death armchair," the voice said. "You're assuming that because you feel miserable she must have felt the same way."

"That's not the point," I said on the verge of yelling my frustration out loud to an invisible presence. "The fact is that she shouldn't be here with the rest of us, for under her circumstances her suicide was justifiable. She doesn't belong to this place where lost souls roam aimlessly."

"There you are being judgmental again," the voice whispered in an irritating tranquil tone that compelled me to pull the top of my hair up with both hands.

"Please, I beg you to stop," I screamed thinking I was being driven to madness by an incessantly tormenting voice harassing my senses from inside my head.

"The only thing driving you crazy is your own consciousness; your awareness of what you did and how you ended up in this place. Witnessing that woman commit suicide in a gentle loving fashion triggered a strong feeling of guilt and remorse in you; and that's why you're overreacting to somebody else's destiny instead of focusing on your own," the voice remarked in a temperate and yet reprehensible tone of voice.

I took a deep breath silently acknowledging the truth of the statement. I realized that in some way, I envied the manner in which that woman was embraced by death. Supported by a loving daughter; assisted by a compassionate professional; and serenaded by the greatest composer that ever lived was stuff that dreams are made on, and made the final moment of her life rounded with a sleep. That voice of intelligence that sneaked into my mind to utter words of wisdom made me realize I still had much work to do before I could find my way out of the S.O.S.

After a long moment of reflection, my thoughts quieted subduing my tempestuous emotions. From the calming silence that ensued, the voice spoke to me again.

"Anyone can choose to end life prematurely; and many a person has what would be perceived as a justifiable reason to do so. But even though exercising this freewill is an individual prerogative, there are consequences associated with it; and that no one can evade," the voice sounded serene and yet authoritative.

I wanted to reply but I was feeling exhausted to engage in an argument I knew I wasn't going to prevail. However, I couldn't help thinking that most suicides are professed to be dishonorable acts committed by craven desperate people. But the case I'd just witnessed was different; at least from a standpoint of logical common sense determined by her utterly helpless situation. In my case, as well as many others I'd encountered in the S.O.S., I felt powerless in the face of life's daunting challenges and quit life out of weakness and desperation. But that woman's ordeal was different; it extrapolated far beyond the level of emotional vulnerability. Her ailing physical body already had given way to slow installments of death with high aching interests. Therefore, expediting a process that was already taking place seemed like a reasonable solution to an unsolvable problem. Why, then, there had to be consequences associated with such a common sense act, especially when it was carried out so beautifully?

"There are no shortcuts to evolution," the voice continued after a long pause. "Of course freewill allows anyone to act as she deems fair or necessary. However, for the sake of fairness, one cannot reach advanced realms of existence in the mysteriously infinite Universe at the same velocity as others who have taken a long route to reach the desired destination. It is a matter of cosmic principle."

"But that woman was already dying," I insisted on advocating for her case.

"I am not judging her decision," the voice replied.

"It sounds that way," I said.

"Because you're seeing with judgmental eyes. The reason she is here in the S.O.S. is simply because she did commit suicide, and this is the transitional orbit for those who choose this exit route. In the end, she'll be appraised based on her own merits and nothing else. But right now, this is where all who exit the physical plane through voluntary action must land. It's just a transitional period, though many, because of the nature of their particular cases, will linger around quite a bit longer."

I remained silent wondering what my particular case was and how much longer I would have to stick around the S.O.S.

"In the last evolutionary stages of a massive star, it does not need to know when it will erupt into a powerful and luminous stellar explosion that will transform it into a supernova," the voice remarked at millisecond sequence to my thought. "The only thing that matters is the process of turning into an extremely bright dwarf star afterwards. In your case, all that matters is to know that, eventually, you will find your way out of here in the most fitting and timely fashion. After all, in due time, all suicides orbit out to other opportunities to life."

Those were the last words the sovereign voice said for the time being; and in my turn, I didn't have anything else to say either. I kept walking through the barren, gloomy, fetid, and chilly street consumed by a feeling of despondence. It felt as though I'd been roaming about that nightmarish place for a very long time toward what it seemed like a never-reaching destination. Nevertheless, I had no choice but to keep moving forward, for it was the only direction that would lead me out of that seemingly endless situation.

I was about to sit down on the sidewalk to get some rest when I noticed a signpost that captured my attention instantaneously. A rotting wooden rod with an arrow on top was scripted with barely legible fading gray letters. As I walked toward it, I could feel my eyes widening open at the faster beating pace of my heart, until I got close enough to be able to read the sign. The word *Exit* was etched in very thin cursive writing on the arrow pointing toward the winding corner of the circle. Without hesitating, I followed the arrow's direction with great anticipation.

Like a brief appearance of the Sun through passing dark clouds, my eagerness suddenly disappeared behind the foggy odorous alleyway I found myself in. I felt as if I'd been duped by the sign that led me to what it looked like an even more sinister region of the Suicide Orbit Sector I had grown used to. Suddenly,

I started hearing the same wailing sounds I heard when I first arrived in this deplorable region. This was no exit, but the reentering gates of the suicide hell I was so desperately trying to escape. I thought of turning around and running back, but as I'm pivoting to reverse my direction, it was so blindly pitch black that it looked like an invisible wall of darkness had blocked the way. I panicked and cried inconsolably.

"The darkest hour is just before the dawn," the autonomous voice whispered inside my head.

I was instantly reenergized and resumed moving forward. Soon, the alley led to an equally dismal street where the dissonant sounds of wailing were disturbingly voluble. As I moved on through the chilly haze, the bawling became more accentuated to the point I could feel in my gut the utmost distress of the beings emitting the sorrowful sounds. All of a sudden, the mist began dissipating and I could see throngs of people writhing on the swampy ground with their arms stretched up toward me while howling as though they asked for help in the language of despair. I tiptoed around them concerned about not stepping on anyone, and at times I had to yank my leg away from grabbing hands. Then, I looked at the other side of the street and noticed there were fewer and more scattered troubled souls lying about on a more solid ground. I crossed to the lighter side of wretchedness.

With the tormenting sounds of lamentation insidiously filling the air with gloom, I waddled through the muddy street trying to get to the other side as quickly as possible. Once I stepped on the sidewalk, I immediately noticed a lady in a fetus position cowing on the corner whimpering and mumbling incomprehensible words. I stopped and stared at her with enhanced curiosity. Although I could not see her face, the tune of her muttering sounded oddly familiar to me. I scrutinized her from afar, tilting my head from side to side attempting to recognize the familiarity of the sound. Unable to identify it, I slowly moved closer and stood a couple of feet away from her, immobile, staring at her for the longest time. Suddenly, the whimpering and mumbling stopped. I could tell that she knew that I was standing there watching her. A piercing silence ensued accompanied by an uncomfortable awkwardness. I was about to move away when she unexpectedly raised her head from under the embracing arms lying on her bent knees. Then, when she looked at me, I was utterly flabbergasted.

"Mother!" I shouted shaken with a mix of shock and joy.

"Oh Lucy, Lucy my baby girl," she mumbled with trembling purple lips. "I am so sorry."

"Of course you had to be here," I said speaking to myself rather than to her. "Come, come with me. I'm going to help you out of this miserable place."

"You can't," the autonomous voice in my head spoke while my mother stared at me giving me an optical illusion that she was the one speaking to me.

"Why not?" I questioned.

"Because you're edging the boomerang point and she's very far away from it," the voice replied while my mother stared at me with loving eyes. "You're heading toward the exit of the Suicide Orbit Sector, whereas she's traveling in a different direction before she can find her own exiting way."

"I cannot leave my mother in this condition by herself in this dreadful place," I said immersed in deep eye contact with her.

"You'll have to, just as she left you by yourself when you were a child," the voice said.

"I can't," I protested.

An eerie silence prevailed as my mother slowly lowered her head tucking it in between her folded arms atop her bent knees.

"Here we have a quintessential distinction of disparate cases in this triage realm of existence," the voice resumed speaking after a long pause. "If you compare and contrast the state of the lady you met earlier who committed medical assisted suicide with your mother's case, you understand why that lady was lying peacefully in the armchair while your mother is dejectedly forsaken on a filthy street."

"No, I do not understand," I said in staccato fashion to emphasize my resentment with the way my mother's condition was portrayed.

"Then I'll explain it to you," the voice sounded composed and determined to close the matter so I could move on. "That lady's decision to commit suicide did not exert a negative impact on anybody's life but her own. In fact, she had the loving support of her daughter and the assistance of a professional guiding her crossing over. That's why she lay placidly in her suicide deathbed. Conversely, your mother's decision, though triggered by despair, was driven by selfishness and brought forth dire consequences to an innocent child who was left behind to fend for herself. As I mentioned earlier, in due time all suicides orbit out to other opportunities to life; but the cases like your mother's require a more challenging and circuitous path."

I released a deep mournful sigh of surrender. Now I understood what he meant and I acquiesced to my mother's unfortunate kismet. Looking at her rolled into a ball of her diminished self brought tears to my eyes. I made an involuntary motion to touch her hair, but something inside me stopped my arm as I reached out to her.

Perhaps, if I could overcome my own trial with premeditated death, I'd be empowered to help my mother. Maybe, if I managed to succeed in my efforts and find my way out of the S.O.S., I'd be able to come back to help her escape as well.

I plucked some chutzpah from the core of my being and set off walking in the direction the arrow indicated without looking back. The farther I moved along, the clearer the environment became. Soon the dark clouds dissipated, the foul odor faded away, the disheartening sounds petered out, and the disturbing images that haunted my vision before vanished in the horizon of a new landscape. Without realizing the gradual transformation, I found myself in an amber color sandy desert that seemed to extend for light-years, though there were a few nearby dunes that hampered some of the scope of my perception. In spite of the relief from the tormenting sights of misery and the desperate howling sounds, I felt discouraged to be in a desert, alone.

"Remember, you are never alone," the affable voice spoke softly in my head.

I simpered and resumed walking. Much sooner than I expected, I arrived at one of the very large sand dunes I was focusing on reaching. By estimating the width of the base and the height of the dune, I realized that I had the option of either going around or climbing it. They seemed equidistant to the other side that I wanted to reach. Oddly, for reasons unbeknownst to me, I knew I had to conquer that dune, but I had no idea why. It didn't matter as long as I followed my intuitive guidance. However, unsure of which way to choose, I stood there pondering on what decision to make.

"If you are on the right path, it will always be uphill," my friendly voice companion said.

I nodded and started climbing what I perceived as some sort of a magic dune. There was something mysteriously intriguing about that humungous mole of sand in the desert. By the time I reached its short zenith I found out why. Down below there was a small oasis with one solitary palm tree. I gasped and remained agape and perplexed with the sight before my eyes. It was not the quaint inviting oasis that captured my enthrallment, but what was written on the shiny surface of its pond. In large thin gray letters, exactly as it was written on the arrow signpost I'd seen earlier, the word *Exit* was etched on the clear water surface. I rushed down eager to find out what it was all about, for it was a sign that I likely had reached the boomerang point I'd heard about, whatever that meant. As I walked gingerly toward it, I reached a point in which I began experiencing a strong magnetic pull that drew me to the pond as if I'd entered the event horizon of a colossal black hole. At that point, my movement toward it became involuntary and irreversible. Undoubtedly, I'd reached the cusp of a major transitional stage.

"Drink the water from the pond," the voice commanded.

I kneeled on the pebbly ground, stooped over the pond, and with both hands cupped together, I scooped the lukewarm unsullied water and drank it with gusto. Instantaneously, my mind exploded like a potent volcanic eruption sending debris of hallucinatory lava through a seemingly infinite space. Then, in the midst of an awe-inspiring hallucinogenic experience, I casually glanced at the pond and fell deep into a fast rotating downward vortex that shredded me into nothingness.

The next leg of my suicide journey had just begun.

PART III

BEYOND

❮37❯

"Congratulations!" A pleasant baritone voice greeted me as soon as I regained consciousness. "You have completed a full circle of the Suicide Orbit Sector and have qualified to be boomeranged to the inner orbits of The Great Circle of Life. You may take this now."

Astonished, I looked at the sparkly and pulsating golden key that magically appeared in my right hand. The luminous vibrating object appeared to have a life of its own that directly affected mine.

After going through a spaghettification process that seemed to have shredded my being into smithereens of nothingness, I felt dazed and confused. I didn't have the slightest idea of where I was or how I'd ended up there. The specter of a man standing in front of me looked somewhat familiar; someone I might have come across in the past but only a vague sensorial memory of the interaction remained. As for the environment around me, it was exactly where I was standing before drinking from the pond at the center of an oasis in the desert, except for two distinguishable differences. The most striking was the long and shiny metallic runway that looked as if it extended through infinity along the desert unhampered by dunes. I stared at it filled with bewilderment, for the smooth layer of the mysterious airstrip vibrated so intensely that, like the golden key in my hand, it appeared to have a life of its own. The other conspicuous detail was the small deep-red hexagon-shaped small building that pulsated like a heart beat—and it was located smack dab where the oasis stood before.

"I must be still hallucinating," I mumbled to myself feeling as if I were riding on a massive theta brainwave.

"You have managed to fix the kinks holding you back, and now you can proceed on your journey back to life," the man standing by me said with genuine enthusiasm as if he had earned the honor himself. "The key you hold in your hand will open the right doors for you in the cosmic quantum realm of possibilities. You've merited it. Go ahead and make good use of it now."

"Goodness, what's going on with me?" I muttered while gawking at that magnificent golden key that throbbed in my hand as if it were a live being. "There must have been some mind-altering substance in that water I drank that's triggering this bizarre sensorial experience."

"Do you remember that warped oxidized key I handed to you when you first entered the Suicide Orbit Sector?" He asked me.

I nodded while staring at the mysterious key in my hand.

"That key represented your state of being then, and this one represents you now. The first opened the S.O.S. entryway, whereas this one will unlock unprecedented possibilities."

Seemingly, that splendid vibrating key in my hand started out opening my memory bank. Now I remembered that man I met as I'd just arrived in the S.O.S. region. I recalled his telling me that the old oxidized key he handed to me at the time would turn on the engine of a derelict car abandoned at the end of a narrow street alley, but only after completing the S.O.S. circuit. I recalled looking at the decrepit condition of the car thinking that would be impossible to get that piece of junk started, much less move. However, he did say that if I managed to fix it, which he didn't explain how and it made no sense to me at the time, the vehicle would be ready for me to use at a future date when I'd need it.

"Come with me," he said beginning to walk inside the vibrant red hexagon structure where the oasis used to be. "There is something I want to show you."

I followed him into the vermilion building that I could feel pulsating under my feet at every step I took. The odd small hexagon-shaped hangar resembled the chemical structure of a molecule, but it felt more like an organic body part; a heart or lung that contracted and expanded rhythmically. I had no doubt I was under the influence of some mind-altering psychotropic substance.

"Voilá!" He said while pulling off a large radiant golden cover hiding a vehicle underneath. "Do you remember it?"

"Yes," I replied monosyllabically not knowing what to make of what he was showing me.

"Well, now you can take it to the runway and take off," he said with evident glee and excitement.

Flummoxed, I stared at the same dilapidated car he'd shown me a long time ago and I felt my hope dissipate piecemeal.

"What do you think?" He asked with undisguised zest.

"If this is the representation of what I've become, I'm afraid I haven't changed much at all," I said with my eyes fixated on the worn-out vehicle feeling just like the car looked.

"Oh no, you don't understand," he said. "You hold the key in your hand now. This vehicle is no longer what it used to be, and it just looks this way because you haven't turned it on yet. All you have to do is take it to the runway, turn the engine on, and take off to a new adventure."

I simpered without saying a word. Then, I started walking around the old car scrutinizing its decaying rusty body, smudged flat tires, broken steering wheel, and an overall appearance of decrepitude that it would make it stand out even in a jam-packed junkyard.

"You have managed to orbit the entire circuit of the S.O.S. without flailing. You're no longer corroded in your ethereal body; your will has not been flattened; your spirit hasn't been broken; and your sense of purpose has not decayed. You have been regenerated and you're now ready to move on," he said displaying undeniable satisfaction.

"How am I going to get this…vehicle to the runway?" I asked with skepticism while looking at what seemed to be falling apart in a state of inertia.

"It's already out there waiting for you," he said.

"What do you mean it's out there waiting for me? It is right here before my eyes," I said befuddled.

"What you see here is merely a representation of your past. Outside on the runway your present awaits to take you into your future," he clarified.

Spurred by uncontainable curiosity and fueled by eagerness to move on, I dashed out to the metallic runway with unbridled anticipation. But as soon as I stepped out of that magical throbbing-with-life building, my steps came to a screeching halt when my startled eyes gawked at the vehicle representation of my present. Marveled by the breathtaking sight, I kept gazing at it with a sense of wonder, amazement, and perplexity. It was what in my physical historical time in the late twentieth century would be called a futuristic transportation. Sitting on the enigmatic runway with its angled front facing a seemingly infinite horizon, a shiny golden boomerang-shaped vehicle looked ready for takeoff. Suddenly, the energetic golden key I held in my hand began vibrating faster; and as it did, the numinous vehicle respond-ed by igniting the engine on its own. Agape, I observed the bright golden fast-moving small wavelength flowing between the key in my hand and the boomerang vehicle on the runway. It was as though the paranormal wavelength functioned as an umbilical cord connecting two complementary elements of the same entity.

"Do you have any other questions?" He asked.

"What's this all about?" I questioned with ample generaliza-tion in the midst of my perplexity.

"You're about to be transported to inner orbits of The Great Circle of Life; and that's the reason the vehicle that will take you there is in the shape of a boomerang," he explained.

"I don't get it," I said.

"The essential characteristic of the boomerang is to return to the point of origin from which it departed. No matter how far off track it goes, it always returns to the original source from which it was released. From life to death and back to life again," he said while I remained mesmerized observing the exchange of colorful wavelengths between the golden key and its matching part. "We are all boomerangs."

Awestruck, I felt irresistibly drawn to the boomerang ve-hicle as if some overpowering magnetic force sequestered my will. I could no longer discern whether it was the key in my hand or I who vibrated so intensely. I'd become one and the same with it, until I blended with a radiant ray of light moving in the direc-tion of the golden boomerang.

"Have a great journey," I heard his fading voice say as if it had come from a far away region I no longer existed in.

By the time I reached the boomerang-shaped vehicle, I was in a state of high ecstasy and consumed by ineffable joy. I en-tered it like an aroused phallic ray of light penetrating the tender early moments of dawn. The climax of the present felt real as I was unified with my destiny. I was ready to take off and find out what was in store for me in the future.

Suddenly, a mellifluous crescendo whirring sound tickled my ears before reaching deafening decibels. The temperature started rising at the same time the ground underneath vibrated at extraordinary tempo. Soon, the boomerang I'd become one with sped up through the metallic runway at dizzying velocity before disappearing into the infinity ahead. I was on my way to where space and time no longer copulated in the confinements of a cosmic affair. I was being catapulted to another existential paradigm. I was about to be boomeranged toward the inner orbits of The Great Circle of Life.

◄38►

The velocity reached an inconceivable level of perception. I felt like a photon traveling at the 186,282 miles per second speed of light in a long journey toward a dimension where time and measurements of distance are meaningless. I'd lost my sense of self and I could only identify individual manifestation through the buzzing sounds, visual experiences, tactual vibrations, enchanting fragrances, and the sweetest tastes I experienced every time a violet ray of light flashed in nanosecond sequences. Compared to the hallucinogenic experience I had when I drank from the pond in the oasis, this was an incomparably far beyond transcendental episode that forever altered my understanding of what it means to exist as an inclusive quantum unit of the immeasurable whole.

"Approaching the event horizon of the Akashic Field," I detected the fine-tuned phonons of sound waves appearing to come from the dark matter of infinite space. I had no idea what to make of the message; and yet, I felt so at ease within this new experience that I remained unfazed. I interpreted it to be a mere announcement of my new destination.

In the meantime, I was basking in the delightfully uncanny occurrence. I felt like a particle of cosmic dust succumbing to an overpowering celestial suction pump invisibly attached to a magenta nebula. Whirling and whooshing through a thick cloud of gas, I was pulled into an entirely brave new world of synesthesia. In this new exceptional paradigm, I could actually hear the colors surrounding me speak the audible language of the electromagnetic spectrum, as well as the voices of fragrances entering my nostrils as though they were my ears.

By the time I became aware of this unparalleled extrasensory perception, the most seductive music I'd ever heard possessed whatever infinitesimally small sense of self I had left. Like a singing mermaid luring a sailor through her magical spell, the harmonious melody enraptured me in an ecstatic dance in which music and listener become one and the same. Eerily consumed by an ecstatic orgasmic experience, the rhythm penetrated me as if I were a wild mare that had willingly surrendered to a stallion in a musical intercourse. My ethereal body contorted, moaned, and begged for more of that ineffable pleasure in which the music and I were unified into one inseparable experience. It was the most sublime of all love-making acts I'd ever experienced. Tempo, timbre, melody, rhythm, harmony, dynamics, and form; yes, I gave myself away to all seven elements of music in an orgiastic musical bacchanal.

Exhausted and satisfied, I reposed to the gentle tune of an ensuing soft-playing harp. By then I'd noticed that the velocity I was traveling seemed to have diminished significantly. Perhaps, it was the afterward soothing effects of my intense copulation with music. After the ecstatic quasi-sexual intercourse musical experience, the pace had slowed so much that I began feeling dozy. As my eyelids fell shut gently over my somnolent eyeballs, I heard the most idyllic a cappella children's choir singing melodious hymns that seemed to be coming from a heavenly place. Gradually, my breathing started synchronizing with those angelic singing voices in a magical lullaby that led me to a dreamland.

"It is so good to have you here with us," a lovely dark-haired boy greeted me as I arrived in a new mystical world.

Gently awakened by his greeting voice, I opened my eyes and immediately noticed I was surrounded by mountains dotted with towering evergreens that seemed to touch the sky.

"Welcome to this multiverse of possibilities," the boy said.

"Multiverse," I mumbled between my teeth.

"Yes, you have entered a Universe within countless Universes. That's why it's called a multiverse, you silly," he said giggling in adorable impish fashion.

"I thought I'd just fallen asleep," I said.

"Yes, of course you did. It's the main passageway to this realm of possibilities," the boy said walking closer to me. "Come, I want to introduce you to my friends."

I held his offering outstretched hand and walked along with my pleasant and well-mannered young host. At first I had some difficulty keeping up with his mirthful energetic pace, but somehow holding his hand felt like a booster cable that energized the battery of my spirit. The farther we moved the more captivated I became by the magnificent environment around me. Basking in the glory of the surrounding spectacle of nature, I was enthralled listening to the sublime language of dazzling colors that vibrated audible living energy; and the subtle sounds they emitted infused the atmosphere with purified air that breathed in deeply.

"Where are we going?" I asked casually; not particularly interested in the answer, but mostly to strike a conversation.

"That one in the middle," he said pointing at the largest mountain amidst a cluster of others in that surrealistic environment.

Involuntarily, I halted my steps under the spell of my bewilderment, but my guiding companion was unaffected by my natural impulses and kept his peppery feet moving forward. As we headed toward the pointed destination, I marveled at the chain of green mountains and the crystal-clear wide bodies of water meandering around them. High above, a splendorous azure sky seemed to be in constant motion, as though inhaling and exhaling life onto the realm below. I felt everything moving in synchronistic harmony with Oneness; and absolutely nothing, not even the gentle sounds of my footsteps crushing dry leaves on the ground were left out of the exceptional experience of being alive.

As my young companion began whistling a merry tune, I looked around, took a long deep breath, and absorbed to the core of my being the splendor of the moment. I felt enormously privileged to be there in the now of then. I relished in the sight of those magnificent mountains while focusing on the mysterious one in the middle. I stared at it feeling awestruck. Although it resembled all the others, the tallest of them all had a luminosity that distinguished its presence within the breathtaking panorama. I felt as though I was walking toward Mount Olympus to make acquaintance of Zeus and have a rendezvous with the gods.

"We are almost there," he said briefly pausing his cheerful whistling to give me an update.

After ambling pleasurably through a timeframe that could not be measured by traditional standards, we arrived at the coveted destination.

"They arrived, they arrived!" A little blond girl in pigtail braids shouted with untrammeled enthusiasm as soon as she spotted us approaching from the distance.

It was a matter of time for me to be surrounded by dozens of screaming with excitement children. They quickly encircled my companion and me while chattering loud and lively. Without my even noticing, they initiated a mass-walking motion in which we all flowed as one toward the base of the imposing mountain where a boy sat alone by a bonfire. As we got closer, he stood up and started walking toward me with a beaming grin.

"Welcome," that's all he said looking into my eye with his penetrating emerald gaze.

Agape, I gasped staring back at him. I could see and feel joy exuding from his eyes that were inexplicably familiar to me.

"I know you. Where have I seen you before?" I asked recognizing his countenance, the sound of his voice, and, even more accentually so, the energy of his presence.

"We're childhood friends," he said with a broad smile that conveyed his joy of seeing me again. "We've been connected through kinship of soul."

"Of course, of course," I repeated in disbelief identifying my hitherto invisible childhood friend who was always there for me when I needed him the most.

At that moment, I immediately remembered his presence in my life; the critical connection that guided me through the most troubling times in my childhood. There I was, standing before my nameless imaginary friend who'd played a fundamental role in my coping with the trying years of my early earthly life.

"That's right," he said winking at me obviously aware of my realization. "In the past, I helped you get through emotional turmoil. This time, however, my role is to lead you to those who can assist you to discover a new sense of purpose and direction in the mysterious grand scheme of life. Come, let's sit by the fire and I'll explain to you everything you need to know before embarking on this new leg of your journey."

◀39▶

Facing my nameless imaginary childhood friend with the majestic mountain in the background, I sat at the circle around the fire with some three dozen children. Hearing the crackling of the firewood and the aromatic scent of burning oak infused in the nightly air, I wondered whether the summer camps I never had an opportunity to participate in my miserable childhood were similar to this type of gathering. Regardless, at that moment all it mattered to me was to be surrounded by my pure-natured companions in a lovely atmosphere. But as soon as the conversation began, I realized that the story telling in this juvenile group was no fairy tale.

"Our small tribe of spiritual children rejoices in the honor of serving as the ushers to the entry way to higher orbits of evolutionary possibilities," my still nameless but no longer imaginary friend said.

Stooping over myself with my elbows lying on my crossed legs, I listened to him with attentive interest. I felt as though I was experiencing a second chance to a unique kind of childhood; a spiritual childhood, as if my soul were in the fledgling stage of development.

"In the spirit of childhood innocence of mind and purity of heart lie the beginning of an individual's evolutionary journey," my friend continued. "We carry within us the seeds of virtue, joy, purity, trustworthiness, and other favorable conditions for spiritual nobility to germinate. It is the essence of the intrinsic characteristics we embody that bestows upon us this dignified responsibility. Thus, at the feet of this majestic mountain we call Hope is where the journey begins."

I didn't say anything, but I couldn't help thinking that hope was something I definitely did not have when I was a child on Earth. I thought I'd find it in death, but it was a delusion of my weakness. It took me a long torturous time to reach the point in which it seemed I finally had a shot at it; a chance for redemption.

"This mountain represents a unique type of journey, similar in pattern to the temporal existence you had in the limited and illusory physical reality on Earth," he said. "Here, too, it begins in childhood, which we represent at the base of the mountain. As you go up this symbolic evolutionary ladder, you go through the naturally occurring developmental phases of growth similar to earthly life patterns."

"Adolescence and adulthood," I blurted it out unwittingly.

"And the very important elderhood," he added.

I looked at him recalling my challenging childhood days when he comforted my battered soul and imparted his wisdom on me. At that moment around the campfire, I realized that childhood was inherently imbued with an intelligence of creation in its preparatory stage of development. I sighed and raised my chin up to take a peek at the obscured top of that monumental mountain. I wondered whether the magical mystery of the unknown was visible from its zenith.

"The top of the mountain that you look at is the equivalent of a worthy elderhood. It is there that the magic of the mystery unfolds its panoramic vision," he said looking at me as I continue to stare up above. "But to reach elderhood, you must go through an entire developmental process; and in the case of this mountain, it's all about reaching the summit. And like any other progression, you must navigate each stage along the way until you reach your destination."

I mulled over his words as if they were the very first stage.

Suddenly the campfire was completely silent. Other than the intriguing sounds of crickets and the seemingly thousands of fireflies sparkling all around my surroundings, the place took on a quasi-solemn atmosphere. I correctly interpreted it as a prelude to some important announcement.

"The gates of Hope are now open to you," my friend said and I could feel joy emanating from each syllable he uttered. "As the ones in charge of introducing you to the Guardians of the Akashic Records, it's time for you to climb the mountain. We'll lead the way."

In extraordinary synchronism, all the children stood up as one entity, as if each were a limb of the same collective body. I remained seated watching them as they circled me and stretched out their hands down in my direction as a sign of help for me to rise; not to my feet, but to the occasion.

Somehow the prospect of climbing such a formidable mountain felt like a daunting task to me, for it was an intimidating journey to embark on. Besides, if this were going to be anything like a human life journey, I'd better brace myself for some serious emotional impact. And after having just completed the entire loop of the Suicide Orbit Sector, I was still in a state of shock and self-reparation.

"Don't fret," my friend said likely noticing my trepidation. "We'll show you the way up the mountain. It is our hope that as you examine the records along the way, you'll be able to transform your concept of what life is supposed to be. You shall learn from the valuable information of life registered on the Akashic Records."

I took a deep breath and got to my feet feeling ready to move on. As soon as I stood up, the children closed in the circle around me in a very tight space. When they were a couple of feet away from me, a chink unexpectedly cracked in the middle of the circle allowing me to pass through to the other side. As soon as I stepped out through the gap of the surrounding children, I was transported to yet another different reality. My nameless friend and all the children were still there smiling at me, but they were on the other side of a thin luminous veil that separated two distinct realms of existence. At that moment I realized that I was on my own again on the upward path of the majestic mountain.

◄40►

Unlike my inauspicious initiation to the Suicide Orbit Sector, this new passageway was a delightful contrast. The air was fresh and exuded gardenia fragrance in an environment vividly green and filled with invigorating energy. Walking amidst harmless roaming animals while heeding the soothing sounds of exotic birds and cascading waterfalls in the distance, I treaded along feeling comfortably at ease.

As I moved upward the radiant towering mountain, I marveled at the shimmering light vibrating all around it; like a protective aura that enveloped me as well in its mantle. I felt welcome and at the same time grateful to have been jettisoned from the penitent S.O.S. and, as I'd been told, boomeranged to the inner orbits of The Great Circle of Life. I was being offered a second chance to be alive again, though I had no idea how this new life would unfold. Regardless of the circumstances, I was determined to do my utmost to take full advantage of the unique opportunity for redemption.

After walking tirelessly up the pathway circling the mountain, I came across extraordinarily new beautiful scenery as I reached higher grounds. At the distance, as if it were hanging on the edge of the horizon, a magnificently bright yellow star with a vibrant violet corona sequestered my attention. Equally captivating was the illuminated verdant valley below where meandering crystalline rivers traced their courses around large swaths of lush forests. Flanking the sovereign bicolor star, two enormous silvery crescent moons rose from opposite ends of the sky as if they fulfilled some stellar protective function. Scattered among the celestial spectacle, countless shiny moving cosmic entities zoomed by one another at extraordinary speed; like electrons around the nucleus of an atom. I was in awe at how they manage to miss one another at such large number and extremely high speed. I decided to sit down on a bench nearby facing the breathtaking panorama and allow myself to be immersed in such colossal splendor.

"Wow, that was a close encounter," I shouted out loud watching luminous miniscule cosmic bodies change their trajectory at the nanosecond moment of impact. I marveled at the mysterious timely perfection of their motion. Perhaps, the timing in life's events operated in similar fashion.

Feeling as though I were in an incredibly realistic high-definition visual amusement park, not only was I taking great pleasure in my newfound entertainment, I was rejoicing in the tranquility of my solitude in that magical environment. It'd been a long time since I had the luxury of enjoying peaceful moments surrounded by spectacular beauty. Just being there watching numerous fast-moving objects crisscross the sky was in itself an immeasurable source of satisfaction. After doing time in a low frequency realm, this was a most welcome reward for the torment I endured in the Suicide Orbit Sector. But as I was basking in the glory of a heavenly spectacle with gusto, suddenly one of those tiny electron-like particles got off the cosmic traffic track on a threatening tangent that made me gasp.

"Oh goodness, what's going on?" I blurted out loud noticing what had turned into a bright white comet with a lengthy fiery tail heading in my direction at unimaginable speed. By the time I finished my sentence, the massive celestial body crashed right next to me generating an explosion of intense light and heat that temporarily blinded me while making me feel like a morsel of melting wax. Then, to my astonishment, as soon as I was able to see again, sitting right next to me there was an oriental-looking older man wearing a white garment with a golden belt around his waist. His effusively radiant purple eye pupils looked straight into the regal yellow star enshrined in its violet corona.

"Isn't the view absolutely superb," he said speaking his first words to me. "Aren't we fortunate to be a part of it?"

His comment struck me as an odd statement, for I wasn't really sure how I, a repenting suicide, could be a part of such splendor. Nevertheless, I liked the fact that he referred to it using the pronoun "we." In his turn, considering how abruptly he arrived and came into being right next to me, I supposed he was entitled to his share of the fortune to belonging to such exceptionally beautiful power. I piggybacked on his comment and went along for a feel-good ride.

"Isn't everything fortunate to be a part of it?" He added.

I could tell right away that he was replying to my musings and letting me know that nothing was left out of the landscape; not me, anyone, or anything. I took interest in my new enigmatic unexpected companion.

"Shall we?" He said while standing up.

"Shall we what?" I asked looking at him still seated.

"Get going," he said beginning to move.

"Going where?" I asked disclosing slight irritation with not knowing the destination he was referring to. Besides, I was enjoying my well-deserved respite before his arriving.

"You ask too many questions," he said turning his back to me and walking away briskly. "But if you want answers, you'd better follow me and keep your ears, eyes, and mind wide open. As for your mouth, I suggest keeping it closed for the time being.

Instinctively, I stood up in a hurry and sped up my steps to catch up with the fast moving older man. Although he looked like a mid-septuagenarian, he had the dynamism of someone half the age appearance of his being. He was a tall broad-shouldered slender man whose stealthy steps and subtle strut made him look like an anthropomorphized version of a royal feline. His posture and gait exuded strength, confidence, determination, and an un-wavering sense of self-worth. He moved as if he were a noble specimen of the realm of creation.

"I suppose you crashed next to me for a reason," I said try-ing to start an ice-breaker conversation. "Do you mind telling me what is this all about?"

"I'm your assigned mentor and guide in your journey through the Akashic Records," he said moving at a steady pace. "My duty is to lead you through a learning process that shall help you reach the top of the mountain. If you manage to accomplish the task, then you shall have a chance to be boomeranged to the inner orbits of The Great Circle of Life."

"What's the Akashic Records?" I asked unaware of it.

"It is the cosmic record-keeping of everything that ever was, is, or ever will be," he responded in the most simplistic compre-hensive fashion. "It is the perennial records of all that happens in the spacetime continuum. It is the memory bank of life."

"Like an esoteric library of the Universe?" I pondered.

"Oh no, it's so much more than that," he said. "It's infinitely more expansive and realistic than you could ever imagine. Ex-amining even a miniscule detail of the records can offer an exis-tential transformation of unprecedented proportions. It's a unique opportunity to experience, albeit vicariously, the history of any-thing or anyone that ever traversed through the spacetime continuum. It's like reading, or more accurately I should say living, the Book of Life."

"And you're telling me that I'm going to have access to such an authoritative source of knowledge?" I asked feeling the muscles in my face contracting with anticipatory excitement.

He halted his steps to a standing still and turned to the side to look at me. I could feel my eyes stretching wide open as soon as I noticed, for the first time, his magnanimous face. Agape, I stared at him and felt as though I'd been hypnotized by his powerful magnetic purple gaze. His aged handsome masculine countenance revealed an expressive contradictory duality; an exotic mix of sternness and gentleness; of angel and demon; of fire and water; of male and female; all blended harmoniously into one being. The energy exuding from his facial features adorned by his long white mane captivated my attention; and his dazzling amethyst-like eyes spoke of millenary wisdom. I was so mesmerized that for a moment I'd forgotten about my question.

"Will I?" I manage to utter while bewitched by his gaze.

"Just enough to get what you need to know to continue on your journey," he replied. "On that note, let's keep moving."

It wasn't exactly the answer I expected to hear, but learning that I'd have a chance to take a peek at such expansive records was exciting to me. However, I was curious and felt like I needed some basic preliminary information. After all, I was on a life-and-death journey toward an unknown destination, and all I knew was that I was climbing in pathway circles toward the top of the mysterious mountain.

"So that you know, I paid heed to your suggestion to keep my mouth closed," I said as a self-excusing disclaimer. "But I can't help asking you for some basic orientation into the nature of the Akashic Records. I just feel like I need to know what I'm supposed to expect."

"I've already told you what the Akashic Records is: a comprehensively unified information center of the memory of the cosmos; life, mind, and spirit," he said keeping up his fast moving pace. "As for expectation, expect nothing and your expectation will always be fulfilled."

"I'm sorry I asked," I said apologetically embarrassed.

"That's alright," he said. "I'll grant you a final analogy of what the Akashic Records is like until you get to experience it for yourself."

I smiled silently articulating my appreciation.

"In technological terms, think of the Akashic Records as if it were a cosmic quantum computer whose operating system is pervasive in every subatomic particle of nature, therefore recording everything on its database. It runs on the software of truth of all the facts registered on the records. Examining it is tantamount to playing a virtual reality game in an altered state of mind, except that there is nothing virtual about it. It's real history in real time."

I didn't need to ask or hear anything else. I was already agog to start this journey; and my guide likely sensed it.

"You must bear in mind that the truth can be quite uncomfortable and even painful at times," he uttered the unexpected caveat in a casual and yet serious tone of voice. "Traveling through the Akashic Field to review the records can often be a dizzying experience."

"I understand," I said.

"No you don't; at least not yet," he contested my false sense of assurance.

We continued walking upward around the mountain until we reached what looked like the entrance of a deep cave. Puzzled, I turned my head to a slight oblique angle in order to take a glimpse inside the place. I was stunned to see a long corridor with a pulsating violet pathway leading to a blindingly bright golden gate. I realized right away it was the exact same tonality of yellow and purple as the shining star and its corona. It was as though the star existed inside the mountain just as it did outside.

"Well, here we are at the entrance of the Hall of Justice; one of the many subsections of the Akashic Records. Are you ready to be introduced to the guardian of this hall and be initiated in the learning of truth?" He asked perfunctorily what it sounded to me like a solemn question.

I didn't voice an answer. Instead, I started walking inside the cave; and from the moment I stepped in, the magnetism of the gate pulled me in its direction. With my feet barely touching the ground, I glided through the purple haze as if I moved on a magical conveyor belt walkway. Whatever timeframe it took me to get to the mystifying gate I could not stipulate. All I know is that when I got there my elder oriental companion was already waiting for me with a familiar golden key in hand.

"The time has come," he said.

Then, he unlocked the gate and an incredibly bright light came bursting forth in an overwhelming wave of luminosity and heat that blinded me instantly. By the time I was able to see again, I was standing next to my mentor in front of an imposing blindfolded woman holding a scale while raising a golden sword up above her head with her right hand.

"Welcome to my domain," the goddess-like woman said while gently touching the tip of her sword on my right shoulder.

◁ 41 ▷

"The first thing you need to learn as you embark on your guided journey through the Akashic Records is about justice, for it is a fundamental supporting principle of life," the giant woman with cascading blond hair said reverentially. "You must always honor its sacredness."

While my mentor bowed as soon as she finished her statement, I looked around noticing I'd been transported to a totally different dimension. From the moment he unlocked that gate, I became aware that everything about my surroundings had changed: the temperature, the colors, the smell, the sounds, the texture and visual perceptions; all revealed the nature of a distinctive experience of reality. And then there was that colossal woman whose blindfolded eyes I could not see; and yet, I could feel her looking into my eyes as if ferreting out the secrets of my soul. I realized I was in evaluation mode.

"Justice is the common thread tying together all the elements of behavioral nobility," the blindfolded lady said. "It's what determines the direction and destiny of individuals and nations. Although justice is inherent in nature, it's often corrupted by the actions of pseudo-intelligent beings."

I was so mesmerized by my surroundings, especially the arresting sight of the massive lady, that I could barely pay attention to her words; much less comprehend what she was talking about. But for the sake of learning what her words had to do with my upcoming journey through the Akashic Records, I decided I'd better engage in dialogue with her to keep myself focused.

"But justice is such a broad concept," I remarked. "How can I narrow it down to the level of my individual behavior?"

"Why would you want to narrow down something that is so expansively wide and all-encompassing?" She said questioning my limited perspective. "The justice I allude to cannot be narrowed down to any level; not social, economic, political, legal, or any other degenerate representation of what can only be effectuated by the merit of actions. I'm talking about the robust trunk and deep roots of a grandiose tree, whereas you're thinking of brittle twigs and dry leaves of a shriveled shrub sprouting out of a shallow ground."

"Either a tree or a shrub, I still don't understand how it applies to me," I said feeling snubbed by her analogy.

"In the same way it applies to everything and everyone else," she said while lowering her mighty sword toward the ground for the first time. "Everything you think, say, and do affects your weight on the scale of justice. It's constantly recalculating and readjusting the balance of your life's account without your even knowing it's happening."

"I see. It's like a checks and balance system that keeps record of debts and credits, but based on a value system of deeds instead of monetary worth," I said beginning to feel relaxed around her. "Like the concept of *karma* in Hindu philosophy."

"You can be as simplistic or sophisticated as you wish to be, as long as you understand the authentic meaning of what I'm referring to as the spirit of justice," the magnanimous lady said. "But at a deeper level of understanding, justice is the soul of the Akashic Records and the heartbeat of its kinetic energy. It exists in and by itself without requiring any extraneous force to set its motion forward. Except for the actions of the subjects, there are no other determinant factors for the outcome of justice. It is the principle upholding truth and the imperative in the evolutionary process of everything that lives. In essence, justice is the manifestation of consciousness."

Apparently, the intellectual acumen of the giant lady was as immense as the materialized manifestation of her being. I have to say that I was having a difficult time following her profound train of thought. Perhaps, I was so focused on myself and the circumstances of my situation that I failed to grasp the broader meaning of her message. Fortunately, she made sure that I would not miss the underlying purpose of the conversation.

"The reason I'm explaining to you the function of justice within the context of the Akashic Records is because the records respond to its intrinsic powerful nature. After all, nothing could be more righteous than a spontaneous response to the energy that initiated the end result effect. And as you examine the records, you'll see how this all play out in a complex canvas of rightness," she said while turning sideways to face my mentor.

"Is there anything else Lady Justice would like to address?" My mentor asked her after bowing to the goddess-like entity.

"The most important thing to bear in mind is that everything that exists in the past, present, and future is a manifestation of justice; the natural outcome of all thoughts, words, and deeds. Your pupil must remember this as she peruses the records," she said stepping to the side. "You may now proceed to the Hall of History."

He bowed to her while signaling me to do the same. Then, moving backwards without turning our backs to her, I followed my guide inside the enigmatic cave.

We moved down the long corridor on the shiny amethyst ground that vibrated intensely with heat, brilliance, and life. We strolled silently side by side hearing the micro sound bites of our footsteps punctuating our motion, even though I wasn't really touching the ground, but rather gliding along as if I stood on some sort of magic moving carpet. Far ahead at the end of the walkway, the bright entrance hall pulled me in by a strong magnetic force. Astonished, I noticed my ethereal body involuntarily swinging as if it moved to the silent rhythm of the light wavelengths coming my way. As I danced with what had captured me, I watched the colorful clouds of gas blending into one another in an ineffable kaleidoscopic pleasure. Breathing the fresh fragrant air emanating from the fusion of light, I proceeded confidently ahead toward the universal destination of the unknown.

"We've reached the event horizon of the Hall of History," I heard my mentor's voice as I felt a more poignant suction pull. "Allow the entirety of your being to surrender to this gravitational force and the transport will be effortless."

I did exactly as I was told. And yet, the transition happened to be much more turbulent than I anticipated. Before I could even take my next breath, I realized I was in the middle of a bloody and brutal battlefield.

◄42►

This was definitely not what I expected. After having experienced an extraordinary transition from a dreadful low frequency orbit to a dynamic vibrating sphere, this new turning point was a major substandard occurrence. Ending up in a place like the one I landed on was a blatant contrast to my erstwhile experience.

In an instinctive act of survival, I hurled myself to the muddy ground to duck from the whizzing bullets flying by me as I stood smack dab in the middle of crossfire. Aghast, I witnessed bombs bursting in the air as the fiery flare of explosions echoed amidst the desperate loud cries of human agony. I gasped when I looked to my right and I saw a young man's body perforated by machine gun bullets lying lifeless over the trench. I was as horrified as I was disappointed to be back to the infamous Suicide Orbit Sector without any warning.

"I feel deceived," I said to my mentor who stood next to me with an impassive expression in his face. "You could have at least warned me about having to go back to the S.O.S."

"There was no need for issuing any warnings," he said calmly. "After all, you are neither in the S.O.S. nor in danger.

Thus, issuing warnings against perils that do not exist would be foolish. You're completely impervious to this brutal madness around you."

"What do you mean impervious?" I said covering my ears as a loud explosion blasted nearby echoing deep inside my head.

"You are now journeying through the Hall of History at such a high vibrational level that makes you imperceptible to all senses. Not even the most acute sensorial capacity could detect your presence in this space and time," he said clearly indifferent to my alarm. "You cannot be seen, heard, or felt in any way; and definitely not able to be harmed."

I slowly moved up from my hunkered down position to stand next to him. I glanced around and everything looked so lively and real that I was in disbelief. It took me quite some time to realize that I was experiencing the most vivid nightmare imaginable. I was eye-witnessing in real time a barbaric interaction without being in any way part of it. Only as an in attendance observer I existed in that spacetime zone.

"What is going on here?" I asked utterly puzzled.

"This is July 1, 1916, the first day of *The Battle of the Somme*; the bloodiest battle of World War I," he said without showing any emotions as bombs exploded and bullets zoomed by nonstop. "On this first day alone, dozens of thousands of lives were lost; and by the end of the battle five months later, more than a million soldiers had been killed or wounded."

I was flabbergasted. As I witnessed the unspeakable carnage in terrified awe, the agonizing loud wailing triggered by hot shrapnel burning inside soldier's bodies made me feel sick, sad, and sorry. The smell of gun powder mixed with the nauseating odor of charring human flesh set off unpleasant recollections. For a moment, I was sure that I'd been transported back to the dark and grim regions of the Suicide Orbit Sector. My olfactory sense recognized a similarity between my current environment to that of the S.O.S. However, soon it dawned on me that I was witnessing a historical event in real time; something that actually happened in human history. I was present in the past. I could feel the skin on my forearm crumpling up with goose bumps as I realized that the reality of the S.O.S. was but a parallel existence to the human experience. Everything looked and felt similar. While in the S.O.S. it was the sulfuric acid stench emanating from the ground, here I experienced eye-burning and throat-scratching toxic billowing plumes of used up ammunition.

"This is a form of mass suicide," my mentor said interrupting my self-absorbed musings. "And the human species has been committing this collective type of suicide for time immemorial."

"This is all very strange," I mumbled as we walked amidst soldiers dashing out of their trenches in droves firing weapons at their charging enemies. They moved by and through us as if they were neutrinos; the subatomic particle with mass close to zero that rarely reacts with normal matter. We were in the middle of a bloody war in real time history, but invisible and unaffected by the circumstances of the occurring madness.

"In the beginning, they engaged in this maddening practice of self-destruction using bows and arrows, spears, swords, and a vast array of murderous weapons that they wielded with expert savagery," he said as we walked in the midst of heavy bombardment. "This particular war, however, marks the dawn of a new era of armed conflicts that forever changed the nature of war."

"How so?" I asked as an adolescent-looking man is sprayed with bullets splattering blood on my impervious ethereal body.

"Because it was the beginning of ingenious developments in weaponry technology," he said pointing at the lifeless body of the young man riddled with bullets as if he were an example of what he was talking about. "From machine guns and flame throwers to submarines and airplanes, a slew of new weapons and strategies to employ them for maximum casualties permanently transformed the consequences of warfare. It was at this time in the beginning of the twentieth century, that science and technology established a criminal partnership with mass murder. This is when intellectual prowess gave way to suicide of common sense; and that's what you are here to examine in your first tour through the Hall of History in the Akashic Records. Keep this in mind as we move along."

Until that moment, I'd never thought about suicide as anything else but an individual human being taking her own life. But after listening to my mentor, I realized that morals and values could also be self-annihilated by nefarious human behavior. I could not stop thinking about ethical principles such as common sense, goodwill, empathy, solidarity, among many other idolized human aspirations committing suicide vicariously through human iniquitous ingenuity. I concluded that when intellectual achievements far outweigh the emotional competence of the species, a strange form of suicide of honorable values die a most ignominious death.

"Perhaps there is some sort of an etheric DNA in the human spirit that is coded for warfare," I said continuing my reflections out loud. "Some sort of survival of the fittest instinct born out of necessity to exist."

"If this is the case, then the code must be urgently edited, otherwise a grand scale calamity shall befall on the species in times yet to come," he said and the ominous tone of his voice made me shiver. "The abysmal gap between technological achievements and emotional-spiritual underdevelopment has become so expansively wide that threatens to sink humanity into a black hole of self-destruction; a hole they dug all by themselves. It will be the ultimate kind of collective suicide."

"Do you really think that widespread collective suicide in the form of a major warfare is possible?" I asked feeling somewhat relieved to be already extricated from the physical world.

"Possible? No, I meant inevitable. Unless there is some drastic transformation in human consciousness followed by immediate reparatory action, what you are witnessing here will be amplified to unimaginable proportions," he said as I visually scanned the ongoing terror happening all around me. "Be it the gap between sophisticated intellect and underdeveloped empathy, or obscene wealth and degenerate poverty, every time there is great disparity between extremes, the likelihood of a dangerous outburst is but inevitable."

"How ironic, then, that economic expansion and intellectual achievements get all the credit for the remarkable successes of modern industrial-technological civilization," I said noticing that I'd become at least temporarily indifferent to the bombings and wailings of despair, as if getting used to suffering desensitized me to its existence.

"The irony lies on the fact that what's perceived as success has become the ultimate failure; that freedom has become the ultimate slavery; that democracy has become the ultimate deception; that unity has become the ultimate divide; that life has become the ultimate death," he said in solemn staccato tempo. "But the greatest irony of all is that a truly successful option has been available all the time but passed by completely unnoticed."

"Like us in this battlefield of history," I remarked as soldiers staggered by me unaware of my existence.

"Like light lost in the darkness of a black hole," he added.

After what it felt to me like a grim conversation, we walked quietly through the boisterously violent battlefield. At that point, I'd become oblivious to the murderous suffering happening all around me. Perhaps, I'd come to accept that I was journeying through a historical event in the past; a *fait accompli* that could not be altered by my thoughts or sentiments.

"Considering the prospects of the future in the twenty-first century with climate change, overpopulation, pandemics, wars, and widespread hatred, I kind of feel grateful to be dead," I said breaking the silence by releasing my suppressed angst.

He stopped abruptly and gave me an admonishing look that made me regret my off-the-cuff comment.

"I mean, I know how much the world changed after this war, and when I left the Earth things were not going too well," I said attempting to minimize the unintended backlash of my previous statement.

He stood there silently staring at me with reproaching eyes.

"What's the matter?" I asked dodging my eyes away from his excoriating gaze with a great deal of embarrassment.

"Never again I want to hear you say that you're grateful to be dead," his stern voice reprimanded me in earnest. "If you ever say it again or even think about it, you will be boomeranged back to the S.O.S. region and forfeit the opportunity to move toward the inner orbits of The Great Circle of Life. This is not a request; it is an imperative requirement."

I wanted to verbalize an apology but my embarrassment muted my words. Without his giving me any explanation for his staunch reaction, I understood that life and not death was to be exalted in gratitude, as the latter was merely a transitional phase to another living experience. Besides, it was a craven attitude not to want to participate in a transformative opportunity for self-development, regardless of how challenging it could be. If anything, I should be grateful to have another chance to redeem myself for having committed suicide.

"We're about to cross a threshold of the Hall of History in the Akashic Records field," he said after resuming walking.

"Where are we going?" I asked with anticipation.

"To the follow up stage of this event," he replied.

"The Second World War?" I said somewhat surprised to continue running the war circuit.

"Yes, the ensuing worldwide war when scientific knowledge begot a most formidable weapon," he said and I felt the chilling effect of his words creeping up my spinal cord. "If the First World War marked the beginning of technology in the modernization of warfare, the second proved that it can put an end to all life with the push of a button. Since then, collective suicide has been hanging, precariously, in the balance."

After having this most surrealistic experience in a brutal battlefield, I didn't feel ready to embark on another similar adventure. And yet, I knew that I had no business analyzing situations or trying to direct my own path when I had no idea where I was supposed to go. Since the day I committed suicide, my perception of what reality was had changed significantly. I was learning to trust and surrender to my kismet, believing that everything that happened to me was exactly what I needed to experience. As Lady Justice said, justice is a force of nature that operates according to its own basic rule: every action generates an equivalent reaction. And if going to another bloody battlefield was my fate, then my sole responsibility was to embrace it wholeheartedly.

"See that last trench over there?" He asked signaling with his chin a mold of dirt in the distance.

"Yep," I replied, though my view of the trench in the midst of foggy smoke was minimal at best.

"It is there that the level of frequency changes and new wavelengths will take us to the event horizon of another dimension," he said keeping his pace against an infantry of charging soldiers that passed by and through us as if we were not there.

"Once we reach the perimeter, the gravitational force of the Akashic Field will pull us in to another era."

"Should I brace myself for impact?" I asked apprehensively.

"You won't even notice that you crossed the illusionary line separating the now and then in spacetime," he said.

Eventually, we reached the trench that was supposed to be some mysterious frontier of reality. As soon as we stepped into the trench, I felt myself free-falling into a deep sleep, until my consciousness was gently awakened elsewhere.

When my mentor indicated that we were heading for the examination of the live record of the Second World War, I expected to be transported to some explosively violent combat zone. However, to my gratifying surprise, I woke up in a large conference room where studious-looking men convened around a large table in what looked like an important meeting. Sitting on a black leather couch across the room, I yawned while stretching my arms outward. Unwittingly, I hit my mentor who was sitting right next to me.

"I thought we were going to examine the live record of World War II," I said. "But this doesn't look anything like it. Where are we?"

"We are at the apex of World War II right now," he replied.

"You could have fooled me," I said glancing around the room where many men, some in white scrubs, others in ornate military uniforms, and a few wearing suit and tie, assembled around a long rectangular conference table.

"The battleground is just where the murderous actions take place. But it is in meeting rooms like this that wars actually begin and end," he said. "You are witnessing a momentous time in the history of wars because these men are planning to end a war that will either end all wars or life on Earth as it's been known."

"It sounds much more serious than it looks," I remarked.

He stood up and started walking toward the conference table where the dutiful men gathered. Then, while the men discussed in animated fashion, my mentor circled the table in slow steps as if he analyzed; not the content of the men's conversation, but the importance of their decision to the future information of the Akashic Records.

"As World War I marked a significant transition from all wars fought before the beginning of the twentieth century, the Second World War ensured that either grand scale wars become obsolete or humanity will," he said still pacing around the table where the seated men spoke their minds to one another. "The First World War inaugurated weapons capable of delivering high number of casualties, but the second determined that a third world conflict would be the last."

I immediately realized what he was talking about, and the magnitude of what those men were discussing at the table. Although my landing in the middle of a battlefield of the First World War was a fear-provoking experience, the consequences of the activities taking place in that room was even more frightening. Instead of young men falling to their deaths riddled with bullets and flesh-burning shrapnel, here older men decided when and where to blast a devastating weapon to wipe out a large number of people out of existence. This was the control center of mass destruction; the place where rationality committed suicide.

"In the first decades of the twentieth century, the new scientific discoveries in the field of quantum physics forever changed humanity's relationship with nature," he said stopping by the head of the table where a four-star general fervently voiced his arguments. "But when this scientific knowledge merged with the development of military operations, the situation became grave and irreversibly dangerous. Only one event was more detrimental to the welfare of humanity than splitting the nucleus of the atom to unleash the inordinate amount of destructive energy it generates."

"For God sake, what could possibly be more damaging?" I asked puzzled about the existence of anything that could be more ruinous to humanity than the effects of nuclear war.

Slowly, he walked back toward me to answer my question.

"Long before scientific knowledge allowed for the splitting of the smallest constituent unit of ordinary matter, something much more important, though equally small at the cosmological scale, had long been shattered into smithereens," he said looking into my eye as though he waited my ensuing reaction. I obliged.

"I cannot fathom what that would be," I said.

"Long before the advent of quantum physics that transformed humanity's relationship with nature, men and women had already dramatically altered the relationship they had with one another. By allowing their unfettered greed and pathological selfishness to prevail over the unity of the species, human beings, mere atoms of the cosmos, were split into a multitude of self-centered units that engendered a self-annihilating path leading to collective suicide. Alas, the enormous devastation triggered by splitting the atom is a direct outcome of the damage produced by the splitting of humanity into individualistic units disconnected from the whole."

It had never occurred to me that humanity could be split into small units of itself; as if individuals were subatomic particles of cosmic nature. What I inferred from what he just said was that divided humankind had turned into some sort of self-destructive entity that would sooner or later explode like an atomic bomb putting an end to the civilization it had developed over millennia. By building walls of discrimination, indifference, and exploitation of their fellow humans, the species had created the conditions necessary to ignite cataclysmic events, which widespread wars were but classic examples. But with the ability to apply nuclear fission as a weapon of unprecedented destruction, a decisive turning point seemed to have checkmated intellectual prowess putting an end to the game of armed conflicts.

"Look, they are about to make the dreaded decision," my mentor said signaling at the conference table where the agitated men discussed in earnest.

I glanced at the table where a few men made decisions about the deadly destiny of hundreds of thousands of people, and the subsequent toxic consequences for years to come. The military personnel looked restless as if they were eager to take action. The civilian members of the group, however, suggested dropping the bomb in unpopulated areas in order to display the potency of this new weapon to intimidate the enemy into eventual surrender. But in spite of the scientists' cogent arguments of the ensuing devastation and high casualties that a nuclear weapon explosion would generate, the hawks of war at the table prevailed and the decision to obliterate the Japanese cities of Hiroshima and Nagasaki was sealed in unspeakable tragedy.

"Let's go," my mentor said standing up abruptly.

"Go where?" I asked feeling the tension building up.

"Witness this wretched historical event in real time."

"You mean, eyewitness it in the middle of the action? Like we did on the battlefield of World War I?" I asked feeling a great deal of apprehension.

"Of course," he responded totally blasé. "How else could you learn about the experience and the consequences of such a devastating transgression?"

I knew that I was supposed to go along without questioning or balking. But in this case, being smack dab in the middle of a nuclear blast was not something I was prepared to endure, even as a non-physical entity. I cringed just thinking of it as I felt the anxiety of the moment taxing my nervous system.

Suddenly, the men at the table stood up and walked out of the room. They looked resolute and ready to take action. I glanced at my mentor hoping to find a cue to what to do next. He remained impassively watching them leave without budging.

"Aren't we supposed to go?" I asked.

"We're already there," he replied.

As soon as he finished speaking, a most boisterous explosion shook the grounds as if a 9.0 Richter scale earthquake had shattered the ground asunder. I looked out the window and I saw a colossal ball of fire billowing up into a monstrous mushroom while waves of excruciating heat spread like a tsunami of flames. As soon as it reached the building I was in, it disintegrated instantaneously as I watched the fast moving inferno continue on its path of unimaginable devastation. Lost in the midst of blinding brightness and scorching heat, I was amazed to notice that I could clearly see the utter annihilation taking place around me. I saw buildings, trees, and people vaporizing into nothingness leaving behind a trail of unspeakable obliteration. And ahead of the path of destruction, the tsunami of flames rolled along consuming everything in a formidable display of thermodynamic power. I was horrified wondering if this was what religious texts described as Armageddon.

"Keep going in the direction of the gamma ray waves," I heard my mentor saying, though I could not see him. "Don't even dare to resist this overwhelming power."

"Where are you?" I asked stretching my arms around hoping to touch him in a fog of brightness and intense heat.

"I've blended in with the frequency of the gamma rays, but I don't have time to explain it to you right now," he said in clear pitch. "Keep moving forward and observe the details of this experience. I'll be providing additional information along the way."

Like steam spewing out of a copper kettle filled with water under extreme high heat, I wafted along with ease in the direction the intense airstream took me. As I moved away from the epicenter of the explosion, I realized that the catastrophe sprawled through the pathway of destruction. People who had not been close enough to ground zero to be vaporized instantly, moaned in agonizing pain as their skin peeled off their bodies like a thin layer of ice melting on sizzling asphalt in the summer heat. Above, where it used to be a blue sky, an ominous ballooning dark cloud of smoke covered the entire scope of my vision. Below, dilapidated buildings spread out in the distance like a desolate urban desert where once a prosperous city flourished. It was the most ghastly sight my eyes had ever seen. At that moment, I only wished that I'd be able to delete that traumatizing memory from my mind at a later time.

"In an all-out nuclear war, the immediate obliteration of cities and decimation of populations is just the prelude of ensuing catastrophes following a nuclear explosion," my mentor's voice reverberated in the bleak atmosphere. "Deadly illnesses caused by the fallout of widespread radiation; severe global environmental effects triggered by nuclear winter; and increased ultraviolet radiation are but a few of the consequences of such an abhorrently irresponsible act. Even the basic functionality of modern technology will be affected due to altered electromagnetic pulses."

"It's just awful!" I bawled.

"Indeed. It is a tragedy of unimaginable repercussion that could last decades if not centuries, depending on the number of nuclear bombs unleashed in the atmosphere."

"I'm feeling terribly hot," I said wondering whether his words or my experience of the heat waves prompted my profuse perspiration.

"Of course you are," he remarked in a matter of fact tone of voice. "One megaton nuclear weapon can produce temperatures of about 100,000,000 degrees Celsius at its center, which is about four to five times hotter than the center of the Sun. Yes, you'll surely break a sweat at 180,000,000 Fahrenheit."

"My goodness, this is a terrifying weapon of nightmarish proportion," I remarked stupefied with both the information he provided and my uncomfortable experience.

"Indeed it is. And the most terrifying aspect of this weapon of mass destruction lies on its very existence; and the fact it is in the hands of an irrational angry species filled with hatred and in constant conflict with rivaling enemies," he said.

Since I was exploring the Akashic Records at a time in the past, I started wondering what could happen in the future when adversary nations developed much more advanced versions of this dreadful weapon of insanity. Considering the large number of nuclear warheads spread around the planet at the time of my physical life, if another world war were to happen again that would be the end of life on Earth. As soon as I had this thought, my apprehension was exacerbated by my mentor's suggestion.

"Are you ready for a tour of the future?" He asked.

"A tour of the future," I repeated implicitly asking for more details.

"Yes, to find out what's going to happen in the future. Remember, you can examine the Akashic Records at any stage of the spectrum of time," he said. "The direction in time you want to travel is only relevant in relation to your purpose."

I suppose most people would do anything to take a good glimpse into the future. Based on what I was experiencing at that particular present moment, I should have wanted to go into the future, or any other time that was not that present. And yet, I remained reluctantly silent avoiding answering his question.

"Are you ready to go?" He asked again.

"Do I have any other options?" I replied already aware of the answer.

"Nope," he said succinctly outright.

I released a resonant sigh of resignation, and without saying another word, I acquiesced in silence.

By the time the flames of the tsunami of nuclear devastation had reached the far boundaries of destruction, whatever particle I had become accelerated upward through the morose mushroom cloud above. As I sped through the somber haze of radiation, I completely lost any sense of time, space, or self. I wondered whether I'd recover them once I reached my next destination; wherever that happened to be in my tour of the future.

"Breaking news!" I heard on a television set in what looked like a hotel room when I woke up from a dizzying nightmare. I rubbed my eyes in a state of confusion unaware of where I was and with a vague recollection of my dreadful dream. But as soon as I paid attention to the broadcast announcement, I realized that nightmares seemed to come in tandem as I transitioned from one into another.

"Following the breakdown in the peace talk negotiations in Geneva earlier this morning, the North Korean-Sino-Russian alliance has declared war on the United States and its NATO allies," the visibly stressed out middle-aged anchorman conveyed the news with a trembling voice. "In the midst of the ensuing diplomatic frenzy, Pakistan declared war on India and Iran reiterated its determination to push Israel out into the sea. The President of the United States will address the nation at any moment to announce that we have entered the early stages of the Third World War."

I had no idea where I was or how I'd gotten there; but wherever it was, it sounded like a very dangerous spacetime region to be. I got up and walked toward the T.V. for a close-up view of video footages of people ransacking supermarkets, bottleneck traffic on highways, rampant chaos on the streets, until, suddenly, the screen went pitch-blank with only the civil emergency signal issuing the red alert warning: "Imminent enemy nuclear attack in progress. Seek fallout shelter without delay."

Feeling like I'd just woken up from a nightmare into another, I was disoriented and could not fathom what was going on. Then, I heard a series of loud explosions and the lights went out leaving the room in complete darkness. I shuffled my feet blindly through the room toward the closed curtain window and pulled it open in one swoop. I wished I had not. Outside in the distance, a number of engulfing fire balls that ballooned into mammoth radioactive mushrooms popped up throughout the horizon in a ghastly sight of utmost devastation. Staring at the destructive scene absolutely aghast, all of a sudden I remembered where I was supposed to be at that moment; and even aware that I was already dead, I felt terrified.

"You can close the curtain now and come back here," I heard my mentor's voice inside the room and I felt relieved to learn I was not alone. "You'll not need to experience this tragedy first hand as you did the previous episode. In fact, this is not an actual event; at least not yet. It's just one of the many alternatives in the far-reaching realm of probabilities."

Although it was completely dark and I could not see him, I followed the sound waves of his voice and ended up sitting right next to him on a couch. Feeling the vibrational warmth of his presence next to me immediately assuaged my troubled mind and jittery emotions. However, I remained puzzled by his statement that what I saw outside the window was not an actual occurrence.

"If what's happening outside is not actually taking place, then I'm either hallucinating or experiencing another realistic nightmare," I said disturbed by the incongruent connection of his words with my sensorial perception. "And what about the loud blasts I heard before I walked to the window to see what was happening? And the tremor I felt under my feet? Didn't they happen either?"

"Well, they did and they did not," he said.

"Wait a minute. They either did happen or not; it just cannot be both," I said thinking he was pulling my leg. "Something either happens or doesn't."

I could feel his standing up and moving about in the dark space. The slow and gentle pace of his footsteps punctuated the enigma that captured my curiosity.

"Since you'll be journeying through the field for awhile, there is something very important you need to learn about the Akashic Records," he said pacing back and forth in the darkness. "In the Akashic Field where past, present, and future merge into an indistinguishable continuum nonlinear motion, what has been lived through and what's taking place in the moment are both recorded as established events of occurrences. The future, however, because it hasn't come to pass yet, can exist only in the realm of probabilities; that is, there are countless possibilities of reality depending on the choices made in the present as it travels in time toward the undetermined future."

"This is very confusing," I remarked with discouragement.

"Actually, it's quite simple," he retorted dismissively. "Think of time as if it were a book of fiction you read leisurely. At the turn of every page your memory records the words and images of the passages you read, even as it's happening at the actual time of the reading. As for the chapters ahead, you can only imagine what they'll be like based on what you've read so far; like the possibilities of outcomes. Thus, the excitement of wanting to know how the plot will turn out is what keeps you turning the pages eagerly wanting to find out how the story will unfold. It is the not knowing that keeps you engaged in the reading. If you were to know the denouement of the story beforehand, you'd likely toss the book aside, for you'd be robbed of the excitement of not knowing what will happen next. Likewise, the mysterious meaning of the future would be nullified by the knowledge of it before it ever happened."

"Interesting analogy," I remarked with a tinge of sarcasm. "But what does it have to do with the dual nature of your statement that what's happening outside is and is not happening simultaneously. After all, it's impossible for me to know and not know the conclusion of a book at the same time."

"Because the book is closed within the timeframe of the story it tells, whereas the future is unbound by the limitation of an ending as time goes on *ad infinitum*. This lack of boundaries and time's inherent interconnectedness with both past and present turns the endless future into a mere realm of probabilities where countless possibilities can become reality," he said as I noticed his footsteps moving toward me. "Thus, according to the probabilistic nature of the future, what you saw happening outside the window is just one possibility of reality among many others."

"Are you trying to tell me that I, or anyone, can create a positive outcome of the future right in the here and now?" I asked beginning to like the possibilities of the conversation.

"Indeed. It's quantum probability in action. The superposition theory of quantum mechanics suggests that until something happens, everything is possible in a superposition of states of reality," he said in professorial style that extrapolated beyond the practical purpose of my question.

"Well, in that case I would like to see a different possibility for the apocalyptic terror taking place out there," I said directing the dialogue back to the pragmatism of the possibility of the moment.

Suddenly, like restored electricity after a long power outage, the light abruptly came back on and brighter than before. I glanced around and my mentor was nowhere to be seen. I started walking about noticing right away that this was not the same space I was before the darkness took over. Although it also resembled a hotel room, this one was a spacious and elegant suite in contrast to the shoddy place I was in before. As I perused my new environment, I spotted an adjacent atrium with a wall-to-wall jumbotron screen facing a velvety white couch with a matching marble coffee table with a golden remote control on it. Feeling somewhat skeptical of such auspicious environment, I approached the couch with seemingly undue caution. When I sat down, my ethereal body sank into ineffable softness of what it felt like the gentle comfort of a fluffy cloud. After a long period of indulgence in the relaxation that my sitting produced, I picked up the remote control and turned the large television set on.

"Breaking news!"

A beautiful young anchorwoman flashing a pearly smile said looking straight into the camera with her bright blue eyes, which in the jambotron screen made her look like she was physically in the room with me.

"Today, after years of cooperation and coordinated efforts, Earth's community of nations reported that climate change has been successfully reversed to its natural sustainable standards. Furthermore, the committee in charge of the negotiations announced that they've been able to conciliate controlled population growth with the economic needs of societies everywhere on the planet," she spoke with demonstrable glee. "Considering the dismal situation we were in the early decades of the twenty-first century, these developments have shown what humanity is capable of achieving as we approach the dawn of the twenty-second century. The future has never looked so promising."

To my astonishment, instead of the intermittent obnoxious commercials following television programs, as soon as the news broadcast ended it was replaced by soothing cello music accompanied by stunning natural sceneries. It was as though the advertisement was about the beauty of the natural world and the comforting emotions that music elicits. I was enthralled.

Tickled by my irrepressible curiosity, I stood up and walked toward the window to take a look outside. I pulled the curtain gently apart with both hands; and as I did, a dazzling azure sky greeted me with enchanting splendor. I was mesmerized by such a magical environment. A towering waterfall cascading down into a large lake surrounded by low rise dwellings brought an immediate smile to my face. Cable cars transported jovial-looking people up and down the arboreal streets in a lively green town where happiness seemed to have settled in its permanent home. Not far away from the lake, a turquoise open sea adorned with glistening white sand that reflected the bright light of the shinning Sun as if in a gesture of gratitude for its luminosity. Children playing merrily at the shore line; adolescents surfing the crystal clear barreled waves; adults ambling on the decorative sidewalk, and older folks sitting on beachfront benches pointing out at fishing boats offshore harvesting bountiful seafood to nourish that self-sustaining community. Inland, on the opposite direction of the ocean, a wide river meandered around the quaint countryside creating a vivid visual effect that everything was moving in perfect synchronistic motion. Farther away in the distance, meadows and agricultural fields extended all the way to the foothills of a majestic mountain with snow topped peak. It was the most picturesque vision of a community establishment I'd ever seen.

"What do you think?" I heard my mentor's voice coming from the couch where I was seated before walking to the window.

"I could easily get used to this way of living," I said moving back toward him. "What I'd really like to know is how this superposition state of reality can come into being."

He rose from behind the white couch like an archangel emerging from a hallowed cloud. Looking at me with his soul-piercing purple slanted eyes, he pointed to his heart and tapped on his chest three times.

"It can't be that simple," I said understanding what his body language communicated.

"No, it isn't," he said. "But it's the answer to your question."

"Oh please, it sounds so schmaltzy and cliché; you know, it's all in your heart thing," I said disparagingly.

"But it is the truth," he said in a sincere tone of voice that contrasted with my derisive remark. "Not 'the heart thing' as your sarcasm insinuates, but that universal unifying energy that glues together all the loose fragments of delusional individual separation from the whole. The only reason the state of reality you witnessed outside does not exist is because the people of the Earth, mere cosmic atoms of the Universe, have split themselves with the divisive tools of selfishness, greed, indifference, and unrestrained desire to conquer others and rule over nature. By exploiting the most vulnerable elements of life, including their own kind, they have negated themselves of unimaginable possibilities in the quantum superposition of available states of realities. If only they'd learn that in the heart lies the nucleus of the energy that glues the building blocks of life together."

"You make it sound like humanity has developed into a self-destructive atomic bomb of a sort that detonates within the individual human," I remarked beginning to believe my own words.

"Yes, but with a much more powerful destructive nature, for it is destroying the very essence of what it means to be human," he said stepping closer to me. "Isn't it the ultimate form of collective suicide?"

I wasn't sure what to make of his comment, but it made sense to me in a strange way. Since splitting the atom is what unleashes the indescribable destructive power of the atomic bomb, his rationale that doing the same to the cosmic human atom seemed like a feasible hypothesis. According to the fundamental science of physics, what ignites an atomic explosion is the severance and release of the energy that maintains the nucleon of the atom together in one unified unit. Once this binding energy is broken apart, an outburst of massive proportion takes place. Something of equal power must hold the cosmic human atom together; and releasing it ignites the self-destructive power he talked about.

"Like the atoms of matter are held together by the strong nuclear force binding protons and neutrons in the atomic nucleus, the spiritual cosmic atom manifested in humankind also has its equivalent," he remarked. "Just as the strong nuclear force is the strongest of the four fundamental forces of nature, the spiritual atomic manifestation of the essence of the Cosmos also has its counterpart."

"And what could that possibly be?" I inquired with interest.

He pointed to his heart and tapped on it three times.

"Love? Is that what you're referring to?" I asked frowning.

Without saying a word, he started walking toward the window. Then, he turned around and beckoned at me to join him.

"Look at that," he said staring outside at the splendorous scenery. "Just as countless atoms come together to form a particular unified matter, what you see out there is the materialized result of the cosmic human atom unified by their own version of the strong force that keeps nuclei together."

"Are you telling me it's all about love?" I requested further explanation of his theory.

"Yes, it is love; not love in the superficial meaning of the word, but the inherent bright light that shines within like a Sun that cannot be obscured by the darkness of selfishness, greed, and indifference. Indeed, it is the powerful energy of love that is the gluon holding together what the madman wants to split into fragments of isolated units, therefore unleashing unimaginable destructive power. If the love that binds that community together were to be severed by the delusion of separation of the parts from the whole, a devastating transformative chain reaction would ensue and that place would look like the downtrodden inner cities you knew in your earthly existence."

"I'm so glad to learn that there is much hope for humanity," I said to myself realizing that I was examining the future section of the Akashic Records.

"Don't count on it just yet," he said and his words felt like a bucket of ice-cold water dumped over my tepid optimism. "Remember that in the realm of the future everything you see in the Akashic Records is but umpteen possibilities; like quantum superposition of multiple states of reality."

Suddenly, a terrifying feeling of despair crawled up my spine when I recalled the other ghastly possibility I'd witnessed in a nuclear holocaust. I kept looking at that idyllic setting wondering how in the world such drastically different possibilities could coexist side by side as feasible manifestations of the future.

"It's time to go and explore other aspects of the records," he said breaking the silence that my self-indulging angst had created.

"Can't we stay here just a little longer?" I pleaded wistfully beholding the lovely scenery outside while feeling uneasy about not knowing what my next destination would be like.

"It's time to move on," he said unreceptive to my longings.

"Where are we heading to now?" I asked apprehensively.

"Backwards," he said.

"Backwards!" I exclaimed in disbelief. "Going backwards seems contradictory to the natural flow of life."

He chuckled while nodding his head sideways.

"Listen, backwards does not really exist in the continuum trajectory of spacetime; and neither does forward for that matter. In fact, past, present, and future all converge in the now where all journeys begin and end. Haven't you ever noticed how a moment ends and another automatically begins? It's like a concatenation of quanta of time that links it all together into infinity. It is your mind and the limited linear perception it has of time that differentiates what is inseparably connected. The chronological delusion comes from your memory that can take you back to the past, just as your imagination can lead you to the future. But in the end, it's all one unremitting experience that always begins and ends here and now."

I was feeling too tired and antsy to make sense of what he was talking about. Besides, I was so enamored of that paradisiacal panorama that I was having a hard time letting go. The present felt soothingly comfortable and I didn't want to leave. But if I had known in advance of the extraordinary journey I was about to embark on, I wouldn't have hesitated even for a second to leave behind that communal sanctuary that existed in the superposition of multiple state of realities in the realm of the future.

The past was yet to come.

From the latter decades of the twenty-first century, I started moving backwards toward the past not sure how far back I was going to go. Nevertheless, I was so enthralled with what was happening to me that not knowing felt like an added bonus.

Sitting in a large and comfortable burgundy armchair, I realized I was inside a seemingly infinite light metallic cylinder that looked like a see-through subway car in a magic time tunnel. In front of me, my mentor sat in a golden armchair facing the opposite direction. Suddenly, I felt a gentle pulsation underneath and I realized that both armchairs were securely placed on a fast-vibrating indigo monorail whose matter I could not detect. With my back to the direction of the motion, at first I felt disconcerted with the atypical pattern in which I would only be able to see the scenery outside once it'd already passed by me. My traveling companion sitting opposite to me, however, he was going to see all the changes ahead of time; or at least from my perception of time. It was as though the past came to my present as if it were the future coming from behind. In spite of the oddity, I was unfazed and excited about this new leg of my journey into the past that would feel like the future yet to come; a uniquely dichotomous experience of time.

"Get ready for takeoff," my mentor said as if he were in command inside some invisible cockpit. "At first the high escape velocity will feel a little dizzying, but once we cross the first barriers of time we'll reach manageable speeds that will allow for observable chronological events."

As soon as he finished speaking, I noticed a very low frequency sound in the distance; almost imperceptible at first, but growing in a steady crescendo tempo until it became identifiable. A calming a cappella singing of a beautiful female choir started resonating inside of me; like a melodic anesthetic inducing me to a state of total relaxation. Buoying in sound waves while drifting through pleasant musical notes, I looked at my mentor in front of me but he was no longer there. In his place, an incredibly luminous colorful kaleidoscope rotated counterclockwise. Mesmerized by its hypnotic motion, I sensed it was emitting electromagnetic waves that blended with the sound waves I floated on as the rotation of the kaleidoscope picked up momentum. Suddenly, I felt as though I'd been caught in a confluence of sounds and colors that span at astonishing speed in circular motion. If it weren't for the soothing singing voices, I'd probably be helplessly nauseated in the ever-faster spiraling movement I was swept in. But instead, I felt nothing but an ineffable ecstatic sensation as if I'd been amalgamated into a numinous dance of light and music. Then, I felt the colorful musical nebula I'd become a part of burst out into a stupendous explosion; and from its dust, the birth of the past came into being. My journey through the past had begun.

"Pay attention to the details of what you see," my mentor who was visible to my eyes again said. "I'll fill you in additional information when necessary. In the meantime, make use of your five limited senses to absorb everything you experience."

At first the sceneries were zooming by me so fast that I could barely identify them in any logical way. Then, unexpectedly, they started slowing down and I realized I had been traveling back from the seventh decade of the twenty-first century to the last decade of the twentieth century.

"The reason you were unable to perceive what was passing by you is because it was part of the future you don't know about yet," he said tilting his head toward the transparent cylinder he faced as if observing what was coming next. "From now on, you should be able to discern what you see."

It was one of the most bizarre experiences I'd ever had. At first there was an assortment of colorful images laden with inherent emotions I could feel deeply in my entrails as my eyes observed them passing by. As soon as that ethereal backwards motion crossed the century mark, I felt the commotion of a time that was changing so dramatically that the very essence of humanity was being altered; like some sort of cultural epigenetic transformation of human nature.

After unprecedented sociopolitical upheavals that had brought the world to the brink of self-annihilation, societies and nations had been divided into antagonistic ideological factions. At the same time, rapidly evolving technological developments were forever transforming both individual and communities everywhere on the planet, while decimating the latter in the process. Soon, technology was conditioning both human behavior and social relations as well. Madly infatuated with the advent of the World Wide Web and the lightning-fast widespread means of electronic communications, it was easy to observe how the populations of that time had become utterly oblivious to the impending dangers of the achievements of their technological adventure.

I was so deeply immersed in my thoughts and consumed by emotions about the last decade of the twentieth century that I didn't even notice a couple of decades of time had passed by me. By the time I looked outside through the cylindered transparent window of that otherworldly vehicle I traveled in, I was stunned to see a different type of sociopolitical commotion. Long-haired youngsters dressed in worn out blue jeans were wreaking havoc to the conventional cultural norms they seemed determined to overthrow. There were protests everywhere against unwarranted discriminations, genocidal wars, social, political, and economic injustices; but above all, it was a massive campaign to topple an economic system and way of life that they knew it was both inhumane and unsustainable. Never before had such a large number of heirs of the rulers turned against their own establishment. It was chaos for the sake of rescuing the world from chaos. My jaw dropped open as I gasped watching unarmed young students being shot dead on the grounds of institutions of higher learning by armed soldiers of their own government. But when I saw a man stepping on the moon, my romantic image of the Earth dissipated as quickly as the chimerical aspirations of the revolutionary youth faded away.

"It is too powerful of a system to overcome," my mentor muttered watching the sceneries of history fly by; and presumably, my thoughts, too.

"Maybe," I replied defiantly hopeful.

"Definitely," he said wiping out any glimmer of hope I had. "Those idealistic youngsters were summarily turned into valuable cogs of the very system they intended to tear down. The mighty ubiquitous economic system turned the quixotic hippies into the petulant yuppies; and that's how this chapter of history ended."

All of a sudden a wave of melancholy washed over me. I felt as though hope was like a shadow that follows us, but every time we turn around to seize it into reality, it disappears leaving no traces that it ever existed.

The historical landscape kept changing uninterruptedly. Now a lighthearted environment, almost mawkish in nature, contrasted with the previous cultural hullabaloo. Colorful suburban houses with happy-looking children playing in manicured front yards highlighted the scenery. Clearly, this was a time of growth and wealth, at least to the few privileged that always seem to harvest most of the bounty of the season of prosperity. Alas, the progress I was witnessing came on the footsteps of unspeakable suffering and widespread devastation, as the change of scenery revealed.

"How sad that we have to unleash so much destruction just to have to rebuild a world in ruins," I said watching graphic images of European cities completely obliterated by the ravages of World War II.

"It has been the norm for time immemorial. You'll see as we move along into the past that this is a regular cyclical pattern of history," he said as dispassionately as if I had made a comment about the weather. "It's the perennial struggle for control of resources, influence, and dominance over perceived or concocted enemies."

"But no destruction has ever been of such magnitude," I said now seeing a number of maimed people helplessly roaming about the hellish rubbles of Hiroshima the day after the first nuclear bomb was detonated over a civilian population.

"Not yet," he said looking at me askew probably noticing my dismay. "I mean, in the superposition realm of probabilities there is a possibility for anything to happen."

I turned my gaze away from him and looked out again. As time moved backwards through the clock of history, I saw the culprit reasons that led to the catastrophic events that inaugurated the era of nuclear mass destruction. With a great deal of consternation, I watched the widespread misery and desperation of large number of people troubled by a sudden economic collapse, and I thought of how cyclically volatile the dominant economic system is. The great prosperity of the 1920s paved the way to the Great Depression of the 1930s. With unbridled greed in the driver's seat of the fast moving pursuit-of-profit-vehicle, the strident crash of the economic system was anything but a surprising event. In the ensuing years, an international economic meltdown drove millions into abject poverty. As a remedial recourse, another major armed conflict was needed to stimulate the economy again back to its dysfunctional cyclical pattern of disorder. I felt disheartened thinking about the endless miserable merry-go-round of boom and bust, war and peace, progress and destruction, and other conflicting dualities that continuously disrupted even a remote sense of enduring harmony.

"Isn't it remarkable what intellectual ingenuity can produce?" He said derailing my tortuous train of thought, which offered some relief from my morose musings.

"Are you being sardonic?" I asked unsure of what he was referring to.

"Not at all. Intellectual capacity is, indeed, a remarkable tool; and a very powerful one for that matter," he said crossing his legs and taking on a more relaxed conversational stance. "The problem, however, is that when this tool is wielded by unbalanced executors of this power, it risks becoming an instrument of self-destruction."

"In this case, then, such a powerful tool should not be granted to unstable beings," I remarked.

He took a deep breath and released a glum-tuned sigh.

"Perhaps, it is the irony of nature that intelligence must be bestowed upon those least prepared to wield it wisely."

"I guess that would mean that God lacks intelligence or discernment, otherwise He would not make such a blunder," I pointed out letting mockery ooze through my words.

"Let me see if I can explain it in a succinctly direct manner that might make sense to you," he said. "Like a smart beautiful lady that is systematically abused by her lover, mishandled intelligence may also become disenchanted with itself and be compelled to take actions that can be detrimental to its benefit. In other words, intelligence may be driven to commit suicide, too."

I liked neither his analogical innuendo about me nor I understood what he meant by intelligence committing suicide. I looked at him silently trying to express both sentiments with my eyes. He heeded my gaze well.

"Like the organic human brain whose primary function is to keep the body working at optimum capacity, the principal utility of intelligence is to promote the continuous development of those wielding its power. When this noble role of intelligence is corrupted by ulterior motives, intelligence dies by turning against itself in a suicidal like way in which only the appearance of it remains. The evidence of this act is revealed through the annihilation of those who mishandled intellectual power."

"I don't understand," I said feeling more confused than ever.

"There's nothing really to understand," he said. "All you have to do is observe."

I turned my head toward the outside where the past passed by my present moment in real time. As I watched the yonder years flash by my eyes with vivid images of history, my mind seemed to go in the opposite direction. I thought of my experiences witnessing nuclear holocausts and I realized what he meant by intelligence committing suicide. It seemed evident that when intelligence is mishandled by corrupting ulterior motives, it loses its fundamental function for development, progress, and self-preservation. Instead, it dies in the minds that miscalculated its overwhelming power. The intelligence that pursues knowledge and turns it into either a commodity for profit or a means for manipulating minds, hearts, and nature is an intelligence doomed to perish. And if intelligence were akin to some sort of ethereal brain of the spirit, then the development of weapons of mass destruction and the unremitting slaughter of the life-sustaining environment are undeniable evidences that intelligence has become brain dead.

Suddenly, that chamber like vehicle I traveled in came to an abrupt halt. I looked outside and a bright red neon light flashed on the platform announcing we'd arrived at the early 1920s.

"Why did we stop?" I asked my traveling companion.

"We're getting off here for a brief educational tour," he said.

"Educational tour," I repeated flummoxed.

"Yes. It's an opportunity for you to learn how intelligence, like everything else, hangs in the balance of superposition of possibilities," he said standing up and beckoning at me to do the same.

"Are we taking an educational tour of the early 1920s?" I questioned looking up at him while still seated. "What's so special about this time in history?"

"Because it was during this time that intelligence pried opened the Pandora's Box containing the mysteries of the Universe and unleashed a chain reaction of unprecedented consequences," he said moving in the direction of a gate-like threshold of colored light emitting gentle buzzing sounds. "But if instead of sitting there asking me harebrained questions you just stand up and follow me outside, you will be able to see it for yourself."

I got to my feet right away and dashed to catch up with him before he crossed that magical liminal border of spacetime.

◄46►

As soon as we walked through that luminous passageway, I was surprised to find myself in what looked like a scientific laboratory. I guess I was expecting to end up in a place more akin to the mystical threshold I'd just crossed; somewhere more colorful, vibrant, and resonant. Instead, I'd walked into a bland, listless, and quiet room with a large blackboard filled with indecipherable mind-bending mathematical equations.

"Where exactly are we?" I asked looking around puzzled by an environment that did not match the excitement of the paranormal portal I'd just crossed.

"Without getting into the complexes and unnecessary details that will not serve your purpose, all you need to know is what this room represents: the place where revolutionary discoveries came into being; a kind of knowledge that radically transformed the understanding of nature, science, technology, and the still untapped potential to transform human consciousness," he said while pacing slowly toward the blackboard.

Within my mind, the sounds of his words mingled with the images of the hieroglyphic-looking equations on the blackboard I gazed at unblinkingly.

"Look at this," he said pointing at the mind-boggling language of science. "What you see here are ground-breaking mathematical equations that reveal the reality of the invisible world."

I moved next to him while looking at the convoluted mathematical equations skillfully arranged with symbols, numbers, and Greek letters in a mesmerizing language I could not comprehend.

"This is the language of quantum mechanics," he said staring at my confounded face. "Quantum mechanics is the study of matter and energy at the atomic and subatomic level. This language explains the connections linking the infinitesimally small precincts of the subatomic world to the unimaginably large scale of an infinitely expanding cosmos."

"I find it impossible to make sense of such a recondite language; and it's even harder to imagine that it evinces factual knowledge," I said staring at the magnificently structured code of communication revealing scientific truths.

"You don't have to understand it. All that is required of you is to know about the message this language conveys. Everything in it contains verifiable truths corroborated by scientific observations and perceived in everyday life," he clarified.

I had no idea why this was relevant to my personal quest. However, if there was one thing I'd learned by then was to flow with the unfolding of events without attempting to interfere with their outcome. I decided that I'd just listen to him and try to glean as much information as I could about a seemingly incomprehensible field of knowledge.

"When looking at any solid object, it is nearly impossible to imagine that it is composed of countless particles that are a billion times smaller than the naked eye can detect; and with an enormous amount of empty space within and between them. In fact, it's even more disturbing to learn that the particles themselves are composed of more empty space than actual matter. In essence, this is what an atom is in a nutshell: a tiny particle bound together with a lot of empty space between the parts," he said beginning to pace back and forth in front of the blackboard.

His talk captured my attention right away. Beginning to feel like a traditional student in a classroom, I took a seat with anticipatory excitement to attempt learning what moments earlier seemed like an inconceivable task.

"After Einstein's famous mathematical equation proving that energy equals mass times the speed of light squared, quantum mechanics validated it at the subatomic level that there is no distinction between energy and matter. Since then, a brave and dangerous new world came into being. It was a matter of time for scientific knowledge to split the strong force within the nucleus of the atom to release unimaginable amounts of energy; and the world has never been the same again," he said halting his steps as soon as he finished his last sentence.

"This is all very interesting, but I don't understand how or why this is relevant to my personal quest, or even to the subject of intelligence committing suicide as we discussed before we stepped out here," I said getting fidgety. "As fascinating as this topic is, I cannot relate it to anything that's applicable to me."

"This is exactly why we had to stop by this era before continuing on your journey," he said sitting on the table with one leg dangling sideways. "There is a subtle element of this knowledge that is evading you as it has done so to numerous others. It is the failure to realize how the infinitesimally small particles relate to you in the context of an immensely infinite Universe. The relevance lies on the ridiculously short time you exist in an equally miniscule space you occupy."

"I still don't get it," I said beginning to feel frustrated.

"Putting it bluntly, you are but a subatomic particle of the cosmos among billions of billions of others with insignificantly short lifespan participating in an endless recycling process of energy," he said and the tone of his voice revealed his growing impatience with my inability to grasp the concept he was trying to explain. "In fact, you are nothing but cosmic dust that missed an opportunity to recycle to a higher energy level."

His words hit me in the gut of my suicide guilt. I was not prepared for his response and that was not what I was bargaining for when I engaged him in conversation. He probably noticed my consternation, for when he spoke again both the tone of his voice and demeanor had clearly changed.

"In the realm of elementary particles you must first get rid of preconceived notions about what is short time or long time. A millionth of a second may seem like an unimaginably short time; and yet, for an elementary particle it is an exceedingly long time.

Conversely, a million years is but a fleeting blink of an eye in the cosmological time scale. With this immeasurable range in mind, where does an eighty-year life expectancy fall in this abysmal chronological disparity of existential time?" He questioned looking at me in the eye as though waiting to read my answer. "I suppose you now understand what I meant, and I trust you didn't take umbrage to my words; or to my intent for that matter."

I didn't reply. I was consumed mulling over the inordinate disproportion of lifespan of different types of lives and forms of energy. At that moment I realized I was but a cosmic particle manifested as individualization deluded by separation from the whole. Perhaps, I was a cell of a vast web of life in constant and continuous recycling mode. Cells replace themselves uninterruptedly and without the interference of any other force external to their own recycling nature. In that sense, I felt like a cell among billions of likewise particles of cosmic life popping in and out of existence in a millionth of a second or a million years. And somehow learning about the enormity of the breadth and depth of life altered my perception of being an autonomous independent self separated from the whole. I was amazed to realize how my understanding of the minuscule microscopic world and the colossal cosmological scale facilitated my acceptance of the insignificance of myself when separated from the whole.

"The advancements in quantum mechanics in the early 1920s and beyond have been a great missed opportunity for humanity," he continued. "While science and technological innovations benefited tremendously from this knowledge, the other fundamental aspects of an intelligent being were dismally neglected. Realizing how the very small interacts with the very large in utmost synchrony should have led to an awakening of consciousness. But instead…"

"Instead…" I hinted for an elaboration.

"Instead, it became a fascination with the scientific ability to unravel the mysteries of life and how to manipulate it,' he said.

"Isn't it a natural impulse of intellectual curiosity in the pursuit of self-improvement and knowledge?" I asked.

"Yes, it is. But when it's corrupted by intellectual hubris, economic interests, or as tool for manipulation and control, then the pursuit of improvement moves backwards; that is, it devolves and it becomes a dangerous endeavor. This is when the knowledge acquired turns against itself and weapons like the nuclear bomb come into being, among countless other means of self-destruction," he concluded.

"What other means?" I asked in an effort to understand the full breadth of his thinking.

"The list is endless. From the widespread use of chemicals and pharmaceutical products to the alienation and manipulation of the masses through electronic means, the misuse of such a powerful tool spawned from scientific knowledge can have devastating consequences for the future and continuity of life," he said as if he were issuing a warning. "But since the ultimate purpose of intelligence is to function as a self-preservation tool and evolutionary progress, when it goes astray from its intended path, it destroys itself through the very results it generates."

"It commits suicide," I muttered to myself.

"Yes, but only to those through whom intelligence can no longer exercise its natural comprehensive functions," he said. "Separating the intellectual from the emotional centers of human intelligence is tantamount to splitting the nucleus of the atom, which triggers similar explosive consequences for the fate of the species. In other words, it leads to the suicide of an intelligence that failed to observe the fundamental principle of wholeness."

Looking at those most intricate mathematical equations on the blackboard that explained how life functions at the subatomic level, I wondered about similar formulations explaining the incomprehensibly boundless Universe. But I didn't indulge in my curiosity trivia for too long. Instead, I made a decision based on the realization that my insignificant individuality bestowed upon me. If it is true that I'm nothing but a cell of an immense cosmic body, then I would choose to be like a T-lymphocyte; a T-cell that plays a vital role in the immune system of the body that's supposed to guard against virus-infected and cancerous cells. However, having committed suicide myself, I wondered whether the intelligence inherent in a protective T-cell had already died in me by default.

"It is time for you to explore another dimension of the microscopic realm and learn about its enormous relevance to the grand scheme of life," he said getting on his feet ready to go. "What is invisible to the naked eye can often do more damage than what is perceived by your limited senses. And what seems relatively big, in comparison to a large scale of measurements, is in reality quite diminutive and yet equally dangerous."

"It sounds intriguing," I remarked.

"Good," he said. "It's time for you to experience how it all plays out. Let's go inside the biological lab to explore a vast world of microscopic life."

Curious and excited about my next learning experience, I stood up and followed him toward the only exit door in the room. I stopped before it noticing the vivid neon green color sign above it that read: Dark Room. Leery, I looked at him silently pleading for some reassurance.

"It's just a dark room; like those they used to process negative films into good quality photographic prints," he said with a dismissive blasé attitude in the face of my obvious concern. "Before you can develop a fine photograph, you must first see the distorted negative image."

I tightened my lips and felt my tense nostrils siphoning in a deep breath of anxiety. I couldn't help recalling the horrifying experiences I had in the Suicide Orbit Sector, and I was afraid I was about to face something similar again.

"Don't worry about it," he said evidently noticing the apprehension stamped in my face. "You're in a higher frequency environment now. Embrace this experience for what it is: an educational opportunity to further your trajectory back toward the inner orbits of The Great Circle of Life."

"Thank you," I said in appreciation for the reminder of what the underlying purpose of that journey was meant to be.

"Are you ready to enter the Dark Room?" He asked.

With my eyes closed, I nodded in agreement without saying a word. By the time I opened my eyes, I'd been transported to a bizarre microscopic world of gargantuan possibilities.

◄47►

As soon as we walked through the closed door as if it were a transparent passageway devoid of matter, I noticed right away that even the slightest glimmer of light had vanished into pitch black darkness. At the same time, I felt an overpowering compression reduce my ethereal body to an infinitesimally small size. In a matter of lightning speed time inconceivable to my perceptual senses, I'd shrunk into a microscopic existence.

Soon, grotesquely looking creatures began appearing before my eyes leaving me scared out of my wits. First there were large worm-like organisms in various shapes and forms wiggling by as though they danced seductively trying to capture my attention. I immediately intuited that I had to avoid them at all cost. And because the environment was so dark, the various colors of those creatures revealed their peculiar contours and motions in detail. But when the last one zoomed by and I thought the worst was behind me, a much smaller and yet more terrifying looking species came dashing in my direction. Unlike the first batch of strange living things that went by me somewhat unthreateningly, the ensuing ones were clearly on a warpath mission. I could sense that the purpose of their existence was to invade, take over, multiply, and destroy me from the inside. Some were roundish shaped with menacing spikes protruding like mortal spears that could pierce through me with ease. I felt as though I was a female egg surrounded by a school of swimming spermatozoids vying to fertilize me with life. But unlike life-giving sperms, those wicked microscopic beasts were agents of death; and if they invaded me, it would be the end of whatever life form I'd become.

"You are now experiencing existence at the cellular level," my mentor said as I was about to scream when one of those despicable spiky things tried to penetrate me. "And don't worry about the viruses harassing you. You are enveloped in a protective protein, immunoglobulin that is, which is produced by the immune system in response to the presence of foreign substances called antigens. Antibodies recognize and latch onto antigens in order to remove them from the body."

"What about the other ones; the worm-looking and roundish creatures that first went by me?" I asked still feeling alarmed by the ongoing experience.

"Those were bacteria. They are a type of biological cell; a member of a large group of unicellular microorganisms that can be found in both organic and inorganic compounds, some of which can cause serious diseases. They were the first life forms to appear on Earth and they are present everywhere in nature," he explained trying to mollify my trepidation.

"Despite their size or characteristic, they all look very creepy to me," I said trying to regain my composure.

"And yet they are very different in nature. Unlike bacteria that are live unicellular organisms, viruses, at least in a classical sense, are not alive. While they're made of proteins and genes like living things, they need to interact with living host cells to reproduce. Viruses can infect all types of life forms, from animals and plants to microorganisms, including bacteria and archaea. When infected by a virus, a host cell is forced to produce thousands of identical copies of the original virus at an extraordinary rate," he continued his detailed explanation of the bizarre experience.

"Even as I stand reduced to the size of a cell, all these weird creatures look pretty small compared to me," I remarked observing them with cautious attention.

"Although they are cells in their own right, bacteria are only about one tenth the size of a human cell; and viruses are even smaller, about a hundredth the size of a cell. And yet, some of them can do irreparable damage if not eradicated from the hosting cells in due time," he said emphasizing the latter's lethal danger. "Viruses are tiny compared to all other living things, but they are giants compared to molecules and atoms; and they're capable of delivering devastating harm to a living organism."

"How can such a tiny thing wreak so much havoc to an infinitely larger organic system with a robust defensive mechanism?" I questioned more as a comment than expecting an answer.

"Here is when we get to the core of the reason for your visiting the Dark Room," he seaid almost prophetically.

"What do you mean?" I asked with apprehension.

His cellular shaped consciousness that was floating freely through the dark space came to a sudden halt. Standing next to me exchanging energy equivalent of an eye contact, he revealed a different representation of the Dark Room in a much larger scale I could not have fathomed.

"Because everything in nature is relative to the existential frequency it manifests through, it shouldn't have been necessary for you to embody the size of a cell to realize that within the context of an infinite and ever-expanding Universe, human beings are like cosmic cells," he said what I correctly interpreted to be the preface of more important information to come. "And just as these armies of dangerous enemies composed of miniscule matter can cause the downfall of a healthy physical body, virulent energies expressed through human behavior can act like deadly viruses. Their disease-causing activities exert similar destructive effects on a much larger entity: the planet Earth."

I wanted to make a comment but he didn't give me a chance to interject.

"Since you considered wanting to be like a T-lymphocyte; a T-cell that plays a defensive role in the protection against virus-infected cells, I thought it'd behoove you to know that among the billions of various human beings on Earth, many are deadly viruses carrying the genetic codes of pestilence and destruction in their unworldly DNA. Like a perilous virus acting as the microscopic biological agent of death, some humans are dangerous types of viruses operating at a different behavioral scale. And the more they multiply, the more damage they inflict on the ailing hosting entity; be it the social body or the planet itself."

I didn't recall sharing with him my passing thought about choosing to be a T-cell in the individual context of my minute separate existence. But at that point in my journey, I knew that my thoughts and even my very sense of self were sort of a public domain I could not privatize. In any case, the concept of a certain category of humans exercising hazardous viral functions on Earth captured my interest and brought forth important questions.

"Are you telling me that some humans exert similar malignant functions like these hideous microscopic organisms zooming by me right now?" I asked watching a flood of viruses and bacteria flow by seemingly eager to infect any vulnerable cell.

"Oh, much worse than that," he said with unhesitant promptitude. "These small biological agents you observe now invade cells in order to force them to reproduce countless copies of their harmful genetic code. The human virus, however, assails itself while dividing and replicating its malicious codes of self-destruction; and they do it with awareness of their deliberate deleterious actions. In fact, they are so vicious that they create their own artificial viruses so they can continue inflicting distress to others and their environment whenever and however they can. They are mercilessly wicked."

As soon as he finished his sentence, I remembered a time in my earthly life when my mother and I went to a local food bank that had been shut down by a malicious computer virus. The manager said that they'd been randomly targeted by a widespread electronic virus attack for no particular reason. He also said that he felt lucky not be one of the many victims that had to pay a ransom to recover their valuable information. Unfortunately, the engineered electronic virus was not the typical case my mentor was referring to.

"Although an organic body can have billions of cells communicating with one another on a regular basis, the germs, bacteria, and viruses present in the organism don't necessarily trigger noticeable symptoms if a healthy immune system is in place. On the other hand, the human virus poses a deadly threat in and by itself because it destroys the only immune system that can halt its malevolent spread."

"What is the immune system against the human virus?" I asked puzzled by the analogical references.

"Elevated consciousness; the enlightening awareness of the harm it generates through irresponsible actions fueled by greed, selfishness, and indifference to the consequences of reckless behaviors. By obstructing, ignoring, and sometimes rationalizing the insignificance of the damage produced, the human virus infects and destroys the fauna, flora, water, air, and the lives of individual human cells through an unnatural way of life that is inconsistent with the norms of healthy living," he said sounding to me like an inquisitor of a guilty species. "And as they replicate the malicious code of their existence, their arrogant sense of intellectual superiority that falsely ensures them that they can solve the very problems they create, their home planet and its extraordinary biodiversity declines at alarming rates, until it succumbs to an untimely death."

Suddenly, I was overwhelmed by a wave of immense sadness. I remembered how my earthly husband and his business and political hoodlums did everything in their power to exploit, swindle, oppress, and rob both individuals and nations in any way they could for their own personal gains. They were the quintessential human pathogens diseasing the wholeness of the social body with their virulent selfish ambitions. They were the enemies of life that divided the human species while replicating the malicious codes of their shallow existence, until the inevitable demise of natural life succumbed to the malevolence of their nature. They represented the pathogenic disgrace of the Earth.

"This brings us to the two fundamental purposes of this temporary existential microscopic experience you're having right now," he blurted out unexpectedly ending my silent soliloquy diatribe.

"And what could that be?" I asked still feeling morose.

"Firstly, that you realize that your erstwhile individual human experience was, in a cosmological sense, very similar to this cellular experience you're having right now; that is, an infinitesimally minute manifestation of life among billions of others," he said pausing for a brief moment as if giving me time to ponder. "Secondly, and more important to the purpose at hand, is the realization that even within such a miniscule existence, you have the choice of functioning as either a toxic bacterium, a deadly virus, or a protective T-cell of whatever organism you happen to embody at the time. And even though all are contributing elements to the evolutionary process of life, one carries much more weight of responsibility to preserve life than the others."

"I've already stated what I choose to be," I said defensively. "However, I'm afraid that by committing suicide I might have acted more like a pernicious virus than a life-saving T-cell."

"No, you didn't," he said sounding self-assured. "A virus infects and destroys healthy cells, whereas you eliminated only yourself in the face of what you perceived to be insurmountable obstacles. Killing yourself was like confessing that life was too much for you bear. A pusillanimous act, no doubt, but it was not virulent in nature."

"Well, in this case, where do I go from here?" I asked.

"Let's get back to exploring the Akashic Records to find out," he answered while moving and pulling me along through a puissant microscopic gravitational force.

First the darkness took over and then a torrential flood of vivid red liquid gushed me away at the sounds of deafening heartbeats. Like a twig flowing down a mighty river hitting rocks along the way, I bounced off the walls of tributary veins at astounding speed. At each consecutive pumping of the heart, I was hurled farther and faster than before; to the point I could no longer feel whether or not I was changing locale. It seemed as though I'd run a full orbit around that mysterious body; and it all happened in a quasi-imperceptible moment.

"We're just making the transition to a different existential dimension," I heard my mentor's voice in my mind. "Once we traverse out of the microscopic matter world, you won't even remember you've been here, because it all lasted in such an indiscernible amount of time that your memory won't be able to register it; only the Akashic Records will."

Next thing I knew I was sitting in the same armchair in that anomalous cylindrical vehicle moving backward through time. Feeling like I'd just woken up from a peculiar nap, I looked at my mentor sitting in front of me while rubbing my drowsy eyes.

"I have no idea how long I slept," I said placing my hand over my yawning mouth. "And I had a very bizarre dream."

"What did you dream about?" He asked perfunctorily without showing interest in whatever I was going to answer.

"I don't remember," I said.

"Maybe you didn't dream at all; or maybe you didn't even fall asleep," he said with a chuckle. "In any case, we are here and now on our backward journey through the records of time. In fact, we're about to cross the millennial milestone; right before the century that forever changed the history of ensuing centuries."

I stretched my arms slightly outwards feeling befuddled by unclear memories roaming through my mind. Making a great deal of effort to suss out the uncanny sensation of having existed in miniscule corporeal matter in a microscopic world, soon I realized it was a futile attempt that led to naught. In the meantime, at that very moment before my eyes, I watched historical images passing by me from behind revealing extraordinary transformations. Like watching a virtual reality newsreel, I saw the beginning of a century that in a surprisingly short period of time developed technology that forever changed the world and even altered the nature of the human species. The progress was astounding: in mere fifty years, the twentieth century went from wagons powered by horses to spacecrafts powered by nuclear energy; from bicycles to airplanes; and eventually from the telegraph to the internet. It was as though time accelerated and took humanity along for a ride in a vortex of technological advancements that human civilization was ill-prepared for.

"We have a long way to go, so we're going to pick up some speed," my mentor said leaning against the transparent cylindrical window looking what was coming ahead. "But don't worry. You won't miss a beat."

With the twentieth century past forward me, I started seeing the deplorable circumstances of the factory system where men, women, and children toiled all day long in the most inhumane conditions. It was the rise of an industrial ruling class composed of factory owners and financiers commanding vast armies of exploited people living in slave-like conditions. I saw the Luddites protesting and dismantling the machines they erroneously perceived to be the enemies, instead of those who owned them. Discontent and discord led to rebellions and new revolutionary thoughts demanding structural change of a society gone astray.

As the years rolled by toward the early days of that era, I noticed how one revolution against exploitation led to another as situations did not seem to change. From the French Revolution that toppled an abusive monarchical regime promising *liberté, egalité, fraternité*, a notable hero of the historical event, Napoleon Bonaparte, crowned himself emperor and went on an expansionist war campaign. It seemed that all revolutions, be it of political, social, or economic nature all ended up in stagnant states that perpetuated the human tragedy. I sadly realized there was something terribly wrong with human nature.

For a brief moment I had a flash of recollection of what I thought was a dream I'd had recently. But with new historical landscapes moving so fast from behind me, my attention reversed to what was happening outside. Based on my observations, it was clear to me that the entire eighteenth century had passed subtly by leaving behind only the music of Johann Sebastian Bach as if to remind me that, despite the inherently virulent human nature, some individuals were like T-cells in a virus-infected collective human society body. They helped counterbalance the prevailing negativity assailing the world through their uplifting art, spiritual intelligence, and loving hearts.

"Oh my God!" I exclaimed out loud as soon as a magnificent picturesque scenery appeared outside. After seeing so many troubling historical events, the new sight was reinvigorating to my vision. I watched in awe the turquoise water rhythmically washing ashore over shimmering white sand in an idyllic tropical setting. Far in the distance, semi-naked bronze-tanned people sauntered about on a sunny day in an evident display of carefree exhilaration. Inland, tall green peaks with cascading waterfalls tumbling down into a large pool of granite black rocks bestowed paradisiacal status to the place. If ever there was a Garden of Eden as described in the Book of Genesis, this setting was its most unadulterated representation.

All of a sudden I gasped. Looking down far into the horizon where the turquoise blue sea met the crimson setting Sun, a swarm of white serpents wiggled their way through the ocean toward the garden island. As they got closer, I could see in the salivation around their exposed venomous fangs that they were ravenous beasts. Their eyes looked determined to conquer, annihilate, and poison the Garden of Eden they intended to obliterate.

"May I go there? Can I witness that event in real time?" I pleaded with great anticipation while watching a first contact between peoples of worlds apart.

"Integration, the ability to be present in a particular time and space, is a basic component of the journey through the Akashic Records," he said. "However, not all requests are granted since some are based on individual merits."

"May I?" I insisted ignoring his remarks.

"In this case, yes," he said making me feel relieved and eager to integrate into that turning point moment in history. "However, be forewarned there will be future requests that won't be granted to you."

Although I inferred that some of my merits were lacking in quality, which did not make me feel good, the excitement of the occasion supplanted my momentary disappointment.

"Go ahead," he said. "You may go now. I'll be here waiting for you."

"Well, how do I get there?" I asked trying to read his casual body language.

"You open the door and go," he replied insouciantly.

"What door?" I asked irked by his offhand answer.

Without saying a word, he stood up and slowly pivoted around himself before sitting down again.

"What's that supposed to mean?" I asked beginning to feel my irritation escalating.

"The doors are all around you," he said leaning forward to look deep into my right eye. "In the spheres of the spacetime continuum, there are countless doors through which to enter other dimensions of reality. Opening these doors is a cinch; unless, of course, the door you want to enter is inaccessible to you."

"But how do you open doors you cannot see?" I asked displaying impatience in the tone of my voice.

"You close your eyes and visualize where you want to be while holding the doorknob in your mind's eye. Then, you open your eyes and the door at the same time; and just like that, there you are where you intended to be. It's that simple."

I followed his clear-cut direction. As soon as I turned the doorknob in my mind's eye, I was transported in timely synchronistic fashion to a new reality I could now experience vividly.

There I was, walking among them utterly imperceptible to their senses. In my turn, however, I could clearly see the intricate details of the natives' countenances. I could smell the stench of the sweaty unclean white bodies donned in heavy velvet garments under the sweltering Sun. I could hear the tropical birds chirping in the palm trees, and even taste the salty sea air while feeling the soothing ocean breeze caress my face with gentleness. Being in an actual time and space of an event that had occurred centuries ago was an exhilarating experience. It felt as though I was in some sort of esoteric amusement park where I was able to learn about history by eyewitnessing the event firsthand.

Standing a few feet away from the interaction between two oppositely different cultures was a memorable learning experience. It was not the linguistic barriers that seemed to complicate their reaching even a modicum of mutual understanding. It was the abysmal gulf separating two drastically different ways of experiencing life that isolated the two parties in their cultural silos. While one culture embraced a carefree lifestyle of total independence, freedom, and indissoluble bond with the natural environment, the other only saw opportunities to profit, dominate, oppress, and control those who once were free, self-reliant, and content. Indeed, it was impossible to find a common ground of understanding when one group coerced the other to sell that which the latter deemed incomprehensible to do. Humans belonged to Earth and not the other way around.

The serpent had arrived in the Garden of Eden, and it brought with it a literary litany filled with imaginary myths and convoluted parables open to all sorts of interpretations, including the validation to tyrannize. The serpent became the forbidden fruit itself. It transformed everything in its own image while wreaking havoc in paradise.

As I stood there eyewitnessing the ingenuous welcoming people's first encounter with the wicked white serpent, I felt myself spinning around the axis of time recalling the future to come. Soon, the venomous nature of the serpent would poison both the people and the environment that it'd eventually own and control. Expansive horizons would turn into megalopolis where millions of people crowd in confining vertical spaces. The freedom to be would turn into the slavery to have. Alas, the temptation to take a bite on the apple of illusion that the serpent hawked as progress proved to be as irresistible as it was devastating in the long run. And because I'd seen the future beyond my own time, I knew the serpent could potentially transform the Garden of Eden into a Gulf of Extinction. The symbolic serpent representing the original sin of morbid greed and selfishness would reassert its perennial dominance in a brave new world of chaos.

Watching heart-wrenching sceneries in which pristine areas were juxtaposed to the deplorable conditions they looked like a few centuries later, I felt emotionally glum and intellectually baffled. Where once was a stunning turquoise water bay surrounded my towering green mountains, four centuries after the arrival of the serpent it had turned into a murky swamp of toxic waste. At that moment I started formulating a theory of intellectual suicide. After all, what intelligence would destroy that which sustains its own existence? Or perhaps, the inherent malevolence in human nature acted as some sort of deadly virus that consumed anything and anyone infected with its lethal pathogenic effects. As I kept rotating in place viewing the images of history revolving around me like a 3D virtual movie theatre, I realized that all the numerous horrific events characterizing the course of history were but gradual suicidal steps of mass scale.

For some reason that experience at the early sixteenth century was not as thrilling as I'd anticipated; to the contrary, it upset me that it corroborated the concept of the virulent nature of the human species. I decided it was time for me to go back to that magical vehicle so I could keep on going back in time in order to move forward in my progress. Now aware and adept to the dimensional crossing technique, I walked in with closed eyes toward the ethereal door I wanted to open.

"How was it?" My mentor asked me as soon as I showed up in front of him.

"Hmm, let's say that I'm ready to proceed to the next leg of this weird backward journey," I said agog to move on.

"Forward or backward; slow or fast; up or down; and who is to say what is the right or wrong way to go?" He remarked in philosophical context. "In the infinitely expanding realm of spacetime where life and death dance to the tune of an eternal symphony, a perennial recycling process occurs. How can you determine where the dance begins or ends?"

"I guess you can't," I mumbled inaudibly.

"Sometimes even the serpent eats its own tail in a symbolic illustration of eternity in the perpetual cycle of life and death, as the ancient symbol of the *ouroboros* represents," he said surprising me by referring to the imagery of a serpent as I had concocted in my mind earlier. "The serpent will do what's required of it at a particular time and space, until it swallows itself up to start something anew in a different chronological locality. So you, like the serpent, regardless where you find yourself to be right now, you could be either at the end or the beginning of something new as well. And not knowing which is which is where the magic of living lies. This is when the natural alchemical process of life unfolds."

Backward or forward; fast or slow; down or up; suddenly they all became one and the same to me, with no one having precedence over the other. And at that point in my journey, the flow of the motion was the only thing that mattered.

I did not know how long it'd been since we started that strange journey backward in time. What I did know was that a very long time had gone by since my last stop without my even noticing it. I was disappointed thinking that I might have missed opportunities along the way. Perhaps I'd fallen asleep again, but this time without dreaming; or at least not anything worth remembering. I was perturbed by the peculiar experience and in desperate need of clarification.

"There is a reason for speeding up through some stretch of time in history," he said clearly anticipating my upcoming question. "In fact, there is a reason for everything."

"Could I get at least a hint for the reason to hie through hundreds of years of history in this bizarre backward journey through time?" I beseeched my travel guide and companion.

"Sometimes it's not the number of years or any measurable amount of time that matters, but what is accomplished with whatever allotment of time is granted to you. One year of light is worthier than hundreds of years of darkness," he said evading my straightforward question.

"But isn't darkness an equally necessary partner in the dance of evolution? By omitting it from my educational experience, I feel like I'm being deprived of opportunities for learning," I said resolute for an explanation.

"Oh, don't you fret about darkness," he said with an ironic mirthful undertone. "There will be plenty of it throughout your journey. In fact, there will be so much darkness that you'll grow sick of it. We're just trying to maximize the usage of time in your exploration of the Akashic Records bypassing doldrums years."

Not exactly the answer I expected to hear. Besides, the idea there would be so much darkness ahead in the backward path in time was somewhat disconcerting to me. And yet, I knew I should not let the information disrupt my determination or ruffle the equanimity of my spirit.

"As it was, the Dark Ages lasted about a thousand years. There was no reason to take too much time exploring a millennium of intellectual, spiritual, moral, and ethical decay," he said leaning back in his armchair while placing his hands behind his head. "Besides, I thought it'd be a good idea to spare you from witnessing the agony of people being burned alive at the stake because their correct ideas and visions contradicted the falsehoods of the Church's ideology. I must add that the religious piracy of the crusades was not terribly amusing either. And if all that were not bad enough, you were spared from watching the bubonic plague wiping out nearly half of Europe's population."

"Sure, but I also missed experiencing the beginning of the remarkable transformations of the Renaissance; that fertile period of uplifting rediscoveries in cultural, artistic, political, and economic rebirth after such a long period of darkness," I said bemoaning what I perceived to be a missed opportunity. "It would have been good to eyewitness it."

"It's important for you to remember that a time of darkness, even as long as a millennium is always followed by a time of light," he said. "But for your purpose and due to your time constraints, you're better off moving straight ahead to a pivotal period that shall prove to offer a much more valuable lesson for you. You do not have any time to squander, for that is what life is made of; and remember, you have a life to recover."

I didn't say another word. I turned my attention outside watching the images come from behind me at extraordinary speed; and they were changing dramatically. After a series of indistinguishable sceneries, the esoteric newsreel of history started slowing down until it came to a complete stop.

"We're getting off here," he said standing up and beckoning at me to do the same.

"What's about this time and place?" I asked watching a village in the desert occupied by armored soldiers.

"It's the time and place of the birth of hypocrisy at its most ignominious state," he replied.

"It sounds intensely disturbing," I remarked raising an eyebrow with anticipatory curiosity.

"Let's get out there and find out," he said.

◄50►

As soon as we passed through the thin barrier separating the temporal field of perceptual realities, we found ourselves walking toward a legion of heated marching Roman soldiers. Holding long spears and with sharp-cutting swords dangling from the waist under the elaborate armors they wore, they passed by and through us as if we were drifting molecules of the air they breathed. The sound of their footsteps pounding on the dry ground resonated in the distance, as they gradually disappeared amidst clouds of dirt their stomping lifted. Soon, they vanished like wraiths in thin air of a barren land.

"Where are we?" I asked.

"Bethlehem," he replied. "At the time of the execution of a loving man whose crime was to spread kindness and goodwill among his people. Ironically, his future followers would commit countless crimes while claiming to represent the one who endured the unwarranted crime in the first place. Both the castigation meted out to this man and the punishments delivered to others in his name are among the greatest travesties of human history. The tragic event of this man's execution has been distorted, corrupted, and misrepresented for the selfish interests of religious, political, and other groups that contributed to besmirching humanity's reputation as an ethical species."

As soon as he finished speaking, the first thing that came to my mind was the memory of the priest I encountered in the Suicide Orbit Sector. The perverted dark wolf hidden under the white sheep cloak of a religious garment was the quintessential of hypocrisy to me. But soon I'd realize that there was much more to ignominious behavior than isolated individual abuses.

Before I could even notice, we were walking in a bustling street market where people seemed agitated and behaved as though they were perturbed. Even the smell of grains, meat, fish, and unwashed people unpleasantly blended in the inauspicious atmosphere of commotion. But it was when a rooster crowed three consecutive times that my mentor called out my attention.

"It's time to heed the conversations around us," he alerted me as we stopped to eavesdrop the chatting on the street.

"They say the carpenter will be crucified today," an elderly lady filling a bowl with grain said to the shopkeeper. "Poor soul; and I've seen him do so much good around here. He is a loving, humble, simple man who has done nothing wrong."

"Under the Roman Empire rules what's right or wrong is irrelevant," the shopkeeper remarked. "Anyone who poses even a remote threat to the ruling power is doomed to be crucified in some way. And the influence of this man on people is getting so widespread that some are even calling him a king."

"He is no king. He's just a common man with an uncommon heart. He's no threat to no one," the elderly lady protested.

The shopkeeper put down the grain sac he held in his hand and looked into the woman's eye before speaking. "In a heartless world, his uncommon heart is the greatest threat of all."

I listened to the exchange with a mix of befuddlement and excitement. It was clear whom they were talking about and what was about to take place that day. Suddenly, a throng of people started rushing down the street toward a narrow alley. My mentor nudged me slightly with his elbow and we moved along with the agitated crowd.

"Move, get out of the way!" A centurion yelled while pushing and shoving people to the side to open the way for a parade of human cruelty.

It was a brutally inhumane scene to witness. Stumbling along the cobblestone alley carrying a heavy wooden cross to which he'd be nailed alive, the lanky bearded man seemed indifferent to the unspeakable suffering he was enduring. His face awash in blood dripping from the thorns of a wreath deeply pierced into his head, he moved as though he stood aside from his tortured body; like a witness to the event as my mentor and I were. And in spite of the dire ordeal of his misfortune, I noticed that the light in his eyes shone like bright stars in the darkness of his suffering. He looked like he had made peace with his destiny; perhaps aware of the powerful impact his life and death would exert in the world for millennia to come.

"This is a ghastly sight. Why am I witnessing this barbaric act?" I asked feeling sick to my stomach while trying to figure out the purpose of the experience.

"What you're witnessing is not merely a man's suffering, but a symbolic representation of what humanity is capable of doing to life, which is what this man represents," my mentor replied with his eyes fixated on the grisly scene. "But the reason for your witnessing this is just a prelude for what comes next; and that's where the purpose lies. Come, let me take you to the place that will unravel the mystery of this leg of your journey."

To my astonishment, we stepped on the alley right between the man carrying the cross and the Roman soldiers whipping him mercilessly. We went all the way to the Calvary and watched closely the gruesome torture of an innocent man. As he winced at every pounding of the hammer on the nails perforating his flesh, I closed my eyes to avoid feeling nauseated by the sadistic spectacle. Once attached to the mortuary structure, the soldiers lifted him up and, ironically, that raised his status as a man of power for centuries to come.

I was absorbed in my thoughts when my mentor signaled me to follow him. Although the walk felt brief in time and short in distance, we had covered quite some ground in both domains. It seemed like we had moved a few years ahead of that repugnant occasion. Soon, I found myself in unfamiliar territory in an isolated desert area. Following my mentor, I cautiously ducked to avoid banging my head against the low entrance of a narrow cavern on the foothills of a hill. Inside, a man wrote nonstop on a lengthy scroll.

"Who is this?" I asked.

"This is one of the apostles of the man you witnessed being crucified some years ago. He is pouring out through his writings all his recollections, opinions, and interpretations of what that extraordinary man exemplified. The other apostles did the same. But as imagination gives way to exaggeration, they all wrote in recondite language and convoluted parables of what they perceived to be the teachings of the man who never wrote a single word about his noble purpose."

"Apparently, the good man was so immersed in living by example that writing down his teachings might have seemed like an unnecessary endeavor," I remarked.

"Obviously, his disciples didn't think so," he retorted immediately after I finished my sentence.

"Is it in the writings that you find the ignominious hypocrisy you referred to earlier?" I asked.

"Not the writings per se, but turning them into what arguably became the most powerful tool for manipulation, oppression, and thievery," he said as we backed out of the cave slowly. "The ignominious hypocrisy lies in the fact that a man who preached about loving thy neighbor as thyself had his teachings misappropriated for the selfish interest of unscrupulous people, institutions, and cultures for centuries."

We resumed walking side by side without saying a word. It seemed obvious to me that he purposefully maintained the silence to induce my mind into reflective mode. And it worked. I started out thinking of the Catholic Church; a quasi-monarchical institution that ruled over the pious, the poor, and the penitent while aligning itself with the powerful and oppressive European monarchies. The Vatican City and its enormous wealth became the capital of the central government of the Roman Catholic Church; the Holy See, as it was named to exert authority over their dutiful followers all over the world. In this city, an opulent church building that resembles the luxurious architecture and ostentatious furnishings akin to the most lavish palaces among the wealthiest monarchs, established itself as a bona fide religious empire. It's a far cry from the teachings of the man who's purported to have said that is easier for a camel to go through the eye of a needle than a rich man to enter the kingdom of heaven.

As we kept walking quietly through what seemed like an endless barren land, I thought of all the other denominations of the Christian faith. Very likely inspired and motivated by the exorbitant financial successes of the Catholic Church, many others emerged as profitable Christian enterprises in their own right. They established an assortment of interpretations of the faith; even a new bizarre theology to authenticate their pseudo-religious privileges, which was suitably christened "prosperity theology." Supported by this novel convenient conviction, various Christian denominations purported that their financial advantages as religious leaders were legitimate manifestations of the will of God for them. The outcome of this wickedly ingenious strategy is that many an evangelical pastor has become obscenely wealthy while enjoying celebrity status, both of which they flaunt shamelessly. But prosperity theology warrants the claim that the Lord wants the faith tricksters to be wealthy, in frontal contradiction to the example of the same Lord who objected and condemned the accumulation of what could not be taken to the kingdom of heaven; the realm of love he envisioned. Using the assumed holy book as if it were a shaft with which to drive the pious herd as wished, the impious impostors of faith manipulate the deficient of intelligence and meek in spirit at will. And in order to solidify their stronghold, they forged iniquitous alliances with powerful political groups, influential economic enterprises, and often times with brutal tyrannical regimes.

"What do you think?" My mentor asked me breaking the silence while derailing my train of thought. I knew he was aware of what was going on in my mind.

"I'm beginning to realize that there are many ways to commit suicide; and I'm not talking about the self-inflicted ending of biological lives, but the suicide of morals and principles," I said pensively. "Maybe there is something intrinsically dysfunctional about humanity; some sort of a self-destructive mechanism that tends to destroy that which is most valuable."

"The agony of existing between two intolerable conditions; the uncertainties of life and the certainty of death, is often all it's needed to trigger off suicide attempts. In the case of morals and principles, corruption becomes the weapon with which to commit suicide. As for a person, the mind becomes a prison in which the bars of guilt, fear, anxiety, resentments, among other negative emotions supersede the calling of life that exists outside the self-inflicted imprisonment. But in the end, suicide, as you've already learned, cannot forge an escape from the duality of life and death; or corruption and nobility, or whatever the case may be," he said picking up his walking pace toward the sunset.

"I wish I had not committed suicide," I blurted out.

"But you did, and by experiencing regret you're only building a prison in your mind with those dreadful bars that will keep you locked up for as long as you remain remorseful for actions you cannot undo," he said as the twilight heralded the approaching evening. "On the other hand, you have the option of being born again through self-forgiveness. Actually, I venture to say that was precisely what the crucified man meant about entering the kingdom of heaven; and forgiveness might well be the key to opening its gate."

I digested his words in silence with only the shuffling sounds of our feet on the sandy ground interfering with the quietness. The high temperature of the desert was beginning to give way to a temperate early evening breeze. In the distance, the only remnant of the existence of the Sun was its multicolored shinning light shooting up from behind the skyline. Bedazzled, I watched that splendid vibrant vista in the desert having an inkling that the worst was behind me; that somehow I'd already crossed the arid regions of the road leading to my redemption.

"It seems that you have earned a time of reward," he said abruptly as if he were being spoken through.

"What's that supposed to mean?" I asked with a great deal of curiosity and anticipation, for I'd long forgotten what the true meaning of reward was.

"An experience beyond the limited spacetime dimension," he replied. "You've been through the S.O.S. and you had your brief tour of history. And in all, you've responded quite well to the challenges of these restorative experiences. Therefore, you've earned the right to explore the inner boundaries of The Great Circle of Life and the opportunity to survey regions of the Akashic Records where the spacetime dimension ceases to exist."

I wanted to ask questions, but I decided to keep quiet instead. Although what he said sounded like an exciting adventure, at that point I was much more concerned about the end of my expiation. Somehow I felt that I was making good progress toward my sense of atonement with myself and the life that manifested through me. After learning that it's impossible not to exist in some shape or form, my unswerving objective was to take another crack at life; just another chance and I'd make good of it.

In the meantime, I was ready to claim my reward time.

<h1 align="center">◄51►</h1>

Perhaps it was the lightness of being that exerted the uncanny experience of being a photon of a beam of light. Zooming through what seemed like an endless cosmic highway with the speed limit of 186,282 miles per second, I could feel a commanding gravitational force pulling me toward the center of an astronomical vortex as a spectacular cosmological display of life paraded before my stunned eyes. From infinite numbers of all sorts of subatomic particles to mammoth macrocosmic celestial bodies, they all moved by me with each leaving behind one single message: everything, included me, was part of an indivisible whole whose only differentiation was the individual uniqueness through which the whole expressed individualizations of itself. At that moment it became clear to me that nothing existed independently, but it was all isolated manifestations of the sum total.

"This is a mind-blowing experience!" I shouted watching trillions of traveling neutrinos fly by through matter as if it were not there. "And it never seems to end!"

"And it never began either," my roving companion said moving by next to me as if we were individual atoms of a common molecule.

I wasn't sure what he meant by "it never began either," but it made sense to me that something that does not end likely never had a beginning either. It is one of those undecipherable mysteries that should remain that way.

"It's remarkable that I can experience consciousness at such a miniscule level of existence," I said referring to another mystery that should also remain unfathomable. "And that I can see particles as infinitesimally small as neutrinos; and hear their dashing by me as if they were moving microscopic motor vehicles on a cosmic highway."

"Sensory systems are relative to the conditions that allow their scope of perception," he said. "In the extremely limited confinement of the human existence, the five rudimentary senses are so narrow in function that they barely meet basic requirements of perception. This is due to designed restrictions in the human brain so the sensory receptors can only capture a certain amount of discernment of what is seen, heard, smelled, touched, or tasted. It is built that way so the human experience can fulfill its limited ephemeral function. It is the evolutionary process of individual manifestations of life with minimum awareness of comprehensive reality."

I listened to his succinct and yet thorough explanation while hearing the distinct sounds of subatomic particles whooshing by. At that level of sensorial perception on Earth, I'd be able to hear the sounds of an ant going about yards away with utmost precision; or clearly see a bacterium floating amidst molecules in stagnant water. As I thought about it, I marveled at how human scientific ingenuity evolved over the centuries to develop powerful observational tools like microscopes and telescopes, which allowed for the investigation of the extremely small and the inconceivably immense. Also, it made me wonder about those ill-fated people who had to go through life without hearing or vision; and some even without both. Such a deprived sensorial condition was as unimaginable to me as the wondrous possibility of seeing and hearing it all that I was experiencing at that extraordinary moment.

"Listen!" He said as I felt the soothing sounds of melodious harp music entrancing my being. "We're getting closer to The Center."

I knew it even before he said anything. The harmonious tunes of vibrating harp strings played by some angelic fingers heralded the approaching of a higher frequency. I surrendered to its calling while basking in the glory of that transcendental cosmic expedition toward the beginning of a new destination that would lead to another, and another, and another…It was then that I became fully aware of the impossibility of finding refuge in suicide. Either at the micro or macroscopic level of existence, all energy is continuously recycled into the whole that spits out renewed manifestations of its essence. Be it a microbe, a fern, a bee, a horse, or a human being, not a single form can become completely disconnected from the life that expresses itself through it. In the grand web of life, not a thread is independent from the whole.

"Here we are!" His voice exuded exuberance. "This is the best vantage point to The Center without being there."

Mesmerized, I gazed at the brightly illuminated nucleus that vibrated with life at the center of an aureole orbit. Around it, umpteen multicolored electron-like particles circulated rapidly in a dazzling display of perennial kaleidoscopic motion. If there were a physical heart of nature, what I was watching agape ought to be it.

"Like everything else within the vast scope of measurements, your perception of The Center is relative to the standpoint from which you observe it," he resumed in timely synchrony with my thoughts. "As a subatomic particle, the perception is that of an atom, whereas if you perceived it as a star you would likely see a ginormous elliptical galaxy instead. And yet, regardless of how The Center is observed, the essence remains unadulterated."

"Can we go all the way in there?" I asked beholden to the object of my awe eager to experience that astounding display of power at a closer range.

"This is as far as you can go at this time," he replied.

"When can I go then?" I insisted eager to know the answer.

He remained quiet as if his silence were an answer in itself.

"When?" I insisted.

"Whenever the time is right," he replied pithily.

Although it saddened me to hear it, I realized that I'd already traveled a long way in both time and space and should not be morose. To the contrary, the fact that I was standing at a premium vantage point to the center of The Great Circle of Life was a tremendous reward that would behoove me to be grateful. Nevertheless, my curiosity about what that center was like and why I was there to witness it could not be diminished.

"Before you are able to explore the nucleus of that magnificent cosmological atom, you must first examine your own," he said casually.

"My own what?" I asked flummoxed.

"Your own atomic existence; all the experiential elements that have molded you into becoming who you are at every passing moment," he said. "It will help you understand both your own nature as well as the nature of life itself."

"And how do I go about examining the atomic nature of my miniscule existence?" I asked.

"By examining your own individual Akashic Records to sort out what's been done and what's yet to be achieved," he said while moving toward a confluence of colors that gradually developed into distinct mass.

"Oh my God!" I bellowed immediately startled by the unexpected apparition. A colossal bright colored rainbow pulsating with life materialized before my eyes as I stood there utterly flabbergasted.

"Go ahead and cross over the bridge," he said softly. "It is your personal record to explore. When you're done, I'll be here waiting for you to introduce you to a brief peek into the nucleus of The Great Circle of Life. Once you sneak a quick look and see what is available to you, then anything is possible."

Without hesitating or saying another word, my photon self flowed forward blending with the shinning colors of the rainbow that arched above a cerulean background of possibilities.

◀52▶

At first it felt like something I'd experienced before. It was like watching a newsreel of past events and situations that were embedded in the memory of cosmic history. However, as I paid closer attention, I realized that the occurrences flashing before my eyes were no ordinary chronicles. They were the records of all my journeys through numerous and various manifestations of life. I was watching me in the past in the same way an astrophysicist observes the formation of a supernova that already happened billions of years ago.

Although the display of images occurred at a seemingly fast time, as each passed by I could experience the consciousness of every thought and emotion the scenes related to my past elicited. From my early existence as a crude rock in the Earth's continental crust to a vine protruding from the top of a mountain where a bald eagle often perched, I was able to identify both the highs and lows of the entire evolutionary process of the individualization of life that I represented. More importantly, however, I was able to understand how life blends within itself in interconnectedness with all the living forms around it. This became crystal clear to me when the image of an oak tree that I used to be appeared on the dark matter of the cosmic screen I watched the show of my life's journeys. The beautiful oak tree I once was had a large trunk that entwined around itself with its bulky roots jutting out widespread above ground. The branches stretched outward creating a welcoming shade with its lively green foliage over a playground where giggly children played in a public park. I was astonished to realize how much I'd learned and grown in my arboreal existence.

At first it seemed that the oak tree, like the nearby shrub or the fern next to it, stood there inactive in a passive rooted existence oblivious to everything around it. But it was just not so. From the consciousness perspective I'd reached to be able to observe my erstwhile oak tree life form, it was clear to me that I, the oak tree, was an integral part of the interplay of energy in that park. Not only I provided comfortable shading, a resting ground by the base of my trunk, and exquisite beauty to my surroundings, I absorbed everything happening in the radius of my arboreal aureole. The mirthful laughter of children, like the sound of rain coming down to soak my roots, nurtured a different kind of roots I had that were deeply ingrained in the spiritual soil all life sprout from. I could feel the titillating tickling of ants crawling up and down in their well-organized movement; and I could even hear their communication as they engaged with one another along their methodical march. Every now and then, those pesky squirrels jumped around my branches squeaking loud while excited children pointed at them gleefully. In the midst of this swirling life extravaganza, the wind gently blew through my branches dancing with every leaf to the tune of the soothing sounds they created together. And at night, a flock of hummingbirds sheltered in the cozy nests housed in my being, until the children came back to play again in the morning. Indeed, in that vast dome of life, I was astonished to realize how much consciousness a single oak tree in a park can surreptitiously harbor.

Without noticing any transitional time, I saw myself soaring up high in the sky imbued with extraordinary freedom and power of perception. The regal flying bird with a white crown of feathers majestically set on its avian head was me; and I was enthralled with the experience. Surveying the ample valley and its meandering rivers from high altitude, I patiently hunted for my next meal as my wide wingspan allowed me to glide freely among the surrounding mountain tops as if in alignment with Earth's axis. Suddenly, my telescopic vision spotted a rattlesnake slithering through narrow spaces between rocks in a desperate attempt to evade the inevitable. The reptile's survival instinct seemed to have sensed my hunting mission, as my own survival needs were at play. Knowing where my supper was hiding, I didn't rush to capture it just yet. Instead, I maneuvered my wings to an angle that allowed the wind underneath to pull me up to even higher altitudes so I could behold the Sun setting behind the mountains in the distance. After a long circumventing pleasure flight in pure atmosphere, I landed on a solitary vine on one of the mountains along the valley. As soon as my talons touched the fabric of the vine, I felt a recognizable familiarity with what I used to be. It was at that moment that I realized that all manifestations of life in me were perpetually intertwined into a common thread of an infinite web I belonged to. It was that awareness that propitiated an extraordinary opportunity: my existential status was elevated to the rational branch of the animal kingdom.

Although the motion picture records of my personal Akashic Records revealed several of my experiences in the mineral, floral, and faunal realms, for some reason unbeknownst to me I was consented to revisit only one of each category. By the time the human experience episode came about, the intensity level knob had been turned up to the highest plateau of unsettling emotions.

◄53►

We were madly, madly in love. We fell in love the very first time we laid eyes on each other. I believe we were around 5-years-old when that happened. I still remember the first time I saw him. Our families were camping in the woods next to a cascading waterfall after a long day hiking back to our tribal community. It was hunting season and all the young men were out fulfilling their role as providers for our communal needs. Once they returned, it would be the older adult's turn to clear out and prepare the food supply while the young men would enjoy their rewarded free time in the Sun. Meanwhile, the elders enjoyed their well-deserved respite after a lifetime fulfilling their duties to their people. It was a perfectly well-balanced work arrangement in which all exercised their responsibilities and enjoyed ample pleasures of living.

After that evening running around the pond getting sprayed by the falling water we became inseparable. Even as a child, I knew that special day was one of the most important of my life. I remember looking into his bright brown eyes and seeing me in him; and I could feel the reciprocity in the experience. We were like the complementing elements of a single unit; the yin and yang; the male and female; the proton and the neutron; the strange quark and the charm quark inside a symbolic atomic nucleus of love. That evening with the full moon shining on us like a cosmic spotlight reflecting its light on the water of the pond, I instinctively knew I was embarking on the most extraordinary experience of my life at a very young age. There was no doubt in my mind that this boy and I were soul mates.

By the time we reached our mid-teens, our incommensurable love for each other gave way to unbridled love making. As the magical conductor of destiny would orchestrate, we made love for the first time on the grass by the same waterfall we first met as children. Right by the waterfall that sprinkled our naked satiated bodies with refreshing droplets of delight, we cemented the bond of our souls with the union of our flesh. We were growing in love more intensely with every passing day, as if time were a special nutrient that nourished our immeasurable affection and commitment to each other unremittingly. Hence, we grew up being the best of friends. We were lovers. We were soul mates. We lived a dream life of great love and romance in an unheralded paradise. And then one day, one tempestuous day, unexpected vanquishers of happiness interrupted a sublime dream and turned it into the most agonizing nightmare.

It was getting dark when I realized it was time to return to the village. I had been gathering herbs all day when I noticed the ominous clouds somberly marching through the horizon. As soon as the first raindrops hit my head, I decided to rush back carrying the large leather pouch filled with the many herbs I'd collected. With the sinister-looking clouds moving at accelerated pace in my direction, I felt as though I was being pursued by a formidable force of nature that could not be reckoned with. Running faster through the trail in the dense forest, the prickly protruding shrubs scratched my body leaving trails of blood drops and rain mix on my soft skin. Scared and perturbed by an ominous presentiment, I ran faster toward my village. As soon as I arrived, pandemonium had already broken loose. Not even the loud clatter of thunder could muffle the sounds of my people's despair.

"Don't just stand there; run, run for your life," an elder woman who first saw my arriving said as she moved in the opposite direction.

"What's going on?" I asked as she grabbed my hand attempting to take me along with her.

"Beasts, beasts like we've never seen before are here to devour us," she said picking up the pace while looking at me with eyes stretched out wide by fear.

"Wait!" I said halting my steps. "What beasts are you talking about?"

"White beasts, with chains and deadly weapons," she replied trying to continue moving away from the village. "They are taking all the young men, women, and children with them. You need to run fast."

And run fast I did, but in the direction of the plundered village. Amidst the deafening sounds of thunder and firing muskets, I dashed through the bedlam calling out my lover's name in a desperate attempt to find him. Watching bloodied bodies of children, women, and men strewn all over the place, I tensely looked at them terrified of recognizing my best friend among the fallen victims. Suddenly, strong arms ensnared me from behind lifting me off my feet. I was now a captured casualty.

As the burly bearded white man placed the shackles on my ankles, I watched my people run through the jungle chased by an angry mob of sickly pallid men. I never thought that one day I'd see a reversed role in which our young hunters would flee from their conquerors as if they were game. Alas, they ran in vain. Soon the white huntsmen caught up with them and the human preys were held in bondage; a live human catch that would serve as fodder for their economic greed in usurped faraway lands.

They lined us up in side by side columns chained together by the neck. After walking for miles hearing the agonizing cries and piercing whimpering sounds of my people, I spotted at the distance several ships awaiting the precious human cargo of the most ignominious commercial enterprise in human history: the slave trade. With my head firmly secured in the iron loop around my neck, I kept looking for my love in the darkness of that nightmarish scenario of unspeakable terror. Every now and then I'd call out his name hoping to hear his voice amidst the sounds of suffering. No such luck. I was frightened, tired, cold, hungry, and soaking wet. Horrified, I watched my humiliated people head to the shore where they would be tightly packed in ships like slimy sardines in corroded containers.

They unchained us before boarding so the deckhands could properly organize the human cargo for the weeks-long transatlantic voyage. The tallest were selected for the greatest breadth of the vessel, and the short sized and youngsters were stowed in the fore part of the ships. Once the lower deck was filled to capacity, the rest were stowed on the upper deck maximizing every inch available with a breathing human being of dark skin color.

Suddenly, as I'm getting ready to step on the ramp to come onboard, I heard my love calling out my name from inside the ship. I shouted his name back and instinctively ran toward him like a metal drawn to an irresistibly potent magnetic force. But as soon as I began running, a big fat white man with a handlebar mustache smacked me in the face knocking me flat on the ramp. Lying on the tilted plank, I looked into my best friend's eye from the distance and I was mortified to perceive what he was about to do. Unhesitatingly, he dashed toward my aggressor who stared at my protector with utmost hatred and fury. My love kept moving toward the corpulent white beast unfazed by his threatening demeanor, as if the oppressor's odium and rage fueled his determination to charge with reckless abandon.

"Ahoy, ahoy," a sailor shouted watching the brewing confrontation developing from afar.

Shortly before the sailor's warning, my loving protector literally jumped on the much larger man straddling the human fiend as soon as he hit the ground. Yelling uncontrollably as if he'd lost his mind, he pounded his tightly clinched fists on the man's chubby bloody face nonstop, even after the battered man had lost consciousness. Then, the inevitable outcome I dreaded exploded in the sound of a firing musket. My love looked at me for the last time and his dying eyes gently smiled at me as I whispered to him with trembling voice: "I love you so much, so much." Staring at me with his glowing brown eyes, he stooped over and fell face down into the water with a gaping hole in his back.

"Move on, move on," my love's assassin commanded the wretched human private property to board quickly as if nothing significant had happened. Weeping and sobbing frantically watching my love's dead body floating in a red pool surrounded by turquoise water, I tried to jump to be with him but I was immediately restrained, beaten, and chained to the upper deck bow.

I'LL NEVER COMMIT SUICIDE AGAIN

Perhaps I'd become maddened by the intensity of unspeakable suffering. But for the rest of my surviving days as another human being's property, never was I pained nearly as much as losing my love and best friend that day. Although I felt deep-seated commiseration for the millions of my people who were kidnapped, exploited, tortured, and murdered by a wicked invasive species, the excruciating grief set off by the abrupt and cruel separation from the love of my life was unmatched. Collectively, we'd been deracinated from our ancestral lands, endured the slave trade and servitude for centuries, and never were able to regain fully our legitimate rights and dignity. But in the desolate solitude of my individual existence, the unexpected brutal loss of my love felt as though my soul had been uprooted from the core of my being. I felt empty and survived the remaining decades of my miserable life that way.

After eighty-five years of a mostly anguished survival, on my last living day on Earth I realized I'd never recovered from the unbearable loss of my love. Thus, as I lay on my deathbed, I decided that if there were a continuation of life beyond the mysterious threshold I was about to cross, I was going to seek out my soul mate and would not rest until I found him. But if my consciousness of life were to be completely obliterated at the moment of my death, then all the suffering I endured was all that pertained to the fleeting human existence. In that case, there would be nothing to regret or fear, for the emotional memory of my sufferings would dissipate like a fog in the first rays of dawn. On the other hand, in the odd chance that life would survive the demise of my old aching body, I was determined to find the one who lit the fire of love in my heart leaving inextinguishable flames ablaze.

As I felt my heartbeat slowing down announcing the approaching of my final breath, he appeared to me as when we first met by the waterfall. He looked at me in the eye, smiled, and, without uttering any words, he said: "The one you seek is seeking you, and we shall find each other again at a time and space yet to be determined by the magic of destiny."

At the exhaling puff of my final breath of life, I smiled back at him with exuberance of certainty that, no matter how long it'd take to be with him again, the wait would be worthwhile.

◄54➤

"How was it?" My mentor asked me as soon as I returned to the spacetime dimension he waited for me.

Mentally confused and emotionally discombobulated, I felt as though I'd just woken up from a terrifying nightmare. I didn't know what to say to him. My memory was foggy and my heart weighed heavily in my chest as if a solid iron pendulum directed the blood flow with its swaying motions. Suddenly, a vague recollection of what I'd experienced surfaced to my consciousness, but the only thing I could detect was a conflicting duality of immense joy juxtaposed to immeasurable sorrow.

"Would you like to share your experience?" He asked again.

"How can ineffable joy coexist in the world with unimaginable affliction? Why the cost of love must be so high?" I replied with my eyes glancing vaguely upwards while looking deep down inside myself.

"Is that it? All you had was a philosophical experience?" He said downplaying my remarks.

"I'm not sure what it was," I said still trying to make sense of the experience I couldn't fully recollect. "It was an existential tribulation that made me wonder about the value of life and death; love and hatred; joy and pain; justice and inequality; and all the contradicting dualities that seem to govern the human experience."

"And what's the take away of your personal experience?" He asked continuing to probe into the issue as if he looked deep inside of me as I did.

"I'm afraid that after realizing the enormous disparity of opposites in the wide gamut of human emotions, I've found legitimate reasons to validate my decision to end my earthly life. After so many blows, at some point the levee breaks out and the water inundates the troubled soul that drowns while yearning for some respite."

"So, you embarked on an exploratory journey of your individual Akashic Records and all you end up with is a pseudo-validation for quitting your life?" He remarked with undisguised sarcasm. "Might as well have gone back to the Suicide Orbit Sector, and stayed there."

"Maybe I should have," I said feeling glum.

"That can be arranged, if you wish," he said.

"No, of course not," I replied immediately realizing the foolishness of my hasty comment. "I just felt so immensely sad to have experienced such intense love just to lose it in equally intense fashion. It seems that when pain reaches its zenith everything else, even life itself, loses meaning and the desire to continue living fades away."

"But as you should have learned by now, you cannot escape the challenges of pain or the life that allows it to exist, even after getting rid of the physical body. You were convinced that the anguish that tormented you would dissipate once you killed yourself; and yet…," he said looking me in the eye without needing to finish his sentence.

Yes, my suicide did not in any way, shape, or form stopped my suffering; to the contrary, it aggravated it to a significant degree. After roaming aimlessly through an existential dimension in which anguish was sovereign, I was finally able to move up and away from the lower frequencies domains and still could not find the peace of mind I so desperately wanted. It felt as though my search went far beyond self-mitigation, but extended to other parts of me that had been severed abruptly before reaching a fortuitous consummation. It became apparent to me that suffering, that universal condition of the human experience, cannot be completely eliminated any more than the secrets of life can be unveiled by scientific progress. Like a coreless magical onion in which each layer removed by latest knowledge only leads to another layer of new questions to be answered, each life cycle ended, naturally or by force, only leads to other layers of new discoveries; new adventures; and new loving experiences. The perennial challenge to reach the core of the being struggling with pain was an endless endeavor; a Sisyphean task.

"There is no rest for the spiritual warrior," he said unexpectedly. "Those in the pursuit of power are always engaged in worthy efforts, for they know that it is in the perseverance of the battle that victory is accomplished. And since life is always recycling itself in all its multifaceted variations, the futility of suicide can only prolong the necessary challenges that evolution calls for. Be it a goal, a project, a love affair, or even life itself, the voluntary killing of any worthy endeavor in the face of difficulties is a form of suicide and a crime against oneself; a crime whose consequences can be even more devastating than the challenge that triggered the slaying of the cause."

"Is that what it is: one needs to be brave to be able to love; to endure all sorts of vicissitudes just to see it all recycled into the orbit of life to start it all over again in a perennial pattern of suffering," I said feeling downhearted with that dismal perspective. "Was Nietzsche really right about eternal recurrence?"

Instead of saying something meaningful, as I expected, he just looked at me and smiled as if I had made some jovial comment.

"What's the matter?" I asked feeling annoyed with his unexpected reaction.

"Would it have bothered you if the eternal recurrence was a continuous return of love, joy, and no pain?" He asked no longer smiling.

"Of course not," I replied wondering where he was going with such allusion to my obvious response.

"But if the eternal recurrence of love were to be always followed by pain, would you no longer be interested in experiencing it, ever?" He asked and his furrowed brow seemed to purposefully challenge my self-assurance.

I was surprised that I hesitated to answer. In fact, I remained quiet for a long time mulling over the new hypothetical option presented to me. It felt like a Trojan horse of love filled with a great deal of pain.

"Would you or would you not?" He insisted that I answered in straightforward fashion.

Surprised and taken aback by my own hesitation, suddenly I had an emotional recollection of the immense love I'd experienced in the examination of my personal Akashic Records. At that moment my chest was immediately filled with ineffable joy. As I reached the apex of a most gratifying emotional memory, the recollection was brusquely short-circuited by a devastating wave of sorrow that blacked out the experience of exhilaration.

"I suppose you cannot have one without the other," I finally blurted out the expression of my jumbled thoughts and conflicting emotions. "It seems it's all an eternal recurrence of love and loss and life and death repeating a perennial pattern in a turbulent swirling of endless occurrences."

"You still haven't answered my question," he said as soon as I finished speaking. "Now that you're aware of the inseparable divergent duality, would you choose love and life knowing that both will inevitably come to an end leading to great sorrow?"

"Oh yes," I whispered with assertive conviction while vaguely recalling the life and love I'd lived and lost.

"Very good," he said sounding like a pleased teacher whose favorite pupil had just succeeded in a challenging educational assignment. "Now I can show you about eternal entanglements; the state of affairs in which love and life are inseparably connected—forever!

◀55▶

I didn't know what to make of it when he spoke about the merits of the ability to love at the highest vibrational frequency.

"Like the nucleus of an atom that compose the molecules of life, love lies at the core of the nucleus of light; not light from an electromagnetic spectrum sense, but the radiance of the highest possible form of intelligence that illuminates the dark shadows of ignorance," he said as we strolled on a green pathway toward the top of the mountain.

I listened to him while beholding the magnificent panorama around me. I had neither an inkling nor recollection of how we ended up in such an exquisite setting. The bright blue sky above was like an enveloping aura of an environment teeming with life everywhere. Rocks, trees, birds, and all sorts of animals roaming freely on the slopes of the towering mountain, all seemed to be unified as if they were complimentary parts of one another in an empyrean whole. And even though we were moving toward the summit, the rarefied air was highly charged with oxygen molecules. Every time I inhaled, I could feel the ethereal atmospheric purity passing through my nasal cavities and filling my lungs as it nourished the blood of my spirit. But spectacular vistas and exquisite experiences aside, the most exceptional value of that journey was the mysterious purpose of my mentor's intention in what he attempted to reveal to me.

"It takes a great deal of mettle to choose to live and love, for both demand overcoming a myriad of challenges and poignant pain," he said. "It's not for the faint of heart. It is for the brave in the pursuit of self-empowerment."

"I'm sure bravery has its merits, but why would anyone choose that which will generate suffering?" I questioned.

"Because it's the right thing to do," he replied. "In fact, it is the only thing to do."

"Choosing should be the right thing to do; the exercising of freewill. Whether one chooses life and love or death and indifference, it should be a prerogative of individual freedom," I argued subtly defending my own suicide case.

"Not if you aspire to grow and attain higher levels of frequency of your soul," he said. "And since you must live in order to love, and you can only love if you live, this entwined duality becomes a necessary requirement of the evolutionary process of the human species. Thus, anyone exercising the freewill not to live or love is missing out on the opportunity to grow."

Suddenly, I noticed that we had made significant headway on the path upward to the top of the mountain. Now I could see the tiptop of the majestic peak covered with a mantle of vivid white snow; like a veil barely hiding the face of a beautiful bride of nature. Behind it, a vibrant hue of orange rays of light blended in with the blue sky creating an exquisite visual work of art. As I walked toward the summit, I felt as an integral part of the surrounding beauty, as if I were both the artist and the creation.

"Those who idolize the powerful representations of glorified life, such as saints, martyrs, and wise enlightened beings, often times fail to realize how these consecrated entities got to become the way they are. If it were not through self-deserved acquisition of personal power, the reason for idolatry would cease to exist, for anyone could obtain it without merit or effort," he said halting his steps to look me in the eye. "It is in the relationship of the ephemeral nature of life with the anguish inherent in the experience of uninhibited love that the elixir of self-empowerment is alchemized. Thus, aware of the hardships intrinsic to the process, only a daring few venture to reach out for it willingly."

"For who would bear the whips and scorn of time," I mumbled the words of Hamlet to myself.

"Only the meritorious few; those who voluntarily choose to overcome the heartache and the thousand natural shocks," he said using the words of the same passage of Hamlet I'd mumbled."

"As if enduring a life filled with anxieties and pain would be something to choose to go through voluntarily," I said recalling my latest experience visiting my personal Akashic Records. "Sometimes the heartache and the thousand natural shocks are just too much to bear."

"But grief should be the instructor of the wise. Sorrow is knowledge: they who know the most must mourn the deepest," he said as we resumed treading uphill. "In order to experience the highest knowledge and greatest love, one must be willing to learn what the opposite end of the spectrum is like, and that's no easy feat. However, the rewards of overcoming the trials and travails of a challenging life are unimaginable under the limited human perception."

"Like what?" I asked impulsively.

"Like life and love becoming eternally entangled in a magical existence of oneness," he said. "The knowing, at the empirical level, that nothing and no one is ever eliminated because it's all a perpetual cycle of recurrence and entanglements."

"It does sound psychedelically magical," I remarked sardonically unaware of the depth of the meaning of his words.

He simpered nodding his head sideways. Then, without saying another word, he turned around and we resumed moving toward the top of the mountain.

The closer we got to the peak, the brighter and more vibrant the mountain became. It felt as though it was the mountain that was moving under my feet leading us to the iridescent summit. At every step of the way up toward the crown of that majestic mountain, the incandescent surroundings intensified its luminosity as I could feel the pleasant heat percolate through my porous ethereal skin. The crescendo increase in temperature was assuaged by a gentle breeze that, like the heat, passed through me leaving behind a sense of refreshment. Meanwhile, all around me the mystical sounds of nature sang songs of life as phonons of joy seemed to fill the vacuum of space. I had no doubt I was approaching a special locale; a place where beginnings and ends meet at the shared transitional point; the dimension where life and death become indistinguishable from each other.

"Here we are," he said with his voice exuding exalted pride basking in conspicuous elation. "Soon you'll be able to take a glimpse through the clouds of illusion that have obscured the light of truth from your view."

Mesmerized by the dazzling golden and purple nebula that enveloped me at the top of the mountain, I realized I was moving in a counter clockwise orbital motion around the summit. Although everything around me was clearly shifting at extraordinary speed, I could not feel the slightest motion; and neither was I able to see what was inside the massive radiant circle gyrating below. But looking up above through the expansive golden and purple royal aureole, I could see countless distant galaxies moving as though they were engaged in a cosmic dance to the sound of a life-creating orchestra. The combination of sounds and colors vibrating around and within me exalted my perceptual experience to an exhilarating state of being. At that moment I knew that I, too, was participating in that cosmic dance as an integral part of everything that existed in the past, present, and future.

"We're now orbiting the outer boundaries of the event horizon of The Great Circle of Life. Soon we'll reach the cosmic vantage point from where you'll be able to see only what you need, but nothing else," he forewarned me.

"Nothing else?" I asked with a smidge of wistful curiosity.

"Only what's necessary for you to learn before continuing on your journey to redemption," he said.

I was mulling over his words when I noticed that the speed of the nebula's circular motion was dwindling piecemeal, until it came to a complete stop. Startled, I looked at him with a frown silently asking for an explanation for what was happening.

"This is it. We've reached the cosmic vantage point; the front row seat to look into The Great Circle of Life," he said as if heralding a momentous occasion. "This is the closest you'll ever get to it for now; at least until you make yourself suitable to be immerged into it. In the meantime, it's time for you to take a furtive glance at what lies beyond life and death."

◄56➤

The luminous celestial sphere gyrated gently around a bright beam of light functioning as a visible axis. Shooting multicolored rays from both poles into infinity, the translucent circle revolved around itself as if dancing to some cosmic music my auditory ability could not detect. Although the sphere's radius was immeasurable, the view inside was impeccably clear and laser point sharp. I could see for miles as if the object of my observation were within a few feet from my face. Astounded by my enhanced visual perception, I wondered what I'd be able to see inside that ginormous celestial crystal ball.

"The cosmic vantage point is the place from where you can see the nature of life as it is," he said in sync with my thoughts. "But more importantly, from here you'll be able to see the true nature of your being."

Even though I was consumed with curiosity to learn anything I could about my true nature, whatever that was supposed to be, I did not say a word back. The only truth I knew about myself was that I didn't know myself at all. I'd spent my whole life on Earth chasing a sense of security in a place where chaos rules. Unable to find the false sense of security outside myself, always searching for comfort as a remedy to the ills of my soul, I'd lost touch with whoever I was that I'd never made acquaintance with. Since childhood all my energy was devoted to learning how to cope with economic deprivation, emotional instability, and psychological impairment. Although by dint of necessity I'd developed good survival skills, never I felt like I'd gained much ground in the expansion of my personhood; and that's probably why I committed suicide. Had I been able to muster the strength to overcome the emotional and psychological challenges of my ephemeral human existence, it's unlikely that I'd ended up in such an inauspicious place as the Suicide Orbit Sector; a dreadful dimension with unique challenges of its own. But at that point what had happened in the past didn't matter anymore. Now I was about to take a glimpse at the truth; at least the truth about myself. Standing on the edge of my destiny, there was no other way to go but forward.

"There you are," he said pointing out to a blob of crimson cloud that rotated inside the enormous crystalline circle. Both moved in synchronistic slow counter-clockwise motion as if they were one and the same.

I squinted, frowned, and then rubbed my eyes trying to see even the slightest image of myself in the midst of the dense colorful swirling mist. I couldn't see anything but a large and formless nebulous cloud of multihued gases.

"You have to be patient and wait for the haze to disperse into the cinematic view of your personal Akashic Records," he said with his pointing indicator finger now rotating in the same direction of the crimson cloud as though he stirred it into shape. "But be attentive, for the images will appear in series and you'll be able to take only a glimpse at them. As I told you earlier, this is all you're allowed to see at this time."

Suddenly, like a cloud in the sky metamorphosing into similitude images, the thick vapor of gases started dissipating while shaping up into a row of human forms moving in a straight time-line.

"Oh my God!" I gasped realizing that every one of those individual humans was me. A loutish-looking Neanderthal dragging a dead beast by its tail into his dark cave; a Roman centurion engaged in battle with blood splattered face and a deep oozing gash on his sword-holding right arm; an innocent native child running through open meadows toward a gathering of tepees by the riverbank; an aristocratic lady being catered by negro slaves in lands far away from her place of birth; a slave tied to a post wailing in agony while getting whipped by her master; an industrialist exploiting helpless laborers; a trollop eking out a living with the sale of her sex-battered body; a heartless mobster committing murder for money and revenge; a lighthearted vagabond wandering through sparsely populated villages; a hermit monk meditating on a mountain top; a caring nurse tending to the wounds of injured soldiers; a child; a man; and a woman in a myriad of human life experiences in different spacetime periods.

"I never thought there could be so many varied aspects of me," I said in awe.

"These are only a fraction of the whole you've incorporated into the person that has become who you are now," he said while gazing at me with loving eyes. "Be it a bacterium, an insect, a plant, a reptile, or a human being, life is a magical energy that cannot be deracinated, even when it's forcefully attempted to stop its perpetual flow. All the fine threads of its complex web are so intricately intertwined that is impossible to disentangle them. As for death, it is nothing but the temporary illusion life gives out at transitional points of its perennial renewing process."

I turned my eyes back toward the center of the circle but now the only image standing there was the current me. I felt as though I was looking into a mirror and, for the first time, seeing myself in all my flaws and qualities blending into a whole of paradoxical perfection.

"You have come a long way from the unknown beginning where it all originates as you move toward the unknown future that never ends," he said as I kept my eyes focused on the center of the circle looking at the image of myself inside. "Each leg of the spiritual journey leads to the next in a recurrent recycling process of each individual manifestation of life. And as this mysterious progression unfolds, deeply rooted connections are established with those you develop loving relationships; and often even those with whom you had inauspicious interactions that contributed to your growth. Either uplifting or unconstructive relationships develops, entanglements of individual energies of life take place, until resolutions to conflicts or amalgamation of loving bonds complete their course."

"And which one applies to the one I see right now?" I asked while looking at the image of myself in the eye. "Do I have a conflict with myself that needs a resolution, or am I working on a loving bond with the individual I am meant to be?"

"Both," he replied succinctly.

"Both? It seems contradictory to me," I said.

"Not at all. It's actually the norm. Everyone forms positive and negative entanglements along the journey, even with oneself. For instance, when you decided to end your former life on your own terms, you unwittingly created a situation that now demands a resolution. And that's the very reason you are here now looking into yourself after enduring a challenging tour through the outer orbits surrounding The Great Circle of Life."

"What about positive entanglements? Is there any for me to be cheerful about?" I questioned feeling slightly downhearted by his truthful remark about my suicide.

The silence that ensued was long and so unnerving that it compelled me to turn my eyes away from the circle to look at him. I was stunned to see his shinning smile illuminate the entirety of his being, as if an aura of radiant light had been lit around him with Prometheus sacred fire. I kept waiting for him to answer my question; but instead, he gazed at the center of the circle as if he were hypnotized. Perplexed, I immediately looked back in the same direction and I gasped when I saw his bright image where mine was a few moments earlier.

"Look," he said with his voice now coming from his image inside the circle. "Here comes a parade of loving entanglements you've cultivated in the course of your many lives."

I was mesmerized in the face of what I witnessed. Like water steaming up into vapor under the laws of thermodynamics, he started evaporating slowly upward while morphing into a swirling multicolored cloud that enveloped him until his image completely vanished in the kaleidoscopic mist. Then, emerging from the middle of the vibrant multihued dense gases, a parade, as he had said, began appearing from the point in the center of the circle where he once stood. I placed my left hand over my mouth ajar and, almost inaudibly, I uttered through my teeth: "Oh my God! That's him!" I said as soon as my great love from the time before I became a slave showed up flashing a most luminous smile while looking at me with loving eyes. Moved by unrestrained joy and excitement, I yelled and beckoned at him to draw his attention. And even though he was clearly seeing me and aware of my reaching out to him, he did not reply in any way. My motioning hands gradually lost their energy as they succumbed to my sad disappointment.

"He is fully aware of you, but the subtle frequency barrier between the two of you does not allow for interaction; only observation," my mentor's voice echoed from the same place where my loved one stood with an exuberant smile. "Enjoy this gift for what it is; a brief and yet ever enduring moment."

I smiled back at him trying to communicate my love with a joyful grin. Oddly, I could feel our connecting through the penetrating eye contact we maintained while smiling broadly at each other in silence. And despite the out of the ordinary distance, our bonding felt so strong inside of me that I could feel his breathing blend with my own. As I'm beginning to indulge in that meaningful silent connection, he raised his right hand and waved good-bye to me. Suddenly, my eyelids drooped heavily over my moist eyes and my beaming grin turned into a gloomy pout. But as soon as I felt my mood sliding down the melancholic slope, the multicolored nebula started rotating counter-clockwise at a significant speed obscuring his image while at the same time creating a new one. At that moment I felt my facial muscles stretching my eyes wide open with new excitement.

Soon, an array of beings with whom I'd established loving bonds in times long gone by showed up at the center of the circle. Popping up from a myriad of tiny bright specs of light, they showed up in orderly progression greeting me with enthusiastic silent luminosity. Although appearing in brief sequences of existence in which they smiled and waved at me before giving way to the next one, each of the countless individuals I encountered left a lasting feeling of exhilaration; each unique, valuable, and perennially permeated in the core of my being. All those I'd befriended, loved, helped and who helped me, we'd formed an indissoluble bond; an entanglement of friendship forged by the life-giving fire of love. Right then I realized that, like every moment of a fleeting existence, every relationship held its own power of uniqueness and its own everlasting nature, for it never ceased to exist once it came into being. It was as though the closer it got to the center of The Great Circle of Life, the more intense the frequency of the experience of love became. It was at that moment of realization that the most astounding parade of familiar faces began appearing before my eyes. From the nucleus of the incandescent nebula, they blossomed like roses in the springtime of a new era of my existence.

"Mr. Burton!" I blurted out astonished to see my loving step-dad smiling at me with great joviality.

Although his smile-stretched lips did not move, I could hear his voice in my head; I could feel him inside of me as if he and I were one. At every glitter I detected in his eyes, a different sound resonated in my inner ears, each conveying a message of love to me. I made a conscientious effort to send thought-formed musical messages of my affection for him with my eyes, and he instantaneously replied with a subtle wink as though to assure me that he'd received the melody of my love. It was one of the most extraordinary and sublime exchange of feelings I'd ever experienced; and yet, I wanted more out of the encounter with someone to whom I was so grateful. I wanted to hear his voice and feel the warm embrace of his loving paternal arms enveloping me with fatherly protection. Alas, it was to no avail. The more I tried to reach out to him the more his image faded away from view.

"Be content with what you got," a voice spoke in the depth of my ears. "You cannot yet be where he is. The frequency of the electromagnetic field of your being is not high enough to reach him. In the meantime, just observe what unfolds before your eyes right now, and enjoy the extraordinary gift of this moment."

I felt imbued with innocent euphoria; as if I were a child waking up in the morning of my birthday party with uncontained anticipation. I could feel my heart palpitating faster inside my chest in crescendo drumbeats of excitement heralding a coveted event. Then, in a nanosecond of imperceptible existence filled with perpetual life, I heard the loud joyful clamor of a voice I had heard so many times in my life.

"I know it's you!" I screamed with excitement of seeing someone I'd known since the early days of my earthly life. Although I'd always felt his presence and heard his voice inside of me in the numerous unspoken conversations we shared, this was a special encounter with my invisible childhood friend. Other than a vague recollection of interacting with him at the base of a majestic mountain in what felt like a distant dream, seeing him at that moment felt vividly real. His beautiful angular face accentuated by well-defined cheekbones and salient nose disclosed a blend of masculine maturity disguised in an impish boy. The lanky dark-haired lad with luminescent green eyes exuded the same positively dynamic energy I recalled from my many interactions with him. He was a beautiful radiant child.

"C'mon, speak to me like you used to," I pleaded as he stood there smiling and making funny faces at me.

Not a sound came out of his mouth; only bright laser-like green light darting out of his eyes accompanied by a jubilant smile. I was about to feel disappointed with the lack of verbal communication when he started waving good-bye and gradually disappeared into a blue vapor mist. Disappointment gave way to sadness, until I felt a strong hand gently touch my right shoulder.

"I remember your presence," I said turning toward the tall handsome man embracing me from the side. "You stopped me from jumping off the cliff that night. I could not see your face then, but never would I forget your touch."

He smiled at me and his pearly teeth shone brighter than the high-beam headlights of my car on that nerve-racking evening. I kept looking into his eye waiting for him to say something to me, but unlike the time we first met, he did not utter a single word. Suddenly, as we maintained a most deeply intense eye contact, I felt as though I was being drawn into a vortex of a multi-being experience in which many existed in one. Feeling woozy and confused, his eyes became like a reflective screen where I saw a multitude of familiar loving faces, including my invisible child-hood friend, Mr. Burton, and even the guides that assisted me in my dreadful journey through the Suicide Orbit Sector, among many others my soul recognized an indissoluble connection. I realized that I was the one separated from the whole.

"I want to be with you all," I said wistfully.

"We do, too," a voice echoed in my mind. "Are you willing to do whatever it takes to make it happen?"

"Anything," I said with unwavering conviction.

"Good! In this case, let's get you back to where you came from," the commanding voice resonated in the depth of my be-ing.

"What?" I said out loud still maintaining eye contact with the countless changing eyes reflected in one person. "How can I be with you if I have to go back to a different time and space? I want to move to the center of The Great Circle of Life where you all are."

"Yes, that's what we want as well; and that's why you need to go back to where you came from," the multi-unison voice reverberated in a canyon-like vacuum space inside of me. "It just happens to be the path of your journey back home."

"It's because I committed suicide, isn't it?" I asked feeling rejected.

"It is because it's what you need to do. There is neither judgment nor punishment for the decisions you've made in your life. It's just a matter of working your way closer to the orbit of the center where we exist. This is about merit and nothing else."

An eerie silence ensued. Looking into his multi-expressive right eye I could see the truth of his words. Although I didn't understand why a detour on my path was necessary to get back to my desired destination, I had absolutely no doubts about the relevance of the requirement I had to abide by.

"Will I have to go through the Suicide Orbit Sector again?" I asked with frightful anticipation to the answer.

"We certainly hope not. It's entirely up to you and the decisions you make."

"I shall never go through that dreadful place again," I said while releasing a deep sigh of relief infused with self-confidence. "I want to be where I belong."

As soon as I finished uttering my last words, a heavy iron curtain immediately dropped with a loud thump inches away from my eyes. In an instant, my surroundings became pitch-black. All of a sudden, I was immersed in darkness again.

Before I could even notice any transition, I was back to where I came from; but this time there was bright light above me.

◄57➤

The light above my head flickered nonstop as I gradually regained consciousness and awareness of my surroundings. I stared at it through half-open eyes disturbed by its consistent trembling motion, which made me feel quite uncomfortable. Dazed and confused, I watched those elongated cylinders on the ceiling sputtering steady glare instead of stable clarity. Somehow they represented my state of mind at that moment.

"This one was a close call," I vaguely overheard as if the sound came from miles away.

"Keep pumping her stomach until it's completely drained," I heard a man's voice while feeling his presence next to me. "And make sure the intravenous fluids are flowing at all times. She's not out of the woods just yet."

His statement got my attention. I made an effort to open my eyes as wide as I could and glanced through the corner of my scope of vision. There was a man donning white scrubs talking to a woman clad in a light green outfit. I immediately realized that I was lying in a hospital bed in the emergency room. With intravenous needles attached to my arms, oxygen tubes inside my nose, and hoses running down my throat all the way to my stomach, I could feel the churning in my belly amidst the intermittent pumping and suction motions. I looked back up to the ceiling but those annoying fluorescent lights disturbed my distraught and somnolent eyes. I closed them to avoid the flickering disturbance; and as I did, I realized I was regaining a modicum of alertness. However, there were two conflicting recent memories competing for prominence in my mind, and I wasn't sure which one was the genuine experience I had last.

"Attempting to commit suicide overdosing on Benzodiazepine is not something someone who is seriously committed to killing herself would do," I listened in a nurse standing nearby whispering to a colleague in discreet manner.

Now I remembered clearly. I had attempted to commit suicide. But contrary to what the nurse erroneously inferred, I was dead serious about putting an end to my life. What she did not know was that I purposefully intended to fade into death's embrace in the arms of the man who was usurping my dignity, while hurting the other perpetrator who betrayed my love and confidence. I was hurt, angry, and vindictive in my intentions. Perhaps that was the reason I did not succeed.

On the other hand, I had a blurred recollection of being elsewhere. A theta brainwave level remembrance of a strange world of umpteen possibilities; a place where heaven and hell coexisted with each other, and either could manifest its reality based on both the merits and needs of the observer of possibilities. I felt as though I'd dreamed that I journeyed in orbital motions around a vacuum where the center of a circle reigned sovereign in the cosmos full of life. I recalled that the closer I orbited to the center, the more light and heat emanated from within me as if I reflected the very nature of that mysterious sphere. Conversely, the farther I orbited away from that magical ring of light, the more miserable my experience of life became. I began wondering whether I'd gone through what it's known as near death experience. In any case, I had no doubt I'd travelled full circle to the starting point of my returning to the center I'd dreamed about.

"Good morning," the handsome young doctor greeted me walking into my hospital room in the morning. "I have good news for you. I've just dropped off your release papers at the front desk and you'll be able to go home by late afternoon. I'll keep you here a little longer just as a precautionary measure."

"How long have I been here?" I asked mumbling my words and squinting to shield my eyes from rays of light coming through the gap between the curtains.

He looked at me as though wondering whether releasing me from the hospital was the right thing to do. I felt embarrassed not being aware of the passing of time.

"You were admitted to the emergency room at 11:45 last night," he said reading from a clipboard in his hand.

I turned my face to the other side and closed my eyes feeling utterly disoriented. With indistinct memories of journeys through strange dimensions of reality inundating my mind, I drowned in a sea of confusion and uncertainties. How could so many happenings unfold in such a short period of time? And to make matters worse, I had a crystal clear recollection of my planning and executing my suicide strategy, which conflicted with hazy memories of existing elsewhere for what felt like a long period of time. Yet, not even twelve hours had passed. There was something mystifying with my recent experiences of time and events intersecting into one reality.

"Excuse me, doctor," a nurse said walking into the room unexpectedly. "You need to contact the front desk right away."

After the doctor left the room, she looked at me awkwardly and the tension in her eyes did not match the tone of her voice.

"Don't worry, ma'am. Everything will be alright."

She smiled fidgeting her fingers while looking at me in silent uneasiness that felt rather unnerving. Suddenly, I became preoccupied with the potential urgency of the moment.

I felt relieved when the doctor returned some half-hour later, though it quickly dissipated when he talked to me.

"I'm afraid you won't be able to go home this afternoon after all. There has been an incident in your house that is under police investigation. The place has been cordoned off."

"What happened?" I asked instinctively attempting to sit up.

"You'll learn all about it later," he said in a dismissive tone coated with quiet concern. "I've been informed that the detectives will want to talk with you once you're fully recovered. In the meantime, you need to get some rest. Do you have any relatives in the area that you could spend time with until this issue is resolved?"

"Relatives? Oh no, I don't have any relatives," I said wistfully. "But I do have a friend, Samantha."

"Well, we'll need to get in touch with her and have her pick you up and sign the release papers," he said.

After spending two weeks at Samantha's home, I was finally allowed to go to my house; but not before visiting with the investigators of the crime that took place the evening I attempted to commit suicide. Although it felt terribly embarrassing and cumbersome having to reveal the private details of my miserable marital life, the information I provided was crucial for the closing of the case. On the other hand, I learned about what took place after I was taken away by an ambulance to the emergency room of the hospital. Apparently, even before I filled in the detectives with the lewd details of my husband's business shenanigans, they already had concluded what happened that evening, and the contribution of the information I provided helped validate the results of their investigation: it was a murder suicide case. Based on the details of their re-enactment of the crime scene, my husband, Daniel, shot Anthony Menlo several times before putting a bullet in his own head. Because of the prominence of the victims, the criminal case headlined on all media outlets across the country and abroad. Although it was an embarrassment for me as well, I took solace on the fact that I was handsomely compensated for my discomfiture. In addition to inheriting Daniel's vast assets, a celebrity attorney took interest in the case and filed several lawsuits in my behalf against the estate of Anthony Menlo, which added many more millions of dollars to my already cash-stacked bank accounts. I would spend the rest of my life financially independent and free.

Since that tragic evening and the humiliation of having my personal life exposed in the media for public consumption, I became a recluse multi-millionaire whose life's aspirations had changed dramatically. In addition to losing interest in romantic relationships, the mundane pleasures of life no longer enticed my sensorial appetite; and neither did the travails of an increasingly troubled world bothered me anymore. I was a changed woman; a person transformed by the experience of death, which I'd experienced in a threefold way: my suicide attempts, the murder-suicide of my perpetrators; and, the most poignant of all, a hazy recollection of having experienced death in another realm of existence. Although I had but occasional spurts of flashing memories of events I could not account for, somehow they exerted a life-altering effect on me. At last I'd found the answer to the proverbial cliché question: what's the meaning of life? The answer was now clear to me: the meaning of life is to prepare for death.

Having experienced deprivation and abundance; poverty and wealth; freedom and subservience; love and loathing; and to an incomprehensible extent even life and death, I was now free to live the rest of my life without fear. I learned to welcome death without wanting to die, though there were days when not wanting to die felt like a daunting task. However, even when I felt morose and pestered by life's challenges and unforgiving assails, I strove not to allow negative thought-seeds to germinate in the soil of my mind. I kept reminding myself that in due time everything passes away; everything, even life itself. Thus, instead of giving in to the disempowering vulnerability that suffering often triggers in the battered human soul, I chose to alchemize my pain into a sharp tool with which to chisel my own destiny toward the ultimate goal of preparing for what I'd learned to be the ultimate meaning of life.

Alas, I must admit there were days when living felt like an impossible undertaking. Even the drudgeries of everyday life held the potential for igniting the explosive keg of pent-up emotions. In fact, one day later on in my life when I was experiencing excruciating emotional anguish, I was seduced by the idea of attempting to commit suicide for the third time. Unbeknownst to my senses, I felt compelled to drive to the coastal cliff where I intended to kill myself for the first time at the tender age of twenty. I reenacted the exact same scenario and walked to the edge of the abyss where life and death hung in the balance. But this time when I looked down at the darkness where roaring waves crashed violently against the rocks, I was reminded of the futility of such a foolish idea. Eerily, I felt a gentle touch of a hand on my right shoulder. I smiled before turning around to head back to my Bentley Flying Spur Sedan.

Walking toward my car's bright headlights that looked like a pair of luminous eyes gazing into my soul, I whispered against the wind that blew softly through my hair and beyond: "I'll never commit suicide again."

About the Author

Sebastian de Assis is a writer, teacher, philosopher, intellectual artist, and a consummate bibliophile with an unquenchable thirst for acquiring knowledge.

A graduate of the University of Hawai'i at Manoa and California State University at Dominguez Hills, he has lived in several countries and traveled extensively through Europe, South and North America, Africa, and the United States. He is fluent in Spanish, Portuguese, and French.

He lives in Oregon where he reads and writes in his personal library while listening to J. S. Bach, Miles Davis, and other inspiring music that nurtures his spirit.

For more information about the author and his work visit www.sebastiandeassis.com.